BELLAROO CREEK!

Three brave women, three strong men…
and one town on the brink

Bellaroo Creek in the Australian Outback
town in need of rescue! But when three single
women appear with a few adorable kids in tow sparks
start to fly! The town and its rugged cattlemen realise
that just have got more than they bargained for!

town, three heart-warming romances—
an unforgettable journey!

CATTLEMAN'S READY-MADE FAMILY
by Michelle Douglas

MIRACLE IN BELLAROO CREEK
by Barbara Hannay

PATCHWORK FAMILY IN THE OUTBACK
by Soraya Lane

THE CATTLEMAN'S READY-MADE FAMILY

BY
MICHELLE DOUGLAS

First published in Great Britain 2013
by Mills & Boon, an imprint of Harlequin (UK) Limited,
Eton House, 18-24 Paradise Road, Richmond, Surrey TW9 1SR

© Michelle Douglas 2013

ISBN: 978 0 263 90132 0
ebook ISBN: 978 1 472 00513 7

23-0813

Harlequin (UK) policy is to use papers that are natural, renewable and recyclable products and made from wood grown in sustainable forests. The logging and manufacturing processes conform to the legal environmental regulations of the country of origin.

Printed and bound in Spain
by Blackprint CPI, Barcelona

At the age of eight **Michelle Douglas** was asked what she wanted to be when she grew up. She answered, 'A writer.' Years later she read an article about romance writing and thought, *Ooh, that'll be fun.* She was right. When she's not writing she can usually be found with her nose buried in a book. She is currently enrolled in an English Masters programme for the sole purpose of indulging her reading and writing habits further. She lives in a leafy suburb of Newcastle, on Australia's east coast, with her own romantic hero—husband Greg, who is the inspiration behind all her happy endings.

Michelle would love you to visit her at her website: www.michelle-douglas.com.

To the Valley Girls
for the support, the laughter and the champagne.

CHAPTER ONE

ARE YOU LOOKING FOR A TREE CHANGE?
Do you long for fresh air and birdsong?
Do you relish fresh-picked produce?
Do you hunger for a gentler pace of life?
RENT A FARMHOUSE FOR $1 A WEEK!
If you're a community-minded family, why not rent a
farmhouse for $1 a week in beautiful Bellaroo Creek?
We can promise you a fresh start and genuine country
hospitality.

CAMERON MANNING PACED from the fence to the empty farmhouse and back again. He checked his watch. The second
hand hadn't moved much from the last time he'd looked.
With a curse, he threw himself down on the bench, squat-
ting beneath one of the Kurrajong trees that screened this
farmhouse from the rest of his property, and drummed his
fingers against his thigh.

Where was the woman?

The slats of the bench, badly in need of a nail or ten, bit
into his back. It would've been more comfortable to sit on
the veranda, but here the deep shade screened him. It'd give
him a chance to contemplate his new tenants unobserved.

He scowled. If they ever turned up.

To be honest, he didn't much care if they did or not. All he wanted was Tess Laing's signature on his contract so he could hightail it out of here again. He had work to do. Serious work.

He leaned forward, steepling his hands under his chin as he glared at the farmhouse. Now that he had the cattle station on the western edges of his property sorted and in the capable hands of an under-manager, and he and station manager Fraser had dealt with all that needed overseeing for the operation of the sheep station and the planting and harvesting of the wheat crop, the only item left remaining was the canola contract.

He needed that locked in.

Once it was he'd be free to leave this godforsaken place. He'd shake off the dust of the poisonous memories that not only plagued his dreams at night but his waking hours too.

He leapt up, a familiar bitterness coating his tongue and the blackness of betrayal settling over him like a straitjacket. For the first time in his life he understood his father's retreat from the world. He recognised the same impulse in himself now. He gritted his teeth. He would *not* give into it.

Blasting out a breath, he glanced at his watch. 3:30 p.m. The woman had said she'd arrive somewhere between two and three o'clock. He slashed a hand through the air. Lucky she wasn't an employee.

Lucky for her, that was. He could fire an employee. He wrenched his gaze from the forty hectares of lovingly improved land that stretched out behind the farmhouse. Land he'd spent the last two years painstakingly improving—turning the soil, digging out rocks, fertilising…backbreaking work. And now…

He seized the contract he'd tossed onto the bench, rolled it up and slapped it against his legs. Once it was signed he could shake the dust of Bellaroo Creek from his feet for good. After that, his mother could deal with the new tenants.

And good luck to them.

He paced some more. He threw himself back to the bench

and kept his gaze firmly fixed on the road and not on those contentious forty hectares. Finally a car appeared at the end of the gravel road, moving slowly—a big, solid station wagon.

Cam didn't move from his spot in the shade, not even stirring when the breeze sent a light branch dancing across his hair, but every muscle in his body tightened. He dragged in a breath and counselled patience. He would explain the inadvertent mix-up to Tess Laing. He would *patiently* explain that a mistake had somehow seen his forty hectares included in her lease on the house. He would get her signature to turn those forty hectares back over to him. End of story.

If the mix-up had been inadvertent—an *honest* mistake. Bile burned his throat. Honesty and his family didn't necessarily go hand in hand. He expected betrayal from Lance. His nostrils flared and his lips thinned. He would never underestimate his little brother's treacherous resentment again. He would never again trust a word that spilled from Lance's forked tongue. But his mother, had she…?

An invisible hand tried to squeeze the air out of his lungs, but he ignored it to thrust out his jaw. Mistake or not, he needed that land. And he *would* get it back. He'd talk this woman out of whatever ridiculous hobby farm idea she'd come out here with. He'd offer her a fair price to lease the land back. He'd make whatever bargain he needed to. His hand curled around the contract. Once he had her signature, Kurrajong Station's obligations would be met. And he'd be free to head off for the far horizons of Africa.

Lance, Fiona and his mother could sink or swim on their own.

The car finally reached the farmhouse and pulled to a halt. He rested his elbows on his knees, eyes narrowed. Would she be some hard-nosed business type or a free-spirited hippy?

Three car doors were flung open and three passengers shot out from the car's interior like bottled fizzy water that had been shaken and then opened—a woman and two children. All of them raced around to the front of the car and bounced from one foot to the other as if they'd been cooped up for too long.

He studied the woman. She didn't look like a hard-nosed businesswoman. She didn't look like a nature-loving hippy either. She looked…

In her red-and-black tartan skirt, thick black tights and black Doc Martens she reminded him of a ladybird. Her movements, though, were pure willy wagtail—light, graceful…cheeky. In fact, she looked like a university student. He sat up straighter. She couldn't be old enough to have two kids!

He turned his attention to the children—a boy of around seven and a girl a year or two younger. He had a vague recollection of his mother mentioning their ages as being a real coup for the school. It was the main reason the committee had chosen this family from the flood of applicants.

A frown built inside him. They might be a coup for the school, but right now they were a disaster for him.

Finally he allowed himself a grim smile as the woman shook out her arms and legs as if she'd spent too many hours in the car—granted it was a bit of a hike from Sydney to Bellaroo Creek—and then moved to rest her hands on the front fence, a child standing either side of her. Her dark hair shone in the autumn sun. It made him realise how brightly the sun shone in the soft autumn stillness of the afternoon.

The boy glanced up at her, indecision flitting across his face. 'What do you think?' He glanced back at the cottage. 'Did you know it would look like this?'

Cam pursed his lips at the edge of disappointment lacing the boy's words. The little girl moved closer to the woman as if seeking reassurance. Cam straightened. If they hated the place they'd happily sign the whole kit and caboodle back over to him! That'd solve everything.

'I had no idea what it'd look like.'

Her voice sounded like music.

She beamed down at the children and then clasped her hands beneath her chin. 'Oh, but I think it's perfect!' She knelt on the ground, heedless of the danger to her tights, to put an arm about each of them.

The little girl pressed in against her. 'Really?'

'You do?' The little boy leaned against her too.

'Oh, yes!'

Cam wondered where she came by such confidence and enthusiasm. She was from the city. What did she know about country living?

Unless she'd known about those forty hectares before times and knew of their value. Unless Lance had already got to her, somehow. Unless—

'Look at the size of the yard. Just think how perfect it'll be once we've mown the lawn and trimmed back that hedge of…' She gestured with her head because it was obvious she didn't want to let go of either child.

'You don't know what it is,' the boy accused.

'I have no idea,' she agreed with one of the widest grins Cam had ever seen.

Plumbago. He could've told her, but something hard and heavy had settled in his stomach. He could've at least mown the lawn for them, couldn't he? He might've been flat out with organising the cattle station, the wheat crop and mustering sheep, but he should've found the time to manage at least that much. He mightn't want these new tenants—his mother had manipulated him superbly on that front—but that wasn't this woman's fault, or her children's.

'But won't it be fun finding out?'

'I guess.'

'And just imagine how pretty the cottage will look once we've painted it.'

She was going to paint his cottage?

'Pink!'

'Blue!'

'Cream!' She grinned back at the kids. 'We'll draw straws.'

He hoped she rigged that one.

The little girl started to jump up and down. 'We can have chickens!'

'And a dog!' The little boy started to jump too.

'And a lemon tree and pretty curtains at the window.' The woman laughed, bouncing back upright. 'And…?'

'And we'll all live happily ever after,' they hollered together in a chorus, and Cam found he couldn't drag his eyes from them.

It was just a house on an average acre block. But it hit him then what this property represented. A new start. And he knew exactly what that meant.

With everything in his soul.

The woman clapped her hands, claiming his attention once more. 'I think we should sing our song to our new perfect home.'

And they started to sing. The children held a wobbly melody and the woman harmonised, and they so loved their song and grinned so madly at each other that Cam found his lips lifting upwards.

'The house loves us now,' the little girl whispered.

'I believe you're right.'

'I love a veranda,' the little boy said and Cam knew it was his way of saying he approved of the house…of their new start.

The woman smiled *that* smile again and Cam had to shift on his bench. 'Right,' she said, dusting off her hands, 'what we need now is the key.'

That was his cue.

He hadn't meant to sit here for so long watching them without declaring himself. He'd only thought—hoped—that a moment's observation would give him the measure of his new tenants. Except… He found himself more confounded than ever.

'That'd be where I come in.'

Both children literally jumped out of their skins at his abrupt declaration and he found himself wishing he'd cleared his throat first to give them warning of his presence.

The little girl ducked behind the woman, her hands clutching fistfuls of the woman's shirt. The boy wavered for a moment or two and then moved in front of the woman, face pale and hands clenched, but obviously determined to protect her. It was a simple act of courage that knocked Cam sideways. His heart started to pound.

The woman reached out and tousled the boy's hair and pulled him back in against her. She kept her voice solidly cheerful. 'Aha! You'll be our emissary from the town.'

Not quite, but… 'I have your key.'

'Good Lord!' She planted her hands on her hips as he emerged more fully into the sunlight. 'Look at the size of you. I bet you're a big help to your mum.'

And beside her both children immediately relaxed, and he found himself careful to keep the smile on his face and to move towards them slowly. 'Actually, I guess I'm your landlord. I'm Cameron Manning.'

She frowned. 'I thought Lorraine…'

'My mother.'

'Ah.' She nodded, and then a cheeky grin peeked out. 'The mother you're such a big help to, no doubt.'

Actually, there was every doubt in the world on that head.

'I'm Tess, and this is Tyler and Kristina—Ty and Krissie for short—and we're very pleased to meet you.'

She held out her hand and he moved the final few feet forward to shake it. With such dark hair—nearly black—he'd thought she'd be pale but she had skin the colour of deep golden honey. Her palm slid against his, smooth and cool. Large brown eyes surveyed him with undisguised intensity as if attempting to sum up the man beneath the bulk.

She smelled of liquorice and cool days, and when he finally stepped back Cam found his heart pounding.

'Can you ride a horse?' Tyler asked, awe stretching through his voice.

'I can.'

'I want to be a cowboy when I grow up.'

'Then you've come to the right town,' Cam said, though he could hardly believe that he spoke them. He hadn't meant to be so welcoming. He'd meant to be businesslike and brisk. But that boy had stepped in front of his mother when he'd thought she'd needed protecting. There were grown men who were afraid to take Cam on physically. At six feet three and sporting the kind of muscles that hard work on the land developed, he understood that reluctance.

He was big and he was strong. Yet, still, this little boy had faced his fear and Cam couldn't ignore that.

'Auntie Tess—' the little girl tugged on the woman's sleeve '—I've gotta go.'

Auntie? She wasn't their mother?

'Right.' She stared at him expectantly. 'The key?'

He recalled how he'd considered talking them out of this property. The contract he'd left sitting on the bench fluttered in the breeze. He considered Tyler's act of courage and Krissie's excitement about chickens and the way Tess had quieted the children's fears with a song.

A new start. He knew all about the need for those.

He fished the key out of his pocket and handed it over.

The three of them raced to the front door of the old farmhouse. Cam retrieved his contract and then stood under the Kurrajong tree and dragged in a breath. Okay, the house was neither here nor there. He had no plans for it. Those forty hectares, though, did matter and he wanted—needed—Tess's signature on the dotted line.

And he wasn't leaving until he had it.

He followed them into the house.

'Bags this room!' Tyler shouted from the corridor off to the right. 'It has a view of the front and I can see who's coming, which is good 'cause I'm the man of the house.'

That almost made Cam smile again, only he remembered how pale the boy had gone when Cam had appeared unannounced.

The toilet flushed, the sound of water running in a tap and then Krissie raced down the corridor too. 'Auntie Tess, this is your room! And this one is mine 'cause it's right next to yours!'

Cam let out a breath as he glanced around. The yard might need some TLC, but the women from the Save-Our-Town committee had cleaned this place to within an inch of its life. The furniture might be mismatched—favouring comfort more than elegance—but there wasn't a single dust bunny in sight. 'Coffee?' he called out, wanting Tess to know he'd followed them into the house.

'Excellent idea,' she called back.

He strode into the kitchen and put the jug on to boil. The farmhouse wasn't fancy by any means, but it had a certain homey charm. He had the impression that Tess would turn it into a home in the blink of an eye.

What on earth was he talking about? He shook his head. She already had, and he wasn't sure how. It took more than a smile and a song to make a home.

Didn't it?

He let himself out of the back door, the contract burning a hole against his palm as he moved down the steps to stare out at those magical forty hectares. She was paying a dollar a week in rent for all that. It was enough to make a grown man weep.

He straightened. He had a canola contract to fulfil—he'd given his word—and he wasn't going to let anyone steal it out from under him. His lips twisted. He didn't doubt for a moment that one person in particular in Bellaroo Creek would try to do exactly that, but would his mother be party to such duplicity?

'You better get that particular look off your face quick smart or you'll give Ty and Krissie nightmares for a month.'

He blinked to find Tess holding a mug out to him. He frowned. 'I was supposed to be making those.' He'd meant to make a stab at the country-hospitality approach first before bombarding her with his demand. Besides, she had dark circles beneath those magnificent eyes of hers. If she'd left two hours from the other side of Sydney this morning she'd have driven for the best part of eight hours.

The least he could've done was make her a cup of coffee. And mow the lawn. And trim that hedge of plumbago.

'No matter, and sorry but I put milk in it before I thought. If you want sugar—'

'No, this is great,' he said hastily. 'Thanks.'

Her lips twitched. 'You didn't strike me as a sugar-in-their-coffee type.'

What was that supposed to mean?

She stared out at the fields and drew a breath deep into her lungs. 'Oh, my, look at it all!'

His skin tightened. His muscles tensed.

'You live in a beautiful part of the world, Cameron.'

'Cam.' The correction came out husky. The only person to call him Cameron was his mother. 'But you're right.' He nodded towards the fields. 'It's beautiful.'

And by rights it should be his. He spun to her. 'There's something—'

'I want to apologise for being late.'

He blinked at her interruption. 'No problem.'

'We had one threat of car sickness.'

He grimaced.

'And I took a wrong turn when we left Parkes. I started heading towards Trundle instead of Bellaroo Creek.'

'That's in completely the opposite direction.'

'That's what a man on a tractor told us.'

He shifted his weight, opened his mouth.

She pointed back behind her with an infectious grin. 'Do you know somebody left us a cake?'

He found one side of his mouth hitching up at her delight. 'That'd be my mother. I'd know her sultana cake anywhere. It's her speciality.'

'Then you must stay for a slice.'

He adjusted his stance. 'Look, there's something I need to talk to you about.'

Her gaze had dropped to take an inventory of his shoulders and he could feel himself tensing up again, but at his words her eyes lifted. She sipped her coffee. 'Yes?'

'It's about that land out there.' He gestured out in front of them.

'Wow! Look how big the yard is!'

With whoops, Ty and Krissie swooped down the back steps and into the yard. Cam winced at how overgrown it all was.

'What kind of tree is that, Auntie Tess?'

She shaded her eyes and peered to where Krissie pointed. 'Tell me?' she shot out of the corner of her mouth and it made him want to laugh. 'Please?'

'Lemon tree,' he answered in an undertone.

She turned and beamed at him. It cracked open something wide inside him—something that made him hot and cold at the same time. Before he could react in any way whatsoever, she set her coffee to the ground, danced down to the lemon tree and the children with her arms outstretched as if to embrace them all. But he could've sworn she'd whispered, 'Smile,' at him before she'd danced away.

'It's a lemon tree!'

The children cheered. They all started rattling off the things they'd make with the lemons—lemonade, lemon butter, lemon-meringue pie, lemon chicken, lemon tea—as if it were a litany they'd learned off by heart. As if it were a list that made the world a better place.

And as he watched them Cam thought that maybe it did.

'Where do you live, um…Mr…?'

He gazed down at Krissie with her blonde curls, and her big brown eyes identical to Tess's, and recalled the way she'd jumped when he'd first spoken. *Smile.* 'You can call me Cam,' he said, making his voice gentle. 'If that's okay with your auntie Tess.'

Tess nodded her assent, but he was aware that she watched him like a hawk—or a mother bear hell-bent on protecting her cubs.

'You can see my house from here.' He led them towards the line of Kurrajong trees at the side fence and gestured across the acre field to his home beyond.

'Wow,' Ty breathed. 'It's big.'

It was, and the sandstone homestead was a point of local pride. 'My great-great-great-grandfather was one of the first settlers in the area. His son built that house.'

'Is it a farm?'

'It is. It's called Kurrajong Station because of all the Kurrajong trees. It's large for these parts at six thousand hectares.' It wasn't a boast, just pure fact.

'What do you farm?'

That was Tess. He eyed her for a moment. He sure as hell hoped she didn't have any interests in that direction. 'Cattle, sheep and wheat mostly.' And just as soon as he had his forty hectares back he'd be branching out into canola. Diversification would ensure Kurrajong's future. And once that was all in place, he could leave.

For good.

'Are we allowed to play in that field?'

Ty glanced up at him hopefully. Cam bit back a sigh. He didn't have anything against the Save-Our-Town scheme in principle. He mightn't want to live in Bellaroo Creek any longer, but his station's prosperity did, to some extent, hinge on the town's ongoing existence. It was just that in practical terms…

So much for his jealously guarded privacy.

Still, they were just kids. They wouldn't disturb his peace too much. And kids would be kids—they'd want to explore, kick balls, run. Besides, he sensed that these kids needed more kindness than most. Rather than declare the paddock out of bounds, he found himself saying, 'You'd better wait till you've made friends with my dog first.'

Ty's face lit up. 'You have a dog? When can we meet him?'

Cam shoved his hands in his pockets and glanced at Tess. 'Tomorrow?'

She nodded. 'Excellent.'

Her cap of dark hair glowed in the sun and her eyes were bigger than they had any right to be. He gave himself a mental kick and turned back to the kids. 'I want you both to promise me something. If you see a paddock with either cows or big machinery in it, promise you won't go into it. It could be dangerous.'

They gazed up at him with eyes too solemn for their age and nodded.

Lord, he didn't mean to frighten them. *Smile!* 'We just want to make sure you stay safe, okay?'

They nodded again.

'And you shouldn't go outside your own yard or this paddock without letting your auntie Tess know first.'

Tess watched Cam as he talked with the children. His initial gruffness apparently hid a natural gentleness for all those smaller than him. Not that there'd be too many who'd be larger! The longer she watched, the more aware she became of the warmth stealing over her.

She shook it off. She wanted this move to be perfect. She wanted to believe that everyone in Bellaroo Creek would have

Ty and Krissie's best interests at heart. She wasn't going to let that hope lead her astray, though. Too much depended on her making the right decisions. She swallowed, her heart still burning at the children's reactions when Cam had startled them—their instinctive fear and suspicion.

She gripped her hands together. Please, please, please let moving to Bellaroo Creek be the right decision. Please, please, please let the children learn to trust again. Please, God, help her make them feel secure and safe, loved.

She relaxed her hands and crossed her fingers. After the initial shaky start, it certainly looked as if the kids had taken to their laconic neighbour. After all, not only did he know how to ride a horse, but he had a dog too. True hero material.

Her gaze drifted down his denim-clad legs and a long slow sigh built up inside her. He could certainly fill out a pair of jeans nicely. With cheeks suddenly burning, she wrenched her gaze away. For heaven's sake, she hadn't moved to Bellaroo Creek for that kind of fresh start!

Besides—she glanced up at him through her lashes—Cameron Manning was a man with something on his mind. She'd sensed it the moment he'd stepped out of the shadows of the trees. She had relaxed a little, though, when he'd handed over the key. She had no intention of handing it back. She'd signed a legally binding lease. She'd paid the first year's rent up front. All fifty-two dollars of it.

The children ran off further down the backyard to explore, but even while she sensed he wanted to talk, she didn't suggest they go inside to do just that. She wanted to keep an eye on Ty and Krissie. She wanted them to know she was nearby. She wanted to share in the joy of their discoveries. She had every intention of smoothing over any little concerns or ripples that threatened their well-being.

That was her first priority. That mattered a million times more than anything else at the moment. Joy, love and hope—

that was what these kids needed and that was exactly what they were going to get.

She shot Cam another half-veiled glance. Still, if he was happy to talk out here… 'I—'

'You're their auntie Tess?'

She blinked.

'Where are their parents?'

Ah. She'd thought the entire town would know their story considering she hadn't been reticent about the details in her application. In fact, she'd shamelessly used those details in an attempt to tug on all the unknown heartstrings that would be reading their application.

They walked back towards the house. Tess swooped down to pick up her abandoned coffee from the grass. She chugged back its lukewarm contents and then let the mug dangle loosely from her fingers. 'Why is your surname different from your mother's?'

'I'm the son from her first marriage.'

Right. She nodded towards the children. 'Their father and mother—my sister—died in a car accident three months ago.'

He stilled. 'I'm sorry.'

He sounded genuinely sympathetic and her eyes started to burn. Even now, three months down the track and a million tears later, she still found condolences hard to deal with. But Cameron's voice sounded low and deep—the tone and breadth midway between an oboe and a cello—and somehow that made it easier. She nodded and kicked herself back into an aimless meandering around the yard.

'Are you interested in farming? In keeping cattle or horses or growing a crop?'

The abrupt change of topic took her off guard. 'God, no!' She hoped he didn't take her horror personally, but she didn't know the first thing about farming. She didn't know much about vegetable gardens or keeping chickens either, she supposed, but she could learn. 'Why?'

'Because there's been a bit of a mix-up with the tenancy agreement.'

Her blood chilled. Just like that. In an instant. Her toes and fingers froze rigid. He couldn't kick them out! *He'd given them the key*.

The children loved this place. *She'd* made sure they'd fallen in love with it—had used her enthusiasm and assumed confidence to give it all a magical promise. Ty and Krissie weren't resilient enough to deal with another disappointment.

And they didn't deserve to.

'I mean, yes,' she snapped out as quickly as she could. 'Farming is exactly the reason we're out here.'

He frowned. In fact, it might be described as a scowl. But then he glanced at the kids and it became just a frown again. 'I beg your pardon?'

She didn't like the barely leashed control stretching through his voice, but he was not kicking them out. 'What I'm trying to say is that I'm fully prepared to learn farming if that's part of my contract.'

She'd gone over the contract with a fine-tooth comb. She'd consulted a solicitor. Her chin lifted. She'd signed a legally binding contract. She *had* understood it. The solicitor had ensured that. She wasn't in the wrong here. A fine trembling started up in her legs, but she stood her ground. 'I'm not going to let you kick us out.' She even managed to keep her voice perfectly pleasant. 'Just so you know.'

'I don't want to kick you out.'

That was when she knew he was lying. Even though he'd been kind to the children. Even though he'd handed over the key. This man would love it if they left.

Didn't he want to save his town?

By this stage they'd reached the back fence. She set her mug on a fencepost, and then leant against it and folded her arms. 'It's been a long day, Mr Manning, so I'm going to speak plainly.'

He blinked at the formality of her *Mr Manning*. And she saw he understood the sudden distance she'd created between them.

'I signed a contract and I understand my rights. If there's been a mix-up then it hasn't been of my making.' She folded her arms tighter. 'Whatever this mix-up may be, the children and I are not leaving this house. We're living here for the next three years and we're going to carve out a new life for ourselves and we are going to make that work. This is now our home and we're going to make it a good home. Furthermore, you are not going to say anything in front of the children that might upset or alarm them—you hear me?'

His mouth opened and closed. 'I wouldn't dream of it.'

He leaned towards her and he smelled like fresh-cut grass, and it smelled so fresh and young that she wanted to bury her face against his neck and just breathe it in. She shook herself. It'd been a long trip. Very long. 'Then smile!' she snapped.

To her utter astonishment, he laughed, and the grim lines that hooded his eyes and weighed down the corners of his mouth all lightened, and his eyes sparkled, the same deep green as clover.

Her breath caught. The man wasn't just big and broad and a great help to his mum—he was beautiful!

The blood started to thump in a painful pulse about her body. Four months ago she'd have flirted with Cam in an attempt to lighten him up. Three months ago she'd have barely noticed him. It was amazing the changes a single month could bring. One day. In fact, lives could change in a single moment.

And they did.

And they had.

She swallowed. The particular moment that had turned her life on its head might not have been her fault, but if she'd been paying attention she might've been able to avert it. That knowledge would plague her to her grave.

And men, beautiful and otherwise, were completely off the agenda.

She snapped away from him. He frowned. 'Tess, I'm not going to ask you to leave. I swear. This house is all yours for the next three years, and beyond if you want it.'

She bit her lip, glanced back at him. 'Really?'

'Really.'

'Still—' she stuck out a hip '—you're less than enthused about it.'

He hesitated and then shrugged. 'My mother has, in effect, foisted you lot on to me.'

She glanced at the house and then back at him. 'Isn't the house hers?'

'Not precisely.' He exhaled loudly. 'My father made certain provisions for my mother in his will. She has the use of this house along with an attached parcel of land for as long as she lives. When she passes the rights all revert back to the owner of Kurrajong Station.'

'You?'

'Me.'

She pursed her lips. He met her gaze steadily. She wanted to get a handle on this enigmatic neighbour of hers. Was he friend or foe? 'Don't you want to help save Bellaroo Creek?'

'Sure I do.'

'As long as you're not asked to sacrifice too much in the effort, right?'

'As long as I'm not asked to give up a significant portion of my potential income in the process,' he countered.

'How will our being here impact negatively on your income?' Her understanding was that the Save-Our-Town scheme only offered *unused* farmhouses in exchange for ludicrously cheap rents. If their farmhouse was unused he couldn't possibly be losing money. In fact, he'd be fifty-two dollars a year richer.

Her lips suddenly twitched. Cameron Manning didn't

strike her as the kind of man who'd stress too much over fifty-two dollars. Not that she needed to stress over money either. It hadn't been the cheap rent but the promise of a fresh start that had lured her out here.

He drew in a breath and then pointed behind her. She turned. 'Forty hectares,' he said. 'Forty hectares I had plans for. Forty hectares my mother had promised to lease to me.'

She slapped a hand to her forehead. 'They were allotted to me in my tenancy agreement? That's the mix-up you're talking about.'

'Yep.'

'And you want them back?'

'Bingo.'

She laughed in her sudden rush of relief. 'Oh, honey, they're all yours.' What on earth did she want with forty hectares of wide, open space? She had a house and a back-yard and a whole ocean of possibilities enough to satisfy her.

She clapped her hands. 'Hey, troops, who's for sultana cake?'

CHAPTER TWO

IT TOOK TESS until her second bite of sultana cake to realise she hadn't allayed her sexy neighbour's concerns.

She stiffened. Umm…not sexy. Taciturn and self-contained, perhaps, and, um… She dragged her gaze from shoulders so broad they made her think of Greek gods and swimsuits and the Mediterranean.

Sleep, rest, peace, that was what she needed. The last month had been a crazy whirlwind and she quite literally hadn't stopped. The two months prior had been a blur of pain and grief.

She flinched at the memory and brushed a hand across her eyes. Bellaroo Creek would bring her the rest and the sleep she craved, but peace? She wasn't sure anything on earth could bring her that.

And she wasn't sure she deserved it.

Cameron hitched an eyebrow. 'A penny for them.'

She stiffened again. Nu-huh. But the exhaustion made her silly—an after-effect of the nonsense she'd used all day to keep the children entertained and in good spirits. 'Are you sure you can afford a penny when I'm only paying you a dollar a week in rent?'

His green eyes gleamed for a tantalizing moment. It made him look younger. She dragged her gaze away and rose. 'I'll just check on the kids. The promise of cake should've had them sprinting inside.'

On cue, the pair came racing through the front door. 'We found a lizard,' Ty announced, breathless with excitement.

'Will it bite us?' Krissie asked, wide-eyed.

She directed the question at Cam. He'd obviously become the source of trusted information. Tess's chest cramped as she stared at them—took in their simple wonder.

'That'll be Old Nelson, the blue-tongue,' Cam said, leaning back in his chair, one long, lean leg stretched out in front of him.

Krissie's eyes widened even further. 'He has a name?'

'Wow, awesome!' Ty breathed. 'Will he bite?'

'Only if you poke him or try to pick him up.'

'Can we take our cake outside, Auntie Tess?'

With a laugh, Tess assented. She watched as they left the room and her chest burned. If only Sarah could see them now. If only—

'You okay?'

She jumped, swung back patting her chest. 'Tired,' she said. She sat and forced a smile. She'd become good at that over the last couple of months—smiling when she didn't feel like it—but she could see it didn't fool Cam. She shrugged. 'They've been through so much, but for this moment they're happy and…and that's no small thing.'

He stared towards the front of the house and then glanced back at her. 'They're great kids, Tess.'

She nodded. 'They really are.' And they deserved so much more than life had dished out to them. Focusing on the negatives wouldn't help anyone, though—least of all Ty and Krissie. She sipped tea. Cam had made a pot while she'd sliced the cake. It was the best tea she'd ever tasted.

She lifted her cup. 'This is seriously good.'

'My mother was the president of the Country Women's

Association for a hundred years. Believe me, she made sure her sons knew how to brew a proper pot of tea.'

She made a mental note to join the CWA. But for the moment… 'You want to tell me why you're still so worried about your forty hectares?'

His eyes widened a fraction, but he held her gaze with a steadiness she found disconcerting. 'I had a contract drawn up. I need you to sign it before I can start planting.'

He whipped out a sheaf of papers, literally from thin air as far as her tired brain could tell. He flicked through to the final page and pointed. 'I need your signature here.' He handed her a pen.

She lowered her cup back to its saucer and dropped her hands to her lap. 'I'm not signing anything I haven't read.'

'Fair enough.' He placed the contract in front of her and leaned back.

'And I'm not reading it now when I'm so tired.'

He frowned.

'And if there's something I don't understand, I'll be consulting my solicitor for clarification.'

He was silent for a long moment and the silence should've sawn on her nerves, but it didn't. After a day of chatter and noise in the confines of the car, the silence was heaven.

'You don't trust me,' he finally said, nodding as if that made perfect sense.

'I don't know you. Once upon a time I'd have been prepared to take spur-of-the-moment risks and trust my gut instincts, but I won't now Tyler and Krissie are in my care.' She leant towards him. 'Are you saying you trust me?' She waved a hand in the direction of the back door and his precious forty hectares. 'By all means start planting tomorrow. I'll keep my word. I'll get the contract back to you by the middle of next week.'

His lips twisted but his eyes danced. 'Nope, don't trust you as far as I could throw you.'

Given his size and the breadth of his shoulders, she had a feeling he could throw her a long way if he so chose.

This time it was he who leaned in towards her, and that fresh-cut-grass scent danced around her and it was almost as relaxing as silence. 'But I do need to get started on the planting soon if I'm to meet my obligations.'

'I promise not to drag my feet.' She wanted to be on good terms with her neighbours and the townsfolk of Bellaroo Creek. She just had to make sure she didn't risk the children's futures in her eagerness to fit in.

Without thinking, she reached out and touched his hand. He immediately stiffened and she snatched her hand back, her heart suddenly thundering in her ears. 'I, uh… You said you'd bring your dog around to meet the children. Why don't you aim to do that tomorrow morning some time—say, ten o'clock? I'll try and have your contract read by then.'

'If you need more time…'

Her pulse rate refused to slow. 'No, no, it's obvious that time is of the essence. Besides, the kids will no doubt be up early and we have a midday meet-and-greet luncheon at the community hall, so I should have plenty of time in the morning to go over this contract of yours.'

He rose in one swift motion. 'I'll see you at ten.' And then he was gone.

She heard him say goodbye to the children. She supposed she should've followed him to the door to wave him off, but the strength had leached from her legs and she found herself momentarily incapable of even rising from her chair. She'd spent nearly ten hours in the car today. She was dog-tired. She'd just turned her entire life on its head—hers and the children's. And if this move didn't work out…

She shook that thought off. This move had to work out. In the meantime, she refused to allow her sexy neighbour to unsettle her.

She frowned. He *wasn't* sexy.

She glanced at her empty plate, and then at Cam's and realised he hadn't touched his cake—he hadn't even broken off the tiniest corner. She hadn't been hungry for the last three months—ever since she'd received the phone call informing her of Sarah's car accident. But now…

She stared at the cake. She pulled the plate towards her and then poured another cup of tea. She devoured both, slowly, relishing every single delicious mouthful.

The children made instant friends with Boomer, Cam's border collie.

'Will he fetch a ball?' Ty asked, pulling a tennis ball from his pocket.

Cam's mouth angled up in a lopsided smile as he surveyed Ty and Krissie and their barely concealed eagerness. 'Believe me, he'll fetch for longer than you'll be prepared to throw.' With whoops of delight, the children raced around the backyard with Boomer at their heels.

He had a way of smiling at her kids—and, yes, somewhere in the last month she'd started thinking of them as hers—that could melt a woman where she stood. 'Morning,' he finally said, the green of his eyes strangely undiluted in the mid-morning sun.

'It will be,' she countered, 'if you'll teach me the trick to making a perfect pot of tea.'

He laughed and it was only then she saw that while his eyes might be the purest of greens, shadows lurked in their depths. Shadows momentarily dispelled when he laughed.

He followed her into the kitchen. 'One demonstration coming up.'

He should laugh more often. 'Jug's just boiled,' she said, shaking the odd thought aside. Cam might well laugh a hundred times every single day for all she knew.

'Did you fill the jug using hot or cold water?'

'Hot. It makes it come to the boil faster.'

'There's your first mistake.' He poured the contents of the jug down the sink and refilled it from the cold tap. 'Cold water has more oxygen than hot. That's key for the perfect cuppa.'

She sat and stared. 'Well, who'd have known that?' Other than a chemistry professor. And a president of the CWA… and her sons.

He sat too, his eyes twinkling for the briefest of moments. 'It's important to be properly trained in country ways.'

'I never doubted it for a moment.' She leapt up to glance out of the kitchen window to make sure the children were okay. When she swung back she could've sworn he'd been checking out her backside.

His gaze slid away. Her heart thumped. She'd imagined it. She must've imagined it. She frowned, scratched a hand through her hair and tried to think of something to say.

'Did you get a chance to read the contract?'

Of course she'd imagined it, but the shadows were back in his eyes with a vengeance and it left a bitter taste in her mouth, though for the life of her she couldn't explain why. 'Yes.' She took her seat again.

'And?'

The contract had been remarkably straightforward. It hadn't asked her to give up her firstborn or sign her rights away to the house and the acre block it stood on. It simply requested she sign over the attached forty hectares of land and to waive her rights to any profits he accrued from the use of the land. Except…

On the table, one of his hands tightened. 'You have a problem?'

She hauled in a breath and nodded. 'I do.'

'You want more money for the lease?'

She hated the derisive light that entered his eyes. She pushed the contract towards him. 'I made my amendment in black ink. That's what I'm prepared to sign.'

Blowing out a breath, he pulled the contract towards him

and flipped through the pages to the end. And then he stilled and rubbed his forehead. 'You don't want any payment at all?'

She rubbed her hands up and down her arms. What kind of people was he used to dealing with? 'Of course I don't want any payment! I'm not entitled to any payment. Rightfully the land is yours. If you want to pay anyone a fee for leasing the land, then pay your mother.'

He sat back. 'I've offended you.'

Why did the wonder in his voice suddenly make her want to cry? Since Sarah's death, the silliest, most unexpected things could make her cry. 'You will if you keep going on in that vein.'

Her voice came out husky and choked. His gaze lowered to her mouth and it gave her a moment to study him. He had a strong jaw and lean lips and she couldn't tear her eyes away. She could keep telling herself that he wasn't sexy, but he was. His eyes darkened. A pulse throbbed in her bottom lip, swelling it and making it ache. The heat in the air between them sizzled with such unmistakable intensity it made her head whirl. With an oath, Cam pushed away from the table. He seized the teapot and started making tea. She closed her eyes. She'd been surrounded by death, preoccupied with it. Life wanted to reassert itself. This—her body's rebellion at her common-sense strictures—was normal.

The explanation didn't make the pounding in her blood lessen any, but it did start to clear the fog encasing her brain.

She jumped when Cam set a mug of tea in front of her, his face a mask. 'I'm sorry. I didn't mean to offend you. I'm just used to paying my own way.'

She wasn't. Not really. Her cold realisation dissipated the last of the heat. She'd always relied on staff or assistants to take care of her day-to-day needs. But she could learn. She *was* learning.

He hooked out his chair again and sat. 'A free ride feels wrong.'

'It's not a free ride. A free ride is if I also did the planting for you. You'd discussed that land with your mother. You had her permission to use it. Like you said, the fact it ended up on my lease agreement was simply an error or an oversight. Cameron, I have no plans for that land. I'm not losing out on anything.'

He didn't say anything.

'Besides, don't knock a free ride. I'm getting one—a dollar a week rent! Who'd have thought that was possible?'

His lips turned upwards, but it wasn't really a smile. 'You've brought two school-age children into the area. You're boosting the school's numbers and increasing its chances of remaining open. The town will think it a very good swap.'

Speaking of children... She rose and went to the window again to check on them. She laughed at what she saw. 'Are you sure they won't wear Boomer out?'

'I'm positive.' He eyed her as she took her seat again. 'They are safe with him. I promise.'

'Oh! Of course they are. I didn't mean...' She could feel herself starting to colour under his stare. The thing was, most days she felt as if she didn't know a darn thing about parenting at all. Maybe she did fuss a little too much, worry too much, but surely that was better than not fussing enough.

That was when the idea hit her.

He leant towards her, his eyes wary. 'What?'

She surveyed him over the rim of her mug. 'You're obviously not very comfortable with me just handing the land back to you.'

'You could make a tidy profit from the lease.'

'Believe me, the one thing I don't need to worry about is money.' Sarah had seen to that. 'But maybe,' she started slowly, allowing the idea to develop more fully in her mind, 'we could do a kind of swap. I'll give you the land...'

'In exchange for what?'

She rose and went to the window again. She loved those

kids. Just how fiercely amazed her. She'd do anything for them. *Anything.* And what she needed to do most was provide them with a positive start here in Bellaroo Creek.

Cam stared at Tess as she peered out of the kitchen window again. She had a stillness and a straightness, even when agitated, that he found intriguing.

And she had the cutest little butt he'd ever seen. There'd probably been a hint of its perfect roundness in her tartan skirt yesterday if he'd been looking, but there was no hiding it in a pair of fitted jeans that hugged every curve with enviable snugness.

And today he was definitely looking!

For heaven's sake, he was male. Men looked at—and appreciated—the female form. It was how they were wired. It didn't mean anything.

But he hadn't looked at a woman in that way since Fiona, and—

With a scowl, he dragged his gaze away. He needed to keep on task. Tess was proposing a deal of sorts. He glanced up to find her watching him, her brow furrowed as if she couldn't figure him out. Not that he blamed her.

'You can take the contract and run,' she said. She walked back to the table, seized the contract, signed and dated it and then handed it back to him. 'Nothing more needs to be said. I don't believe you're beholden to me, not one jot.'

Honour kept him in his seat. Tess hadn't taken advantage of the situation as she could've done. As Lance and Fiona would've done. He did his best to clear the scowl from his face. She'd been reasonable and…generous. 'What kind of bargain were you going to propose, Tess?'

'I want to make moving to Bellaroo Creek a really positive experience for Ty and Krissie.'

She hadn't needed to say that out loud. He could see how much it meant to her. He wanted to tell her how much he admired her for it, but he didn't. He didn't want her to think he'd mean anything more by it than simple admiration. Because he wouldn't.

'But frankly I'm clueless.'

That snapped him back. 'About?'

She lifted her arms and let them drop. 'Everything! I didn't even know that was a lemon tree and yet you heard all our plans for it.'

Something inside him unhitched.

'I don't know the first thing about keeping chickens, but Krissie has her heart set on it. I expect I need a…a hutch or something.'

'Henhouse.'

'See? I don't even have the right vocabulary. And what about a vegetable garden? Other than supposing there's a lot of digging involved, I haven't the foggiest idea where to start.' She frowned. 'I expect I'll need compost.'

And, suddenly, Cam found himself laughing. 'Believe me, Tess, the one thing we aren't short of in Bellaroo Creek is compost.'

She gripped her hands on the table in front of her and leant towards him. 'Plus I need to get Ty a puppy, but is a puppy and chickens a seriously bad combination?'

'They don't have to be.' He leaned across and covered both of her hands with one of his own. She stiffened and he remembered the way he'd stiffened at her touch yesterday and was about to remove his hand when she relaxed. Her hands felt small and cold and instead of retreating he found his hand urging warmth into hers instead.

'So you want help building a henhouse and a veggie patch, and in selecting a dog?'

'It has to be a puppy. Apparently that's very important.'

Cam understood that. He nodded.

'And maybe some help choosing chickens?'

She winced as if she were asking too much, but it was all

a piece of cake as far as he was concerned. 'Tess, helping you with that stuff is nothing more than being neighbourly.'

The townsfolk of Bellaroo Creek would have his hide if he didn't offer her that kind of support. Though—his lips twisted—he expected there'd be quite a few single farmers in the area who wouldn't mind offering her any kind of help whatsoever.

'Then…maybe we can agree to being good neighbours. That's something else I can learn to do.'

He frowned, but before he could say anything she leapt up to glance out of the window again. 'And until I manage to get one of my own, may I borrow your lawnmower?'

'Done.'

She swung around and beamed at him. 'Thank you. Now watch me as I make a fresh pot of tea to make sure I'm doing it right.'

She had the kind of smile—when she really smiled—that could blow a man clean out of his boots. Mentally, he pulled his boots up harder and tighter.

'Why can't Cam come to our party?'

Excellent question. Tess glanced briefly in the rear-view mirror to give Krissie an encouraging smile. 'He said he had lots of work to do.'

'I bet he had to take time off work to bring Boomer around to play,' Ty said from the seat beside her. It was his turn in the front. 'His farm is really big, isn't it?'

'Six thousand hectares is what he said.' And Cameron didn't strike her as the bragging type. He was definitely the state-plain-facts type. 'Which I think is really, really big.'

'So he probably has loads and loads of work to do.'

Was that admiration or wistfulness in Ty's voice? She couldn't tell.

A mother would know.

She gulped. 'Good thinking, Ty, I expect you're right.'

His chest puffed out at her simple praise. Blinking hard, she concentrated on the road in front of her.

It only took three minutes to drive from their front door to the community hall in Bellaroo Creek's tiny main street. Across from the hall stood a row of late-Victorian town-houses—tall, straight, eye-catching, but with all their windows boarded up. Whatever businesses had operated from them were long gone. Once upon a time the town had been prosperous. Tess crossed her fingers. Hopefully they could help make the town prosperous again.

Unhooking her seat belt, she turned to the children. 'Ready?' They watched her so carefully. She knew they'd take their every cue from her. The realisation made her swallow. She had to get this just right.

Krissie leaned forward. 'Is this party really just for us?'

'It sure is, chickadee. Everyone is dying to meet us. They're so excited we've come to live in Bellaroo Creek.'

'What if they don't like us?' she whispered.

Tess feigned shock. 'Do you really think they won't like me?'

Krissie giggled. 'Not you, silly.'

'They'll love you,' Ty announced.

She knew what he was really saying was that he loved her and it made her heart swell and her eyes sting. 'And I absolutely promise that they'll love the two of you too.'

They stared at her with their identical brown eyes—eyes the same as Sarah's. They trusted her so much! She racked her brain to think of a way to make this easier for them.

'You know,' she started, 'it can be a bit awkward making new friends at first, and I bet they're just as worried that we should like them too.' She could see that thought hadn't occurred to either child. 'Sometimes it helps to have something ready to talk about. So…when you're talking to someone today you might like to ask them what their favourite thing about living in Bellaroo Creek is, or if they have a dog, or if they keep chickens.'

Both children's faces cleared immediately.

'Ooh!' She clapped her hands. 'I could send you both on a quest to find out what everyone thinks would be the best vegetables to grow in our backyard.'

Ty squinted up at her. 'Because that's important, right?'

'Vital,' she assured him.

He grinned. 'And you could find out how to make Cam's mum's cake.'

She pointed a finger at him. 'Excellent idea!' She straightened her shirt. 'And I'm going to remember to smile nicely at everyone and remember to say please and thank you in all the right places. Ready?'

The children nodded. They tumbled out of the car and, holding tight to each other's hands, they entered the hall together.

Tess blinked. There had to be at least thirty people in here! As well as one seriously long trestle table covered with more sandwiches, pies, quiches, cakes, slices and biscuits than Tess had seen altogether in one place. The sight of all that food, and all those faces, made her head spin. A hush fell over the crowd.

Thirty people, and yet for one craven moment she'd have given anything to swap ten of them for the familiar reassuring bulk of Cameron Manning. Which was crazy because she didn't know Cameron well enough for him to be either familiar or reassuring. But so far Bellaroo Creek consisted of their farmhouse, their lemon tree and Cameron.

All these people will become your community, your friends, too.

First-day nerves, that was all that this was. Taking a deep breath, Tess beamed about the room. 'Hi, I'm Tess, and this here is Ty and Krissie. We can't tell you how happy we are to be in Bellaroo Creek and how much we're looking forward to meeting everyone.'

A tall, straight woman detached herself from the crowd. 'I'm Lorraine Pritchard, and we're all absolutely delighted that you've joined our little community.'

And just like that the silence was replaced with a hubbub of voices, and the three of them were swept into the heart of the crowd. An older woman—Stacy Bennet, the school-teacher—whisked Ty and Krissie off to join a small band of children, stopping by the refreshment table to make sure they armed themselves with a fairy cake each first, and thereby winning herself two friends for life.

'The children will be fine with Stacy,' Lorraine told her kindly.

Of course they would. The same way they'd been fine with Boomer this morning. It was just…she hated losing sight of them, even for a moment. Telling herself to stop being so silly, she turned back to Lorraine. The older woman took her arm. 'Come and meet everyone.'

It'd take her longer than a single afternoon to get every-one's names straight in her mind, but they were all so friendly and kind with their welcomes and their offers of assistance to help her settle in that in under ten minutes Tess felt wrapped in warmth. The glimmer of light that had taken up residence in her heart the moment her application had been accepted now became a fully floodlit arena.

She pressed her hands to her chest and blinked hard.

A group of women surrounded her. One handed her a mug of tea, another handed her a plate piled high with food. They filled her in on what produce was available from the general store and how to set up an account there. They shared their favourite online sites for ordering in school supplies, work boots and make-up. When she asked, they told her the date for the next CWA meeting and promised to meet her there.

Several men came up to her too. One to tell her he was her

man if she ever decided to keep pigs. Another to let her know he could help her set up her own home brew if she wanted. Another introduced himself as the soccer coach for the Bellaroo Creek under tens team and told her that both Ty and Krissie were welcome when training started up in another month.

The entire town, it seemed, welcomed them with arms wide open and friendship in their hearts. Her earlier nerves suddenly seemed ludicrous.

'How are you doing, dear?' Lorraine said, coming up behind her. 'I hope we haven't overwhelmed you?'

'This is…' Tess swallowed and gestured around the room. 'It's just something else. I can't tell you how much I appreciate it.'

'Nonsense! We wanted to welcome you to town in style. Now may I introduce my future daughter-in-law, Fiona?'

'Lovely to meet you.' Tess balanced her mug on her plate and shook hands with the pretty young woman. They exchanged pleasantries for a couple of minutes before Fiona, with a glance back behind her, excused herself. Tess turned back to Lorraine. 'Thank you so much for the cake you left yesterday. I can't tell you how much we appreciated it after that long drive.'

'You're welcome, my dear. I'm only sorry I couldn't be there to greet you in person.'

'That's okay, Cameron deputised honourably in your absence.'

Lorraine's head shot up. 'Cam?' Two beats went by then, 'Oh, I'm so glad to hear it.' Her hand fluttered to her throat. 'I've been meaning to ring him, but… Is he well?'

Tess thought about those broad shoulders and long legs and had to swallow. 'He seemed very well.'

Lorraine leaned forward, her eyes eager. 'Yes?'

She blinked. 'Umm… I mean, he obviously works hard, but he brought Boomer around to meet the children this morning, which was kind of him.'

'Oh!' Lorraine clapped her hands together, her eyes shining. 'Oh, I'm so pleased to hear that.'

She was? She continued to stare at Tess as if eager to hear any news about Cam that Tess was willing to share. Tess lifted a shoulder. 'There was a bit of a mix-up on the lease agreement, but we sorted it out.'

Lorraine stilled. 'Mix-up?'

'Something about forty hectares that belong to Cam, or that he was supposed to be leasing from you or something like that, accidentally being on the lease agreement I signed.'

Lorraine paled. 'Oh...no. Are you sure?'

Tess stilled then too because it was evident that something was wrong. Very wrong. She wanted to ask what it was but manners prevented her. She rolled her shoulders. 'Perhaps I shouldn't have mentioned it.' She forced a wide smile, wanting to ease the other woman's evident anxiety. 'But I promise we sorted it out. He's happy with the outcome and so am I.'

A breath shuddered out of the older woman and she sent Tess a smile that signalled her relief. 'I'm very, *very* glad to hear that. If you see him, please give him my love.'

'Of course.' But...why didn't Lorraine give Cam her love in person?

Lorraine stared beyond Tess and suddenly straightened. 'Would you excuse me for a moment, Tess? I—'

Before she could move, however, a man Tess hadn't met charged up and kissed Lorraine's cheek, before turning to survey Tess. 'Would you introduce me to Bellaroo Creek's newest resident?'

Lorraine bit her lip. Finally she shook her head and said, 'Tess, this is my son, Lance.'

Cameron's brother? Tess hastily set her plate and mug on a nearby table and extended her hand. 'I'm very pleased to meet you.' He was prettier than Cameron with his blond good looks and golden tan, but neither his size nor his presence was anywhere near as commanding.

He grinned at her. He had one of those infectious kinds of grins. 'Oh, ho! The single farmers in the district are sure going to be pleased to meet you.'

She laughed. And he had an easy charm his older brother totally lacked.

She'd met men like Lance before—full of fun, but often not much else. On closer inspection, though, the colour was high on his cheeks and she couldn't help feeling his joviality was forced.

'It's great to meet you, Tess. Welcome to Bellaroo Creek.'

'Thank you.'

'And as I'm not the kind of man to let the grass grow under my feet…'

Really? She didn't believe that for one moment.

'I'd like to talk business with you.'

The hair at her nape prickled. She folded her arms. 'Oh?'

'Lance.' Lorraine laid a hand on his arm. 'This is neither the time nor the place.'

He shook off his mother's touch. 'Of course it is.' He bounced on the balls of his feet, a fine sheen of perspiration filming his top lip and his forehead. 'Now I understand, Tess, that you have forty prime hectares on your allotment that are just going begging. I want to make you an offer you can't refuse.'

Several groups nearby stopped talking and turned to listen. Others moved forward.

'Oh, Lance, I can't believe this of you!' Lorraine hissed. 'I think—'

He held up a hand, his eyes glittering. 'I'd like to lease that land from you at very generous terms.'

Someone nearby snorted. Lance ignored it, but Lorraine's hand fluttered about her throat. 'Lance, please,' she whispered.

He rocked back on his heels. 'What do you say, Tess?'

That was when she realised thirty pairs of eyes watched

her closely, waiting to see what she'd say, and instinct told her whatever she did or said now would seal her, Ty and Krissie's fate in Bellaroo Creek, for good or ill.

And she didn't know what would work for or against them.

She swallowed. She hadn't done anything wrong. All she could do was offer Lance the truth. 'I'm sorry, Lance, but I signed a contract this morning leasing that land to Cameron. I understood he had a right to it.'

Cameron was his brother. Surely Lance would be happy for him?

Lance stared at her, the blood draining from his face. 'But…I need that land more than he does. I *need* that canola contract.'

'Cam's spent the last two years improving that land,' somebody from the crowd said.

He had?

'Yeah, back off, Lance. Cam's earned the right to that land,' someone else called out.

Lance swung back to Tess, his face twisting and his eyes wild with panic. 'You've ruined me. You and Cam both.' His voice rose on each word. 'It's what he wants, and you've been party to that!' He stiffened. 'I hope you're happy?'

Happy? She was appalled!

One of the older farmers muttered, 'One can hardly blame Cam for that.' He lifted his voice. 'And it's sure as heck not Tess's fault. So like Stuart said, back off, Lance.'

Lance pointed a finger at her. Tess swallowed. She opened her mouth just as Ty came barrelling up, shaking, his small hands clenched to fists. 'Don't you yell at my auntie Tess!'

Bursting into tears, Krissie hurled herself at her aunt. Tess scooped her up and held her close, dangerously close to tears herself.

Fiona raced up and took Lance's arm. With an apologetic glance at Tess, she led him away.

Lorraine turned to her, pale, her hands shaking. 'Oh, Tess, I'm so sorry. I—'

Hauling Ty in close to her side, she said, 'Just give me a moment,' before leading the children to a quiet corner where she tried to quieten Krissie's sobs. Not easy when her insides were quivering and all she wanted to do was drop her head and cry too.

The luncheon had been so perfect. She'd started to feel like a part of the community. She'd thought everything was going to work out exactly as she needed it to. And then, bam!

Her head reeled. She found it hard to catch her breath. She closed her eyes and dragged air into her lungs. 'Shh, honey.' She rubbed Krissie's back. 'Everything is okay.'

It would be okay. She'd make sure it'd be okay. A setback, that was all this was.

'Why was that man angry?' Krissie hiccupped.

'It's not so much that he was angry as he was upset. He's very worried about some things.'

Her whole body shuddered. 'Is he going to hurt us?'

'No, honey, he's not.' She hugged Krissie close and then touched Ty's cheek. He was so quiet. 'I promise. Okay?'

''Kay,' he murmured.

'The man was being very silly and we don't need to worry about him at all.' She prayed they'd believe her, that they trusted her enough. Time for a brave face. 'You know what I need?' she whispered. 'A lamington. Are there any?'

'Ones with cream in them.'

'Ooh, yum.' She made her eyes wide. 'Let's go look.'

They each selected a lamington, they each took a bite, and then Tess caught Stacy's eye. 'Don't forget,' she whispered before the teacher reached them, 'I need the names of vegetables.'

They were laughing again by the time they reached the group of other children. Tess didn't doubt there'd be more questions tonight, but for now things were fine.

She moved back towards Lorraine and the group of women who surrounded her. 'Are the littlies okay?' one of the women asked her.

Tess hesitated, her gaze darting back to the circle of children. 'I think so.' She swallowed. She'd given an account of Ty and Krissie's circumstances in her application letter. Not a full account, perhaps, but full enough. She didn't doubt that everyone in the room knew about the death of their parents. 'It's just that they've been through so much in such a short space of time… Little things can unduly upset them.'

'An angry man isn't a little thing. Especially when you're five years old.'

Tess had to close her eyes for a moment. *An angry man.* The shaking started back up inside her. Lorraine touched her arm. 'I can't tell you how sorry I am, Tess. Lance has a lot on his mind at the moment, but that doesn't excuse his behaviour.'

Lorraine was obviously appalled.

'It wasn't your fault.' But… She twisted her hands together. 'Is there anything I ought to know?'

The women surrounding them discreetly melted away, leaving Tess and Lorraine alone. Lorraine gripped her hands together. 'Cameron and Lance have had the most dreadful falling out, Tess. They haven't spoken to each other in over ten months.'

Ten months!

Lorraine's eyes filled with tears. 'I…I certainly didn't expect any of that fallout to land in your lap, though. I'm absolutely mortified.'

The older woman's heartache tugged at her. But… 'That forty hectares?' she whispered.

Lorraine blinked hard and swallowed. 'I knew nothing about it, I promise.'

The shaking inside her started to slow.

'Tess, I can't tell you how sorry—'

She reached out to clasp the other woman's hands. 'There's no need to apologise further, Lorraine.' She had no desire to make things even harder for the other woman. Especially when she'd gone to so much trouble to welcome them to town so warmly. 'Let's forget about it.' She made herself smile and then turned to check on Ty and Krissie again. She prayed there hadn't been any permanent harm done there.

'Honey.' Lorraine moved in close so they were touching shoulders. 'I understand your concern. Your Ty and Krissie have had a lot to deal with, but…children are remarkably resilient, you know?'

She gave a shaky laugh. 'Are they?' She didn't have a clue.

'Yes, I promise. And I promise they'll be okay. All you can do is love them the best you can…as you obviously do. All of us here in Bellaroo Creek will do our best to become a second family to them. It'll all work out in the end.'

The other women, who'd moved back in closer, all nodded and murmured their agreement.

They made it sound so easy.

Why, then, was it proving so very, very hard?

CHAPTER THREE

CAM WENT TO knock on Tess's front door, but the sound of voices out the back had him redirecting his path around the side of the house.

Tess, Ty and Krissie all sat on a bright blue rug beside the lemon tree. They sat in a row—Tess in the middle—with legs stretched out in front of them and their backs to the sun, and him.

The scene hit him in a place he'd thought he'd locked up for good. For three beats of his heart a gnawing, ragged ache threatened to split him open. Reaching out, he steadied himself against the boards of the house. He'd dreamed of being part of a picture like this once. Ten short months ago, in fact, though it seemed like a lifetime ago now.

A family.

His jaw clenched. Lance and Fiona had stolen this from him.

A boulder of a lump stretched his throat. His temples pounded.

No! He refused to be beguiled by this dream again. He would never again open himself up to the kind of betrayal Lance and Fiona had inflicted upon him.

Filling Kurrajong House with a family, that had all been a ludicrous, out-of-reach dream. He'd found that out the hard way, just like his father. Unlike his father, however, he had no intention of burying himself on Kurrajong Station and stewing in 'what might have beens' and regrets, and waiting for death to come claim him. He'd fill the gaps somehow.

He went to swing away, to retrace his steps to the privacy and solitude of Kurrajong where he could wipe this picture from his mind and replace it with his plans for Africa and adventure, but Ty chose that moment to look up at his aunt. In profile Cam recognised the little boy's frown and the way it changed his entire demeanour. Noted the hunching of his shoulders and the way he curled himself around his knees. Very slowly, Cam turned back.

'What if this isn't a good place?'

Tess tousled his hair, and, although he couldn't see her face, he knew detail for detail the smile she'd have sent the young boy. 'How can this not be a good place? Look, we have a lemon tree *and* sultana cake.' She gestured to the tree and then the plate that shared the blanket with them.

Ty's frown didn't abate. Tess's shoulders started to tighten.

'And what about all the nice people we met yesterday? Cam's mum, Mrs Pritchard, was lovely *and* she gave me her sultana cake recipe. Plus you guys were great and we now have the names for all the vegetables we should plant in our veggie garden. And what about Mrs Bennet? You both told me she's the nicest teacher in the world.'

'Yeah.' Ty grabbed a dandelion out of the lawn and shredded it.

'Suzie was nice,' Krissie volunteered, 'even if she thinks chickens are boring. She said we could come and play in her pool in the summer.'

'Nice.' Tess drew the word out, injecting it with what Cam supposed was the appropriate amount of enthusiasm.

'Mikey and Ryan have dogs,' Ty said, but there wasn't a fleck of enthusiasm in his voice.

Cam shifted his weight. What the hell…?

'What if bad men keep yelling at us?' Krissie blurted out.

'Chickadee, that man yesterday wasn't bad.' She gave Krissie a one-armed hug. 'Like I said before, he was upset, that's all. And remember, people yell for lots of different reasons.'

'You don't yell,' Ty said.

'Believe me, if I saw one of Cam's sheep in my veggie patch, I'd be yelling my head off!'

Neither child laughed.

'But that man yelled at you!' Ty burst out.

Someone had yelled at Tess? Cam stiffened. He stepped into the yard. 'Howdy, gang.'

Both children immediately swung around, fear frozen on their faces. Cold, hard anger lanced through him because then he knew—someone had hurt these kids, had frightened them, and he wanted to find out who it was and tear them from limb to limb.

'Hey, Cam, nice to see you.'

Behind the children's backs, Tess mouthed, *Smile* at him, and it suddenly hit him how intimidating he must appear to these two small kids.

He forced his face to relax into a kind of half grin, although his blood burned and the surface of his skin prickled. 'You guys have the nicest spot in the sun. Mind if I join you?'

'We'd like that.' Tess shuffled over. Both children remained glued to her side. 'Want some sultana cake?'

He glanced at the plate, hunger rumbled through him, but he shook his head.

'Did you bring Boomer?' Ty asked.

Cam kicked himself for not bringing the dog. 'Sorry, mate, I didn't. I left Boomer in charge of the sheep.'

'That is one smart dog,' Tess said, and Cam watched as the worst of the fear and shadows slowly drained from Ty's and Krissie's faces.

'I just dropped by to talk lawnmowers. I have a ride-on and thought I might whizz it around this place tomorrow if that suited you.'

Tess shook her head, her hair so dark and her skin so golden it made him ache in familiar and unfamiliar ways. 'Oh, no, you don't, Cameron Manning. I can mow my own lawn, thank you very much. Though, a lesson in how to operate your ride-on would be greatly appreciated.'

It was obviously important to her to do it herself. He bit down on his urge to argue with her, although it chafed at him. He nodded. 'Right.'

'Woo hoo!' She punched the air. 'I get to use a ride-on mower. How much fun will that be?'

Krissie finally smiled.

'So how did yesterday's luncheon go?' He rested back on his hands, deliberately casual.

'Ooh.' Tess rubbed her hands together. 'There must've been thirty people there.'

'It was a Saturday. Everyone would've made an effort.'

Ty scowled. 'You didn't.'

'No,' he agreed. 'But I really wish I had.' And he meant it.

His stomach suddenly rolled. Why hadn't he gone? Eleven months ago he'd have been there. But since Lance and Fiona... Nausea burned his throat. Despite all his precautions he was turning into a recluse like his father.

No! He snapped the thought off. He was leaving Bellaroo Creek so he *didn't* turn into his father. He'd forge a new life for himself—an involved and engaging life. The kind of life he couldn't have in Bellaroo Creek.

Still... The idea of socialising had become anathema and he'd buried himself in station work, rarely going into town. None of that changed the fact that he wished he'd attended yesterday's luncheon.

Who had yelled at Tess and spooked the kids?

'A bad man yelled at Auntie Tess,' Krissie confided.

'Who?'

Ty scowled again. 'His name was Lance and we don't know if we want to live here any more.'

Lance?

He flicked a glance at Tess and a hand reached inside his chest to wring his heart. The raw grief in her eyes as she surveyed the children made his jaw ache. She glanced up, caught his gaze and tried to smile, but he saw the effort it cost her. That was when he realised she couldn't speak for the tears blocking her throat, and he sensed that crying in front of the children was the last thing she wanted. And probably the last thing either Ty or Krissie needed.

'Oh, Lance!' he pshawed. 'You don't have to worry about Lance.'

Krissie bit her lip. 'He's not a bad man?'

He was a black-hearted traitor, but Cam had enough justice in him still to know Lance would be horrified to find he'd become a bogey man to these kids. 'Nah, he's all hot air, you know? He makes a lot of noise, but he wouldn't hurt a fly. I should know, because he's my little brother.'

Relief rushed into both the children's faces and it hit him then how much these kids trusted him. He didn't know how or why—whether it was a carry-over from all of Tess's positivity when they'd arrived on Friday, or because he'd brought Boomer over to play, or the fact he knew Old Nelson the blue-tongue lizard, but it made his chest cramp. He couldn't let these kids rely on him too much. He was their neighbour, nothing more. But instinct told him he'd need to tread carefully—these kids needed kid-glove handling.

He ached to quiz them more about Lance—why he had yelled at Tess—but the kids needed to take their minds off yesterday's incident. They needed to remember the good things about living in Bellaroo Creek. They needed to be allowed to get on with their fresh start without fear and setbacks.

'Now I don't know if this will be agreeable to you guys or not, but because I worked so hard yesterday, and because Boomer's taking care of things today, I get to take the rest of today off.' He rubbed his chin and pursed his lips as if in a pretence of thought. 'So I was thinking you might like to go and check out some chickens and puppies.'

All three faces on the blanket before him lit up. He immediately tried to temper their enthusiasm. 'Today we only look because these things take a lot of careful thought and planning. It's a big responsibility to own an animal and you need to be very sure that the choice you make is the right one for you, you understand?'

All three heads nodded in unison. It struck him how young Tess was—she couldn't be much older than twenty-five. Too young for taking on all the responsibility she had.

Ty jumped up. 'Can we leave right now?'

He suppressed a grin at the young boy's eagerness. 'You'll need time to get ready. I'll pick you up in an hour. Promise you'll be ready?'

'Yes!' Both children raced indoors and Tess laughed. She actually laughed as she watched them and it lightened the unexplained weight that had settled across his shoulders. To see pleasure in her face instead of fear and grief…

She leapt to her feet. He rose more slowly, finding it suddenly difficult to catch his breath. She grabbed his arm, reached up on tiptoe and kissed his cheek. 'I could kiss you, Cameron! Thank you.'

He went to point out that she'd done exactly that, but he couldn't push a single sound out of his throat. He went to tell her to call him Cam, but his full name sounded so bewitching on those charming lips of hers, he found himself saying nothing at all.

And then she hugged him—hard and fierce—and it knocked the sense and the breath clean out of his body. Every sweet curve Tess possessed pressed against him, and his body soaked up her warmth and vigour. It brought him to aching life and sent a surge of primitive hunger racing through him with the swiftness of a rabbit startled in the undergrowth. A wildfire licked along his veins…carrying the same danger that fire did out here in the bush.

Reason screamed at him to move away. Instead, one of his arms snaked around her waist and he pulled her in closer, hugged her back. His hand rested against the top of her hip. He wanted to move his hand lower, he wanted to mould her against him, wanted her soft and pliant and…

He felt rather than heard her quick intake of breath. She stiffened. A heartbeat passed. A heartbeat in which the fire raging through him threatened all of his control, and then she softened against him.

He let his hand drift down to cup her bottom and lift it against him. She arched into him. He groaned. He couldn't help it.

Her hands drifted down his chest, her face lifted to his, her eyes soft and her lips parted.

He wanted to taste her. He wanted to explore the fullness of her bottom lip and—

For God's sake, she hugged you out of gratitude. She wasn't inviting you to maul her like some low-life sleaze!

He recalled the raw pain he'd witnessed in her eyes a moment before and, rather than snap away, he eased her out of his arms gently. 'Sorry, Tess.' His voice came out raspy and hoarse. 'I forgot myself for a moment.'

She blinked twice before the mistiness cleared from her eyes. Her cheeks flushed bright red. 'Oh! I—' She swung away. 'You and me both. I'm sorry. It's been an emotional morning.'

He shrugged and tried to appear as casual for her as he had for the children earlier. 'No harm done.'

She turned back to him. 'No harm done,' she echoed, her eyes searching his to test that truth. They both stood there awkwardly until she glanced at her watch. 'So you'll be back at around eleven?'

He snapped to and nodded.

'Should I pack a picnic?' She smiled impishly and every-thing slowly returned to normal—the colour of the sky, the sound of birdsong, the racing of his pulse. 'You wouldn't be-lieve how much food there was at yesterday's do. And some-how most of the leftovers ended up in my car.'

He stared at her lips—they were more plum than rose. Hunger stretched through him as he took in the fullness of her bottom lip. His pulse began to race again. 'Sounds great,' he said, backing up. 'I'll see you in a while.'

He shot around the house and back towards his homestead. It occurred to him that burying himself out on his station for the last ten months might not have been the wisest course of action after all.

Cam's four-wheel-drive pulled up out the front and Tess hauled in a deep breath and locked the front door. Ty and Krissie raced towards the car with all the alacrity of children promised their heart's desire.

Cam had done that. He'd found the perfect way to remind them of all the exciting potential that living in Bellaroo Creek could bring. They'd gone from the doldrums to delight.

But she should never have kissed him. She most certainly shouldn't have hugged him.

And yet, even now, her body throbbed with a primitive hunger. She yearned to explore each and every line of his powerful body—naked. She craved his hands on her again—gentle hands, knowing hands. Oh, so knowing. Her knees quivered before she could stop them.

Enough of that!

She kicked herself into action and moved down the path, sidestepping Old Nelson who currently sunned himself on the cement path. Cam met her at the gate to take the picnic basket from her. He searched her face. She let him—freely and openly. She searched his face too. It was amazing how much information they could convey to each other without a word. He liked how she looked, and he wanted her in the same way she wanted him, but…

They both sighed and nodded at the same moment. Romance wasn't on the cards for either of them. She didn't know his reasons, but she knew her own. She'd been selfish her entire life—selfish and clueless—but not any more.

I won't let you down again, Sarah. I promise.

'Where are we going?' Krissie demanded the minute Cam started the car and eased it onto the road.

'Our first stop is the O'Connell farm. Blue O'Connell has the best layers in the entire district. He has show chickens too. He takes out the blue ribbon every year at the Parkes agricultural show. What's more, his black lab has had a litter of puppies.'

Ty started talking so fast Tess couldn't understand a word he said.

'Steady, buddy.' Cam laughed. 'We've also a litter of border collie pups—like Boomer—to check out as well as some poodles.'

When they reached the farm, the children literally launched themselves out of the car. They both jumped and danced—at least in Krissie's case—and jumped and hopped—in Ty's— with uncontained excitement. Tess watched them and something inside her swelled. To see their faces alive with hope instead of fear, to see them grinning at the unknown farmer who came to greet them rather than backing up towards her with suspicion clouding their eyes, lifted something inside her.

To see them, for just one moment, truly happy. It made her want to weep. It made her hope. It made her think that coming to Bellaroo Creek had been the perfect plan after all.

'Are you Mr O'Connell?' Krissie asked.

'That I am, little miss.'

'I'm Krissie.' She walked right up to the farmer and held her hand out. 'And we're here to see your chickens.'

Sweet Lord, she must want a chicken badly.

Ty hung back for all of five seconds before bursting forward as well. 'And your puppies too.'

'Well, young folk, that's something I can certainly accommodate. Come right this way.' With a wink and a smile for Tess and Cam, he led the children towards the barn.

'Are you okay?' Cam asked, those green eyes of his seeming to plumb her soul.

'Oh!' She pressed both hands to her chest. 'Oh, Cameron, I think they're going to be fine after all.'

He tipped his hat back—a dusty, sweat-stained Akubra. 'Why wouldn't they be?'

She had to swallow before she could speak. 'The last three months have been just awful. And…'

'And?'

Beneath her hand her heart pounded. 'I didn't know if they would ever be happy again,' she whispered. 'I didn't know if I could help them be happy again, but… But your mum was right. Children are resilient.' This was the beginning of the brand-new start she'd been hoping for. Now she just had to focus on keeping them all on an even keel and making sure they felt secure.

'C'mon.' He took her arm. 'I have a feeling you need this as much as they do.'

They found Krissie sitting in a pen with the silliest piece of feathered nonsense that Tess had ever seen perched on her lap. It looked as if it should be worn on some posh hat for Melbourne's Spring Carnival. Krissie raised her big brown eyes. 'This one,' she whispered, hope so alive in her face it stole Tess's breath.

Cam stiffened and opened his mouth. Tess dug her elbow in his ribs. 'Can't you see it's true love?' she murmured, leading him further into the depths of the barn.

'But it's a show chicken. It won't lay a tuppence worth of eggs.'

'And yet Krissie doesn't care…and neither do I.' She wanted to sing! 'Let's find Ty.'

They found him being licked to within an inch of his life by six puppies. Cute, round, roly-poly puppies. When he saw Tess and Cam he picked one of the puppies up and clambered to his feet. He hitched up his chin. 'I thought about it very long and hard,' he vowed. 'This is the absolutest, bestest puppy in the world for me. I don't need to look any more.'

Cam's mouth dropped open. 'We were only supposed to look!'

But she'd started laughing. 'Cameron, you have a lot to learn about children if you really thought all we were ever going to do today was just look.'

They went home with a chicken and a wire cage loaned to them by Mr O'Connell, a puppy, a dog basket, a collar and lead, and plenty of pet food.

And their picnic.

Tess set up a card table in the backyard to keep the food out of reach of their furred and feathered friends, and two camp chairs for her and Cam. Children and animals cheerfully settled on the blanket until they'd finished eating, and then Krissie and Ty set about introducing Fluffy and Barney to the backyard.

Tess selected a pikelet liberally slathered in butter and jam and bit into it, closing her eyes for a moment to savour it. If she didn't stop eating like this soon, she'd outgrow all her clothes. She took a second bite. 'I can't believe that chicken is following Krissie about as if it's a dog.'

'I can't believe you bought a White Bearded Silky instead of a Leghorn or a Rhode Island or…or anything that's a proven layer. You know that thing is going to lay next to no eggs.'

She just grinned at him. 'Have a piece of sultana cake.'

He had a piece of fruitcake instead. 'And a black Labrador?' He shook his head.

'Labrador puppies are the cutest in the world.'

'They don't stop being stupid until they're about four years old. It'll chew everything it can find, you know?'

'That'll teach the kids to pick up after themselves. And while Barney may not prove to be the cleverest of dogs, I suspect he's going to be loving and loyal.'

'He'll never be a working dog.'

'We don't need a working dog.' She polished off her pikelet and licked her fingers. 'Cameron, I know we're breaking every rule of being proper country folk, but look how happy they are.' She found herself grinning like an idiot. 'How can that be a bad thing?'

He glanced at her and those green eyes of his softened. 'It's not, I guess. Not when you put it like that. I just can't help feeling you've taken on more work than you realise. And I'm responsible for that. If I'd known earlier what would happen—'

'I'm glad you didn't! You're responsible for the kids remembering all the good things they wanted from our move to Bellaroo Creek. You're responsible for them being happy that we moved here rather than afraid. Do you always focus on the negatives rather than the positives?'

He didn't answer. His eyes had lowered to her mouth and there was absolutely nothing negative about his gaze. What if he had kissed her earlier? What would that have been like? She swallowed. Heat circled in slow spirals through her veins. She recalled in microscopic detail the feeling of being pulled up hard against him and the need that had roared through her.

The world contracted about them. She touched her lips—lips sensitised beyond measure. Her index finger traced her bottom lip. It swelled and throbbed…until she encountered something sticky.

Sticky? She closed her eyes in sudden mortification. Jam! She had jam all over her face? No wonder Cameron was staring. She scrubbed it off and when she opened her eyes she found him staring straight out in front of him at his precious forty hectares.

She scowled but it didn't slow the thud of her heartbeat. 'Why did Lance yell at you?'

She shifted on her chair. Lorraine had said Cameron and Lance hadn't spoken in ten months. She didn't want to make that situation worse.

'I will find out so you might as well tell me.'

She slumped on a sigh. 'Fine, but I'll only tell you if you fill me in on what's going down with the two of you.'

His nose curled. It shouldn't look sexy. *It didn't look sexy!* 'I'm surprised nobody filled you in about it yesterday. It's no secret.'

His curled lip told her that while it might not be a secret, he didn't enjoy talking about it. She pulled in a breath. 'Whatever it is, it's certainly upsetting your mother.'

He snorted. She didn't understand that.

'Ten months ago,' he clipped out, 'I was engaged to Fiona.'

She stared. Did he mean the same Fiona who... 'Tall, blonde, ponytail?'

'That's the one.'

She stiffened. 'Oh!'

He smiled but there was no warmth in it. 'Exactly.'

They both stared out at the backyard, silent for the moment. 'I, umm...take it,' she started, 'that you and Fiona hadn't broken up before she and Lance...'

'You take it right.'

Ouch!

She opened her mouth to say something, anything that would offer comfort or commiseration, but he glared at her and shook his head. 'Don't.'

Right. She closed her mouth again.

They were both quiet for a long time. Eventually she moistened her lips. 'Lance wanted to lease the forty hectares from me. When I told him I'd already signed the lease over to you he…became a little upset.'

His eyes narrowed, but he still didn't look at her. 'He wanted to lease that land?'

'Uh-huh.'

His nostrils flared. 'I knew he was behind that.'

Um… 'I'm pretty positive your mother had no part in it, though.'

That made him swing to her. 'Oh, really?' His scorn could blast the skin from a person's frame. She darted a glance towards the children. He swore softly. 'Sorry.'

He raked a hand back through his hair. 'Look, I'm still angry that I didn't see it coming, that I didn't see what was happening right under my nose. That he was—'

He broke off. 'I underestimated him. None of that is your fault, though.'

'I'd have said believing in your family was a good thing, not a bad one.'

He didn't reply. She pulled in a breath. 'Look, yesterday your mother seemed appalled and shocked when I told her about the mix-up with the forty hectares. I doubt very much she feigned that.' She bit her lip and then shrugged. 'I liked her.'

His lips twisted. 'And let me guess, despite my brother's bad behaviour you like him too?'

She thought about that for a moment. 'Hmm, no, I'm not convinced I do. I don't much like being yelled at. He owes me an apology and until I receive one he's a…' He'd stolen Cam's fiancée! She tilted her chin. 'He's a weaselling, snivelling, black-hearted swine.'

Cam stared at her, his jaw slack, and then he threw his head back and laughed. The sound rippled through her, warming her all over. Both Ty and Krissie glanced across at them and grinned. It made Tess realise what little laughter they'd had in their lives these last few months. And probably quite a while before then too if the truth be told.

Oh, Sarah.

At the thought of her beautiful dead sister any desire to laugh along with Cam fled. 'Cam, about your mum…'

His face shuttered closed. 'She's made it clear where her loyalties lie.'

'She loves you!' She couldn't keep the shock out of her voice.

'Then she has a funny way of showing it. Besides—' he rounded on her '—this is none of your business.'

'You should talk to her.'

He didn't say anything. She clenched and unclenched her hands. Lorraine's loyalties were obviously torn—she didn't want to lose either son. Tess understood that, but…

She leaned across and touched his arm. 'I'm serious, Cameron. I think you need to speak to her. I think the farm is in trouble. Big trouble. I think she needs you.'

The same way Sarah had needed her. Only, Tess had let her down and now she had to live with that knowledge for the rest of her life.

'Trouble? What makes you think that?'

She didn't want Cam making the same mistakes she had. 'Lance said he needed that canola contract. He implied the farm was in danger.' She bit her lip. 'He thinks you want to ruin him.'

Cam shook his head. 'I don't much care what Lance thinks any more.'

She understood that, but…

He turned to her. 'Look, Tess, the problems associated with my mother and Lance's station is none of my concern any more. Lance has made that clear through his actions and my mother has made it clear by virtue of her silence.'

She chafed her arms against a sudden chill. Three months ago she'd lost her sister. She'd do anything—*anything*—to have Sarah back for just one hour. And yet Cam was willing to turn his back on the only family he had? Lance might be a lost cause, but couldn't Cam see how much his mother loved him?

He rose. 'I'll bring the mower around tomorrow.'

'Thank you.'

He called out a goodbye to the kids and disappeared around the side of the house. Tess rose to find a cardigan and snuggled into it until she started to feel warm again.

CHAPTER FOUR

CAM CLEANED THE last of the tack. He glanced at the neatly aligned rows of bridles and lead ropes, and at the newly polished saddles, but two hours' worth of rubbing and buffing hadn't helped ease the itch between his shoulder blades.

With a frown, and a muffled curse that had no direct object, he strode out of the tack room and into the machinery shed to leap on a trail bike and kick it into life. He pointed it in the direction of the northern boundary fence and let loose with the throttle, even though he knew Fraser had trawled along that boundary through the week to check the fences.

He belted along the track for ten minutes when, with another muffled curse, he turned the bike back in the direction of the homestead. Dumping the bike back in the machinery shed, he grabbed several assorted lengths of wood and a roll of chicken wire and threw them, along with his toolbox, into the back of one of the station's utes and, with a final muffled curse, headed next door to Tess's.

He might be planning to sever his ties with Bellaroo Creek, but he couldn't leave a lone woman with two dependent kids to flounder on her own. Not on land he was ultimately responsible for. Not when it was his fault she now had a puppy and a chicken to look after on top of everything else.

Talk to her. That was what Tess had said about his mother. He swiped a hand through the air. His mother would always have a home with him. She knew that, even if she chose to never accept it.

I think the farm is in trouble.

That was none of his business any more. He fishtailed the ute to a halt in front of Tess's cottage and the itch between his shoulder blades intensified. He stared out of the windscreen and shook his head. The thought uppermost in his mind, it seemed, wasn't on building a chicken coop or wondering why his mother refused to come out to Kurrajong, but what Tess might be wearing today—jeans or a skirt?

He rubbed his eyes. When he lowered his hand it was to find Ty and Barney barrelling down the side of the house towards him. 'Hey, Cam!'

He pushed his door open and found a grin. 'Hey, Ty, how's Barney settling in?'

'I love him best of all dogs in the world!'

It struck him then that Ty looked just like any other seven-year-old boy who'd just got his first puppy—carefree, excited, his face shadow-free.

'He's a mighty fine-looking puppy,' Cam agreed, realising he'd helped to make those shadows retreat. The knowledge awed him, humbled him. He reached behind him to scratch his back.

Then Tess came tripping around the side of the house and all rational thought stopped for more beats of his pulse than he had the wit to count. Shorts. Tess wore a pair of scarlet-coloured shorts and a pale cream vest top. Her bare arms, bare legs and shoulders all gleamed in the autumn sunlight. She made him think of fields of ripening wheat, of cream and honey and nutmeg, of spiced apples and camping under the stars. She made him think of his mother's sultana cake—his favourite food in the world. He curled his fingers against his palms to stop from doing something daft and reaching out to stroke a finger down her arm.

'Hello, Cameron.'

He swallowed and then simply nodded, unsure if his voice would work.

'Auntie Tess said Barney did really good for a puppy. We've only had one accident.'

Cam winced. 'I, uh…'

Her eyes danced. 'Apologise again and I'll thump you. That puppy has been a source of pure joy.' She glanced at his ute and then planted her hands on her hips and sent him a mock glare. 'Where's my lawnmower?'

He grimaced. 'My station manager is currently lying beneath it trying to fix a fuel leak.'

'Ouch.'

'It should be fixed in the next day or so.' He didn't want her using it if it wasn't a hundred per cent safe.

She gestured with her head and turned. 'Come and join the party.'

He followed her. He didn't even try to keep from ogling the length of her legs or taking an inventory of the innate grace with which she moved. She was like some wonderful and exotic creature who'd deigned to live among the mundane and the humdrum. A creature whose beauty took one out of the mundane and humdrum for a few precious moments.

He wondered what she'd done for a living before she'd moved to Bellaroo Creek—maybe she'd been a dancer. He opened his mouth to ask, but they'd rounded the house and Krissie sat on a blanket with that darn chicken on her lap and when she glanced up and saw him she sent him a grin of such epic proportions it cracked his chest wide open.

He had to swallow before he could speak. 'Did Fluffy have a good night?'

'She slept in her cage in the laundry, but I think she'd be happier sleeping in my bedroom.'

Tess sent him a bare-teethed grimace that almost made him laugh. One could toilet train a puppy, but a chicken…? 'Well, honey, I've come around to build Fluffy her very own house.'

Krissie's bottom lip wobbled. 'Barney slept in Ty's room.'

He crouched down beside her. 'The thing is, Krissie, chickens aren't like puppies or kittens. They like the fresh air and they like to see the stars at night and be able to come and go as much as they please. So, as much as Fluffy loves you, she'll be happier out here in the yard.'

She stared at him and he held his breath. 'She'll get her very own house, right?'

'That's right.'

'A nice one?'

'One that she'll love,' he promised.

Her face cleared. 'I can show you a picture of Fluffy's dream house!' She plonked Fluffy down on the grass and raced inside.

'Oh, good Lord.' Tess groaned. 'I have no idea what she has in mind, Cameron.'

He had sudden visions of a hot-pink Barbie house and gulped. And then he glanced around. A collection of plastic planters in assorted shapes and sizes battled for space from the back of the house to the lemon tree. 'Where on earth did all these seedlings come from?'

Tess planted her hands on her hips. Sweet hips…long, lovely legs…pretty arms. Cam curled his fingers into his palms again. With a silent curse he uncurled them and shoved them into his pockets. Deep into his pockets.

'Everyone has been so kind. At Saturday's luncheon Ty, Krissie and I mentioned we'd like to start our own veggie garden and asked for advice on what vegetables we should grow.'

He shook his head, but he couldn't help grinning. 'I guess you got your answer.'

She grinned back. 'I guess we did.'

Her plum-coloured lips gleamed temptingly in the sunlight. His heart thumped. He kept his hands firmly in his pockets. The itch started up again with a vengeance.

Krissie reappeared brandishing a magazine. 'This one!' She held it up for them to see.

'That's an awful lot of house for one chicken, Krissie,' Tess said.

Krissie's bottom lip wobbled. 'But we'll get more chickens, remember? Fluffy will need friends for when I'm at school.'

She turned liquid eyes to Cam and they melted him on the spot. He rolled his shoulders, risked removing his hands from his pockets to take the magazine and survey the picture more fully. 'Oh, I think we can manage something like this.' He frantically recalculated the amount of wood in his ute with the amount he still had at the homestead.

'Give me a list of what we need and I'll go into the stock and station store to get supplies,' Tess said, as if reading his mind.

It wouldn't be cheap. He grimaced. He should've found a way to talk Krissie into something less grand and—

'We're good for it, Cameron. It isn't a problem,' Tess said, again as if reading his mind, which unsettled him. He normally maintained a quiet reserve that made him hard to read. It had been one of the things Fiona had complained about. But this woman, it seemed, had only to glance at him to know what he was thinking.

But her plump dusky lips curved up with such promise he found he didn't mind at all…or, at least, not as much as he suspected he should.

'Can I help you build it?' Ty breathed, his eyes alight.

'I'll definitely need a helper—a foreman. It's a big job, Ty, and I'll need your help.'

Ty's eyes grew as big as cabbages, his chest puffed out. That awe hit Cam again as he pulled his cell phone from his pocket. Surveying Krissie's dream chicken coop, and doing his best to keep his eyes from the plump temptation of Tess's lips, he placed an order at the stock and station store.

* * *

They spent the afternoon on Phase One of the chicken coop. Tess couldn't believe Cam's patience with Ty or the way her nephew blossomed under his quiet but authoritative guidance. He'd lacked a male role model for so long.

Eventually, though, both children wandered off to check on Old Nelson. And then Ty set about teaching Barney how to play fetch while Krissie fell asleep on the blanket beneath the shade of the lemon tree, leaving Fluffy free to scratch about the yard.

Tess glanced at Cam whistling idly as he nailed boards to the frame he'd built. Something inside her shifted. Ever since that moment yesterday when she'd hugged him, she'd grown increasingly aware of the breadth of his shoulders, of the flex and play of the muscles in his arms, and of the fresh-cut-grass scent that followed in his wake and stirred something to life inside her. Something she desperately tried to ignore.

The sun shone brightly, but not too fiercely, picking out the lighter highlights in his chestnut hair. Fiona had thrown this man over for Lance? Tess snorted. What a loser! The woman quite obviously had her head screwed on backwards. Lance might dazzle with those playboy good looks of his, but when a woman looked at Cam she was left in no doubt that he was all man.

One hundred per cent fit and honed man.

And the longer Tess stared at him, the more that thing inside her stirred and fluttered and stretched itself into heart-beating, mouth-drying sentience.

Thoughts of Lance, though, slid an unwelcome reminder through her. The expression on Lorraine's face—that mixture of anxiety, regret and heartbreak—rose in her mind and she bit back a sigh.

'You want to tell me what's on your mind?'

She blinked, and then realised Cam had caught her out blatantly staring at him. The skin on her face and neck burned. 'Oh…I…nothing.'

'Why don't I believe you?'

He wielded a hammer as if he'd been born to it. She dragged her gaze from muscled forearms lightly dusted with hair, and the pull of lean brown hands. She tried desperately to dispel thoughts of what else those hands might be expert at.

She clenched her eyes shut and counted to five. For pity's sake! She didn't need this at the moment—this wild, desperate ache. She needed to remain focused on the children. On not letting Sarah down. On making amends.

'Tess?'

She went back to tacking chicken wire to the frame of their mansion of a chicken house, the way he'd shown her, but she couldn't resist another glance at him. The brilliance of his eyes struck her afresh. She swallowed and shrugged. 'Oh, I was just thinking about stuff you'd no doubt declare me nosy for contemplating.'

He set his hammer down. 'Like?'

Keep your mouth shut. She set her hammer down too. 'Like how a man who is as gentle with children and animals as you could just ignore that his mother might be in trouble.'

He stiffened as if she'd slapped him.

'I said it was nosy,' she muttered, though she wasn't certain she was actually apologising.

'You're not wrong there.'

Minding her business was the wisest course of action. She knew that. Cam was a grown-up. He knew what he was doing. She swallowed. She used to be really good at minding her own business.

'You must really hate Lance if you haven't spoken to him in ten months.' She shivered. She understood his bitterness. She really did, but… 'How can you stand to live in the same town as him when you bear that much resentment?'

He eyed her for an interminable moment. It made her chest

constrict. 'I'm not planning on staying for that much longer, Tess.'

He hammered in a nail with more force than necessary, and a sickening thump started up in her stomach. 'What?'

He set his hammer back down and glared at her. 'In two months I'll be out of this godforsaken town and Lance can sink or swim under his own steam. I've washed my hands of him and his tantrums and his so-called troubles.'

'But…' Cameron couldn't leave!

'What about your mother?' she burst out.

He picked the hammer up again. 'I expect my leaving will be a blessing for her. With me gone, tensions will ease.' He hammered in another nail. 'Besides, like I told you, my mother has made it clear where her loyalties lie.'

Tess's mouth opened and closed. 'Can't you see her loyalties are being torn?'

'By remaining in the same house as Lance and Fiona she's given them her tacit approval.'

'You mother is not the type of woman who would ever kick her offspring out of her house, regardless of what they've done.' She planted her hands on her hips. 'But that doesn't mean she doesn't love you.' Couldn't he see that? 'Do you really mean to make her choose between the two of you? She's not responsible for the things Lance has done.'

'My leaving means she won't have to choose.'

She glanced at Krissie and an ache exploded in her chest. Cam's anger and bitterness were warping him and tearing him apart. Couldn't he see that? 'Oh, Cameron, it's been ten months.'

He strode around and seized her chin, his eyes blazing. 'And you naively think that time can heal all wounds?'

His fingers were gentle but his voice was hard. He smelled of wood and grass and sweat.

He paused and she swallowed, aching at the pain she sensed behind the flint of his eyes.

He scanned her face and then released her with a shake of his head. 'Why does this matter so much to you?'

She had to take a step away from him. He was too…much. Too much for her senses. Too much for her hormones. And the hardness in him clashed too deeply with the places that grieved inside her. 'I just lost my sister, Cam. I never appreciated her enough. I wish I had but I didn't. And now I've lost her and I can't get her back.'

He paled.

'I have no one now but Ty and Krissie. Don't get me wrong, they make up for everything, but…you have a mother who loves you and I'm jealous.' She tried to smile. He had a brother too, but she left that unsaid. In his shoes, would she be able to forgive Lance?

His eyes darkened, his hand half lifted as if to touch her cheek…and then he wheeled away.

She hunched her shoulders, wishing she hadn't started this conversation. Wishing she'd left well alone. She tried to make her voice bright. 'Where will you go when you leave Bellaroo Creek?'

He turned back. 'Africa. I'm an advisor for a charity whose mission is to increase agricultural production in Third World countries. I've requested a field position.'

'Wow!' She stared at him. 'Just…wow! That's amazing.' She swallowed and chafed her arms. 'What an adventure.'

'I'm hoping so.'

'Is it a secret?'

'I haven't told anyone, if that's what you mean.' He shifted his weight to plant his legs firmly.

She tried another smile and mimicked zipping her mouth shut to let him know she wouldn't say anything to anyone, and she had a feeling he had to fight back a smile of his own. She'd like to make him smile for real. 'We'll miss you, Cameron. You've been just about the best neighbour we city slickers could've had.'

His eyes widened. He blinked and then they narrowed. It made her want to fidget. Did he think she was making some kind of a move on him? Her spine stiffened and her chin shot up. 'You can lose that nasty suspicion right now,' she shot at him. 'Even if I was in the market for something more, I'm not stupid enough to get involved with a man on the rebound.' She folded her arms. 'In fact, I'm starting to think the sooner you leave, the better!'

He grinned then—a true-blue, solid-gold grin that hooked up his mouth and made his eyes dance. For a moment all Tess could make out was the brightness of the sun, the sound of the breeze playing through the leaves of the lemon tree and the force of that smile. She blinked and the rest of the world slowly surged back into focus.

'From where I'm standing, Tess, my suspicion was more like wishful thinking and it wasn't the least bit nasty. In fact, it was pretty darn tempting.'

Heat crept along her veins. She bit her bottom lip in an effort to counter its heavy throbbing. There was nothing she could do about her breasts, though, except to keep her arms tightly folded across them and hope their eager swelling didn't show.

'But I'm severing ties with Bellaroo Creek while you're in the process of establishing them. And while I wouldn't be averse to a purely physical arrangement…'

She shook her head.

'That's what I figured.'

She pulled a breath of fresh country air into her lungs to try to cool her body's unaccountable response to the man opposite; to give herself the space she needed to remember the promises she'd made to herself. 'Romance in any shape or form isn't figuring on my horizon for the next year or two.'

He stared at her, frowned. 'Why not?'

She glanced at Krissie still dozing beneath the lemon tree, and at Ty and Barney wrestling gently in the long grass down by the back fence. 'Because at the moment the children need stability in their lives. Bringing a new man into the mix would freak them out, threaten them.' For the next year or two she meant to focus all her energies on them and what they needed.

For pity's sake! It couldn't be that hard. She'd spent the last twenty-six years focussing on nothing but herself and her music. It wouldn't kill her to put others' needs before her own for a while. In fact, she had a feeling it was mandatory. Anyway, what did she know about romantic relationships? She'd had flirtations, but nothing serious or long-term. She didn't know enough about them to risk Ty's and Krissie's well-being, that was for sure.

'Tess, you're young and beautiful. You're entitled to a life of your own.'

She stared at him. Did he really think she was beautiful?

She started and shook her stupid vanity aside. 'Well, then, hopefully another two years won't make much difference to either of those things.'

'I think you're making a mistake.'

'Ten months,' she shot back. 'I think you're the one making a mistake.'

They glared at each other. 'Speaking of nosy questions…' his glare deepened '…I have one of my own.'

She moistened dry lips. 'Oh?'

He hitched his head in the direction of the children. 'Who hurt them?'

The strength drained from her legs. She reached out but the chicken coop wasn't stable enough to take her weight. She backed up and plonked down on a load of timber Cam had placed to one side, a chasm opening up in her chest. She wanted nothing more than to drop her face to her hands, but if either child glanced her way it would frighten them, worry them, and calming their anxieties was her number-one concern.

Cam swore. She glanced up. With the sun behind her, she

could see his face clearly and the range of expressions that filtered across it—concern, protectiveness…anger.

Who hurt them? Her chest cramped. She'd hoped… 'Is it that obvious?' she whispered.

He eased himself down beside her. 'Not at first.'

She had a feeling he was trying to humour her, to offer her some comfort, but there was no comfort to be had. Not for her.

'Tess?'

She chafed her arms as a chill settled over her, although the sun and the air remained warm. 'Their father,' she finally said. 'It was their father.'

From the corner of her eyes she saw one of his hands clench. She sensed that every muscle in his body had tensed. 'He hit them?'

She nodded.

'And he hit their mother?'

She nodded again.

'The bastard!'

She had to swallow a lump at the pointlessness of it all. 'Oh, Cameron, it's so much sadder than that.' Heartbreakingly sad.

'Did he kill their mother and then commit suicide?'

Her head came up at that. 'No!' The police had been certain. 'It was a car accident.' She swallowed. 'They hit a tree. The police who arrived first on the scene found an injured kangaroo on the road.'

'They swerved to avoid it?'

'I expect so.'

He reached out to clasp one of the hands she had clenched in her lap. 'Tell me the sad story, Tess.'

Why did he want to know? And then she thought about Lorraine, and Lance and Fiona. Maybe something in Sarah and Bruce's story would touch a chord with him. Maybe it would help heal the anger and pain inside him. Maybe it would help him find a way to forgive. Lance might not deserve that forgiveness, but she had a growing certainty that Cam needed to find it inside himself all the same.

His grip tightened and finally she met his gaze. She turned her hand over and without any hesitation at all he entwined his fingers with hers, giving her the silent strength and support she needed.

'As far as I can tell,' she finally started, 'Sarah and Bruce were happy for most of their marriage.' Though God knew she wasn't an expert. 'But two and a half years ago Bruce was involved in an accident at his work where he suffered a brain injury.'

'Where did he work?'

'In an open cut mine in the Upper Hunter Valley. An explosion went off when it shouldn't have. It was all touch and go for a while. He spent four months in hospital and then had months and months of rehabilitation.'

'What happened?' he prompted when she stopped.

She clung to his hand. Unconsciously she leaned one bare arm against his until she remembered that there were still warm good things in the world. 'His personality changed. This previously calm, family-oriented man suddenly had a temper he couldn't control. It would apparently flare up at the smallest provocation.' And then Bruce would lash out with his fists. 'He looked the same, he sounded the same, but he was a totally different man from the one my sister had married.'

'She should've removed the children from that situation immediately.'

Tess stilled. Very gently she removed her hand from his, and went back to chafing her arms. 'We're so quick to judge, aren't we? But how sacred do you hold wedding vows, Cameron? Because my sister took them very seriously. *For better for worse; in sickness and in health.* The accident wasn't Bruce's fault. He didn't go looking for it. He'd simply been in the wrong place at the wrong time. How do you abandon someone who's been through that?' She peered up at him.

'I don't think you'd abandon a woman who'd been through something like that.'

He stared at her and then dragged a hand down his face. 'Did you know about the violence?'

Bitterness filled her mouth and she shook her head. 'I was hardly ever in the country. I was too busy with my career and gallivanting around Europe and making a name for myself to notice anything.'

She'd been off having the time of her life while her sister had been living a nightmare. Sarah had always been so staunchly independent but that was no excuse. Deep down she'd known something had been troubling her sister, only Sarah would deny it whenever Tess had pressed her. Oh, yes, there had been signs. Signs she hadn't picked up on.

Her vision blurred. Sarah had been so proud of Tess's successes, but they were nothing—surface glitter with no substance. Like Tess herself.

'Tess?'

She shook herself. 'I found out about the violence after the car accident, from Sarah's neighbours and Bruce's doctors. From Ty and Krissie.' And from the letter Sarah had left her, asking her to look after the children if anything should happen to her, and leaving her a ludicrously large life insurance policy, enabling her to do exactly that.

She lifted her chin. 'All that matters now is making sure Ty and Krissie feel safe and building a good life for them here. I'll do whatever that takes.'

'Why?'

The single question chilled her. 'Because I love them.' That was the truth. Cam didn't need to know any more than that. She wasn't sure she could bear the disgust in his eyes if she told him the whole truth.

'Miss Laing, there you are! We've been knocking on the front door, but you obviously didn't hear us.'

Tess and Cam shot to their feet as three women came

around the side of the house—Cam's mum, Stacy Bennet and the unknown but well-dressed woman who'd addressed Tess.

Tess urged herself forward and forced what she hoped was a welcoming smile to her lips. 'I'm terribly sorry!'

'It's no matter, dear,' Lorraine said. 'But I want to introduce you to Helen Milton. She's the headmistress of Lachlan Downs Ladies College, which is a boarding school two hours south of here. She's made the trip into Bellaroo Creek especially to meet you.'

Cam rolled his shoulders and remained where he was. Why on earth did Helen want to meet Tess?

'I saw you play when I was in London the year before last. My dear, you have such a rare talent, but it wasn't until I saw you play in Barcelona a few months later that I truly realised it.'

Tess's spine, her shoulders, her whole bearing stiffened. He couldn't see her face, but the fact she made no reply told its own story. He moved to stand beside her.

'Hello, Cameron.'

He glanced down at his mother and his stomach clenched. 'Mum.'

'Oh, no, no, no,' Helen continued, 'you won't be hiding your light under a bushel out here, Tess!'

Tess gripped her hands together, her knuckles turning white. 'Oh, but—'

'You don't mind me calling you Tess, do you?'

'Of course not. I—'

'It'd be a crime for you to bury your talent and I won't allow it.'

Lorraine smiled at him and behind the lines of strain that fanned out from her eyes he recognised genuine delight. 'Tess is apparently not just a world-class pianist, but a classical guitarist of some note too.'

He stared at her. Not a dancer but a musician? It made perfect sense. It explained her innate grace and balance, and the way her whole being came alive when she sang.

She shrugged, colour flooding her cheeks as he continued to stare at her. He nudged her arm. 'Tess, that's really something.'

But she stared back at him with doe-in-the-headlight eyes and he didn't understand, only knew something was terribly wrong. He straightened. 'How about we go inside and I'll put the kettle on?' Tess needed something warm and sweet inside her.

'I can't, I'm sorry—this is just a flying visit. I need to be back at the college by three—I've chartered a plane—but I wanted to introduce myself to Tess while I had a brief window of opportunity.' Helen turned back to Tess. 'Because I have plans for you, my dear.'

'Oh?' Tess's voice was nothing but a whisper.

'Every year we hold a two-week summer camp at the college, and we want you to give music tuition. Heavens, talk about a coup!'

'But…but I couldn't possibly leave Ty and Krissie for two whole weeks.'

'My dear, they can come too. There'll be all sorts of activities to keep them occupied.'

'But—'

Helen's eyes narrowed and hardened. Cam shifted his feet. The headmistress hadn't got where she was today by taking no for an answer.

'Miss Laing, you can't possibly have a problem with wanting to assist the community that has taken you under its wing. Surely?'

'Well, no, of course not.'

His lips twisted. The rotten woman should've gone into politics.

'Excellent!' She took Tess's arm and led her back the way

she'd come. 'I'll email you with all the details. And don't worry, you'll be handsomely reimbursed.'

'How are you, Cameron?' his mother asked, her question stopping him from following.

He rolled his shoulders. 'Fine, and you?'

Her hand fluttered to her throat. 'Fine.'

He shifted from one leg to the other. 'Would you like to come around for dinner one day this week?' The words burst from him. They burned and needled but he didn't retract them.

'Oh!' She swallowed. 'I…I'm afraid this week isn't good.'

'Right.' Exactly the same response as the last time he'd asked her. 'Let me know when your diary clears.'

She opened her mouth, but closed it again without saying anything more. 'I'd better go,' she finally said. 'Goodbye, Cameron.'

'Mum.'

He stared after her and then started in surprise when Ty slipped his small hand inside Cam's. He glanced down. 'You okay, buddy?'

'What did that lady want?'

'I think she wants your auntie Tess to do some work for her.'

'Auntie Tess didn't look very happy.'

No, she hadn't. Why not? If she had a passion for music… Cam cut the thought off and focused on allaying Ty's concern instead. 'I think your auntie Tess is going to be just fine, Ty. She doesn't have to do anything she doesn't want to.'

Ty thought about that for a moment and then nodded. 'Would you like to play fetch with Barney?'

CHAPTER FIVE

CAM STRODE THROUGH the back door of the schoolhouse. If Stacy really wanted to turn that lower field into a play area for the children, they were going to need to talk about drainage, fund-raising and working bees.

He turned the corner and then pulled up short as Tess bolted through the school's front door.

He swallowed. He'd spent two afternoons last week finishing off the chicken coop. Both times she'd invited him to stay for dinner. Both times he'd declined. Since he'd revealed he was leaving Bellaroo Creek, they'd maintained a polite but slightly formal distance.

Which was fine by him. As far as he was concerned the less time he spent thinking about her, the better.

He watched her halt now, press her hands to her waist and drag in a breath. Something was up. Before he could kick himself forward and ask what, she'd set her spine and moved straight for Stacy Bennet's office. 'Hey, chickadee, what's up?'

Before she could enter the office, however, Krissie had hurtled out of it to fling herself at Tess, her face crumpled and her shoulders shaking with sobs. Tess held her against her with one hand while the other caressed the hair back off her face. His gut tightened as he watched her. Her love was evident in every touch and gesture. The set of her shoulders and her bent head told him that Krissie's pain was her own. He had to swallow. He rolled his shoulders, but he couldn't look away.

Krissie's storm was brief. When she finally relaxed her grip, Tess led her back into the office. Had someone frightened Krissie again? Almost without thinking he moved towards the office, halting in its doorway. Tess, Krissie and Stacy all sat on Stacy's sofa, and Tess wiped Krissie's face with a handful of tissues. They didn't see him.

'You want to tell me what happened, chickadee?'

He marvelled at the calm strength in her voice, at her distinct I-can-fix-anything attitude. He shoved his hands in his pockets. Tess Laing was a hell of a woman. He took a step back. She obviously had everything under control. He should leave and give them some privacy. He turned away.

'Do we have money troubles?' Krissie hiccupped.

He stiffened and swung back.

'Heavens, no,' Tess pooh-poohed. 'What's brought this on?'

'Mikey said we must be poor if we're renting a house for a dollar a week. And I know that when you're poor bad things can happen.'

Cam stiffened. A five-year-old should be happy and carefree, not constantly glancing over her shoulder waiting for bad things to happen. A five-year-old shouldn't have so little faith in all that was bright and good.

Neither should a twenty-nine-year-old.

He shook that thought off.

For the first time he truly appreciated the task Tess had set herself.

Tess tucked the child under her arm and pulled her in close. 'When you're a bit older I'll explain life insurance policies to you, chickadee. You'll probably learn all about them at school when you're fourteen or fifteen. But I can promise—cross my heart—that your mum and dad made sure that you,

Ty and me would have enough money so we wouldn't want for anything.'

She'd taken the perfect tone, and she had perfect—

He averted his gaze and wished he'd thought to do that before she'd crossed her heart.

He glanced back to see Krissie turn up a hopeful face. 'Really?'

'Really, truly.'

'Daddy too?'

'Daddy too.'

Tess might've taken the perfect tone, but some sixth sense warned him that she was horribly close to tears. Stacy jumped to the rescue. 'You want to know why your aunt Tess wanted to come to Bellaroo Creek, Krissie?'

She stared up at the teacher with solemn eyes and nodded.

'It's because she knew we wanted you all to come and live out here and be a part of our town. Your aunt Tess knows how nice it is to be wanted.'

The child swung to Tess and Tess smiled at her. 'It's true. Don't you think it's lovely to come to a place where everyone wants to be friends with us? And weren't we talking just last night about all the things we like about living in Bellaroo Creek?'

'You like the fresh air.'

'I sure do.' She nudged Krissie's shoulder with a grin. 'And I'm finding I have a big soft spot for sultana cake.'

Krissie giggled. 'And I love Fluffy and Ty loves Barney. And Louisa and Suzie are really nice, and so is Mrs Bennet,' she added with a shy glance at her teacher.

'So you don't need to get upset about anything anyone says, all right?' Tess said.

Krissie pursed her lips and finally nodded, obviously deciding to trust her aunt. 'Okay.'

'How about you run back to class now, Krissie?' her

teacher said. 'Mrs Leigh is teaching everyone a new song and you wouldn't want to miss out on that, would you?'

With a hug for Tess, Krissie started for the door. Cam suddenly realised he still stood there staring. He tried to duck out of the way, but he wasn't quick enough. 'Cam!' Krissie hugged him, grinning up at him with those big brown eyes of hers before disappearing down the corridor to her classroom.

He gulped and turned back to Tess and Stacy. 'Sorry, I was coming in to talk to you about that lower field. I didn't mean…'

'Well, as you're here now you may as well come in.' Stacy waved him in as she walked back behind her desk. 'You've obviously become good friends with your new neighbours if Krissie's reaction is anything to go by.'

The collar of his shirt tightened. He didn't know what to say, so he entered the room and sat on the sofa beside Tess, careful to keep a safe distance between them. 'You okay?' he murmured.

'Sure.' Tess sent him a wan smile before turning back to Stacy. 'Mrs Bennet, I'm so sorry. I—'

'Stacy, dear, please…at least when the children aren't present. And let me assure you there's no need to apologise. There were always going to be a few teething problems. I knew that the moment I read your application and discovered Ty and Krissie had recently lost their parents.'

Tess's breath whooshed out of her. 'That didn't put you off accepting us into town?'

'Absolutely not! We think you're perfect for Bellaroo Creek. And we think our town has a lot to offer all of you too. What are a few teething problems in the grand scheme, anyway? So don't you go making this bigger in your mind than it ought to be. The children will settle in just fine, you'll see. What we need to do now is sort you out.'

'Me?' she squeaked.

'But before we move on to that, I just want to let you know

that if Krissie has another little outburst like that, then we'll deal with it in-house rather than calling you in.'

'Oh, but—'

'Believe me, Tess, it'll be for the best. I thought it important you came today, just so Krissie knows she can rely on you, but from hereon we'll deal with it.'

'But what if—?'

Stacy held up a hand and Cam heard Tess literally swallow. 'Oh, I'm making a hash of it, aren't I?'

His jaw dropped. He turned to her. 'What are you talking about? You've been brilliant!'

'Cam is right, Tess. You're doing a remarkable job in difficult circumstances. I sincerely applaud all you've achieved.'

Tess shot him a glance before turning back to Stacy. Her spine straightened. 'Thank you.'

'Believe me, you can be the natural mother of twelve children and still feel utterly clueless some days.'

Tess stared, and then she started to laugh. 'I'm not sure that's particularly comforting, but it makes me feel better all the same.' She leant forward, her hands clasped on her knees. 'Okay, so what did you mean when you said you needed to sort me out?'

'Do you really think you'll find it satisfying enough just keeping house and looking after the children?'

'Well, I—'

'My dear, I think you'll go mad. So what I want to propose is for you to run a class or two for our OOSH programme.'

'OOSH?'

'Out of school hours,' Stacy clarified. 'The classes would only run for forty minutes or so. The school has a budget for it, so you would be paid.'

Tess opened her mouth, but no sound came out.

'It'll be a great benefit to the community during term time and great for the kids. More important, however, I expect it will help keep you fresh and stop you from going stir crazy.'

Tess stiffened when she realised exactly what kind of classes Stacy was going to ask her to teach—music classes. Cam stared at her and recalled the way she'd tensed up when Helen had co-opted her for the summer school. He frowned. Surely with her experience and expertise teaching music classes would be a cinch. If she had a passion for music, wouldn't she be eager to share it?

He didn't want to ask any awkward questions. At least, not in front of Stacy, but…

Silence stretched throughout the office. Finally Tess smoothed back her hair. 'I know you're thinking of my piano and guitar training,' she said quietly. Too quietly. 'But piano isn't really appropriate to teach to a large group. As for guitar, that will only work if everyone has their own instrument.'

Stacy grimaced and shook her head.

Tess's hands relaxed their ferocious grip on each other. He stared at them, and then opened his mouth. He could donate the funds needed to buy the school guitars.

'I figured that might be the case,' Tess said.

He closed his mouth again, curious to see what she meant to propose.

She pursed her lips and pretended to consider the problem. He stared, trying to work out how he knew it was a pretence, but he couldn't put a finger on it. He kept getting sidetracked by the perfect colour of her skin and the plump promise of her lips.

'I could do percussion classes,' she said. 'It teaches timing and rhythm and the kids would love it.'

'Sounds…noisy,' he said.

'Which no doubt is part of the fun,' said Stacy. 'What equipment would you need?'

'Any kind of percussion instrument the school or the children have lying around—drums, cymbals, triangles, maracas, clappers. Even two bits of wood would work, or rice in a plastic milk container.'

'We can make some of those in class.'

'Do you have recorders?' Both he and Stacy groaned. Tess grinned. 'I'll take that as a yes. In my opinion recorders get a bad rap. They're a wonderful tool for teaching children how to read music.'

'Oh, Tess, that sounds perfect!' Stacy clasped her hands on her desk and beamed at them. 'Can you start next week? We hold the classes at the community hall and there'll always be a parent or four to help out. Would Tuesdays and Thursdays suit you?'

'I'd love to be involved, and any day of the week is fine with me.'

Cam couldn't tell if she truly meant it or not, but he sensed her sincere desire to fit in, to become fully involved in life at Bellaroo Creek. To give back. His stomach rolled. While he was intent on leaving.

'I know you're busy on Kurrajong, Cam, but I don't suppose you'd take a class?'

He went to say, You can take that right, when Krissie's crumpled face rose in his mind…along with the way Ty flinched whenever he was startled as if waiting for a blow to fall. 'I'll teach judo classes on a Wednesday if you think there'll be any takers.'

Tess spun to him. He refused to look at her. He refused to consider too deeply what that meant for his plans. It'd only be a minor delay. It'd only mean hanging around in Bellaroo Creek for an extra month to six weeks. He did what he could to stop his lip from curling.

'I forgot you had judo training. You received your training certificate before you went off to university, didn't you?'

He nodded. Teaching judo had helped pay his way through university.

'Excellent! That'll be another winner. I can't tell you both how much I appreciate it. I'll be in touch to fine-tune the details,' Stacy said. 'Now, Cam, my lower field.'

'We need to talk drainage and fund-raising.'

She sighed. 'Just as I feared. We might have to leave that all for another day,' she said, leading them to the door. 'But many thanks for coming out here and taking a look. Take care, the both of you.'

Cam glanced at Tess as they set off for the front gate. Was she all right? Dealing with Krissie's and Ty's fears and insecurities had to be taking its toll. He didn't doubt for a moment that she loved them, but... She'd essentially gone from fêted musician to a single mother of two needy children in the blink of an eye. It couldn't be easy. Some days it must be bloody heartbreaking and exhausting. 'Are you okay?'

One shoulder lifted, but lines of fatigue fanned out from her eyes. 'Sure.' When he didn't say anything she glanced up, grimaced and shrugged again. 'Some days it feels as if we take one step forward and three steps back.'

He couldn't think of anything to say that didn't sound like a platitude or the accepted wisdom she already knew.

'I know it'll get better with time.'

But how much time? And how ragged would she run herself in the meantime? He glanced at her again and bit back a curse.

'You did that for Ty's and Krissie's sakes, didn't you?' she said, when they reached their cars. She blinked in the sunlight. 'Offering to teach judo.'

He chose his words carefully. 'I think if they feel they can defend themselves, they'll become a little more...relaxed.'

'I don't doubt that for a single moment, but...'

But? He shifted. 'I don't teach fighting as a good or positive thing to do, Tess. Judo is about self-discipline and learning how to defend yourself.'

'Oh, it's not that!' She actually looked shocked by the idea. 'But...' she glanced around as if afraid of being overheard '...I thought you were leaving town?'

He rolled his shoulders. 'I am. That hasn't changed.' He

wanted them very clear on that. 'But there's still a lot of work to sort out on Kurrajong. Hanging around until the end of the school term means I won't be leaving it all for my station manager to sort out.' He gritted his teeth. What was a month?

Besides, it had struck him afresh in Stacy's office that while he was fighting not to turn into his father, that was exactly what he was in danger of becoming. Just like his father, he'd withdrawn from the community and thrown himself into work on the station. Leaving Bellaroo Creek and involving himself in a cause he was passionate about would ensure that history didn't repeat, but in the meantime he had to fight that inward impulse as much as he could. Even if it meant coming face-to-face with Lance and Fiona some time in the near future.

What would that matter? In three months he'd be in Africa.

In the meantime, he would not bury himself on Kurrajong Station with all of his bitterness and shattered dreams. He thrust his shoulders back. He'd get the chance to explore new horizons, stretch his wings, and shake the dust of this godforsaken place from his boots soon enough.

'You know, I'd kill for a piece of butter cake with orange icing right about now.'

He blinked himself back into the present. 'Sorry, Tess, I'm afraid the town doesn't stretch to a bakery.' Though rumour had it that might change in the not too distant future with Milla Brady coming home. One could only hope.

'It doesn't mean I can't make a cake of my own, though.'

True enough. He opened her car door for her. 'You think it'll cheer Krissie up?'

'It may well do,' she said with a shrug, but a cheeky grin peeped through. 'Mostly I just want one because I'm famished!'

He laughed, noting the way her shoulders had started to loosen.

'I don't know what it is about the air out here, but my appetite suddenly seems to know no bounds.'

'Will you have time for a lesson on the lawnmower this afternoon? It's in perfect working order again and I thought I might bring it over.' It occurred to him that it might be a good idea for Tess to have company this afternoon.

'Oh, that'll be perfect! I'll feed you cake, and you can teach me the fine art of lawnmower riding.'

'Deal.'

He tried to ignore the excitement that curled in his stomach as she drove away. He was teaching her how to use the ride-on, that was all. If he was lucky it might stop her from brooding. End of story.

Cam drove the mower into the backyard. From her position at the kitchen window Tess's gaze zeroed in on those impressive shoulders and the strongly defined muscles of his upper arms, and her breath hitched.

She leaned closer to get a better look. She fanned her face. She jumped when the oven timer dinged.

She wrenched her gaze away. It had been an emotional morning. This was a carry-over reaction from that. She shied away from the 'emotional' part of that thought too. It made her insides start to wobble again, and she was getting tired of wobbling, of feeling the ground constantly shifting beneath her feet.

'Come on through,' she hollered before he could knock on the back door.

She pulled the cake from the oven and, although she sensed him standing behind her, she set the cake on the bench and just stared at it, her mouth watering. She needed to let it cool for at least ten minutes before cutting into it.

Longer if she intended to ice it.

When she finally turned to Cam, his lips twitched as if he

could read her hunger, her greed. He nodded towards it, his eyes dancing. 'I'm impressed.'

Something in his voice… Didn't he think that she could bake? She stuck her nose in the air. 'So you should be.'

Then she grinned. 'I've been practising becoming model-mother material since before we left Sydney.' She tapped an old exercise book—Sarah's recipe book—her sister's hand-writing as familiar as her own. 'There's a wealth of hints and tips in this baby.'

'What is it?'

She handed it to him, and then hitched her head in the di-rection of the yard, grabbing her sunhat as they went. 'C'mon, I'm dying to eat cake so the sooner I learn all I need to about your ride-on mower, the better.'

Barney greeted them with excited barks, leaping up on Tess and practically exploding with delight when she petted him. Fluffy followed behind at a far more dignified pace.

'C'mon, you two.' She scooped the puppy up in one hand and the chicken in her other and popped them both in the chicken mansion out of harm's way. They proceeded to romp down the length of the run together.

Cam stared. 'Who'd have believed it? They've become playmates.'

'I'm convinced Fluffy thinks she's a dog. I'm not sure what she's going to do when we get more chickens.'

'When are you planning on that?'

'Just as soon as I do my research and know what I'm doing.' The last thing she needed was a dead chicken or three. There'd been enough death in the children's lives—and hers—to last them for a lifetime.

'I've some books you can borrow.'

'Thanks, but I have a couple on order at the library.'

Bellaroo Creek had the tiniest library on the planet—full of fat romance novels of which she'd fully availed herself. As part of the Greater Parkes Shire, though, the library had a huge range of books available through the inter-library loan scheme. Her books should arrive within the week.

Cam surveyed her. 'You don't want to accept my help?'

She recalled the heat that had hit her at the kitchen window, the silly flutter in her chest. 'It's not that. It's just the library already has them on order for me.' And she was *not* going to get into the habit of counting on Cam too much. Not when he was leaving Bellaroo Creek. Not when he heated her blood so quickly and assailed her senses so fully she found it impossible to keep her balance around him.

She dragged her gaze from the green promise of his eyes and gestured to the mower. 'What do I need to know?'

He placed Sarah's book on the garden bench Tess and the children had hauled around from the front yard last weekend, and gestured to the mower. 'C'mon, then, up you get.'

He helped her climb on and his hand on her arm was warm and strong. Absurdly, it made her feel strong too.

'Okay, quick overview—handbrake, foot brake and accelerator—' he pointed to each of them '—and this lever here—' he tapped it '—lifts and lowers the cutting blades.'

'Right.' She nodded. It was an auto transmission—easy-peasy.

'People generally run into two problems with ride-ons. The first is stalling the mower because they're trying to set off too fast. The second is setting the cutter blades too low and hitting dirt. So let's work on starting it up and moving forwards first. Ignition is right there.' He handed her a key.

She fitted it to the ignition and it started up first go. She put her foot on the brake, let out the handbrake and then pressed down on the accelerator.

And stalled.

Cam didn't laugh. He just reached over and pulled the handbrake on, hitting her with his heat and the scent of cut grass. 'Okay, let's try that again.'

Even though her heart beat faster, his calm confidence filtered into her.

'Ease your foot gently onto the accelerator.'

She did as he instructed and this time the mower edged forward. She drove to the lemon tree before pulling to a halt again, a ludicrous flush of accomplishment surging through her. She grinned as he strode up to her and he grinned back. It suddenly struck her how sunny it was out here, how clear the sky and how good everything smelled.

He taught her how to reverse. He showed her how to adjust the blade level. 'Okay, show me what you're made of, Tess Laing. Off you go. I want to see you do a lap around the chicken coop.'

She took a deep breath and headed for the chicken coop. She finished the lap, headed for the back fence and then did it all over again.

'Yee ha!' Holding her hat to her head, she lifted her face to the sun and laughed for the sheer joy of it. Who knew a ride-on lawnmower could be so much fun? 'Oh, man, I have to get me one of these!'

She clamped both hands back to the steering wheel as she whizzed around the chicken coop a third time. Barney raced the length of the chicken run beside her, barking madly and wagging his tail. Cam laughed at her, but she didn't mind in the least. This—this mad, fun dash on the mower—felt like freedom.

With the kids having started school this week, she'd started to feel less tense, less…shackled. Until this morning, that was. But…to not have to be on her guard all the time, aware that her every move and word could impact on Ty and Krissie in some unforseen way. That…well, it was heaven.

Not that she didn't miss the children being at home with her, but she relished the downtime from them too. Nobody had told her how much mess they could make, or how noisy they could be, or how grumpy they could get when they were tired or…or just how relentless parenthood was.

And nobody had warned her how much that could take out of a person.

Which went to show what a poor substitute she was for Sarah.

She promptly stalled the mower.

Cam came up, a frown in his eyes. 'What happened?'

She swallowed. 'I, uh, lost my concentration for a moment.' She tried to find that elusive sense of freedom again, but it slipped out of reach. 'Thank you for the lesson, Cameron. I think I have the hang of it now.' She started the mower up again. Something in his eyes made the ache inside her threaten to explode, and she wasn't sure if tears or heat would be the outcome—and she had no intention of finding out. 'I'll just park it up near the house.' She didn't wait for him to say anything, but took off.

She climbed off the mower and checked her watch.

'Somewhere you need to be?'

She suddenly laughed. 'I'm just waiting for that darn cake to cool. I'd planned on icing it, but I'm not sure I can wait that long. I'll put the kettle on in a moment and cut us both a slice. I just want to check the animals' water first.'

Cam settled on the garden bench and picked up Sarah's book. Tess checked the water bowl by the back door and then the one in the chicken coop, letting Barney and Fluffy out to play in the yard.

Cam gave a sudden snort. 'You have got to be joking! Listen to this. "Carrot spaghetti: using a vegetable peeler, create long lengths of carrot to look like spaghetti. Submerge in boiling water for a few seconds and then top with pasta sauce. Children will love it and it's a tasty way to ensure they eat their vegetables."'

She nodded. 'I know. Who has the time for that, huh? Do

you know how long it takes to peel a whole carrot with a vegetable peeler?'

He stared at her. The book dropped to his lap. 'You've tried this?'

'Well…' She heaved back a sigh. 'I just never knew it could be so hard to get kids to eat their veggies. There's loads more tips in there about grating carrot and zucchini and adding it to mince when making rissoles or meatloaf…and grating cauliflower and zucchini into hash-brown mixture and…'

She plonked down beside him. 'Long gone are the days of pulling a frozen dinner out of the freezer and nuking it in the microwave.' And God help her, but she missed those days. A sigh overtook her. 'Do you know how long it takes to grate anything?'

'Hell, Tess.'

She straightened. 'I mean, that's one of the reasons we came out here—so I'd have plenty of time to do exactly that.' Looking after Ty and Krissie was the most important job in the world to her, so what were a few grated carrots between family, huh?

'You're going to send yourself around the twist grating vegetables as if there's no tomorrow.'

It was starting to feel that way, but…

'You know what, Tess?'

She glanced at him and the sympathy and compassion in his eyes made her sinuses burn and her throat ache. 'What?' she whispered.

'I think you need to stop trying to be Sarah and focus on being yourself.'

Her head rocked back.

'And another thing… Why are you so reluctant to continue with your music?'

She froze.

'Why aren't you eager to dive back into your piano and guitar?'

An invisible hand reached inside her chest to squeeze her heart.

'Hasn't it occurred to you that playing again might actually help you manage all your stress and worry?'

'No!' She leapt up. 'You're wrong. So wrong!'

She stood there, hands clenched, shaking, and realised too late how utterly revealing her reaction had been. She forced herself to sit again, doing what she could to hide her panic. 'No.' She moderated her tone. 'You don't understand.'

'Then explain it to me.'

Explain? Oh, that was impossible, but… 'Music consumes me. I… When I play, nothing else matters. For the time being, it needs to go on the backburner until I get a decent handle on my new life.'

All true, but she couldn't look at him as she said it.

He surveyed her for a long moment. It took a superhuman effort not to fidget. 'So you haven't played since you heard about Sarah's accident?'

The yearning rose within her but she ruthlessly smothered it. 'There hasn't been time.' There would never be time. She'd make sure of it. She'd turned her back on that life of selfishness.

His eyes suddenly narrowed. 'Why do I get the feeling you're punishing yourself?'

'Low blood sugar,' she prescribed, jumping up. 'It's beyond time I serve up that promised cake.'

'Tess.'

She halted halfway to the back door and then turned. 'Cam, can we leave this for now? I…I just need to get my priorities straight and my music messes with that too much. I'll sort it out eventually, but in the meantime talking about it doesn't help.'

She hated lying to him. But he was leaving Bellaroo Creek soon and… And it was just too hard.

With a nod, he let it be and she could've hugged him. To

stop from doing anything so stupid, she set up the card table and served tea and cake. Cam ate it with the same relish as she did, and it lifted something inside her.

Eventually they both sat back, sated.

'Tess, about grating all those vegetables.'

His tone made her laugh. 'Yes?'

'I don't think it's necessary.'

'No? Well, c'mon, convince me, because, believe me, if I never see another grated carrot for as long as I live it'll be too soon.'

He sobered, that compassion alive in his eyes again. 'Tess, no matter what you do you'll never be able to make up to Krissie and Ty that they've lost their parents. You can grate from now till kingdom come, but it won't make a scrap of difference.'

Her throat closed over.

'And spoiling them in the attempt will be doing them a grave disservice.'

With a superhuman effort, she swallowed. Had she been spoiling them? 'You think I fuss over them too much, don't you?'

His face softened. 'I think when you're feeling more confident, you'll relax a bit more.'

'So…that's a yes, then?'

He remained silent.

She pondered what he'd said. It should break her heart that she couldn't make up to Ty and Krissie that they'd lost their parents. And it did, but it was strangely freeing too. It gave her permission to focus on the things she could change.

She glanced at Cam. He'd put his exciting plans for Africa on hold for a whole additional month for Krissie and Ty…and for her. She started to smile. 'You're saying I'll never have to grate another carrot in my life?'

'That's exactly what I'm saying.'

He grinned back at her and she couldn't help it. She leaned across and pressed her lips to his.

CHAPTER SIX

CAM DIDN'T PULL away. He didn't even hesitate. He greeted Tess's kiss with wholehearted pleasure. One of his hands cupped her face, engulfing her in his warmth. Tendrils of sensation unfurled in her stomach and drifted out to every corner of her body in slow adagios of delight. Waltzing delight.

And then the tendrils became licks of fire. Cam's free hand curved around the back of her neck and he pulled her in closer, his lips moving over hers more fully, more thoroughly, offering her even more delight, making her even hungrier for him.

Greedy to taste, greedy to touch, she slid her hands to either side of his face and she explored the texture of his jaw and the strong column of his neck until her hands and fingers were as alive as her lips. When he licked the corner of her mouth, traced the fullness of her bottom lip, she opened up to him and he dragged her right into his lap as their tongues danced. She wound her arms about his neck as if she never meant to let him go.

She gave herself up to the thrill of being alive and in his arms. Kissing Cameron was like listening to vibrant, wonderful music. Better yet, it was like *making* vibrant, wonderful music. Music that could fill the soul and send it soaring free, and Tess wanted to soar and fly and swoop and twirl with Cameron and never stop.

She slipped her hand between the buttons of his shirt,

needing to touch firm bare skin. His hand slid beneath her shirt, his caress an omen of bliss. And then they both stilled, so unaccountably in tune with each other that they knew.

They knew this had become more than a kiss. It was about to become something a whole lot more interesting…if that was what they chose.

If.

Tess stared up into eyes so vivid with promise that all she had to do was reach out. She sucked her bottom lip into her mouth and tasted him there. Her body clamoured for more, but…

She shivered. Ty and Krissie.

She gave a tiny shake of her head.

She felt the sigh he heaved back, but he nodded his acknowledgement. He went to lift her off his lap, but she held up a hand to forestall him. She dragged in a breath, counted to three…four, and then removed herself under her own steam until she was sitting beside him again.

'I really shouldn't have done that,' she murmured.

He surveyed her with watchful eyes, but didn't say anything. She bit her lip and then shrugged. 'But while I shouldn't have kissed you, I can't find it in myself to be sorry for it.' She frowned, suddenly realising how selfish that sounded. 'I mean, I'm sorry if I made you—'

'Me neither, Tess,' he cut in.

He leaned back, a grin lighting those ecstasy-inducing lips of his and hunger raged through her.

'I don't see why you shouldn't have done it. I don't have a problem if you want to do it again.' He raised his hands. 'Just saying.'

She laughed and shook her head. 'I shouldn't have done it because I liked it too much.'

'And there's a problem with that?'

It was the same as when she played the piano or the guitar—the world receded and the music took over. And until three months ago, she'd let it. Willingly. Gladly. She'd welcomed it. Only now, she knew how selfish that had been. How unfair it had been to those around her.

No more.

She'd let her selfish obsession keep her from Sarah, when her sister had needed her. She couldn't afford to let Ty and Krissie down in the same way.

'There are just too many strikes against us, Cameron.'

'Like?'

'Like the fact I truly believe Ty and Krissie need stability for a while. I don't think it's fair to ask them to adjust to a new man in their lives just yet. Not after everything they've been through. I don't think that's unreasonable, even if you do. We're just searching for...'

'An even keel.'

She nodded. 'I really don't want to mess this up.'

'Strike One,' he murmured.

She glanced down at her hands and then back at him. 'There are other issues too. You have a grudge in your heart that's bigger than forty hectares of golden canola. Until you come to terms with that, there'll never be room in your heart for another woman.'

He drew back. 'I have good reason for that grudge.'

'Yes, you do.'

'But?'

Couldn't he see how much his bitterness, how much holding on to his grudge was hurting him? 'It's just from where I'm standing—sitting—that's Strike Two.'

He didn't say anything.

She couldn't let it go. 'What Lance and Fiona did to you, Cameron, sucks. But...' She gripped her hands together. 'But has it never occurred to you that maybe they never meant for it to happen, that they never meant to hurt you? That maybe they just fell in love with each other? Maybe he's just as appalled by what's happened as you are.'

Cam dragged a hand back through his hair, making it stand on end. She ached to reach out and smooth it back down.

'Look, Tess, all his life Lance has been jealous of me. Jealous that I had a father with a bigger station than his father's. Jealous that I had two homes I divided my time between. Jealous that I did well at sport and at school. You name it—if it was mine, he wanted it.'

He scowled out at the yard. 'If he spent half as much time working towards whatever it was he wanted instead of resenting me for having it, or stealing it from me, then he might have achieved something worthwhile. I thought he'd grow out of it. Hoped he would. For heaven's sake, he's twenty-six years old! I never thought he would go to such lengths, but...'

His hands clenched. 'But it appears he still wants what I have, so, no, I haven't considered the fact that he never meant to hurt me. I know that's precisely what he was hoping to achieve.'

Bile burned the back of Tess's throat at the expression in his eyes.

'He stole all that I most cherished in this world, and he laughed while he did it. Forgiveness, even if he asked for it...'

He broke off, his face growing grimmer. 'This time he went too far. He involved an innocent third party in his nasty little games.'

All that I most cherished. She swallowed, suddenly nauseous. 'Fiona?' The name croaked out of her.

He gave one hard nod.

She swallowed again. 'Forgive me for saying this, but the fact she, um...canoodled with your brother while engaged to you doesn't exactly cast her in the role of an innocent.'

Did he still love that tall, slim woman with the golden ponytail? The thought left a bad taste in her mouth. If her stomach hadn't been churning so badly she'd have grabbed another piece of cake to override it.

'Lance has always had more charm than was good for

him. He knows how to woo a woman and make her believe he's in love with her.'

She leant towards him, though she was careful not to touch him. 'But maybe he really loves Fiona.'

He turned to her then and raised a dark eyebrow. 'When he's finished with her, he'll dump her.' His lips compressed into a hard, grim line. 'He'll break her heart. All just to get back at me.'

That didn't ring true. Oh, she didn't doubt for a moment that Cam believed it, but… 'They looked very together at the luncheon…as in a definite couple. Cameron, it's been ten months. Your mother obviously thinks they mean to marry.'

He didn't say anything for a long moment. 'Even if what you say is true, does that excuse the fact that they betrayed me?'

'Of course it doesn't! But maybe it'd prove that they never meant to hurt you, and that has to count for something.'

'If it were true, perhaps it would.'

She ached for him then, for the pain she sensed bubbling beneath the surface, his utter sense of betrayal. Forgiveness would bring him peace, if only he would consider it. Ten months. Surely that was long enough. But some wounds, she knew, never healed.

She smoothed her hair back, longing to make him smile. 'Do you know you kiss like an angel, Cameron? And that by holding onto your grudge you're depriving some woman out there of the most divine kisses, all because you won't forgive Lance?'

He stared and then a laugh shot out of him. 'I didn't realise you could be quite so persistent.'

'Dog with a bone,' she agreed. Speaking of dogs… She glanced around and then blew out a breath when she found Barney and Fluffy sunning themselves only a few feet away. 'My parents found it one of my less endearing traits.' But it was the reason she'd become such a fine musician.

He leaned towards her, swamping her with his green-grass freshness and all that false promise. She gulped. He didn't mean to kiss her again, did he?

He reached out and traced a finger down her cheek. Her pulse leapt to life beneath it. 'Tess, regardless of what anyone says, you are divine.'

What if she channelled all the energy she'd put into her music into healing this man, into loving him and showing him there was a better way? Would she succeed? Would she—?

She drew back. She didn't have the time or the luxury for those kinds of games. If she only had herself to consider…

But she didn't.

Her skin pimpled with gooseflesh when she recalled the kind of family Sarah had dreamed of having—a wonderful, close-knit family who loved each other, supported each other and did things together. That had all been taken away from her. It had all gone so terribly wrong for her, and for Ty and Krissie too. Tess couldn't let it go bad for them again. Her fingers shook and her throat tightened. She'd failed Sarah once, but she wouldn't fail her again.

Ty and Krissie were the ones who deserved—who needed—all her energy. And she couldn't risk their hearts to such an endeavour. She couldn't let them become so dependent on Cam that they'd be crushed when he left.

When he left…

'And Strike Three,' she said, 'you're planning on leaving town. Unless you've changed your mind on that head.' Her heart gave a traitorous jump.

'I haven't changed my mind.' He stared down at his hands. 'Strike Three,' he agreed.

They sat in silence for a moment. 'So lots of reasons not to kiss,' he said, as if double-checking her resolve.

'Yep.' She couldn't keep the glumness from her voice.

Cam rose. 'I think it's beyond time that I made tracks.'

A protest clamoured through her but she bit it back. He was right.

He set his dusty Akubra on top of his head and touched its brim in a kind of salute. 'I'll be seeing you, Tess.'

It had all the finality of an irrevocable goodbye.

'Let's go down this road,' Ty said, pointing to the right.

Krissie nodded her agreement.

Ty held Barney on his lap, Krissie held Fluffy on her lap, and Tess had a picnic hamper on the passenger seat beside her. It was Saturday. The children had completed their first full week of school, and they'd agreed to spend the day exploring the surrounds of their new home.

Tess turned the car obediently in the direction Ty had indicated. All the roads around here seemed to be unsealed, and some of them weren't in the best of repair. This one was no exception, but she didn't mind driving slowly to avoid the worst of the potholes and corrugations. It gave her a chance to enjoy the scenery.

And the scenery was stunning—long stretches of low hills green with wheat and lucerne. Here and there a river or stream gleamed silver-blue amid the landscape. There were ridges of land dotted with scribbly gums and sheep, and brown fields enclosing brown cattle, muddy dams and dandelions. It was warm enough still to leave the window down and the air was fresh and green, if occasionally dusty.

'Fluffy thinks that'd be the best spot for our picnic,' Krissie announced, pointing to a stand of Kurrajong trees up ahead.

The trees formed a natural glade that sloped down to a river. Tess glanced at her watch. They'd been driving for just over an hour, and, if her sense of direction was anything to go by, they should've nearly completed the loop that would take them back into Bellaroo Creek.

They'd taken the road west out of town and the plan had been to circle around and come back in on the town's northern side. According to her calculations, they couldn't be more than a couple of kilometres from the township.

And it was nearly lunchtime.

And she was starving!

She pulled the car to the side of the road. 'Well spotted, Fluffy. This looks like a fabulous picnic spot.' She hoped whoever owned the land wouldn't mind them trespassing. 'Watch out for cows,' she hollered as the children and animals spilled from the car and raced towards the river. 'And don't get too close to the water!'

She was out of breath when she reached them. And, truly, it was the prettiest spot. They all gazed at it in silence for a moment as if to just drink it in. 'Beautiful,' Tess breathed.

Krissie slipped her hand inside Tess's. 'Do you think Cam has a river on his station?'

'I haven't the foggiest, chickadee, but I expect so. You can ask him next time you see him.'

'At judo class!'

Both children were excited by the after-school activities on offer, but especially Cam's judo class.

'Ninja!' Ty executed a high, flying kick that made Fluffy flap her wings.

'Food,' Tess countered.

They spread out a blanket and devoured their picnic— sandwiches, fruit, date scones and bottles of water—sharing it all with Barney and Fluffy. By the time they were finished, Tess wanted nothing more than to curl up on the blanket and doze in the sun.

'Barney wants to explore,' Ty announced.

'Of course he does,' Tess said, suppressing a grin, a sigh and an eye-roll all in one movement. She glanced at Krissie.

'Fluffy wants to sleep.' She sighed.

Lucky Fluffy.

'Right, well, we'll take our picnic things back to the car and put Fluffy in her cage to sleep.' Tess had thankfully had the foresight to pack the cage and some newspaper. She left the rear door of the car up and wound down all the windows. 'Okay, which way does Barney want to go?'

They walked beside the river. With the children and puppy racing off in front of her, leaving her momentarily chatter free, Tess was at leisure to enjoy the peace. After only five minutes of walking, they rounded a bend and a low sandstone and wrought-iron wall brought them up short.

Krissie turned back to her. 'What is it?'

Tess glanced over the fence. It was so overgrown it took her a moment to make out what it was. When she did her stomach gave a queer little jerk. 'It's a cemetery,' she said, watching both children carefully.

Neither recoiled, and she let out a breath.

'Can we go in?'

Shielding her eyes against the sun, Tess followed the sandstone wall around until she found what she was looking for. 'The entrance is over there.' She pointed. If they'd driven a little further on they'd have happened upon this spot in the car—it was the very end of the road. Her lips twisted. In more ways than one, she supposed, but she determinedly left the gallows humour behind as she walked through the gate.

'Ty, Krissie.' She gestured to the children. 'There are some rules we need to observe in a cemetery. It's very bad manners to walk on a grave, so please keep to the paths.' And there were some, even if they were terribly overgrown in places. Someone was doing what they could to maintain this little cemetery. 'If you want to look at the headstones walk beside the graves, okay?'

Both children nodded solemnly. 'What about Barney?'

'Puppies are exempt, young man.'

They turned in concert to find an elderly woman, half hidden in the shade of a Kurrajong tree, sitting on a camp chair beside one of the graves. 'I hope we're not disturbing you,' Tess ventured.

'Not at all, lovey.'

Tess moved towards her. 'I'm Tess Laing and this is my nephew and niece—'

'Tyler and Kristina, yes, I've heard about you folk and I'm real pleased you've come to settle in Bellaroo Creek. I'm Edna Fairfield. I meant to make it to your luncheon, but my knees aren't as young as they used to be. My husband, Ted, and I own a pocket of land just back that way.' She nodded back the way Tess and the children had come.

After shy hellos, Ty and Krissie raced off to explore. Tess sat on the grass next to the older woman and Barney settled at her feet to nap. 'I'm afraid we've been trespassing on your land. I'm terribly sorry.'

'You're welcome to wander through our holding whenever you want, lovey.'

They sat in silence for a while. Tess finally gestured. 'Is this a private cemetery?'

'Lord, no, it's the Bellaroo Creek cemetery, but folks these days prefer to scatter the ashes of their loved ones on the land. Hardly anyone comes here any more.'

'But you do?'

'My dear mother and father are buried just over there.' She pointed to a nearby grave. 'And this here—' she touched the edge of the grave she sat beside '—is where we buried my darling boy, Jack. He was only a tiny tot—eighteen months—when croup took him.'

Tess read the dates on the headstone and a lump lodged in her throat. Edna had been coming here for sixty years to sit by her beloved baby son. 'Oh, Mrs Fairfield,' she whispered. 'I'm so sorry for your loss.'

'Don't you go wasting your sympathy on me, young Tess. Ted and me, we raised three healthy children and sent them out into the world—good strong folk we're proud of. Into every life there comes some sorrow.' She might be old but her eyes hadn't faded and they glanced shrewdly at Tess now. 'I understand there's been some recent sorrow in your lives too.'

She nodded. Into every life… She glanced at Ty and Krissie, carefully walking around the graves. 'I'm thinking, though, that moving out here means we can start focusing on good things again.'

Please, God.

'I don't doubt that for a moment.'

She couldn't help smiling at Edna's no-nonsense country briskness.

'But, lovey—' Edna sighed after a moment '—I can't help wondering who'll come here and tend my Jack's grave when Ted and I are gone.' She shook her head. 'It's a silly thing to worry about, I know, but it doesn't stop me from thinking about it.'

'I don't think it's silly.'

She didn't think it was the slightest bit silly. She went to say more but suddenly found Ty and Krissie standing in front of her. Holding hands, no less! 'Everything okay, poppets?'

'Can we bury Mummy here?' Krissie asked without preamble.

Whoa!

Okay.

Um…

She glanced at Edna. 'Is it still possible to arrange a plot here?'

'I expect so, lovey. Lorraine Pritchard would be the person to ask. She's the president of the Residents Committee.'

'That's Cam's mum,' Ty said to Edna. 'He's our friend.'

'He lives right next door,' Krissie added.

'He's a good young man,' Edna agreed. 'He helps Ted out every now and again. Means we can still manage to keep a few head of cattle on our land.'

He did? Tess stared at Edna. What would she and Ted do when Cam left?

* * *

Cam's farm ute was parked out the front when they arrived back home. Tess parked beside it and tried to school her wayward heart back into its normal pace and rhythm instead of a ridiculous speeded-up staccato.

'Can we play on the computer?'

She eyed her nephew and her heart expanded. Two months ago he'd been listless with no enthusiasm for any kind of play. Understandable given the circumstances, but now it seemed the world held a whole list of endless possibilities.

She climbed out of the car and crossed her fingers, prayed the worst was behind them now. 'As long as you promise to let Krissie have her turn too.'

He nodded.

'Okay, go on, then.'

He was about to race off, Krissie at his heels, when Cam came around the side of the house. 'Hey, Cam.' He waved.

'Hey, kids.'

Krissie flung her arms around Cam's middle and hugged him. Tess couldn't prevent a squirm of envy.

'We found the bestest cemetery,' she announced, releasing him. 'You wanna come play on the computer?'

He blinked. 'Um... Maybe some other time.' He ruffled her hair. 'I have to chat to your aunt about some stuff.'

Krissie ran off and Cam turned to her with a frown. 'What's so hot about a cemetery?'

'They want to inter their mother's ashes there.'

He pushed the brim of his hat back to stare at her. She nodded. 'I know. It took me off guard too. It's all kind of serious, huh?' She twisted her hands together. Once they interred Sarah's remains in the Bellaroo Creek cemetery, there'd be no going back. For good or for ill, Bellaroo Creek would become their home. For good.

'Are you okay with that?'

'Sure.' As long as Bellaroo Creek flourished. As long as the primary school remained open. As long…

She kicked herself into action. Standing still for too long allowed doubts to bombard her. And what was the use in those? Striding around the car, she retrieved Fluffy and the cage.

'So what's wrong?'

She sent him a swift glance. 'Who says anything's wrong?'

'I do. Your eyes are darker than normal and you have a tiny furrow here.' He touched a spot on her forehead, before taking the cage from her.

She folded her arms. How could this man be so attuned to her and yet be so far out of reach? She clamped her lips shut. He *was* out of reach. *That* was the pertinent fact. Everything else was just…wishful thinking.

'Tess?'

She turned away, swallowing back a sigh, and led the way down the side of the house. 'They want to inter their mother's remains in Bellaroo Creek's cemetery, but they've made no mention of their father.'

She plonked herself down on the garden bench and watched Cam as he placed Fluffy into her mansion of a coop. He was a joy to watch. He might be big, but he didn't lumber about like a bear. He moved with the grace of a big cat.

She forced her gaze away, only turning back when he took a seat beside her. 'And that's a problem?'

She thought about it. 'I don't know. Potentially, I guess. We had Sarah and Bruce cremated, but I had no idea what to do with the ashes. A counsellor suggested I let the children be part of the decision-making process, but they were appalled at the thought of scattering the ashes. So…'

'So you brought them with you.'

'They were very insistent that their mother should come with us.'

'But their father?'

'Not a brass razoo.' She shook her head. 'And I couldn't very well leave him behind, could I?'

'I guess not.' He squinted up at the sky. 'I expect they'll need closure at some point.'

'Lord, I hope so.' She grinned at him. 'Because I'm not sure I want Bruce living on the top of my wardrobe for the next twenty years.'

He laughed as she'd meant him to, but he leaned towards her, and that suddenly seemed dangerous. 'And, yet, why do I get the feeling that if that's how long Krissie and Ty need, then that's exactly where Bruce will stay?'

He smelled like cut grass, dirt and fresh air. It hit her that he smelled like Bellaroo Creek. When he went to Africa, he'd be taking a little bit of Bellaroo Creek with him. The thought should've made her smile.

'I met Edna Fairfield.'

He leaned back. 'Keeping Jack company?'

'Uh-huh.'

She eyed him for a moment. He rolled his shoulders. 'What?'

'She has a very high opinion of you.'

'I have a high opinion of her and Ted.'

'They'll miss you if you leave.'

'When, Tess. *When* I leave.'

She shook herself. 'That's what I meant.'

He had exciting, not to mention important, work to look forward to in Africa. He had the promise of adventure before him, the once-in-a-lifetime experience of immersing himself in another culture and sharing his knowledge, and helping make the world a better place. She couldn't begrudge him his dream, but…

She pulled in a breath. 'I liked her a lot. I don't know much about cattle, but…but could you teach me what to do so I can help them out?'

'Nope.'

She gaped at him.

'Lord, Tess, you think I'm just going to abandon them?'

'Well, aren't you?' He was abandoning all of Bellaroo Creek, wasn't he?

'I've told Fraser to keep an eye on things out there, to help wherever needed.'

His station manager? 'It won't be the same, you know?'

'That can't be helped.'

She supposed he was right.

'If you really want to help Edna out, you'll drop out there when her fruit trees are full and pick the fruit for her...and ask her to teach you how to bottle it, and how to make jam. She'd love that.'

'Excellent.' She'd have to find out when the trees came into fruit. Oh, and she'd better find out what kind of fruit trees they were too.

'Plum and mulberry. And you'll be looking at about November.'

The man could read minds.

'And I also think you should come to judo lessons.'

His sudden change of topic threw her like an unexpected rhythm or an atonal jazz riff. 'You mean...participate? Be one of your students?'

'What would it hurt to learn a few self-defence tactics?'

Nothing, she supposed, but she'd never precisely been the sporty type.

'And you're going to be there anyway, bringing Ty and Krissie to the class. So, why not?'

She saw it then, what it was he was trying to do. 'You think Ty and Krissie will feel safer if I know how to defend myself.' Her heart thumped and her hands clenched.

'I think it's a good idea for every woman to know how to defend herself.'

She chewed her bottom lip.

'Come on, Tess, I'm not talking about grating carrots here.'

He was right. 'It's an excellent suggestion.'

'Good.'

'Now what can I do for you?'

He blinked. And for a moment she could've sworn the colour heightened on his cheekbones. Her heart leapt into her throat and it was all she could do not to cough and choke and make a fool of herself. 'I mean,' she rasped out, gazing everywhere except at him, 'I expect there's a reason you dropped by this afternoon, other than to bully me into taking your judo class?'

He leapt off the bench and strode several feet away. 'I wanted to find out what you had in mind for a vegetable garden,' he said, his back to her, and she knew he felt the same heat, the same urgency, that she did. 'I am getting forty prime hectares practically scot-free, after all. I mean to keep my word, Tess. Chicken coop—tick. Puppy—tick. Vegetable garden—still pending.'

'You didn't just build a chicken coop. You built a chicken palace!' As far as she was concerned, he'd well and truly paid off any debt he'd owed.

He turned and squinted into the sun. 'Are you after a, um, vegetable patch on the same sort of scale?'

She laughed at the expression on his face, though she didn't doubt for a moment that if she wanted it he'd do his best to make it a reality. 'Truly, Cameron, I just want a home for all of these.' She gestured to the ragged array of donated pots and planters. 'And whatever else you think might be a good idea to plant.'

'I was sorting through them when you pulled up. You've a nice variety there.'

'The town's generosity knows no bounds.'

'They want you to stay.'

And she wanted to stay. She had to make this move work. She had to. Her smile faded when she recalled the expression on Edna's face when she'd wondered aloud about who would tend Jack's grave when she was gone. A shiver of unease threaded through her.

'You're not having second thoughts, are you?' he rapped out.

'No!'

'But?'

She swallowed. 'But it didn't hit me until today how tenuous the town's survival is. And I've thrown my lot—and Tyler and Krissie's—in with the town's.' What if the school closed? What if the town did die a slow death? What would they do? It would mean more upheaval and that would be her fault.

'Tess.'

She glanced up.

'Nobody can foresee the future. All you can do is make the here and now meaningful.'

Right. She knew he was right.

'And work with the Save-Our-Town committee to attract even more new blood to the area. Okay?'

She drew in a breath and nodded.

He smiled. 'Now are you going to help me measure out this garden bed or what?'

'Aye-aye, sir.' She clicked her heels together. 'Right after I ring your mother. Apparently she's the one I should talk to about organising a plot at the cemetery.'

He dug his phone out of his pocket and tossed it to her. 'She's on speed dial.' Pulling a tape measure from his hip pocket, he moved away to give her a measure of privacy.

She brought up his list of saved numbers. Lorraine's number was the second on the list.

The first was Lance's.

All you can do is make the here and now meaningful.

She stared at Cameron's back as she placed her call.

CHAPTER SEVEN

LORRAINE ORGANISED A working bee at the cemetery with all the speed and efficiency of a conductor's flourish. 'We can't hold a memorial service there with it looking the way it is! It's beyond time we tidied it up.'

Which was why Tess and the kids found themselves getting ready to return to the cemetery the following Saturday. Tess finally managed to convince Krissie that Fluffy would be much happier staying behind in her chicken mansion rather than attending a busy, noisy working bee. When she rose and turned she found Cam standing directly behind her and her skin flared and her stomach tumbled and a bubble of something light and airy rose within her.

Her heart fluttered up into her throat. She swallowed it back down into her chest and tried to pop the bubble with silent verbal thrusts. *He'll be gone soon.* But her brain refused to cooperate. It was too busy revelling in the undiluted masculinity on display. In low-slung jeans, soft with wear, and a faded cotton twill work shirt—with buttons...buttons that could be undone—he made her fingers itch to run all over him in the same way they did whenever she was near a piano.

She took a step back. 'Hello, Cameron.'

He blinked and that was when she realised he'd been staring at her as intently as she'd been staring at him. Her skin flared hotter. They both glanced away.

'Are you coming with us to the working bee?' Krissie asked.

'Working bee?'

He glanced at Tess. She frowned. Hadn't Lorraine spoken to him? *None of your business.* She cleared her throat and folded her arms. 'The town's organised a clean-up of the cemetery. We're just about to head out there now.'

'I didn't hear about it.'

She unfolded her arms. Well, why not? It—

None of your business. She folded her arms again.

'You have to come,' Ty said. 'It won't be the same if you're not there.'

That was one way of putting it.

Cam smoothed a hand down his jaw. 'The thing is, buddy, I was going to start on your vegetable garden today.'

'But we want to help you do that, don't we, Auntie Tess?'

'We do.'

'And the working bee is for our mummy.' Krissie slid her hand into Cam's. 'Please…you have to come.'

Tess had to choke back a laugh. Talk about emotional blackmail! She clapped her hands briskly. 'Okay, kids, grab your hats and, Ty, make sure you bring Barney's lead.'

The kids raced off.

Cam stared at her. She sucked her bottom lip into her mouth. He followed the action and his eyes darkened. She released it again, her pulse pounding in her throat. She wheeled away to stare blindly at the backyard. 'I don't feel right about you working here without us being around to help. I want to learn.'

'It'll mostly be brute work today.'

'Nevertheless.'

There was a pause. 'Is that a roundabout way of saying you'd like me to come to the cemetery instead?'

'I'd love you to come.' And she meant it. She really wanted him to be part of the working bee, but she wasn't quite sure what that meant. Except she needed to be careful. *Very* careful.

She needed to fight her fascination for this man, or it would all end in tears. If they were only her tears that wouldn't matter, but… She glanced towards the house. 'I think it's only fair to warn you that I expect your mother, Lance and Fiona will all be there today.'

Again there was a long pause. 'You think I'm afraid to come face-to-face with them?'

He stole all that I most cherished.

'I think you've been doing your best to avoid them.' A part of her didn't blame him. She wouldn't want to come face-to-face with the person she loved more than life itself on a daily basis and know they'd chosen someone else. And not just any anonymous *someone else* either, but a sibling. It'd be like ripping a scab off a wound again and again.

She could understand why he wanted to leave Bellaroo Creek. She could even see why he might need to. She couldn't see that cutting himself off from the entire community in the meantime was the thing to do, though. He hadn't done anything to be ashamed of.

'You know—' she planted her hands on her hips '—I think you've made it awfully easy for Lance and Fiona. It wouldn't hurt them to have to see you on a regular basis and feel awkward and ashamed about what they've done.'

He laughed. It surprised her. 'It's nice to have you in my corner, Tess.'

Was that what she was? *You want to be a whole lot more than just in his corner.* She shook the thought off, refused to follow it, tried to focus on the conversation. 'That's your problem with your mother, isn't it? You feel she's not on your side.'

'She's not,' he said bluntly. 'She's always favoured Lance. And, no, that's not jealous sibling rivalry talking, Tess, but…'

Her heart stilled at the expression on his face. 'But?'

'I realised something when we were up at the school the

other day. When my mother left my father, he withdrew into himself. He still managed the farm but he had no social life. He let all his friendships slip; he let his position in the community go. When he died he'd closed himself off so completely that the only person left to mourn him was me.'

She pressed a hand to her chest. 'Oh, Cameron, I'm so sorry.' What a terrible story. And what a sad household for a boy to grow up in. No wonder—

'But I have no intention of following his lead.'

She stared at him for a long moment. 'That's one of the reasons you're going overseas.'

'I might never have a wife and children, but it doesn't mean I can't find meaning in something I'm passionate about. It doesn't mean I can't have adventures and contribute to the world.'

Helping to feed the world would be a huge contribution. Africa would be an amazing adventure. He'd experience the most awe-inspiring things and eventually his heart would heal. Eventually.

'But in the meantime, it's time to stop holing up like a hermit.'

She lifted her chin. 'I think that's an excellent plan.'

He stared at her and then pursed his lips. 'But?'

This is none of your business. She lifted a shoulder. 'Just because things didn't work out with Fiona doesn't mean you'll never fall in love again.'

He shook his head. 'I saw what love did to my father.' His eyes grew grim, dark…shadowed. 'No, thanks, once was enough. I'm not diving into that particular hellhole again. I'll find satisfaction elsewhere.'

She grimaced. Feeding the world was all well and good, but an abstract concept couldn't give you a big fat hug when you needed it. She opened her mouth but he held up a hand. 'Leave it now, Tess.'

She moistened her lips and then nodded. He'd make friends

on his adventure. They'd look after him. For no reason at all, a hole opened up inside her.

'You know,' she started, turning back towards the house, 'I used to be really good at minding my own business.'

One side of his mouth hooked up. 'I don't believe that for a moment.'

The thing was, it was true. She'd been too caught up in her music to notice if anyone had been feeling down or worried. How selfish she'd been! She'd been too self-absorbed to involve herself in other people's problems, in other people's lives. In a way, she'd cut herself off as comprehensively as Cam had.

Her chest burned. Giving up music had been a good thing.

But that bubble of half-happiness half-excitement that had been floating around inside her ever since she'd turned and seen Cameron finally popped.

'Would you like to come with us, Cam?'

'I'll meet you at the cemetery. I'll run back home and collect a few tools first.'

She waved him off as Ty and Krissie piled into the car. She pushed her shoulder back and drew in a breath. A big one. These kids were worth every sacrifice she'd have to make. She'd choose them over music any day of the week— even when they were running her ragged. She'd choose them over a man.

Yes. She slid behind the steering wheel and nodded. This was the life they were meant to be living. *I won't let you down, Sarah.*

Lorraine set the men to work with lawnmowers and whipper-snippers clearing the scrub from around the fence line and mowing the paths. The women and children she set to work clearing weeds from around the graves and scrubbing head-stones clean of moss and lichen. Having never been a part of a working bee before, Tess enjoyed the sense of camaraderie with the dozen or so other workers.

As expected, the handful of children eventually took off to play in the neighbouring paddock—eight children, three dogs and two soccer balls. One of the older women kept an eye on them. 'Don't worry yourself,' she'd said to Tess when Tess had wandered over to check on them for the third time. 'We know out here that at least one person needs to keep an eye on the children to avert potential accidents. And it's a treat for me to sit in the sun like this and listen to the littlies.'

With her fears eased, she'd returned to work pulling weeds from around a grave.

Lorraine came up, touched her arm. 'Tess, I want to thank you for convincing Cameron to come along.'

Tess sat back on her heels. 'I had nothing to do with it. I was only surprised he didn't know about it.'

The older woman's hand fluttered about her throat. She glanced away.

'When the children told him, though, he was more than happy to lend a hand.'

Lorraine turned back with an overbright smile. 'All I can say is that it's lovely to see him here.'

Tess met the other woman's gaze. 'Then you might want to tell him that some time.'

She blinked. 'You think he'd…' She swallowed. 'It's his birthday next Sunday, you know? It's one of those birthdays that ends in a zero. Maybe I…'

Tess didn't want to appear too interested. She went back to pulling weeds. 'Are you planning anything special?' Would she like Tess's help?

'Oh, no, I don't think so. I don't think he'd welcome that.'

The older woman's sigh touched her heart. The secateurs suddenly felt heavy in her hands. What would she do if Ty and Krissie were ever at sixes and sevens the way Cam and Lance were? She suppressed a shudder. She'd do everything in her power to make sure that never happened. If it did, she'd do everything in her power to fix it.

But what if that wasn't enough?

'Listen to me rambling on! Time to get back to work.'

Lorraine moved away to oversee more job delegation. Tess glanced around until she found Cam's broad capable bulk, whipper-snipper in hand, cutting a swathe through the long grass on the other side of the cemetery. He looked at ease, comfortable, in his element, and Tess followed his lead, giving herself up to working in the fresh air beneath an autumn sun that wasn't too fierce.

'Hello, I'm Fiona. We met briefly at the luncheon.'

Tess blinked to find the flawless blonde working on the other side of the grave. She suddenly found herself battling the desire to reach out and slap the other woman or to just get up and walk away.

Whoa!

She rocked back on her heels. 'I remember,' she managed, but something in her tone made the other woman flush.

Be nice! 'Gorgeous day for it, isn't it?'

'Yes.' Fiona didn't immediately set back to work, but stared at a point beyond Tess's right shoulder. 'Cam is looking well.'

Ah... 'Well? Gorgeous more like.' She turned to look too. 'That man is a sight for sore eyes.'

When she turned back she found Fiona staring at her. 'Are you and Cam——?' She broke off. 'Sorry, that's none of my business.'

Tess went back to weeding. She had no intention of satisfying Fiona's curiosity.

'Look, Tess.' Fiona set her clippers down. 'What I really want to know is if he's doing as well as he looks.'

Tess glanced up. 'Why don't you ask him some time? I understand you used to be close.'

The flawless skin suddenly flushed pink. 'Oh! You think I'm a right piece of work, don't you?' She sat with a thump on the side of the grave—a cement rectangle with an angel atop the headstone. Tess kept her mouth very firmly shut. 'I never meant for all this to happen. I never meant to fall in love with Lance and cause a rift between the brothers.'

And yet she had. And from what Tess could see, Fiona wasn't doing anything about it—wasn't trying to bridge gaps or make amends.

'I know Cam is the better man.'

That had Tess's head swinging around.

'The thing is, you see, he never really needed me. He's so strong and honourable and…self-sufficient. I can't complain about the way he treated me—he treated me like a queen—and yet… I never felt I'd made much of an impact on him.'

How wrong Fiona had been! She opened her mouth and then snapped it shut again. She had no intention of betraying Cam's confidence.

'But with Lance…'

Fiona turned to glance at Lance and her whole face lit up. Tess's stomach clenched.

'Lance needs me.' She turned back to Tess, her face earnest. 'I feel I can help make him a better man. I don't expect you to understand because you're strong, like Cam.'

Her, strong? That was laughable.

'Taking on your niece and nephew like you have proves that,' Fiona continued. 'But I'm the kind of person who needs to be needed. And that's why I'm with Lance instead of Cam.'

Couldn't she have found a different man who needed her instead of Cam's brother?

A bustle at the front gates interrupted them. 'It's the CWA with lunch,' Fiona explained, rising. 'I'll go lend them a hand.'

'You do that,' Tess muttered under her breath, pulling out a weed with a vicious tug. No doubt the CWA *needed* her. Man, what a flake! What on earth had Cam seen in her?

Other than her flawless skin.

And her perky blonde ponytail.

Oh, and her model-like figure.

She sat back on her heels scowling at the grave, but after a moment she started to laugh. Oh, did she have the green-eyed monster bad or what? Fiona was probably a perfectly nice woman. And to give her credit, she did seem genuinely sorry for hurting Cam and creating a rift between him and Lance.

Though, from what Cam had said, that rift had been widening well before Fiona had come onto the scene.

Mind your own business.

As for the jealousy, she had no right to that. No right whatsoever.

Cam was more than ready for lunch when it was announced. Breakfast seemed like hours ago and he expected they'd all worked up healthy appetites. He joined the throng around the CWA tables and started loading up a paper plate with sandwiches and party pies.

'Hello, Cam, would you like a mug of tea?'

Fiona. He waited for his gut to clench. It did. A fraction. Not as much as he expected, though. 'Thanks.' He nodded.

'Are you well?'

She was obviously trying to make an effort. 'Never better.' He went to ask her how she was, but his arm was suddenly tugged.

'Cam,' Ty asked, 'can I feed Barney a party pie?'

'Sure you can, buddy. Just make sure it's cooled down first, okay?'

And then he found he'd wandered away from the table and he hadn't made the polite enquiry of Fiona after all. With a shrug, he set off for a spot in the shade of a Kurrajong tree.

'Hey, Tess.' Lance called out from his spot in the sun on the other side of the gated entrance from Cam. 'Why don't you join us?'

Cam's gut clenched up tighter than a newly sprung barbed-wire fence. With his back stiff and rigid, he kept moving towards the Kurrajong tree.

'No, thanks,' Tess called back. 'I prefer the view over here.' And then she was sitting beside him on the newly clipped grass and gesturing at the scene spread in front of them. 'It's really starting to take shape, isn't it?'

The woman stole his breath.

'This working-bee idea is really something.'

He glanced around at the clumps of people settling down to have their lunch and his throat tightened. He'd honestly thought, once, that he could make his simple dream come true in this community. Days like today brought the disappointment home to him afresh. And yet…

He couldn't deny it'd been invigorating working in the sun, side by side with people he'd known his entire life. He glanced at Tess—and some he'd known for less than a month.

'Yeah, I guess it is,' he finally agreed. And if she noticed the strain in his voice, she didn't mention it.

I prefer the view over here.

He found himself starting to grin.

'I think this will be the perfect spot to bury Sarah.' She shrugged when he glanced at her. 'Well, to inter her ashes or whatever it's called. You know what I mean. It's a nice spot for a final resting place.'

He supposed she was right.

'What did you do with your father's remains, Cameron?'

'I scattered his ashes on Kurrajong Station. It's what he wanted.'

She nodded and bit into a sandwich. 'That's nice too.'

What about her parents? Were they still living? 'Will your parents come to the memorial service?'

'I doubt it.'

She lowered her sandwich to her plate and he immediately regretted asking the question. 'Forget I asked,' he ordered. 'It's none of my business.'

She shot him a look that made him laugh, and then she shrugged. 'I don't mind. It's kind of funny coming to a place like Bellaroo Creek. You've all known each other so long that you know each other's histories.'

She turned those big brown eyes to him and he had to swallow. He shifted and covered his lap with his plate, and hoped she didn't notice how tightly he gritted his teeth.

'It's nice,' she finally finished.

'You're fitting in brilliantly.'

She flashed him a smile. 'I'm not feeling insecure, but thank you. I know it'll take time, but so far it's going better than I'd hoped.'

That was okay, then.

'My parents are…distant,' she said, picking her sandwich up again. 'Sarah and I actually came from quite a privileged background, but to be honest I'm not really sure why my parents had children. We were raised by nannies.'

The sweet vulnerable curve of her mouth turned down and her slender shoulders drooped for a moment, and an ugly darkness welled in his gut.

'So, to be honest with you, I don't really know them. Obviously they came to Sarah and Bruce's actual funeral.'

But he could see now that they'd provided Tess with no support whatsoever.

'And I very much doubt they'll ever visit us out here at Bellaroo Creek. They've been living in America these last few years.'

He shifted. 'Privileged, you say?'

She nodded.

'So, you could've organised nannies for Ty and Krissie and kept your career?'

'It's what my parents wanted me to do.'

He saw now that Tess had too much compassion and natural sympathy, too much integrity to have abandoned her niece and nephew.

She rolled her eyes. 'Apparently a daughter who's a concert pianist and fêted classical guitarist has more cachet than one who is merely a mother and housekeeper.'

They should be proud of her and all she'd taken on!

'I couldn't let Sarah down,' she said softly.

He reached out and briefly clasped her hand. 'She'd be proud of you, Tess.'

'I hope so,' she whispered, her eyes suspiciously bright. She blinked and then resumed eating. 'We always promised each other that if we ever had children we'd be hands-on parents—the opposite of our own.'

He understood that perfectly. He couldn't imagine having a child and then farming it out for other people to look after. Even the folk around here who sent their kids to boarding school couldn't wait for end of term time.

'She left me a letter, you know?'

'Sarah?'

She nodded.

'She knew something was going to happen to her?'

'I think after Bruce's accident it really hit home to her how life can change in an instant. She said she wouldn't offend me by asking me to raise Ty and Krissie as if they were my own—she knew I would. She told me all the good things I had to offer them. And then she told me about the life insurance policy she'd organised so we'd never have to worry about money.'

'She wanted to be prepared,' he murmured. In case life ever played her another nasty trick. She'd been smart.

'Which is why you should get married and have kids, Cam. 'Cause, the way things currently stand, if anything happens to you Lance will probably inherit Kurrajong Station, and we can't have that.'

He stared, and then he threw his head back and laughed. 'You never give up, do you?'

'Nope.'

He shook his head. 'Sarah sounds like a hell of a woman, Tess.'

'She was.' Her eyes turned misty and faraway and he knew she no longer saw the cemetery and this golden autumn day. 'She was four years older and became a bit of a surrogate mother to me.'

'And you hero-worshipped her, right?' She'd had the kind of relationship with Sarah he'd hungered to have with Lance. He promptly lost his appetite.

Tess laughed. He loved the sound. 'I expect I plagued her half to death. But I remember…'

She leaned forward, her eyes dreamy and distant again. Thirst snaked through him and the longer he gazed at her, the thirstier he became, but he couldn't tear his eyes away. 'What do you remember?'

'Music was my passion.' She sat back. 'No, it was more than that. It drove me, rode me…obsessed me. I would practise for hours and hours, driven to get a piece just right. I'd stay up into the wee small hours, practising and playing and practising more and more. And Sarah would sit up with me, and when I was about to drop with exhaustion she'd put me to bed.'

His heart started to ache. Ty and Krissie had lost their mother, and that was a terrible thing. But Tess had lost a sister—a much-loved sister—and who had held her in their arms and let her cry out her grief?

Certainly not her parents.

Tears swam in her eyes. 'I miss her so much.'

He reached out to touch her cheek, but suddenly a little dynamo in the shape of Krissie burst up between them. Her bottom lip wobbled as she stared at Tess. 'Why are you crying?'

Tess held her arms open and Krissie threw herself into them. His heart clenched when Tess lifted her face to the sun and dragged in a breath to steady herself.

So strong!

'I was just telling Cam about your mum and I got to missing her.'

'I miss her too,' Krissie whispered.

'I know, chickadee.'

Krissie snuggled closer. 'Tell me a story about when you and Mummy were kids like Ty and me. Were you ever naughty?'

'Never!'

Tess feigned shock and Krissie giggled.

'Except—' she winked '—this one time when we were in high school. We both really, *really* wanted to see this movie— *Charlie's Angels*—and we actually snuck out of school early to go and watch it.'

Krissie covered her mouth with both her hands, her eyes wide.

'What's more, we bought the biggest popcorn we could find and the biggest cola you ever did see.'

'Did you get caught?' Krissie breathed.

'No, but we got the biggest tummy aches, which served us right for being such gluttons!'

Tess tickled Krissie until she squealed with delight and then ran back off to find what the other children were doing.

Cam wanted to hug Tess the way she'd hugged Krissie. He wanted to tickle her until she felt better too.

His lips twisted. Who was he trying to kid? He wanted to kiss her until neither one of them could think straight. But that wouldn't make her feel better, not in the long term.

He blinked to find her eyeing him as hungrily as he did her. His skin tightened, but he ignored it. He had to tread carefully around this woman. She'd taken on a lot. She'd sacrificed a lot, and it would be cruel and thoughtless of him to make her life harder. She didn't deserve that.

She deserved to grow roots and be surrounded by a community that would look out for her. She deserved to be loved by a man who could give her security and a loving family. She deserved a man who meant to stay in Bellaroo Creek.

He crushed his plate into a ball. He wasn't any of those things.

But…

There was one more thing she deserved. 'Tess?'

'Hmm?'

'I think you're making a big mistake.'

She swung to him, brown eyes wide and alert. 'About?'

'Giving up your music.'

Her face closed up. 'I haven't given it up. I'm giving music lessons for the school, aren't I? Ty, Krissie and I sing all the time—I'm teaching them to harmonise. As for being on stage—'

'I'm not talking about being on stage. Tess, when was the last time you played the piano or picked up a guitar?'

She flinched. 'What's that got to do with anything?'

'I think it has everything to do with it.'

'You don't know what you're talking about.'

Every instinct he had told him he was right. Sacrificing something that was such a part of who she was would damage her in a fundamental way. Maybe not this year or the next, but eventually. 'Do you think Sarah would approve of you punishing yourself like this?'

Tess went to leap up, but he grabbed her arm. 'I'm not going to let this lie, Tess. I'm going to get to the bottom of it.'

She subsided back to the ground beside him. 'And what do you think you're going to find when you do? Do you think it's going to be pretty or something you can fix? Because it's not pretty and it can't be fixed. So as far as I'm concerned talking about it is pointless.'

'I mightn't be able to fix it, Tess, but bottling it up won't help either.'

She had to look away then because his eyes told her he

only wanted her to be happy. And she knew his questions came from a good place, not a bad one.

'Tess?'

And he wouldn't leave it alone; she knew that too. If he knew the truth then he'd see that she was right. Even if it did change his opinion of her for the worse.

'Sarah asked me to come home at the beginning of December.' She stared at her hands. 'But I had a whole series of concerts lined up and I put her off for a month.'

A whole month!

'Later, when I did get home…' When it was too late. 'I found out Sarah had been trying to set up a second residence and was in the process of moving the children there.'

She'd wanted Tess to come home and help her. But Tess, in her selfishness and self-absorption, had put Sarah off for a whole month. Who knew what they could've accomplished together in a month, what changes they could've made…what disasters they could've averted. Instead of making a difference in her sister's life, she'd chosen to shine on stage instead.

She straightened. But she wouldn't let Sarah down again. She'd look after Ty and Krissie and give them all the love she had, give them the absolute best lives she could. It wouldn't be enough. It would never be enough. But it was something.

'Hey!'

She blinked at the hard command in Cam's voice.

'Did she tell you why she wanted you to come home?'

'No, but—'

'Then you have nothing to beat yourself up about.'

He was wrong about that. 'She asked so little of me over the years.' *She should've come home.*

'She should've been straight with you. Nothing that happened to Bruce and Sarah was of your making.'

'No, but—'

'And whipping yourself into a frenzy of guilt is ludicrous. You didn't cause Bruce's accident. You weren't driving the car that left the road and hit the tree. Hell, Tess, you're giving these kids a great life. You should be proud of yourself.'

Proud of herself for not being there when Sarah had needed her? Never!

'Depriving yourself of your music—'

She leaned towards him. 'When I chose my music over Sarah, music let me down. I let me down. But, worse, I let Sarah down.' She shook her head. 'I'm not risking that again.'

'Tess, I think Sarah would weep in her grave if she knew all you'd given up.'

Tears clogged her throat. This time when she leapt up, he let her go. 'My life has a different focus now and I'm pleased about that.' *She was!* She pointed behind her. 'I'll go help clear the food away.'

Tess had been working steadily for an hour when Lance stormed up. 'You have no right upsetting Fi!'

She stared up at him. 'Lower your voice,' she snapped. 'You upset my kids again and I will have your guts for garters, got it?'

His mouth opened and closed. He dropped down to sit on the side of the grave she was working on. 'I, uh…I didn't mean to appear so…'

She quirked an eyebrow. 'Aggressive?'

He raked a hand through his pretty blond hair. 'I've never thought of myself as scary to kids before,' he muttered.

'Then maybe you should stop puffing your chest out and beating it in that ridiculous fashion, and learn some manners.'

She swore his jaw dropped to the ground at his feet. She didn't doubt for a single moment that the women in his life mollycoddled him, and she had no intention of joining their ranks.

Still…

She rose, planting her hands on her hips. 'And I didn't

upset Fiona. I suspect she upset herself. I believe it's called a guilty conscience.'

He turned beet-red and glanced away. Interesting. Maybe he wasn't immune to a guilty conscience either.

'Still, at least it appears you really do love her.'

He swung back. 'Of course I love her.' He gazed to where Fiona worked and his face took on a goofy expression. 'I mean, she's the best girl in the world.' He glanced back at her, the blue of his eyes suddenly bleak. 'I didn't mean to...'

She waited but he didn't go on. 'You're wrong about Cam too. He's not trying to ruin you. I doubt he'd ever stoop to something so petty.'

He squinted down at the ground. 'Cam never was petty. But after what I did, who could blame him for wanting his revenge?'

She let the silence speak for her.

He rose with a sick kind of pallor. 'I wish...'

She ran out of patience with him then. 'For God's sake, stop thinking about yourself for once! Have you ever considered actually apologising to Cameron for your appalling behaviour?'

His eyes started from his head. 'Are you joking? He wouldn't listen. I expect he'd deck me!'

'Then you're a stupider man than I thought.' With that, she turned away sick to her stomach. Cam deserved so much more than what any of his family had given him.

It's nice to have you in my corner.

She set her shoulders. Cam mightn't be here for much longer, but for as long as he was in Bellaroo Creek she had every intention of remaining in his corner.

CHAPTER EIGHT

'SHOULDN'T WE BUY Cam a present if it's his birthday?'

Tess glanced at Ty. 'I think you and Krissie should make him a birthday card. I bought cardboard, glitter pens and stickers.' She'd lugged them all the way from Sydney sure they'd find a use for them, and she set them on the kitchen table now. 'Plus, we are making him the best cake in the world.'

'With cream and jam in the middle and sprinkles on top?' Krissie double-checked.

'That's right, chickadee.'

'And I'm going to take my pin-the-tail on the donkey game,' she added. 'I think Cam will love playing that.'

'I'm sure you're right.'

'I know!' Ty's face lit up. 'I can write him a story. We're writing stories at school and Mrs Bennet said I was good at them.'

'Cam would love a story,' Tess agreed. 'And you can make a proper cover for it out of the cardboard and draw a picture on it.'

Hopefully book and card building would keep the two of them occupied for the next thirty minutes while she worked out how to cut her sponge in half, fill it with jam and cream, and then ice it.

Krissie suddenly rose from the kitchen table to press herself to Tess's side. 'Mrs Bennet's leaving at the end of the year. She's re...re...'

Tess's heart clenched at the anxiety that threaded through her niece's eyes. How she wished she could shield them from everything that worried or frightened them. 'She's retiring.' Tess's own heart clenched then too. 'Which means you'll have a brand-new teacher next year.' Please, God, because if Bellaroo Creek couldn't attract a new teacher to town, and the school closed...

Her stomach churned, but she made her voice cheerful. 'And we'll have to make sure they feel as welcome to town as we did.'

'And then we won't be the newest people any more,' Ty said.

Krissie bit her lip. 'Do you think we'll like her...or him?'

Ty glanced up at Krissie's 'or him', his eyes wary. It made Tess's heart burn harder. 'I'm sure we will.' She sent them both her biggest smile. Reassured, they returned to their card and story making.

'That's the best cake in the world!' Krissie said in awe a little while later when Tess stepped away from the cake to admire her handiwork.

'And that's one super-duper card.' Tess picked it up to admire Krissie's handiwork.

'And I'm finished too!'

Ty handed her the book he'd made. He'd stapled the pages between cardboard and had drawn a...um... She'd challenge even Sarah to hazard a guess about that one. 'It looks just like a proper book!'

That was obviously the right response because Ty beamed at her. 'It's a story about a cowboy.'

'Which will be perfect for Cam,' she agreed, glancing again at the cover trying to make out either a cow or a horse or a cowboy.

She clapped her hands. 'Okay, go wash your hands, put on your party clothes and let's go surprise Cam.'

He'd been here yesterday afternoon, building the bed for the vegetable garden. He hadn't let slip for a single moment that he had a birthday today. He'd said he was going to catch up on his bookkeeping.

On a Sunday?

On his birthday?

Oh, no, no. Tess had decided then and there that the least she could do was make him a birthday cake. Somewhere along the line, that had evolved into a full-blown party. Grinning, she went to put on her pink party dress. A party was exactly what they all needed.

Cameron stilled, cocked his head to one side and then frowned. Someone was knocking on the front door.

Nobody knocked on the front door. Ever. The few people who came out to Kurrajong these days came around the back. Fraser would've tapped on the French doors of Cam's study if he'd needed to discuss anything.

More knocking sounded. He pushed away from his computer with a growl and set off through the dim hush of the house. Since he'd taken a bedroom at the back, he rarely came into this part of the house any more. These big front reception rooms with their picture rails, antiques and high ceilings held the memory of too many shattered dreams. He scowled as he strode through them now. He flung the heavy door open, a bitter reproof burning on his tongue...

A reproof he swallowed at the sight that met his eyes. A sight as colourful as a flock of rosellas and just as cheerful.

'Surprise!' Ty and Krissie yelled, almost in unison, and then they each popped a party popper that covered him in coloured streamers, and for a moment he felt just as colourful—as flamingo-pink and butter-yellow as the girls' party dresses and as purple and blue as Ty's best jeans and shirt.

But then the shadows of the rooms behind touched the back of his neck with cold fingers, mocking him with the ludicrousness of any colour surviving within their forbidding walls, and he pulled the streamers from his head and shoulders, and a hard ball settled in the pit of his stomach.

'Happy birthday, Cameron.'

Tess's smile almost melted the coldness. 'How on earth…?'

She waggled a finger at him. 'You needn't think you can keep something as important as a birthday a secret.'

As far as he was concerned, it was just another day.

'And we wanted to give you a party, because you're one of our best new friends!'

The smile Krissie sent him did melt the coldness. And while he wished with all his might that they'd turn around and walk back home, he managed to cover his lack of enthusiasm with a smile. 'A party?'

Ty held up a bag. 'We brought jellybeans and crisps!'

'And Auntie Tess made you a cake.'

He glanced at Tess, delectable in her pink dress, but her smile had slipped. She'd sensed his discomfort. 'I hope we haven't caught you at a bad time.'

He blinked. He straightened. She was giving him an out? He could tell them he was really busy, promise to drop over to their place in a couple of hours… And Tess would turn the children around and walk away, and leave him in peace?

But when he glanced at the kids with their eager shining faces, he didn't have the heart to disappoint them. He could manage a party in this cold, heartless house just this once. It wouldn't kill him. He dragged in a breath and made himself grin. 'A party sounds like just the thing!'

He was rewarded with a smile from Tess that almost knocked him off his feet.

'Your house is amazing,' Ty breathed, glancing around Cam's bulk. He frowned and edged closer to his aunt. 'It's a bit dark.'

He translated that immediately into, *It's a bit scary.* He kept his voice steadily cheerful. 'Well, with only me living here these days I don't use these front rooms much.'

'Auntie Tess was right,' Krissie whispered to her brother. 'We should've gone around the back.'

'But I wanted to see,' he whispered back.

Cam then found himself pushing the door open as wide as he could, beckoning his visitors inside and turning into the reception room to his left and throwing open the curtains as wide as they would go, so the children could take in the room in its entirety, sans shadows. He strode across the corridor and did the same for the other reception room. The children trailed behind him, oohing and ahhing, their eyes wide and mouths agape.

When Tess saw the dark cherrywood baby grand in the second room, she froze. He took the cake from her before she could drop it. He recognised the fear in her eyes, but there was something else there too, fighting for supremacy. She closed her eyes, but not before he saw raw, naked hunger.

With sudden resolution, he turned back to Krissie and Ty. 'It's been a long time since I used this room, but I think it makes the perfect party room, don't you?'

'Yes!'

He set the cake down on a colonial-style hardwood coffee table. He took the bags of party food from Ty and set them there too. 'Then let's get some plates and drinks and then we can really get this party on the road.'

He led them through the formal dining room with its magnificent table-seating for twelve.

Ty gazed at it in awe. 'You must be able to have the biggest parties.'

'Legend has it that my grandparents threw the kind of parties that people spoke about for years.'

There were photo albums showing these rooms filled to bursting with smiling people, dressed in their best. As a boy, he'd pored over those photographs. He'd yearned to be in those photographs, and he'd sworn to bring that kind of gaiety back to Kurrajong House—a dream he'd finally thought within reach when Fiona had agreed to marry him. His hand clenched. How wrong he'd been. He couldn't re-create the gaiety of that bygone era. Not with the kind of family he had.

But he refused to fade away as his father had done.

'Cameron?'

Tess touched his arm. He stared down at her and had to fight the urge to haul her into his arms and kiss her. Falling into her would chase away the ghosts of the past and ease the hurt of shattered dreams, at least for a little while. If he backed her up against the wall, teased her, seduced her…

He could lose himself in her arms and take all he wanted.

And he wanted all right, no doubt about that, but it'd be a despicable thing to do.

She bit her lip—her plump, delectable bottom lip—and her eyes darkened at whatever she saw in his face. The pulse at the base of her throat fluttered. He wanted to press his lips to that spot and—

'The kitchen?' she croaked.

Gritting his teeth, he swung away. 'This way.'

They collected plates, bowls and cans of soda, and headed back to the so-dubbed party room. Cam opened the two front bay windows. A warm breeze filtered through, fanning the lace curtains, a touch of white against the dark wood panelling. While he did that, Tess and the children put out the party food—a big bowl of crisps, smaller bowls of jellybeans and chocolates, a plate of ginger-crisp biscuits, and even a small cheese platter.

He didn't have much of a sweet tooth, but his mouth started to water.

Tess, with her back very firmly to the piano, placed three blue candles on top of the cake and then lit them. She glanced at Krissie and Ty. 'Ready?'

They huddled in around her and at the tops of their voices sang the Happy Birthday song to him, and the longer it went on the wider their grins grew.

'Blow out the candles,' Tess ordered.

He did and they popped more party poppers. Krissie handed him a card she'd made out of glitter and stamps, and Ty handed him a story he'd written about a cowboy, and Cam found himself laughing and eating jellybeans and playing pin the tail on the donkey...and having a party.

He pulled up short when Fraser and Jenny appeared in the doorway a short while later. 'We came to investigate the noise,' Jenny said.

Cam leapt to his feet. 'Come and join us. Tess, Ty and Krissie, this is my station manager, Fraser, and his wife, Jenny, who manages to keep this place clean and running smoothly.' They'd be Tess's nearest neighbours when he left. It would be good for her to know them.

'Lovely to meet you.' Tess beamed at them. 'And you've arrived at the perfect time. We were just about to play pass the parcel.'

Everyone ended up with a snack-sized chocolate except Cam, who won the final prize of a family block of chocolate.

He stared at it—*a family*. He gazed about the room. At the moment they had all the appearance of a family. His heart started to pound, but he pushed the fantasies away. He wouldn't be beguiled by them. Not for a second time. He knew his own strength. He could survive one let-down, but two? He shook his head.

He couldn't deny, though, that for the space of an afternoon Tess and her kids with their laughter and this party had brought a spark of life back into this cold mausoleum of a house.

Krissie slipped a hand inside his. 'Are you having a good party, Cam?'

'The best,' he assured her. 'There's only one more thing that would make it perfect.'

They all swung to him. Tess planted her hands on her hips. 'What could we have possibly forgotten?'

His heart started to thump. She wouldn't thank him for this. At least, not initially, but... He glanced about the room. She'd given him a marvellous memory to take away with him when he left Bellaroo Creek. Instead of seeing his father sitting here in the half-dark, he'd now see Tess in her pink dress and hear the children's laughter.

'Come on, out with it,' she ordered.

He planted his feet. 'I'd like you to play something for me on the piano.'

Wind rushed in Tess's ears. The room shrank in on her. She collapsed onto a footstool.

No! Cameron couldn't ask this of her. He couldn't. It was too cruel. She'd kept her back firmly to the piano because the lure of it was like a siren song.

She knew he didn't mean to be cruel. He couldn't know about the hole that had opened up in her as big and as dry as the Great Western Desert since she'd packed away her guitar and stopped playing the piano

'I don't play any more,' she whispered, aching to sit at that beautiful piano and to fill her soul with music, but—

She'd turned her back on that life. On that person she'd been.

'I don't have parties,' Cam said, 'but I made an exception today and I don't regret it.' He glanced at the children and then at her again. 'Make an exception, Tess, just for today.'

She glanced at the children then too. The hope in their faces tore at her. Didn't they know that if she'd been a better person—if she'd never played music—their mother might still be alive?

Krissie hopped from one leg to the other, clapping her

hands silently, hope filling her eyes—eyes the same shape and colour as Sarah's. Ty came over to where she sat and pressed his hands to either side of her face. 'Please, Auntie Tess? Mummy loved to hear you play.'

Her heart nearly fell out of her chest. It took every ounce of strength she had not to cry. Cam came across and held out a hand to her. She stared at it, swallowed and then reached up and took it, allowed him to help her to her feet and lead her across to the piano.

'What would you like me to play?' she murmured, once seated.

'Whatever you want,' he said, moving to sit across the room from her in an easy chair.

Her hands shook as she played a tentative scale and she had to suck in a breath at the familiarity, at the need growing in her.

Oh, play that one again, Tessie. I love that one. It makes me feel as if I'm flying above the treetops.

Tuning out the doubts, Tess gave herself up to playing one of Sarah's favourite pieces. It filled her up. It made her feel—for a short time—as if she'd found her sister again.

As ever, the music transported her. When she finished she couldn't tell if she'd played it well or not. The stunned faces in front of her told her it'd been good.

Cameron leaned towards her and she imagined she could feel the strength of his regard and his admiration all the way across the room. 'Superb.' And the expression in his eyes made her feel as if she were flying above treetops.

Then she saw a movement by the doorway. Glancing at Cam, she rose and nodded towards his visitors.

Lorraine. Fiona. And Lance.

All the adults rose, but nobody spoke. Finally Jenny cleared her throat. She glanced at Ty and Krissie. 'Would you like to see where Fraser and I live? It's just out the back,' she added to Tess. 'And I can show you the lambs.'

Krissie and Ty leapt to their feet.

'You could come meet the horses too,' Fraser added, winning over one little boy in an instant.

Tess went to start after them, but Jenny touched her arm with a murmured, 'You might like to stay here.'

Tess didn't want to stay. She didn't want to intrude. But she recognised the vulnerability behind the stiff set of Cam's shoulders and the grim line of his mouth. *It's nice to have you in my corner.* She counted the people in the room. She went and stood beside him. She might not even out the numbers, but she'd give him whatever support she could.

Lorraine finally broke the silence. 'Hello, Cameron.'

'Mum.'

'I wanted to wish you a happy birthday, son, and…' She trailed off as if she wasn't sure what else to say.

Tell him you love him!

'If you really wished me a happy birthday,' Cam drawled in a voice so hard it made Tess wince, 'you'd have left your other son at home.'

'He wanted to wish you many happy returns too.'

'They say love is blind. Where Lance is concerned, you're living proof.'

'Oh, Cam, please,' Lorraine implored.

'Please what?' He rounded on her. He glared at Lance. 'I want you off my property now!'

Lance flinched, but he held his ground. 'I came to say I'm sorry.'

The silence grew so loud Tess wanted to clap her hands over her ears.

'For?'

She glanced up at Cam uneasily. She didn't like that edge to his voice.

'For…for breaking up your engagement with Fiona. The thing is, I…I love her.' He swallowed. 'But I'm sorry we hurt you.'

'Love her?'

Cam's scorn almost burned the flesh from Tess's arms and it wasn't even directed at her.

'The only person you love, the only person you've ever loved, is yourself.'

Lance flinched.

'The only reason any of you are standing here now is because your farm is in trouble and you want me to bail you out.'

'You're right. Ever since you walked away from the management of the farm it's all gone to hell in a hand basket, but that's not why we're here. We're here because…' He halted, but Fiona nudged him. 'Because I've never been the kind of brother you deserved. I'm sorry for that. But I never really thought you'd turn your back on me and Mum.'

'I haven't turned my back on Mum.'

The unspoken words, *but I've turned my back on you*, hung in the air.

Cam shifted his gaze to Lorraine. 'That said,' he drawled, 'she doesn't seem particularly eager to spend any time in my company.'

Although he hid it well, Tess could feel the hurt emanating from him. She moved a fraction closer.

'Oh, Cameron, honey, it's not that I don't want to spend time with you! But you refuse to step foot over my threshold.'

'The threshold where Lance and Fiona reside,' he pointed out.

'It's this house!' she suddenly blurted out. 'I find it so difficult being here.'

They all stared at her in varying states of astonishment.

'You hate this house?' Cam shifted, frowned. 'But, why?'

Her hand fluttered about her throat. 'That's all in the past now.'

'Obviously it's not or you wouldn't find it so hard being here. Why?' he demanded again.

Lorraine folded her arms as if to shield herself, and Tess had to fight an urge to go to the older woman.

'You won't like it, Cameron. It does no good to rake over old hurts.'

'The truth,' he demanded in that hard voice Tess found difficult to associate with him.

Lorraine glanced away. Her gaze drifted about the room and she barely suppressed a shudder. 'I was so unhappy here. I…I married your father with such high hopes…'

She dashed away a tear. Tess's throat thickened. Surely Cameron could see what distress he was causing his mother.

'So you had an affair.'

Lorraine drew herself up at that. 'I most certainly did not! I'd left your father for a good eight months before I fell in love with Bill. I left your father because he was unfaithful to me, Cameron. Not once, but multiple times.'

Cam's jaw slackened. 'But he left that house and land for you to use. Even after you'd married another man.'

'Oh, darling, that wasn't due to unrequited love. It was due to remorse. And guilt.'

Tess wanted to take Cam's arm and lead him to a chair to digest the information, to give him time to think and take it all in.

'That's why I never visit this house. It holds so many bad memories for me—a time in my life where I questioned my very abilities as both a wife and a mother. When I left here I…I thought I would never laugh again. That's why I've refused your dinner invitations, Cameron. I simply can't imagine being in this house and not being overwhelmed again by those old feelings. And since the unfortunate business with Lance and Fiona…well…it's been almost impossible to ask you to dinner at my house. I knew you wouldn't come.'

'Unfortunate?' Cam choked out.

'They didn't do it on purpose, son.'

Cam glared at Lance. 'I don't believe that for a moment,'

he said with soft menace. 'I wonder how long Fiona will stick by you, *brother*, when you ruin the farm and have nothing left to your name?'

Lance paled. 'Things have always come easy to you, Cam. You always had good grades, were great at sport and took to farming like it was bred into your bones, but you have no sympathy for those who don't have the same natural aptitude.'

'I have no sympathy with those who sit back and let everybody else do the hard work.'

'It was hell growing up in your shadow!' Lance suddenly yelled. 'I wanted to be just like you, you know that? It's why I took your things. I was hoping they'd give me the key, the magic, but I failed again and again until I decided to stop even trying. And you want to know what the worst thing was? You let me keep all the things I took, when you could've taken them back so easily. Even Fiona. I know you could probably win her back with a snap of your fingers if you put your mind to it, but this time—*this time*—I will fight back.'

'Hey!' Fiona pushed forward to give Lance's arm a shake. 'No, he couldn't. Why do you have so little faith in me?'

'Because you left me for him, so who will you leave him for?'

The words could've been uttered cruelly, contemptuously, but Cam said them with a weariness that simply highlighted their logic.

She stared at Cam with those perfect blue eyes, and Tess wished she could just disappear into the woodwork. She refused to glance up at Cam. She didn't have the heart to deal with the hunger she fully expected to see in his eyes.

'I really wanted to make things work with you,' Fiona said. 'You had such seductive dreams about turning this house into a wonderful family home, but…'

'But you obviously changed your mind and decided my brother was a better bet.'

She shook her head and her perfect blonde ponytail

swished about her perfect face in perfect rhythm. 'I came to realise those dreams of yours meant more to you than I ever did. I was just some idea you had of the ideal wife and mother. I needed more than that. I needed you to need me, but you're so self-sufficient, Cam, that I started to think you'd never need anyone.' She glanced at Tess. 'Maybe I was wrong about that.'

Beside her, Cam stiffened. She wanted to drape herself across him and tell Fiona to *back off!* That Cameron was too good for the likes of her. She didn't. That would be a crazy, stupid move, and she was darn sure Cam wouldn't thank her for it if she did. But one thing became increasingly clear. She was fed up with just standing here while these three made excuses for themselves.

'I'll tell you all something for nothing,' she stated so loudly it made everyone jump. 'Cameron has made my family's transition to Bellaroo Creek so much easier than it would otherwise have been. He's one of the best men I have ever met and he's a valued friend.'

True, true and true.

'Furthermore, I think he deserves a whole lot better from all of you.'

'Tess,' he growled.

'No, she's right,' Lorraine said. 'I shouldn't have let stupid memories keep me from coming out here to check on you, Cameron, and to make sure you were doing okay.'

'I didn't need checking up on or looking after.'

She smiled sadly. 'And there you go pushing us away again.'

He rolled his shoulders and frowned. 'I'm not pushing you away.'

'Tess is right, though,' Lance said.

'It's why we wanted to come out here and apologise,' Fiona added. 'And to hold out an olive branch.'

Cameron said nothing, but Tess stood so closely to him she could feel the tension coiling him up tight.

'We're kin, Cam.' Lance held out his hand. 'That has to mean something.'

Tess held her breath, hoping, praying that Cam would accept his brother's proffered hand. She closed her eyes when he gave a harsh laugh.

'Your farm must be in a real state. You're welcome here any time, Mum, but, Lance…you can go to blazes. If I shake your hand now, how long before you turn around and stick the knife in again? How long before you try to steal another canola contract out from under my nose? I'm just waiting to find you rustling my cattle next. But stand warned. If I do I'll be contacting the authorities. You've burned your bridges as far as I'm concerned. Now get out!'

'What about me?' Fiona whispered.

Cam planted his hands on his hips. 'What about you?'

The scent of cut grass wafted about Tess. She drew it slowly into her lungs to counter the nausea churning her stomach. Did Fiona want him back?

'Do you accept my apology? Am I welcome in your home?'

Cam sent Lance a cruel, hard smile. 'You're welcome in my home any time, Fiona.'

Lance turned white. He seized Fiona's hand and stormed from the room.

Lorraine pressed a gift into Cam's hand and then reached up to kiss his cheek. 'It was lovely to see you, Cameron. I just hope we haven't spoiled your day.'

And then she left and Tess could feel all the energy just drain out of her body, leaving her limp and wrecked. It must be a hundred times worse for Cam. She moved to a chair, pressed her hands together between her knees. Her pink party dress suddenly seemed totally out of place. She eyed Cam carefully. He hadn't moved. She cleared her throat. 'Are you okay?'

He rounded on her then. 'That was all your doing, wasn't it?'

Her jaw dropped.

He flung an arm out, pacing from one side of the room to the other. 'I should've known little Miss Fix-it wouldn't be able to mind her own business, that she'd need to interfere.'

She shot to her feet. The roller coaster of emotions she'd experienced this afternoon crashing through her now. 'Well, even if I did—' which she hadn't, but she'd rather walk on broken glass now than admit it '—I sure didn't make things worse. Oh, no, you accomplished that all on your own!'

He swung back to her. 'Are you telling me you actually believed that line he fed me?'

She planted herself directly in front of him. 'Yes, I do.' And strangely enough she did. It was only now when he was deprived of his brother that Lance could see all that Cam meant to him, and how much he needed him. 'But even if I didn't,' she suddenly found herself shouting, 'he's your brother and he deserves the benefit of the doubt!'

'Just because you feel guilty about letting Sarah down doesn't give you the right to go meddling in my life! Fixing my situation won't be a form of restitution, you know.'

She sucked in a breath. 'At least I'm not hiding from life.'

'What do you call turning away from your music?'

She clenched her hands. 'At least I'm not afraid to let love in my life. At least I put people first!'

Neither of their voices had lost any of their volume and the walls practically rang with their shouts.

'That's just as well because you know nothing about chickens!'

'At least I know how to throw a decent party! Me!' She thumped her chest. '*Me* has got the hang of country hospitality in under a month. You haven't got the hang of it your whole life!'

'Your grammar sucks!'

'And your manners suck!'

She glared. He glared.

She bit her lip. His lips started to twitch.

She snorted. *'Me has got?'*

He rolled his eyes. 'I can't believe I made that chicken crack.'

And suddenly they were both roaring with laughter.

And then Cameron pulled her right into his arms and kissed her.

CHAPTER NINE

RAW, BURNING NEED blazed a path of fire through the very centre of Cam's being and shot out in every direction. He'd ached to kiss this woman ever since…ever since he'd clapped eyes on her. But he'd burned harder and fiercer with that need since the first kiss they'd shared. And he was tired of fighting it.

He revelled in the sweet softness of Tess's lips and the way they opened up at his demand—so sweet and giving as if she sensed his hunger and wanted to assuage it. So unselfish.

The realisation made him slow the kiss down, gentle it until she could catch up with him. Loosening his hold on her nape, he slid his hand through the dark cap of her hair and caressed the skin behind her ear in a slow circular motion, and then followed with his mouth. A shudder rippled through her, filling him with satisfaction, increasing his hunger, but he refused to speed up to meet that demand.

He wanted Tess with him. All the way. He wanted her smiling and satisfied…sated and delighted. A resolution he nearly lost the battle with when her grip tightened on his arms and she moved in closer to press all her softness against him.

He tugged gently on her ear lobe. She gasped and arched into him. He grinned a lazy grin and did it again. She smelled of jellybeans and cake. Breathing her in was a treat in itself. The grin disappeared when she shifted restlessly against him, one of her hands plunging into his hair, her other arm winding around his neck.

He lost all sense of himself then, all sense of time. His mouth found hers and he fell into her, losing himself in the experience of kissing her, touching her, filling himself up with her essence like a man gorging on some vital nutrient he'd been lacking but had suddenly found.

The hunger built and built until kissing and touching was no longer enough. He needed—

A groan broke from him when she tore her lips from his and wrenched herself out of his arms. She stumbled to a sofa on the other side of the room. Seizing a cushion, she hugged it to her chest.

His chest rose and fell as if he'd spent the last hour roping yearlings. He wanted to stride over to where Tess sat, haul her back into his arms and propel this encounter through to its natural conclusion. He almost did, but common sense reasserted itself. Ty and Krissie were somewhere on the premises. This was not the ideal time for making love to Tess. He bit back an oath. 'I'm sorry. The timing on that could've been better.'

She didn't say anything. He wanted her to look at him, but she didn't do that either.

He dragged in a breath, adjusted his stance and tried to quieten the stampeding of his blood. 'Would you like to have dinner with me tonight? Jenny would love to babysit the kids and—'

'No.'

He blinked.

She plumped the cushion up and set it back to the sofa. 'There won't ever be a good time for us, Cameron.'

'But—'

'Do you think I'm the kind of woman who jumps willy-nilly into bed with men I know I have no future with?'

'No, I—'

She walked across and poked him in the chest. 'Do you want me to fall in love with you so you can then break my heart? Will that mend your wounded ego and make you feel powerful and manly again? Will that show Lance that you're over what he did to you?'

Her eyes blazed with a fire he hadn't witnessed before, but her words left him chilled. 'No!' How could she put such a dreadful interpretation on his desire for her? 'You're beautiful, Tess. I find you fascinating and irresistible. I love kissing you.'

Colour flared in her cheeks. She backed up a step. 'That may well be, but it's been an emotional day. I refuse to be the distraction you need to distance yourself from all that's happened this afternoon.'

He stabbed a finger at her. 'You're more than a distraction!' She was wonderful and warm and she could make him laugh even when he was livid.

She folded her arms and lifted her chin. 'How much more?'

A chill trickled down his backbone. For a short time today this woman had brought his old dream roaring back to life. She'd made him wonder if it were still possible. The arrival of his mother, Lance and Fiona had dashed that, had forced him to face reality again.

'You still have no intention of forgiving Lance. You're determined to hold on to your bitterness. What would it hurt to just let it go?'

His gut clenched. 'How can you even ask that?'

She pressed a hand to her forehead. 'There's absolutely no point to this conversation. You have no intention of staying in Bellaroo Creek anyway, have you?'

He straightened and shoved his shoulders back. He wasn't being made a fool of a second time. Not by Lance. Not by Tess. Not by anyone.

She gave a short laugh, obviously reading the resolution in his face. 'Well, in the meantime I won't let you turn me

into some toy you can play with. I might've let my sister
down, but I don't deserve that. And the children certainly
deserve better.'

He wanted Tess in every way a man would want a woman.
If she were free and unencumbered he'd ask her to come to
Africa with him. For fun. For adventure. No strings. His chest
clenched. Maybe…

He closed his eyes. What was he thinking? Tess was all
strings and he wanted no part of that. Besides she wanted
the impossible. Forgive Lance? No chance. He made himself
take a physical step away from her. His chest hurt, his groin
ached, but he held firm.

Without even glancing at him, she headed for the door.

'Tess…' He could hardly speak for the bitterness that
coated his tongue and lined his throat.

She turned in the doorway.

'Whatever else has happened, you've not let Sarah down.
You love her kids as if they're your own. You're giving them
not just a good life but a great life. You've brought them
laughter and joy and hope for the future. You never let Sarah
down. If you'd known the true state of affairs you'd have returned home as soon as you could. And I don't doubt for a
single moment that she knew that. Saying you let her down
by not returning home sooner is the same as saying she let
you down because she didn't tell you the truth sooner. Nobody let anybody down.'

She gripped her hands together, her eyes wide and
wounded. He wished—

He cut the thought off. 'There's only one issue that I suspect would bring Sarah pain. How do you think she'd feel
if she knew you'd turned your back on your music because
of her?'

The confusion that flared in her eyes made him ache to
go to her, to comfort her. But she didn't want the kind of

comfort he offered and he could hardly blame her. When she turned and left, he let her go.

Cam avoided Tess's house for the next week. She attended his judo class on Wednesday. When they'd heard she was doing the class, another two mums had signed up too. The three of them had spent the majority of the class in fits of giggles. He hadn't spoken to her one-on-one, though.

Instinct told him she needed time. He sure did. Time to rebuild his defences. Time to reinforce his plans for the future. Time to forget the impact of their kisses. Because after vowing not to, he'd almost fallen under the spell of that old dream again. Tess brought out that old weakness in him, and he was determined to fight it with everything he had.

Out of sight, though, didn't mean out of mind.

And there was still the issue of her vegetable garden. His debt to her wouldn't be cleared until he'd finished that.

The following Saturday he loaded the tray of his ute with all the tools he'd need—shovels, picks, hoes and a generous amount of cow manure—and headed for Tess's. One good day should see the vegetable bed finished. He'd help her with the planting and give her tips on how to look after it.

And then he could walk away. Job done. Debt cleared.

He pulled in a breath when he arrived, and then set off towards the back of her house. *Don't think about that kiss!* Work, that was what he had to think about. Work and digging and—

He rounded the side of the house and then pulled up short, unable to move another step.

Tess and the kids were dancing around the backyard, singing along to a pop song on the radio. And it wasn't just any old singing and dancing. His chest clenched. They jumped and twirled and swooped with abandon. With complete unadulterated joy at being alive. As if this moment was the best moment that had ever existed and they were going to clutch it and hold it close and cherish it and live it before it could slip away.

It filled him with a yearning that almost buckled him at the knees.

Tess's hips swayed and shook in a sexy rhythm and his mouth dried and his blood pounded. Her simple delight in the dance and the way she occasionally caught one of the children's eyes and how their pleasure fed each other's left him breathless. He'd never seen anything like it.

He'd never experienced anything like it.

His heart started to thump and an ache pounded behind his eyes. He would *never* experience anything like it. This kind of exuberance, rapture, was alien to his family.

Duty, responsibility and self-reliance—those were all the things he'd been taught to value. Not joy. And no matter how much he might hunger for the same kind of closeness with his family that Tess and the kids shared, he knew it was beyond his reach.

Fiona had taught him that. Trying to reach for these heights with her had revealed it for the sham it had been. He had to stick to what he did know—duty, responsibility and self-reliance.

Without a word, he backed up a step, turned and headed for his car.

Tess spun around, arms outstretched as the song came to an end, feeling alive and young and grateful for Ty and Krissie's laughter, when a flash of blue disappearing around the side of the house caught her eye.

She acted on instinct. 'Hey, Cam!' She tripped around the side of the house.

He froze. He didn't turn around. Her heart surged against her rib cage. His back beckoned—so strong and muscled. So capable. Her fingers curled against her palms. 'Anything we can do for you?'

'Hey, Cam!' Ty came rushing around the side of the house with Barney in close pursuit. 'Look, I taught Barney how to shake hands.'

Cameron turned to watch the trick. He smiled, but it didn't reach his eyes. 'That's brilliant, Ty. He's one smart dog.'

Those shadows in his eyes chafed at her. They made her want to go to him and offer herself to him, to offer the kind of comfort he wanted from her.

She glanced at Ty and Krissie, planted her feet and remained where she was.

'I, uh…' He rose from patting an ecstatic Barney. 'Thought I might get a start on digging the bed for your vegetable garden.'

Bed? It brought a whole different picture to her mind that had nothing to do with gardening or vegetables. Heat that had nothing to do with the exertion of dancing surged into her cheeks. It took a moment to unknot her tongue. 'That'd be great,' she finally managed. 'If you can spare the time, that is?'

'Right.'

He didn't move. She didn't move. The air between them vibrated with all that remained unspoken.

With a superhuman effort she managed to shake herself out from beneath the heavy, suffocating blanket that tried to descend over her. She clapped her hands. 'Right! Let's help Cam unload his tools.'

They all set to work. Digging, she decided an hour later, wasn't a bad antidote to restlessness. Other than to issue instructions or to check his directions, she and Cam barely spoke. But as they worked side by side together the tension slowly dissipated. She liked having him in her backyard again. She frowned at that thought. He'd been a great friend.

He'd be a better lover.

Whoa!

She pushed the thought away, thrust her shovel into the

ground, and pushed her hands into the small of her back, groaning as her muscles protested.

Cam sent her a grin that filled her to the brim with renewed energy. 'Sore?'

'No wonder you're so fit if you do this kind of work day in and day out. All I can say is thank God it's lunchtime. I'll go rustle up something to eat.'

A short while later they all sat in the sun munching sandwiches and apples.

Krissie glanced up. 'Auntie Tess?'

'What, chickadee?'

'It's a big vegetable garden, isn't it?'

'Well, I'm not an expert on vegetable gardens, but I think ours is pretty much the perfect size.'

'So can we grow marigolds in there too? Will there be room? Did you know they were Mummy's favourite?'

Yes, she did know. Her throat tightened. She swallowed. 'I think there'll be oodles of room for marigolds. I think marigolds will be the perfect addition to our vegetable garden.'

Krissie, Ty, and the animals all ran off to play.

Cam shook his head. 'You can't eat marigolds.'

She couldn't tell if he was vexed with her or not. 'They do look pretty in a vase, though.' And for taking out to a grave. She eased back on the blanket to survey him more fully. 'Do you always choose the common-sense option?'

'I work the land. Planting forty hectares of marigolds instead of canola will not earn me my crust.'

'What a sight it'd be though.'

He suddenly smiled. 'Wait until the canola blossoms.' He gestured out in front of them at the newly ploughed fields that stretched over a low hill in the distance. 'It will be bright yellow for as far as you can see.'

'Magic,' she breathed. Then she frowned. 'But you won't be here to see it?'

He shook his head.

Wouldn't he miss that? Didn't he want to see the fruits of his labour? She bit the questions back. They'd carefully avoided any mention of the personal today, had found a comfortable footing with each other, and she didn't want to ruin it. 'I'll take a photo and have Fraser send it to you,' she said instead.

She was just about to tip the dregs of her mug of tea out when Ty and Krissie came up. She could tell from the fact they walked rather than ran and by the serious expressions on their faces that they'd just 'conferred' about something. 'What's up, chickadees?' She kept her voice deliberately light and cheerful.

'When are we going to have Mummy's…' Ty frowned, obviously searching for the right word.

'Memorial?' she asked softly.

They both nodded and knelt down on the blanket in front of her.

'Well, Mrs Pritchard is organising a plot for us, and I expect to hear from her about that in the next couple of weeks. Then I'll speak to Reverend Wilkinson, who'll perform the service, but he's only out this way every second week.' How long was a piece of string? Things moved at a different pace in the country. 'So I'm expecting it'll be maybe in a month, possibly two.'

'So, sorta soon?' Ty checked.

She nodded.

They leapt up, evidently satisfied. 'But while we're on the subject…' she started, her throat drying.

They stared at her for a moment and then sank back down to the blanket. Her chest clenched. Maybe she should let this subject rest. Instinct, though, told her ignoring it wouldn't be right.

'Okay, chickadees, we need to talk about your daddy.' Ty's eyes grew wide and wary. Her stomach started to churn. 'Do we want to bury his ashes too? Do we want to put them in the same plot as Mummy's?'

'No!' Ty shot to his feet. 'I hate him! He killed Mummy!'

The blood drained from her face. Her hands started to shake. 'Ty, honey, that's not true.' His bottom lip wobbled. He stood there pale and shaking. Her heart lurched and her eyes stung. She wanted to reach out and hug him to her, but she sensed any such movement would send him running. 'That's not true, Ty. I promise you. You know Daddy was sick.' She'd tried to explain it, but, truly, how much were they expected to understand? Especially when Tess could barely accept it herself. 'It was an accident.'

'No, it wasn't! I heard him say he was going to kill her. He drove into that tree on purpose!'

Tears poured down his face. They started to pour down hers too. 'He only said those things because he was sick. He didn't mean them. And I know he didn't drive the car deliberately into the tree, Ty, because he wasn't the one driving— Mummy was.'

His fists clenched. His face turned red. 'No!'

She tried to take him into her arms, but he wheeled out of her reach and raced away. She started to her feet, but Cam's hand on her shoulder stopped her.

'I'll go after him,' he said quietly with a nod towards Krissie.

She turned and found her little niece with her face buried in the blanket and her shoulders shaking. With a lump in her throat the size of a teapot, Tess lifted the child into her lap and wrapped her arms tight around her.

Ty didn't go far. He'd raced around the front of the house to fling himself down full length on the veranda.

Cam sat next to the distraught boy and hauled him into his arms so he could cry against his chest.

His throat thickened as he rubbed a hand up and down Ty's

back, trying to impart whatever comfort he could. So much grief and pain. These kids had been through so much. Tess was doing a great job, but…

He thought back to this morning's image of them all dancing. Tess was doing a *brilliant* job. It was those moments of joy that would help Ty and Krissie through the hardship of their grief and create bonds that would link them together as a family. He ached to take away all their pain—Tess's included—but that wasn't possible. All he could do was offer his friendship and hope it helped.

Tess. His mind rang with her. She was trying to do so much on her own. And she was achieving so much. If only she could see that she didn't have to lose herself in the process.

Eventually Ty's sobs eased to hiccups. A couple of minutes after that he pushed away from Cam's chest to stare up in his face.

'How you doing, buddy?' Cam asked, his chest cramping at the small, tear-stained face. He found himself wanting to protect this young boy from every kind of harm. All of Tess's fussing suddenly made perfect sense.

'Do you think Auntie Tess is right?' he said without preamble.

He'd give away Kurrajong Station in an instant if it'd mean sparing them all of this. He met Ty's gaze. 'Has your aunt Tess ever lied to you about anything else?'

Ty considered that for a long moment. 'No,' he finally said.

'Then do you really think she'd lie to you about this?'

He considered that too. 'She doesn't want me and Krissie to be mad with our dad.' He glared. 'But I am. I'm really mad.'

'Yeah, I get that.'

Ty gazed up at him, eyes wary. 'You do?'

'Sure I do. Your dad hurt you and Krissie and your mum. It'd make me angry too.'

'Auntie Tess said he was sick.'

'I think your auntie Tess is right. And you know what else

I think? I think that your dad would be very glad that he can't hurt you any more.'

'Even though he's dead?'

Cam nodded. 'Even then.'

'You think he loved us?'

'I think he loved you all very much, Ty. I think he just wasn't able to show it any more.'

Ty rested his head against Cam's shoulder. The trust awed him. The warm weight cracked open a gulf of yearning inside him. He closed his eyes. He understood Ty's anger. It was the same as his anger at Lance. Except Ty's dad had been sick. Lance had no such excuse.

Eventually Ty pushed away and climbed out of Cam's lap. He missed the warmth and the weight immediately.

'I'm going to go and give Auntie Tess a hug.'

'I think that's an excellent plan.'

He followed Ty around to the backyard to find Tess and Krissie, now with Fluffy on her lap, talking quietly on the blanket. Tess turned at their approach. Without a word she opened her arms and Ty raced into them.

What if, like Ty and Krissie's father, Lance died in a car accident? The ground shifted beneath his feet. He planted his legs more firmly and bit back a curse. Lance had burned his proverbial bridges. He was nothing to Cam any more.

That assertion, though, didn't ease the burn in Cam's heart.

He forced himself to focus on the tableau in front of him. Tess held Ty for several long moments and then rose, holding him in her arms. She hitched her head in the direction of the house and Cam nodded, settling down on the blanket beside Krissie.

She glanced up at him with those big brown eyes that were identical to Tess's. With a cluck and a flutter, Fluffy freed herself to scratch about in the grass.

Krissie moved closer and curled up against him as if it were the most natural thing in the world. 'You okay, pet?'

She nodded. 'My daddy was very sick, you know?'

'So I understand, honey.'

'It's very sad,' she whispered, leaning into him. 'And I think we should bury him with Mummy and maybe he'll be happy again.'

She was five, but her generosity and ability to forgive stole his breath. 'I think that's a real nice idea, sweetheart.'

He wasn't sure for how long they sat there, but when Tess materialised in front of him, he glanced down to find Krissie fast asleep. Tess went to take her from him, but he shook his head. 'Let me. You lead the way.'

They put Krissie to bed. He followed Tess back into the kitchen. She grabbed two beers from the fridge and handed him one before leading the way back outside again.

'You okay?' he asked. She looked pale and lines of weariness fanned out from her eyes. She looked as if she could do with a nap herself.

She settled on the blanket, stretching her legs out in front of her before glancing up at him. 'Some days I feel as if we're merely lurching from one catastrophe to another.'

He lowered himself down beside her. It suddenly shamed him to think how he'd tried to seduce her last weekend. She had so much to deal with. 'I held Ty while he cried his heart out and all I wanted to do was make things better for him. I know that's impossible. I don't know how you're managing to do all this with such grace.'

She opened her beer. 'I'm not sure there's much grace involved.'

'I think you're doing an incredible job.'

She turned those eyes on him. Eyes the same as Krissie's. He had absolutely no intention of trying to seduce her again, but what if she moved in close and curled up against him the way Krissie had? He couldn't get the thought out of his mind.

He forced his gaze away. 'I will tell you something,' he

managed. 'Nobody could get them through this as well as you are.'

She took a long pull on her beer. 'Some days are better than others. The gaps between the bad days are getting longer.'

He read her unspoken hope that eventually there wouldn't be any more bad days, but both of them knew bad days came and went. Ty and Krissie, as they got older, would simply learn to deal with those bad days more effectively. With Tess's help.

'So…' She studied him. 'Are you okay?' She asked as if she could sense the confusion bubbling just beneath the surface. It reminded him how well attuned they were to each other's moods. It reminded him that he *wasn't* going to attempt to seduce her again.

'Yeah, sure.'

But even as he said the words he knew they were a lie.

He frowned. 'Krissie…'

She watched him closely, as closely as he often caught her watching the children. It made the ache around his heart ease for some unaccountable reason. 'What about Krissie?'

'Something she said…' He scratched a hand back through his hair. 'She said she thought that if her father was buried with her mother, then maybe he'd be happy again.' His frown grew. 'She *wants* him to be happy.'

'Of course she does. He was her father. She loved him.'

'But he hurt her and Ty so badly.'

'Your father was unfaithful to your mother, but does that make you love him any less?'

His mother's revelation had shocked him, had made him rethink all he'd thought he knew about his father—but, no, it didn't affect the love he bore for him.

'I think a part of Krissie remembers the good times before her father's accident, when they were all happy and life was how it should've been. I think Sarah helped keep those memories alive.'

'You've forgiven him too, haven't you?'

She stared down at her beer and nodded.

He leapt up and started to pace. 'How can you? How can you find that in yourself after everything he did to your sister?' He knew she'd loved Sarah. 'And to those kids? I know how much you love them.'

'I don't see why loving them means I should hate Bruce. I can't forget that Sarah hadn't given up on him. I know *she* still loved him. I can't forget all the years he made her happy or their joy when the children were born. They—'

She broke off to stare at her drink. 'He didn't go looking for that accident. He didn't deserve what happened to him. He'd been a loving husband and father up till that point. And I'm proud of Sarah for sticking by him.'

He opened his mouth but she held up a hand. 'Yes, she should've gotten the children away from that situation sooner, but I'm proud of her for having the courage to try to find help for the man she loved. My sister loved him, Cameron. I cannot hate him. I…I just can't.'

He's your brother and he deserves the benefit of the doubt!

He collapsed back down beside her, her words of last weekend echoing through him. He knew precisely where Krissie's generosity and her big heart came from—from her auntie Tess. 'No wonder you think me a hard, unfeeling brute.'

'I think no such thing!'

'Lance.'

Just one word but comprehension dawned in those melt-a-man eyes of hers. 'That's a bit different. You're an adult and so is Lance, even if he has been acting like a petulant teenager.' She smoothed the rug and glanced away. 'He's learning a very hard lesson now, though.'

I think a part of Krissie remembers the good times.

Cam scowled at the ground. There had been good times, but…

'I think it'll probably be good for him in the long run. He

relies too heavily on his charm, and I suspect your mother has shielded him far more than has been good for him. A bit of hard work and a whole lot of worry may make a man out of him yet.'

His head came up. 'Steady on, Tess, he's not that bad.'

There were days when Lance had made life hell. There'd also been days when he'd made Cam laugh until his sides had hurt. It was why Cam had put up with the hell days—because nobody else in the family had ever laughed all that much. That laughter had been worth a lot.

She leaned back, stared down her nose at him. 'Do I hear you defending him?'

Was he?

If anything happened to Lance while he was in Africa... Cam swallowed. What if something happened to him while he was away? Was this really how he meant to leave things?

He frowned and finally cracked open his beer. 'I guess I am.'

She arched an eyebrow. 'Is that significant?'

He dragged in a breath. 'If Krissie can forgive her dad...' He shook his head. 'Lord, Tess, I can't be shown up by a five-year-old, now, can I?'

'It'd be very poor form,' she agreed.

Somewhere inside him a smile started to build. He held his beer towards her. She clinked it in a silent toast.

CHAPTER TEN

TESS WANTED TO leap to her feet and dance. She wanted to hug Cam.

She suspected the dancing would prove the lesser of two evils.

A new calm had settled over him, certain shadows had retreated from his eyes—not all, but some—and his shoulders had lost their angry edge.

She surveyed them and bit her lip. In fact, they looked broad and scrumptious.

Cam cleared his throat and she realised with a start that she'd been staring at them for too long. She snapped her gaze away and lifted her beer to her lips. 'If you want my two cents' worth…' she started before taking a sip.

'Which you'll give me, even if I don't.'

The grin he shot her and the effortlessness with which he teased her filled her with such a fluttery nonsense of wings she was in danger of floating two feet above the ground. She clutched a handful of blanket and held tight.

'What's your two cents, Tess?'

She surveyed him over the rim of her beer. 'I think you should pay your family a visit tomorrow afternoon.'

'Why?'

'The sooner the better, don't you think?'

He stared at her for a long moment. 'And?'

'And I'll be there,' she finally 'fessed up. She wanted to be there when he faced his family too. She wanted to make sure Lorraine, Lance and Fiona didn't take advantage of him. 'Last weekend at your party it was as if it were you against them and the rest of the world. That's not true. You have friends and I think both you and they should acknowledge that fact.'

Also, her being there would create a subtle confusion she was eager to encourage. Cameron might love Fiona to her dying day, but neither Lance nor Fiona had to know that. They had no right to crow in triumph. It wouldn't hurt anyone to think Cameron had well and truly moved on.

It could hurt you.

She shrugged the thought off. She knew the truth—Cam was leaving. Forewarned was forearmed. She could protect her heart.

'I'm dropping Ty and Krissie off at a birthday party and then popping by Lorraine's to discuss the memorial service. Apparently Lance and Fiona plan to be there to offer their...' She shrugged and rolled her eyes.

'Moral support?'

She bared her teeth. 'Something like that.'

He started to laugh. 'So who exactly is helping who in this scenario?'

She couldn't help but grin back at him. 'Why don't we call it a joint effort?'

His grin was slow and easy and it could make a woman's heart kick straight into triple time without any warning at all. 'What time are you supposed to be out there?'

'One-thirty.'

'I have a few things to do in the morning, but...I'll be out there by two.'

'Excellent.'

'C'mon.' He nodded towards the garden bed. 'Time to get back to work.' He helped her to her feet and she tried to ignore the strength of his hands, tried to ignore the heat he exuded, and the fresh smell of cut grass.

She averted her gaze from the strong, lean promise of his back and threw herself into attacking the ground with the assorted instruments of destruction currently within reach.

'Well, Tess,' Lorraine said, leaning back in the padded wicker sofa that graced her generous back patio, 'that should all be remarkably easy to arrange.'

Tess had just outlined the simple service she and the children had agreed upon.

'No Herculean feats to be performed,' Lance said with a smile.

He almost looked disappointed, as if he sensed Tess's reservations about his character and wanted to prove himself in her eyes. Who knew? Maybe he did. But if she needed any Herculean tasks performed she'd ask his brother, thank you very much.

Fiona leant forward to top up Tess's teacup. 'Do have a scone,' she urged, as if unstinting hospitality might melt Tess's reserve.

It'd take more than a scone and a cup of tea. What this pair had done to Cam—

It's none of your business. She had no right holding a grudge against this pair. Especially when she'd been urging Cam not to and—

Her teacup wobbled. None of her business? Everything to do with Cam felt like her business.

Because he's helped you so much, helped you, Ty and Krissie feel a part of Bellaroo Creek.

That was right. That was all it was.

Her heart started to thump. Why, then, when he smiled at her did her heart grow wings? Why when his eyes practically devoured her did she feel like the most desirable woman on earth? Why when she kissed him was it better than making music?

She'd told herself she'd wanted to be here today to support him, but it wasn't the whole truth, was it? She set her tea down before she could spill it. She'd wanted to be here today to prevent Fiona from getting her perfect pretty little claws into him again. She'd wanted to stake her claim.

Because she'd fallen in love with him.

Her heart throbbed. Her temples pounded. Cam had made it clear to her that she had no claim to stake. Hadn't she been listening?

Of course she'd been listening! She seized a pumpkin scone and bit into it viciously. But how could a woman not fall in love with a man like Cam? He had the biggest heart of any person she'd ever met. He did so much for others, and all of it without fanfare. He had the kind of grin that could melt a woman's resolutions in a heartbeat and the kind of physique that could have her fantasising in Technicolor.

He was so…much. He was everything. And she loved him.

The acknowledgement calmed the dervishes careening through her blood. A hard black ache settled in her heart instead. She set her pumpkin scone back to her plate.

Cam rounded the corner of the veranda and found his family and Tess seated in front of him. In the warm sunshine and the filtered light from a wisteria vine, the tableau looked inviting and almost summery—even with the cool of autumn in the air.

Tess, though, looked pale and his heart lurched for her. Organising this memorial service must be hell. She glanced up and her face relaxed into a smile of pure pleasure. It immediately buoyed him up. He couldn't remember any woman's smile affecting him the way Tess's did. Not even Fiona's.

'Hello, Cameron.'

'Tess.'

His mother shot to her feet, delight lighting her face. 'Cam!'

He moved down the length of the veranda and kissed her cheek. 'Hello, Mum.'

Lance stood more slowly. He nodded to Cam and then turned to Lorraine. 'There's some work I should get done in the eastern paddock.'

Fiona jumped up too. 'I'll help.'

There was no denying that they were trying to make room for him, trying to make things less awkward. He appreciated the effort. Tess had been right. They deserved the benefit of the doubt. 'I'd like the two of you to stay, if you don't mind.'

A tremulous smile appeared on Fiona's lips. It left him unmoved and he suddenly frowned. When precisely had he fallen out of love with her? His heart started to pound. Or had she been right? Had he been more in love with his dream of filling Kurrajong Station with laughter and with a family?

Lance sat when Fiona tugged him back down to the seat beside her. His blue eyes filled with a hope he desperately tried to hide, but Cam had always been able to read his little brother.

Until he'd turned his back on him.

He glanced at Tess and she held a hand out to him. He took it without thinking, squeezed it before releasing it to take the lone chair at right angles to her. The only other spare seat was beside his mother. It wasn't that he wanted to shun her. He just wanted to face his family square on during this conversation—read their faces, gauge their reactions.

'You wanted to speak to us about something, Cameron?' his mother asked.

'I've been thinking about your visit last weekend, and it has to be said that I was discourteous and churlish in response to your offer of an olive branch. If the offer still stands, I'd like to accept it.'

'It still stands!' Lance shot to his feet and thrust his hand towards Cam.

Cam rose and shook it. With a nod he took his seat again. He met Tess's warm gaze, recognised her unspoken approbation. It made him push his shoulders back and lift his chin. Her innate generosity and the sacrifices she'd made had helped him see sense. More than that, though, she'd made him believe he was worth more than he'd ever credited before.

He turned back to Lance before he could become too preoccupied with the dusky fullness of Tess's bottom lip. 'This is just a start. It's going to take me a while to trust you again.'

'I know.' Lance squared his shoulders. 'But it's a start, and I'm not going to screw up this time.'

Cam stretched a leg out. 'Now to the financial situation of this station. I'm not just going to bail you guys out. I'm not a bank and I have my own place to consider. But—' he glanced at his mother '—I am prepared to buy a fifty per cent share of the property and to invest in improving it.'

She bit her lip and nodded. It was an acknowledgement, not an acceptance. This was business. This wouldn't be her ideal scenario, but interest-free loans and working for this station gratis were a thing of the past.

He glanced back at Lance. 'Are you fair dinkum about giving farming a proper go?'

'Yes.'

'Then I'm prepared to pay you a wage to train under Fraser for the next two years. If Mum does decide to sell me half the property, and if you prove yourself, I will let you buy back my share of this station for whatever the current market value is.'

Lance swallowed and nodded. 'I accept.' Fiona nudged him and he broke into a grin. 'In fact, I'm darn grateful, but…'

He had to stop his lips from twisting. Here it came. 'But?'

'Cam, I'd rather work under you than Fraser.'

The steel momentarily left his spine. It was the last thing he'd expected Lance to say. It brought home to him the depth of the younger man's resolution. A breath eased out of him. 'I'm afraid that won't be possible.'

His mother leaned towards him. 'Why not, darling?'

'Because I won't be here.' His gut tightened and he couldn't look at Tess. 'I've accepted a field assignment to Africa with the Feed the World programme.'

'For how long?'

'Two years.'

To his right, he heard Tess's quick intake of breath and his chest started to ache.

'When do you leave?' Lance burst out.

'The end of next month.'

And then all hell broke loose as his mother, Lance and Fiona all broke out in loud voices, talking over each other as they remonstrated with him. Tess leaned across to touch his arm. 'Will you stay at least until the memorial service?'

He didn't know when the service was scheduled, but he knew she wouldn't try to trick him into staying any longer. He trusted her. 'Yes.'

'Thank you. It'll mean so much to Ty and Krissie.'

And her?

'And me,' she added as if she could read his mind.

Then she stood. 'Honestly,' she snapped to his family, 'stop all this nonsense. All his life Cameron has looked after you lot. All his life he's done things for other people. Stop being so selfish and think of him for once. He's entitled to follow his dream and you as his family should be supporting him rather than bellyaching at him and making things difficult.'

She was fierce and fabulous and he suddenly wanted to laugh with sheer exhilaration. But when she turned to smile at him he wanted to close his eyes. He recognised what glowed in the gorgeous brown depths of her eyes. Love.

Love for him.

And he had absolutely no intention of accepting it, of returning it, and that knowledge was there in her eyes too.

Bile burned his throat. Why hadn't he taken more care around her? She was the one person in Bellaroo Creek who wanted what was truly best for him—without agenda and without reference to her own needs or desires. He'd rather cut off his right arm than hurt her. A giant vise squeezed his heart. He hadn't meant for it to happen, but a fat lot of good that would do her in the months to come.

He opened his mouth. He wanted to offer her some form of comfort. Only he knew that'd be useless. Worse than useless.

He dragged a hand back through his hair. She'd wanted to be here today to shield him in whatever way she could from Lance and Fiona's betrayal. That all seemed so small and petty now. If only there'd been someone looking out for her!

'Tess is right,' his mother finally said, waving everyone back to their seats. 'Again.'

'Again?' he found himself asking.

'The day of the working bee at the cemetery I mentioned to Tess how nice it was to see you there.' Lorraine bit her lip. 'She said I might want to mention that to you, and it made me suddenly see how…unsupportive I must've seemed to you. Frankly, I was mortified.'

And because of Tess he now knew why his mother had stayed away from Kurrajong Station for all these years.

'She gave me a right set down that day too,' Lance said. 'Demanded to know if I'd ever actually apologised for my appalling behaviour.' He grimaced. 'It was the kick in the pants I needed.'

Cam turned to stare at Tess. She screwed up her nose. 'I tried really hard to mind my own business, but…'

He leaned across and covered her hand with his. 'I'm glad you didn't. I want you to know that all this—' he gestured around the table '—is due to you. And I'm grateful.'

'So am I.' Lorraine rose and embraced Tess. 'My darling girl, not only are you helping save my beloved town, you've helped save my family.'

With her arm about Tess's waist, she turned to Cam. 'Darling, of course you must do what your heart tells you. You've been involved with the Feed the World programme for so long, and I know you've made a real difference in the lives of those less fortunate than us. It's selfish of us to want to keep you to ourselves, but you must never forget that you always have a home here with us.'

He leant across and kissed his mother's cheek. 'I won't forget.' But it was Tess's fragrance he drew into his lungs as he moved away.

'I think it's beyond time I made a fresh pot of tea. Could you give me a hand, Fiona, dear?'

Cam turned to Tess. He wanted to say something—something that would tell her how much he appreciated all she had done, and how sorry he was for the rest of it.

Her smile and the tiny shake of her head forestalled him. 'I think it's all worked out exactly the way it should've, don't you?'

No.

Oh, it had for him and his mother, and for Lance and Fiona, but not for her. Not in the way she deserved.

'I'm mighty glad you came around today, Cam.'

Lance's words reminded him that he and Tess weren't alone. And he didn't want to say or do anything that might embarrass her in front of Lance or cue anybody in on her pain. Tess was like him. She'd not want a broken heart on display for all and sundry to exclaim and pick over. He could at least do that much for her.

He turned to his brother. 'So am I.' And he meant it more than he'd thought he would.

'Say.' Lance pointed, leading him to the edge of the veranda. 'See that colt in the home paddock? Do you think he's ready for breaking?'

Cam watched the colt moving over the grass with an easy

gait and his tail held high. 'Your call, Lance, but I'd be inclined to give him another six months.'

When Cam turned back, Tess was gone. Every atom in his body shouted at him to go after her. He remained where he was. In his heart he knew there was nothing he could say that would make an atom of difference to either one of them. Letting her go was harder than going after her, but it was also kinder.

Where Tess was concerned he'd already done enough harm.

CHAPTER ELEVEN

TESS WORKED HARD at making the memorial service a celebration of Sarah's and Bruce's lives. The scheduled day dawned cold and still, with barely a breath of breeze to stir the leaves in the Kurrajong trees. Cameron's canola had been planted and, while winter had arrived, the blue skies and constant sunshine made her feel as if she, Ty and Krissie were moving into a smoother, calmer period. Truly a new beginning.

Even though she missed Sarah every single day.

Even though whenever she thought of Cameron leaving Bellaroo Creek her heart trembled and her throat would close over.

Still, at least she would know that somewhere in the world Cam was following his heart. If his heart could never belong to her, then she just wanted him happy.

When the day of the memorial service dawned—with Cam due to leave Bellaroo Creek the very next day—Tess bounced out of bed and lifted her chin. She had so much—a home, two beautiful children, and a bright future. Today she meant to count her blessings, not her sorrows.

The entire town turned out for the memorial service. The women wore their best dresses, and while not all the men owned suits, they all wore ties. It touched her to the very centre of her being.

The minister gave a brief but heartfelt sermon. Lorraine led them all in a stirring version of 'Amazing Grace'. Tess, with Ty and Krissie at her side, gave a eulogy—she spoke about Sarah's generosity, her love for her family, and how much she'd have loved Bellaroo Creek. Both Krissie and Ty told a little story about their mum—even their dad. There wasn't a dry eye after that. They ended the service with a recording of Sarah's favourite song—the Hollies hit 'He Ain't Heavy, He's My Brother'.

A wake was held at the community hall. After refreshments and cake had been amply consumed, Tess strode up to the podium and called the room to order. 'Ty, Krissie and I wanted today to be a celebration of Sarah's life and you've all helped make that possible and I want to thank you from the bottom of my heart.'

Without any effort at all, she found Cam's tall broad bulk in the crowd. The smile he sent her warmed her to her toes. 'We miss Sarah every single day, but we don't want to focus any longer on all the bad stuff about missing her, but on how much better our lives are for having known her. Today, you helped us do that.'

She smoothed her hair back behind her ears. 'Something Ty, Krissie and I have taken to doing at dinnertime is naming something that has made us happy for that day or something that we're grateful for. Every single day I'm grateful that Sarah was my sister, but when she died I turned my back on my music. A very special guy here in Bellaroo Creek, though, showed me what a mistake that was. I'm very grateful to Cameron Manning for that lesson. I want to now play you all a piece that was one of my sister's favourites.'

She moved to the side where she'd stowed her guitar case and retrieved the guitar she'd had couriered from Sydney. She hadn't played it in over five months. She slipped the strap over her head, seated herself on a stool, and looked out at the sea of faces staring back at her. 'Sarah, honey, this one's for you,' she whispered.

She met Cam's eyes, drew in a breath at his encouraging nod, and then her fingers touched the strings and magic filled her. She lost herself to it, pouring her heart into the music.

When she finished she smiled at Ty and Krissie sitting on the floor in front of her. And then at Cam. He was right. The music was a gift, and there was room in her heart for it all—for Ty and Krissie, and for the music. She should embrace it.

'I want to invite anyone who'd like to take part, to come up here and share something that's made you happy or that you're grateful for.'

Cam stared in awe.

Tess Laing was the most amazing woman he'd ever met. If Bellaroo Creek could attract another couple of women with her spunk the town would be safe for the next hundred years. It wouldn't just be saved. It'd flourish!

Krissie walked up onto stage to the microphone. 'You should go down there now,' she whispered to Tess, pointing at the crowd, obviously not meaning for everyone to hear, but the microphone picking it up as Tess adjusted it for her.

With a kiss to the top of the child's head, Tess made her way down to the crowd to stand with Ty. Without consciously meaning to, Cam made his way to her side. She smiled at him, turning automatically as if she'd sensed him there. It made his gut clench.

Did he truly mean to leave this woman?

'I want to say that one thing that makes me happy is my auntie Tess. We do lots of fun things together like singing, and we dance around the backyard and colour-in together. She's not a very good dancer...'

Everyone laughed. Cam remembered seeing Tess dance and shook his head. She was a great dancer.

'But she's going to teach me guitar and I love living with her.'

He held Tess back when Krissie finished. 'Let her do it all under her own steam,' he counselled.

'I'm fussing, huh?'

He didn't interfere though when she bent down to encompass the child in a hug once Krissie had reached them. It wasn't until she righted herself, though, that he saw Ty had moved to the microphone.

'My auntie Tess is awesome, but today I want to say I'm happy Cam has been our neighbour. He's shown me how to stake tomato plants and how to nail chicken wire and how to teach Barney to fetch a ball. I'm going to miss him when he goes to Africa.'

There were a few 'hear, hears' from the crowd and Cam found his throat thickening. He lifted Ty up in a bear hug when he rejoined them. 'Thanks, buddy, I'm going to miss you too.'

'Me too?' Krissie tugged on his sleeve, demanding a hug of her own.

'You too,' he said, hugging her close.

Damn it! Did he really mean to leave these kids behind?

'Me three.' Tess leaned across and kissed his cheek. She backed up pretty quick again too, though, and he didn't blame her. Not if the heat threatened her in the same way it did him.

One by one the townsfolk walked up to the microphone to name the things that made them happy—family, a good wheat crop, a clean bill of health, family, friends who rallied around in times of need, good rainfall, grandchildren, family. *Family*. It figured high on everyone's happiness radar. Not a single person mentioned going to Africa—or any other place for that matter. Bellaroo Creek and family, that was what mattered.

Bellaroo Creek and family.

Cameron stared at Tess and the kids. Could he truly leave them? Did he *want* to leave them?

He stared at his mother. She'd miss him dreadfully. He knew that now, even if she was putting a brave face on it.

Family and Bellaroo Creek.

Lance and Fiona canoodled in a corner like the lovesick couple they were and he didn't even feel a pang. Instead he felt hopeful. Lance was keeping his word and working hard. Having finally emerged from under Cam's shadow, he was even showing some natural aptitude on the sheep-breeding programme. And it was obvious he had no intention of breaking Fiona's heart as Cam had feared.

Family and Bellaroo Creek.

Once upon a time that had been his dream too. When it had failed him he'd turned his back on it, proclaimed it impossible. His heart started to thump. But it wasn't impossible, was it? It was within reach if he had the courage to try for it.

He stared at Tess and Ty and Krissie, remembered the laughter and light they'd brought to Kurrajong House, the life they'd sent flowing through it.

That dream of his wasn't impossible. Oh, it hadn't been possible with Fiona, and all he could do was be thankful that she'd realised it in time.

That dream of his was absolutely possible.

If only he wasn't too afraid to reach for it again.

His heart thundered in his ears. Tess had found the courage to embrace her music again. Could he find the same courage within himself?

He shoved his hands in his pockets and stared hard at the floorboards at his feet. What did he truly want? What would he lay his life down for and be glad to do it?

Tess.

That single word filled his soul.

'I'm next!' He pointed to the microphone. Everyone turned to stare at him. He swung to Tess, seized her face in his hands and kissed her soundly. His lips memorised every single curve and contour of hers and she kissed him back with such unguarded love it fed something essential inside him.

He let her go. He squeezed Krissie's and Ty's shoulders before striding up to the stage and the microphone.

Tess watched Cam adjust the microphone while the blood crashed through her veins.

He'd kissed her.

In front of everyone!

What did he mean by it?

Ty and Krissie grinned up at her. She couldn't help but grin back.

Cam cleared his throat. Her attention flew back to his tall frame and those powerful shoulders and lean hips…and long, long legs with their powerful thighs. Her knees quivered and her heart tripped and fluttered.

His gaze wandered about the crowd until she thought he must've made eye contact with everyone. 'I know every single one of you by your full name. I've listened to you recite the things that make you happy, the things that are most important to you, and the message has come through loud and clear—you love your families, your properties and Bellaroo Creek.'

He shifted. 'All I've ever wanted is to grow a big bustling family at Kurrajong Station, but a year ago that dream came crashing down around my ears and I thought it would never happen. That's when I made my decision to leave. I knew it would be too hard living here day in and day out with that dream mocking me.'

Her heart burned for all he'd been through.

'I want to say now that I'm grateful to Fiona for realising we weren't well suited and calling our engagement off before we made a dreadful mistake. I only wish I could've seen that truth sooner.'

He didn't love Fiona? Her hands clenched and unclenched until, to stop their fidgeting, she gripped them together.

'Because now I know what true love is.'

He did?

When his gaze moved to her, she had to press her hands to her heart to make sure it didn't leap right out of her chest.

'Loving someone means wanting them to be happy, even if it means giving up your own dreams. It means supporting them in the things that are important to them, even if you don't understand that importance.' He suddenly grinned. 'Like White Bearded Silkies and marigolds in a vegetable garden.'

Krissie tugged on Tess's blouse. 'Cam loves us, Auntie Tess.' She grinned as if it were the best news in the world.

''Course he does,' Ty scoffed, as if he'd always known as much.

She swallowed. Had she truly thought they wouldn't welcome another person into their lives? It was obvious that they'd welcome Cam.

Except…

Her heart started to wilt. Loving someone meant supporting their dreams. Cam's dream was to go to Africa—to experience the world, to make a difference. She couldn't stand in the way of that.

'Loving someone means risking your heart, even if you've vowed to never do that again, even if you don't feel ready to take that leap.'

He was going to risk his heart for her, wasn't he? She wanted him to. Oh, how she wanted him to, but…

Africa. His dream.

'I want you all to know that I won't be going to Africa after all.'

Applause broke out along with several cheers. Tess couldn't bear to glance around. Her heart had slumped to her ankles.

'I'm going to fight for the life I want. I'm going to fight for my dream. If that dream proves impossible, I'm going to stay here in Bellaroo Creek anyway. I'm not going to turn my back on the town. This is where I belong.'

He climbed down from the stage and made his way directly

to where she stood. Taking both Krissie's and Ty's hands, he led them away to the far side of the room and knelt down to speak to them. With his back to her she couldn't see what he said. She could only see the smiles that lit the children's faces, their decisive nods, and the hopeful glances they sent her way.

She wanted to close her eyes. She couldn't let him do this. When he rose and beckoned to her, she pulled in a breath and moved towards them. With a smile designed to heat her from the inside out, Cam took her hand. 'You guys go join the party again. Your aunt and I are going to talk.'

And with that he led her out of a side door and away from the noise of the hall until they stood beneath the fronds of a pepper tree that partially hid them from view. He stared down into her face, plucked one of the fronds from her hair, but he didn't say anything.

Loving someone means wanting them to be happy.

'When did you realise I'd fallen in love with you, Cameron?'

He touched her cheek with the backs of his fingers. He kept a firm grip on her hand. 'That day at my mother's.'

'It was the day I realised I loved you.' She paused and bit back a sigh. 'I don't think I'm very good at keeping things from you.'

His lips lifted. 'I'm glad about that.'

She gently detached her hand and moved a couple of steps back until she leant against the hard, rough trunk of the tree. He stiffened. 'I hope you mean to tell me what's troubling you now?'

Oh, how she would miss him!

Behind her, she closed her fingers about the rough bark. She dragged in a breath that hurt her lungs. 'All your life you've taken responsibility for other people. For your father when he cut himself off from the world, and for continuing his legacy in providing your mother with a haven if she should ever need it. For taking on the management of the property your stepfather left to her…and even for helping Lance find his feet. You help Edna and Ted Fairchild run cattle so they can stay in the home they love, and heaven only knows how many other people you help out in a similar way. You're amazing, Cameron, a true-blue hero. I swear I have yet to meet anyone with more decency and integrity.'

He adjusted his stance, legs wide and hands on hips, and her heart stuttered in her chest. 'Why, then,' he said, 'am I suddenly not happy to hear this?'

She ached to rush forward and throw her arms around his neck and tell him how much she loved him, but…

He deserved to chase his dreams.

'Because all your life you've taken on everyone else's responsibilities, but now you have a chance to travel and to find out where you truly want to be.'

'I know where I want to be.'

She wanted to believe him, but… 'Do you know how much responsibility it is raising two kids? Do you know how needy and…and…Cam, we—Ty, Krissie and me—we're *not* your responsibility.' She might not have given birth to Ty and Krissie, but they were hers now and she loved them as if she had. 'I know when you look at us you see a single mum with two kids who need rescuing, but—'

'Garbage!' He slashed a hand through the air, making her blink. 'I look at you, Tess, and I see an incredibly strong woman who manages to make me laugh even when I'm feeling my bleakest and grumpiest. I look at you and see a desirable woman I want to take to my bed and make love with thoroughly and comprehensively.'

She pressed hands to cheeks that burned.

He moved in close until all she could smell was the scent of cut grass and hot man, and all she could see was him.

'I look at you, Tess, and my soul sings and my heart is at rest and there's glitter in my world.'

He reached out to touch her face. 'I don't see a woman

who needs rescuing. I see a woman with a safety net ready for me if I should ever fall. Tess, when I look at you I don't see a responsibility. I see my future. I see my soul mate. I see the woman I love.'

Her heart all but stopped.

His hands clenched, his eyes blazed with resolution. 'I don't know how long it will take me to convince you of the truth of that, but I want you to know I'm going to dedicate my life to doing exactly that.'

'But Africa,' she whispered. She wanted him happy. She wanted him to follow his dream.

'To hell with Africa! It was my consolation prize. I'm not running away. I'm not leaving Bellaroo Creek. And let me tell you another thing.' He jabbed a finger at her nose. 'I'm not making way for some other single farmer to make a move on you.' He thrust out his jaw. 'I'm not going anywhere!'

She stared at him. He stared back, his eyes a glowing, gleaming green. 'Africa is not where I want to be. Wherever you are, Tess, that's where I'm going to make my home—whether that be at Kurrajong House, your little farmhouse or in Sydney.'

He meant it. Every single word.

And she could see the exact moment when he clocked her belief in him. His smile was like drought-ridden land coming back to life after vital rain.

He reached out to cup her face. 'Your eyes tell me you're going to say yes when I ask you to marry me.'

She grinned. She couldn't help it. She reached up to touch his cheek, before moving in closer to wind her arms about his neck. 'Yours tell me you've already asked for the children's permission.'

'They gave it gladly.'

Of course they had. They adored Cam as much as she did. 'My eyes don't lie, Cameron. I love you. My heart is completely and utterly yours.'

Just as his was hers. And she meant to treasure it and keep it safe for ever.

He stared down at her as if her words were magic. She moved against him suggestively. 'So, what do you mean to do with your Bellaroo Creek bride once you have her?'

His head dipped towards her, blocking out the sun. 'I mean to make her the happiest woman on the planet,' he murmured against her lips, before he captured them in a kiss of such pure joy Tess felt as if she were flying and swooping among the treetops.

* * * * *

A woman in a white flowing dress caught Cash's attention. She rushed along the side of the church. Abruptly she stopped and bent over some shrubs. What in the world was the bride doing? Looking for something?

This was certainly the most entertainment he'd had in the past half-hour. He shook his head and smiled at the strange behavior. When she started running down the walk toward his vehicle he tipped his hat upward to get a better view.

The bride spun around. Her fearful gaze met his. Her pale face made her intense green eyes stand out bright with fear. Alarm tightened his chest. Was there more going on here than a change of mind?

She glanced over the hood of his truck. He followed her line of vision, spotting a group of photographers rounding the corner of the church. In the next second she'd opened his passenger door and vaulted inside.

What in the world was she doing? Planning to steal his truck?

He swung open the driver's side door and climbed in.

"What are you doing in here?"

The fluffy material of her dress hit him in the face as she turned in the seat and slammed her door shut.

"Drive. Fast."

RANCHER TO
THE RESCUE

BY
JENNIFER FAYE

First published in Great Britain 2013
by Mills & Boon, an imprint of Harlequin (UK) Limited,
Eton House, 18-24 Paradise Road, Richmond, Surrey TW9 1SR

© Jennifer F. Stroka 2013

ISBN: 978 0 263 90132 0
ebook ISBN: 978 1 472 00514 4

23-0813

Harlequin (UK) policy is to use papers that are natural, renewable and recyclable products and made from wood grown in sustainable forests. The logging and manufacturing processes conform to the legal environmental regulations of the country of origin.

Printed and bound in Spain
by Blackprint CPI, Barcelona

In another life, **Jennifer Faye** was a statistician. She still has a love for numbers, formulas and spreadsheets, but when she was presented with the opportunity to follow her lifelong passion and spend her days writing and pursuing her dream of becoming a Mills & Boon® author, she couldn't pass it up. These days, when she's not writing, Jennifer enjoys reading, fine needlework, quilting, tweeting and cheering on the Pittsburgh Penguins. She lives in Pennsylvania with her amazingly patient husband, two remarkably talented daughters and their two very spoiled fur babies otherwise known as cats—but *shh*…don't tell them they're not human!

Jennifer loves to hear from readers—you can contact her via her website: www.jenniferfaye.com.

This is Jennifer Faye's fabulous first book for Mills & Boon!

To my real-life hero, Eric,
who is the most positive, encouraging person
I've ever known. Thanks for cheering me on
to reach for the stars. You're my rock.

And to Bliss and Ashley.
You both amaze and impress me every day.
Thank you for filling my life with so much sunshine.

I'd also like to send a big thanks to my wonderful
editor, Carly Byrne, for believing in my abilities and
showing me the way to make my first book a reality.

CHAPTER ONE

WHY DO PEOPLE insist on pledging themselves to each
other? Love was fleeting at best—if it existed at all.

Cash Sullivan crossed his arms as he lounged back
against the front fender of his silver pickup. He pulled his
tan Stetson low, blocking out the brilliant New Mexico
sun. From the no-parking zone he glanced at the adobe-
style church, where all of the guests were gathered, but
he refused to budge.

His grandmother had insisted he bring her, but there
was no way he'd sit by and listen to a bunch of empty
promises. Besides, he'd met the groom a few times over
the years and found the guy to be nothing more than a
bunch of hot air. Cash would rather spend his time wrestling the most contrary steer than have to make small talk
with that blowhard.

He loosened his bolo tie and unbuttoned the collar of
his white button-up shirt. Gram had insisted he dress up
to escort her in and out of the church—even if he wasn't
planning to stay.

What he wouldn't give to be back at the ranch in his old,
comfy jeans, instead of these new black ones that were as
stiff as a fence rail. Heck, even mucking out stalls sounded
like a luxury compared to standing here with nothing to do.

A woman in a white flowing dress caught his attention.

She was rushing along the side of the church. Abruptly she stopped and bent over some shrubs. What in the world was the bride doing? Looking for something?

This was certainly the most entertainment he'd had in the past half hour. He shook his head and smiled at the strange behavior. When she started running down the walk toward his vehicle, he tipped his hat upward to get a better view.

A mass of unruly red curls was piled atop her head while yards of white material fluttered behind her like the tail of a kite. Her face was heart-shaped, with lush lips. Not bad. Not bad at all.

Her breasts threatened to spill out of the dress, which hugged her waist and flared out over her full hips. She was no skinny-minny, but the curves looked good on her. Real good.

He let out a low whistle. She sure was a looker. How in the world had boring Harold bagged her?

He couldn't tear his gaze from her as she stopped right next to his pickup and tried to open the tan SUV in the neighboring parking spot. Unable to gain access, she smacked her hand on the window. Obviously this lady had a case of cold feet—as in *ice cold*—and hadn't planned an escape route. At least she'd come to her senses before making the worst decision of her life.

The bride spun around. Her fearful gaze met his. Her pale face made her intense green eyes stand out bright with fear. Alarm tightened his chest. Was there more going on here than a change of mind?

She glanced over the hood of his truck. He followed her line of vision, spotting a group of photographers rounding the corner of the church. In the next second she'd opened his passenger door and vaulted inside.

What in the world was she doing? Planning to steal

his truck? He swung open the driver's side door and climbed in.

"What are you doing in here?"

The fluffy material of her veil hit him in the face as she turned in the seat and slammed the door shut. "Drive. Fast."

He smashed down the material from her veil, not caring if he wrinkled it. He'd never laid eyes on this woman before today, and he wasn't about to drive her anywhere until he got some answers. "Why?"

"I don't have time to explain. Unless you want to be front and center in tomorrow's paper, you'll drive."

His gaze swung around to the photographers. They hadn't noticed her yet, but that didn't ease his discomfort. "You didn't kill anyone, did you?"

"Of course not." She sighed. "Do you honestly think I'd be in this getup if I was going to murder someone?"

"I'm not into any Bonnie and Clyde scenario."

"That's good to know. Now that we have that straightened out, can you put the pedal to the metal and get us out of here before they find me?"

He grabbed the bride's arm and yanked her down out of sight, just before the group of reporters turned their curious gazes to his pickup. Luckily his truck sat high up off the ground, so no one could see much unless they were standing right next to it.

"What are you doing?" she protested, struggling.

"Those reporters don't know you're in here, and I don't want to be named in your tabloid drama. Stay down and don't get up until I tell you to."

His jaw tensed as he stuffed the white fluff beneath the dash. He was caught up in this mess whether he wanted to be or not.

Her struggles ceased. He fired up the truck and threw

it in Reverse. Mustering some restraint, he eased down on the accelerator. Damn. He didn't want to be the driver for this bride's getaway, but what choice did he have?

He knew all about reporters—they were like a pack of starving wolves, just waiting for a juicy story. For their purposes he'd be "the other man." Scandals always made good sales—it didn't matter if you were an innocent bystander or not. In the court of public opinion, when your face hit the front page you were crucified. He should know.

Cash pulled his cowboy hat low, hoping no one would recognize him. He didn't want to draw the attention of the reporters who were searching behind rocks, shrubs and cars. There would be no quick getaway. Slow and steady.

When the bride once again attempted to sit up, he placed his hand on the back of her head.

"Hey, you!" a young reporter, standing a few yards away, shouted through the open window.

Cash's chest tightened as he pulled to a stop. "Yeah?"

"Did you see which way the bride ran?"

"She ran around back. Think there was a car waiting for her."

The reporter waved and took off. Cash eased off the brake and rolled toward the exit. He hadn't had a rush of adrenaline like this since his last showdown with a determined steer.

"What'd you say that for? You're making things worse," the bride protested, starting to sit up.

He pressed the side of her face back down. "Stay down or I'll dump you in this parking lot and let those hungry reporters have you."

"You wouldn't."

"Try me." He was in no mood to play around with some woman who didn't know what she wanted.

Now he needed to get rid of this bundle of frills so his life could return to its peaceful routine.

Before he could ask where she wanted to be dropped off she started to wiggle, bumping the steering wheel.

"Watch it." He steadied the wheel with both hands. "What are you doing down there?"

"Trying to get comfortable, but I think it's impossible. Are we away from the church yet?"

"Just approaching the parking lot exit, but don't get any ideas of sitting up until we're out of town. I'm not about to have people tracking me down and bothering me with a bunch of questions I can't answer."

"Thanks for being so sympathetic," she muttered.

He slowed down at the exit, checking for traffic before merging. "Hey, I didn't ask you to hijack my truck."

"I didn't have any other choice."

"Get cold feet?"

"No...yes. It's complicated." She squirmed some more. "I don't feel so good. Can I sit up yet?"

"No."

The rush of air through the open windows picked up the spicy, citrusy scent of the colorful bouquet she was still clutching. A part of him felt bad for her. He'd heard about how women got excited about their wedding day and, though he personally couldn't relate, he knew what it was to have a special moment ruined, like getting penalized after a winning rodeo ride.

He checked the rearview mirror. No one had followed him out of the parking lot. He let out a deep breath. So far, so good.

He tightened his fingers around the steering wheel, resisting the urge to run a soothing hand over her back. "Where am I taking you?"

"I...I don't know. I can't go back to my apartment. They'll be sure to find me."

"You're on the run?" He should have figured this was more than just a case of cold feet. "And what was up with the reporters?"

"My boss thought the wedding would be a good source of free publicity for my television show."

"You certainly will get publicity. *Runaway Bride Disappears Without a Trace*."

She groaned. Her hand pressed against his leg. The heat of her touch radiated through the denim. A lot of time had passed since a woman had touched him—back before his accident.

He cleared his throat. "I suppose at this point we should introduce ourselves. I'm Cash Sullivan."

He waited, wondering if there would be a moment of recognition. After all, he hadn't retired from the rodeo circuit all that long ago.

"Meghan Finnegan." When he didn't say anything, she continued, "I'm the Jiffy Cook on TV, and the reason those men are armed with cameras is to see this hometown girl marry a millionaire."

Nothing in her voice or mannerisms gave the slightest hint that she'd recognized his name. Cash assured himself it was for the best. His name wasn't always associated with the prestige of his rodeo wins—sometimes it was connected with things he'd rather forget. Still, he couldn't ignore the deflating prick of disappointment.

"I don't watch television," he said, gruffer than intended. "Okay, we're out of Lomas and this road doesn't have much traffic."

When she didn't say anything, he glanced over. Her complexion had gone ghostly pale, making her pink glossy lips stand out. "You feeling okay?"

"No." Her hand pressed to her stomach. "Pull over. Now."

He threw on his right-turn signal and pulled to a stop in a barren stretch of desert. Meg barreled out of the vehicle, leaving the door ajar. She rushed over to a large rock and hunched over. So this was what she'd been doing when she ran out of the church. Must be a huge case of nerves.

He grabbed some napkins from his glove compartment and a bottle of unopened water. It was tepid, but it'd be better than nothing. He exited the truck and followed her. He wasn't good with women—especially not ones who were upset and sick.

"Um...I can hold this for you." He reached for the lengthy veil.

He didn't know if he should try talking to her to calm her down or attempt to rub her back. He didn't want to make things worse. Unsure what to do, he stood there quietly until her stomach settled. Then he handed over the meager supplies.

"You okay now?" he asked, just before his cell phone buzzed.

His grandmother. How could he have forgotten about her? This bride had a way of messing with his mind to the point of forgetting his priorities.

He flipped open his phone, but before he could utter a word Gram said, "Where are you? Everyone's leaving."

"I went for a little ride. I'll be there in a few minutes."

"Hurry. You won't believe what happened. I'll tell you when you get here."

He hated the thought of going back and facing those reporters. Hopefully there'd be too much confusion with the missing bride and the exiting guests that they wouldn't remember he'd been the only one around when Meg had disappeared.

He cast a concerned look at his pale stowaway. "We have to go back."

Fear flashed in her eyes and she started shaking her head. "No. I can't. I won't."

"Why? Because you changed your mind about the wedding? I'm sure people will understand."

She shook her head. "No, they won't."

He didn't have time to make her see reason. "I have to go back to the church. My grandmother is waiting. I can't abandon her."

Meg's brow creased as she worried her bottom lip. "Then I'll wait here."

"What?" She couldn't be thinking clearly. "I can't leave you here. You're not well."

"I won't go back there. I can't face all of those people... especially my mother. And when the press spots us together they'll have a field day."

"You can hide on the floor again."

She shook her head. "We were lucky to get away with that once. With all of the guests leaving, the chances of me staying hidden are slim to none."

She had a good point, but it still didn't sit right with him. "Leaving you here in the middle of nowhere, in this heat, isn't a good idea."

"This isn't the middle of nowhere. I'm within walking distance of town. I'll be fine. Just go. Your grandmother is waiting. There's just one thing."

"What's that?"

"Leave me your cell phone."

He supposed it was the best solution, but he didn't like it. Not one bit. But the chance of discovery was too great. Not seeing any other alternative, he pulled the phone from his belt and handed it over.

"You're sure about this?" he asked, hoping she'd change her mind.

She nodded.

"Then scoot around to the other side of that rock. No one will see you there—unless that veil thing starts flapping in the wind like a big flag."

"It won't." She wound the lengthy material around her arm. A look of concern filled her eyes. "You will come back, won't you?"

He didn't want to. He didn't want anything to do with this mess. All he wanted was to go home and get on with his life. But he couldn't leave her sick and stranded.

"I'll be back as fast as I can."

Meghan Finnegan watched as the tailgate of the cowboy's pickup faded into the distance. The events of the day rushed up and stampeded her, knocking the air from her lungs. How could Harold have waited until she'd walked up the aisle to tell her he'd suddenly changed his mind?

He didn't want her.

And he wanted her to get rid of their unborn baby—a baby they'd agreed to keep secret until after the ceremony. Meghan wrapped her arms around her midsection. She loved her baby and she'd do whatever was necessary to care for it.

She sagged against the rock before her knees gave out. Sure, she knew Harold hadn't wanted children—he'd made that clear from the start. And with her rising television career she'd accepted that children wouldn't fit into her hectic lifestyle. But this was different—it had been an accident. When she'd told Harold about the pregnancy a few weeks ago he'd been stunned at first but then he'd seemed to accept it. What in the world had changed his mind?

The sound of an approaching vehicle—perhaps departing wedding guests—sent her scurrying behind the out-crop of large rocks. She wasn't ready to face the inquiring questions, the pitying stares or the speculative guesses. At twenty-eight, she'd prided herself on having her life all planned out. Now she was pregnant and she didn't have a clue what her next move should be.

She sank down on a small rock and yanked out scads of hairpins in order to release the veil. At last free of the yards of tulle, she ran her fingers through her hair, letting it flow over her shoulders.

She glanced down at the black phone in her lap. She should probably call her family, so they didn't worry, but there was no way she was going to deal with her mother, who would demand answers. After all, her mother had been instrumental in planning this whole affair—from setting up her initial date with the boy-next-door who'd grown up to make a fortune in the computer software business to making the wedding plans. In fact the preparations were what had finally pulled her mother out of her depression after cancer had robbed them of Meghan's father less than a year ago.

Not that all of the blame could be laid at her mother's feet. Meghan had been willing to go along with the plans—anxious to put her father's mind at ease about her future before he passed on. And, eager at last to gain her mother's hard-won approval, she'd convinced herself Harold was the man for her.

Then, as the "big day" approached the doubts had started to settle in. At first she'd thought they were just the usual bridal jitters. But Harold had started to change—to be less charming and thoughtful. It had been as though she was really seeing him for the first time. But her options had vanished as soon as the pregnancy strip displayed two little pink lines.

Meghan's hand moved to her barely-there baby bump. "It's okay, little one. Mommy will fix things. I just need some time to think."

First she had to call her family. She carefully considered whom to contact. Her middle sister Ella? Or her little sis Katie? At the moment they weren't all that close. Since their father's death the family had splintered. She'd hoped the wedding would bring them all together again, but nothing she'd tried had worked.

Never having been very close with her youngest sister, she dialed Ella's number. The cell phone rang for a long time. Meghan had blocked Cash's number and now she worried that her sister might think it was a prank call or, worse, a telemarketer and not answer. Maybe that was for the best. She could leave a message and have no questions to field.

"Hello?" chimed Ella's hesitant voice.

"Ella, it's me. Meghan."

"Meghan—"

"Shh…don't let anyone know you're talking to me. I'm not ready to deal with Mother."

"Wait a sec." The buzz of people talking in the background grew faint, followed by the thud of a door closing. "Okay. I'm alone. What happened? Why'd you run off? Where—?"

"Slow down."

Her first instinct was to tell Ella she was stranded on the side of the road. In the past they'd shared all sorts of girly secrets—right up until Ella's engagement had ended abruptly seven months ago. Her sister hadn't been the same since then. Now, it wouldn't be right to burden her sister with her problems—not when Ella still had her own to figure out.

Meghan heard herself saying, "Don't worry. I'm fine. I'm with a friend."

"But why did you run out on the wedding? I thought you wanted to marry Harold? He acted so broken up and shocked when you took off."

"What?" Her mouth gaped as her fingers clenched the phone tighter to her ear.

"Harold barely held it together when he told the family that he didn't have a clue why you ran out on him."

"He knew…"

That low-down, sniveling, two-faced creep. Her blood boiled in her veins. How could he turn the tables on her when he was the one who'd done the jilting?

He was worried about his image. It always came back to what would look best for him and his company. Why should he take any of the blame for the ruined wedding when she wasn't there to defend herself?

"Meghan, what did he know? Are you still there?"

"He lied," she said, trying to remain calm so she didn't say something she'd regret later. But she couldn't let her sister believe Harold's lies. "He knew exactly why I left."

"It's okay," Ella said as sympathy oozed in her voice. "I understand you got cold feet. Remember I was there not that long ago—"

"I didn't get cold feet. There are things you don't know."

"Then tell me."

"I can't yet. This is different from when you called off your engagement. And it seems to me you've been spending all of your time hiding in your bakery."

"This isn't about me." Ella sighed. "Harold hinted that the stress of planning such a large wedding might have driven you over the edge."

"But that's not what happened." Why hadn't she seen this side of Harold a long time ago? Had it been there all along? She'd thought he was honorable and with time he would accept the baby.

"It doesn't matter. Just come home. The whole family is worried. Mother is beside herself. She says she'll never be able to step outside again because she's too embarrassed."

"And what do you expect me to do?" she asked, tired of being the oldest and the one expected to deal with their mother. "Nothing I say will make her less embarrassed."

In fact it'd only make it that much worse when her strait-laced mother, a pillar of the community, found out her unwed daughter was pregnant by the boy-next-door—the same guy who'd dumped her and their baby at the altar.

"But, Meghan, you have to—"

"No, I don't. Not this time. You and Katie are going to have to deal with her. I need some space to figure things out. Until I do, I won't be of any help to anyone."

Ella huffed. "So when are you coming home?"

She wanted to go to her apartment and hide away, but she wouldn't have any peace there. And there was no way she was going to her mother's house.

"I don't know. I have two weeks planned for the honeymoon so don't expect to see me before then. I'm sorry, Ella. I've got to go."

There was nothing left to say—or more like nothing she was willing to say at this point. She knew Ella was worried and frustrated, but her sister was smart and had a good head on her shoulders. She'd figure out how to manage their mother.

As Meghan disconnected the call her concern over her family was replaced by nagging doubts about the cowboy returning for her. She glanced down at the new-looking phone with a photo of a horse on the display. Surely he wouldn't toss aside his phone with his photos and numbers inside?

He'd be back…

But then again she'd put her faith in Harold and look where that had gotten her. Pregnant and alone. Her hand moved to spread across her abdomen. She'd barely come to terms with the fact there was a baby growing inside her, relying on her. And she'd already made such a blunder of things.

CHAPTER TWO

CASH ARRIVED AT the church in time to witness the groom taking his moment in the spotlight, blaming everything on Meg in order to gain the public's sympathy.

The nerve of the man amazed Cash. Meg was distraught to the point of being physically ill, and here was Harold posing for pictures. His bride might have walked out on him, but Harold sure didn't look like the injured party. A niggling feeling told him there was more to this story than the bride getting cold feet.

Ten minutes passed before he pried Gram away from consoling the groom's family and ushered her to his pickup. At last they hit the road. Gram insisted on regaling him with the tale of how the bride ran out of the church without explanation and all the wild speculations. Cash let her talk. All too soon she would learn the facts for herself.

When he reached the two-lane highway he had only one mission—to tramp the accelerator and get back to the sickly bride. By now she must think he'd forgotten her.

Nothing could be further from the truth.

"Cash, slow down," Gram protested. "I don't know what you're in such an all-fired-up rush for. There's nothing at the Tumbling Weed that can't wait."

"It's not the ranch I'm worried about."

He could feel his grandmother's pointed gaze. "You aren't in some kind of trouble again, are you?"

He sighed, hating how his past clung to him tighter than wet denim. "Not like you're thinking."

He glanced down at the speedometer, finding he was well beyond the limit. He eased his boot up on the accelerator. As his speed decreased his anxiety rose. It was bad enough having to leave Meg alone, but when she didn't feel well it had to be awful for her.

At last he flipped on his turn signal and pulled off the road.

"What are we stopping for? Is there something wrong with the truck? I told you we should have gassed up before leaving town."

"The truck's fine."

"Then why are we stopping in the middle of nowhere? Cash, have you lost your mind?"

"Wait here." He jumped out of the truck and rushed over to the rock.

Meg wasn't there. His chest clenched. What had happened to her? He hadn't seen any sign of her walking back to town. Had someone picked her up? The thought made him uneasy.

"Meg!" He turned in a circle. "Meg, where are you?" At last he spotted her, on the other side of the road. She gathered up her dirty dress and rushed across the road. "What in the world were you doing?"

"I thought if any passing vehicles had taken notice of you dropping a bride off on the side of the road, it might be wiser if I moved to another location."

It seemed as though her nerves had settled and left her making reasonable decisions. "Good thinking. Sorry it took me a bit to get back here. Picking up my grandmother took me longer than I anticipated—"

"Cash, who are you talking to?" Gram hollered from inside the truck.

"Don't worry," he said, "that's my grandmother. Your number-one fan."

"Really? She watches my show?"

"Don't sound so surprised. From what Gram says, you've gained quite a loyal following."

"I suppose I have. That's why the network's considering taking the show national."

So she was a rising television star. Maybe Harold hadn't been up for sharing the spotlight? Cash liked the idea of Meg being more successful and popular than a man who played up the part of an injured party to gain public sympathy.

"Cash, do you hear me?" Gram yelled, her voice growing irritated.

"We'd better not keep her waiting," he said. "If she gets it in her mind to climb out of that truck without assistance I'm afraid she'll get hurt."

Meg walked beside him. "Your truck could use a stepladder to get into."

"When I bought it my intent was to haul a horse trailer, not to have beautiful women using it as a taxi service."

He noticed how splotches of pink bloomed in her cheeks. He found he enjoyed making her blush. Obviously Harold, the stuffed shirt, hadn't bothered to lather her with compliments. No wonder she'd left him.

"Before I forget, here's your phone." She placed it in his outstretched hand. "I hope you don't mind but I called my family."

"No problem." He knew if she were his sister or daughter he'd be worried. Turning his attention to his grandmother, he said, "Meg, this is my grandmother—Martha Sullivan. Gram, this is—"

"The Jiffy Cook," Gram interjected. Her thin lips pursed together. Behind her wire-rimmed glasses her gaze darted between him and Meg. "You stole the bride. Cash, how *could* you?"

His own grandmother believed *he* was the reason the bride had run away from the church. The fact it had even crossed her mind hurt. He'd have thought Gram of all people would think better of him and not believe all those scandalous stories in the press.

Before he could refute the accusation Meg spoke up. "Your grandson has been a total gentleman. When he saw me run out of the church with the press on my trail he helped me get away without any incidents. I'm sorry if it inconvenienced you, Mrs. Sullivan."

Gram waved away her concern. "It's you I'm concerned about. Has this thing with my grandson been going on for long?"

Any color in Meg's cheeks leached away, leaving her pasty white beneath the light splattering of freckles across the bridge of her nose. "I…ah…we aren't—"

"Gram, we aren't together. In fact until she ran out of the church I'd never seen Meg before. She needed a lift and I was there. End of story. No one else knows where she is."

"My goodness, what happened? Why did you run away?" Gram pressed a bony hand to her lips, halting the stream of questions. Seconds later, she lowered her hand to her lap. "Sorry, dear. I didn't mean to be so dang nosy. Climb in here and we can give you a ride back to town."

Seeing alarm in Meg's eyes, Cash spoke up, "We can't do that, Gram."

"Well, for heaven's sake, why not? She obviously needs to get out of that filthy gown. And we sure aren't going to leave her here on the side of the road."

"I can't go home," Meg spoke up. "Not yet."

"But what about Harold?" Gram asked. "Shouldn't you let him know where you are? He looked so worried."

Meg's face grew ashen as she pressed her hand to her stomach. She turned to Cash, her eyes wide with anguish. She pushed past him and ran off.

"Meg—wait." He dogged her footsteps to a rock in the distance.

When she bent at her waist he grabbed at the white material of her dress, pulling it back for her. He'd hoped the nausea had passed, but one mention of the wedding and she was sick again.

Was she overtaken by regret about leaving old what's-his-name at the altar? Had her conscience kicked in and it was so distressing that it made her ill?

He considered telling her what he'd witnessed when he'd gone back for Gram, but what purpose would it serve? Obviously the thought of the wrecked wedding was enough to make her sick. Knowing the man she must still love had turned on her wasn't likely to help.

When she straightened, her eyes were red and her face was still ashen. She swayed and he put a steadying arm around her waist. He had no doubt the hot sun was only making things worse.

"I'm fine," she protested in a weak voice. "There's nothing left in my stomach. Just dry heaves."

He didn't release his hold on her until he had her situated in the pickup next to his grandmother. "Gram, can you turn up the air-conditioning and aim the vents on her?"

Without a word Gram adjusted the dials while he helped Meg latch her seatbelt. Once she was secure, he shut the door and rushed over to the driver's side.

He shifted into Drive, but kept his foot on the brake. "Where can we take you, Meg?"

When she didn't answer, he glanced over to find her

head propped against the window. She stared off into the distance, looking as if she'd lost her best friend and didn't know where to turn. In that instant he was transported back in time almost twenty years ago, a little boy who needed a helping hand. If it hadn't been for Gram…

"We'll take you back to the Tumbling Weed," he said, surprising even himself with the decision.

"Where?" Meg's weary voice floated over to him, reassuring him that he'd made the right decision.

"It's Cash's ranch," Gram chimed in. "The perfect place for you to catch your breath."

"I don't know." She worried her bottom lip. "You don't even know me. I wouldn't want to be an imposition."

"With there just being Cash and me living there, we could use the company. Isn't that right, Cash?"

"You live there too?" Meg looked directly at his grandmother.

Gram nodded. "So, what do you say?"

Cash wasn't as thrilled about their guest as his grandmother. Meg might be beautiful, and she might have charmed his grandmother, but she was trouble. The press wasn't going to let up until they found her. He could already envision the headlines: *Runaway Bride Stolen by Thieving Cowboy.* His gut twisted into a painful knot.

"You're invited as long as you keep your location a secret," he said, his voice unbending. "I can't afford to have the press swooping in."

"Oh, no," Meg said, pulling herself upright with some effort. "I'd never bring them to your place. I don't want to see any of them."

Honesty dripped from her words, and a quick glance in her direction showed him her somber expression. But what if she started to feel better and decided she needed to fix her reputation? Or, worse, made a public appeal to what's-his-name to win him back?

Then again, she wouldn't be there that long. In fact it was still early in the day. Not quite lunchtime. If she rested, perhaps she'd be up to going home this evening.

Certain she'd soon be on her way, he said, "Good. Now that we understand each other, let's get moving."

The cold air from the vents of Cash's new-smelling pickup breathed a sense of renewed energy into Meghan. She was exhausted and dirty, but thankfully her stomach had settled. She gazed out the window as they headed southeast. She'd never ventured in this direction, but she enjoyed the vastness of the barren land, where it felt as if she could lose herself and her problems.

Instinctively she moved her hand to her stomach. There wasn't time for kicking back and losing herself. This wasn't a vacation or a spa weekend. This was a chance to get her head screwed on straight, to figure out how to repair the damage to her life and prepare to be a single mother.

The thought of her impending motherhood filled her with anxiety. What she didn't know about being a good parent could fill up an entire library. The only thing she *did* know was that she didn't want to be like her own mother—emotionally distant and habitually withholding her approval. Instead, Meghan planned to lavish her baby with love.

But what if she failed to express her love? What if she fell back on the way she'd been raised?

"Here we are," Cash announced, breaking into her troubled thoughts.

The truck had stopped in front of a little whitewashed house with a covered porch and two matching rocking

chairs. The place was cute, but awfully small. Certainly
not big enough for her to keep out of everyone's way.

Cash cut the engine and rounded the front of the truck.
He swung open the door she'd only moments ago been
leaning against. She released her seat restraint as Cash
held out his hands to help her down. As the length of her
dress hampered her movements she accepted his offer.
His long, lean fingers wrapped around her waist. Holding
her securely, he lowered her to the ground in one steady
movement.

She tilted her chin upward and for the first time noticed his towering height. Even with her heels on he stood
a good six inches taller than her own five-foot-six stature.
His smoky gray eyes held her captive with their intensity.

She swallowed. "Thank you."

"You're welcome." His lips lifted in a small smile, sending her tummy aflutter.

Before she could think of anything to say he turned to
his grandmother and helped her out of the vehicle. Martha rushed up the walk, appearing not to need any assistance getting around. Meghan could only hope to be so
spry when she got on in years.

Martha, as though remembering them, stopped on the
porch. "See you at five o'clock for dinner."

She'd turned for the door when Cash said, "Wait, Gram.
You're forgetting Meg."

"Not at all. She's invited too." She reached for the doorknob.

"But, Gram, aren't you going to invite her in?"

Martha turned and gave him a puzzled look. "Sure,
she's welcome. But I thought she'd want to get cleaned up
and changed into something fresh."

"Wouldn't she need to go inside?"

Martha's brows rose. "Um...Cash...you're going to have to take her to the big house."

"But I thought—"

"Remember after you built the house we converted your old room into my sewing room? She could sleep on the couch, but I think she'd be much more comfortable in one of your guestrooms."

This wasn't what Meghan had imagined. She'd thought they'd all be staying in one house together. The thought of staying alone with Cash sent up warning signals.

"I don't want to be a burden on either of you. If you could let me use your phone, I can call and get a ride."

Cash shot her a puzzled look. "I thought you didn't have any other place to hide from the press?"

"I don't." She licked her dry lips. Softly she added, "I'll just have to tell them..."

"What? What will you tell them?"

Panic paralyzed the muscles in her chest. "I don't know."

"Why *did* you run out on your wedding?" His unblinking gaze held hers, searching for answers.

"I...ah..."

"Why *did* you abandon the groom at the altar? Do you want him back?"

She glared at Cash. "I'm not ready to talk about it. Why are you being so mean?"

"Because that is just a small taste of what's waiting for you. In fact, this is probably mild compared to the questions they'll lob at you."

"What would a cowboy know about the press?" she sputtered, not wanting to admit he was right.

"Trust Cash," Martha piped up. "He knows what he's talking about—"

"Gram, drop it. Meg obviously doesn't want to hear our thoughts."

Meghan turned her gaze to Cash, waiting for him to finish his grandmother's cryptic comment. She'd already had her fiancé dupe her into believing he was going to marry her—that he cared about her. But if he had he wouldn't have uttered those words at the altar. Everything she'd thought about their relationship was a lie. And she wouldn't stand for one more man lying to her.

"What aren't you saying?" she demanded. "What do you know about the press?"

His jaw tensed and a muscle twitched in his cheek. His hands came to rest on his sides as his weight shifted from one foot to the other.

"I'll let you two talk," Martha said. "I've got some things to do."

The front door to the little house swished open, followed by a soft thud as it closed. All the while Meghan's gaze never left Cash. What in the world had made her think coming here was a good idea?

"I'm waiting." The August sun beat down on her in the layers of tulle and satin, leaving it clinging to her skin. Perspiration trickled down her spine. She longed to rub away the irritating sensation, but instead she stood her ground. She wouldn't budge until this stubborn cowboy told her what his cryptic comments meant.

Cash sighed. "I overheard your fiancé talking to the press and it sounded like you'll have a lot of explaining to do."

He'd turned the conversation around on her without bothering to explain his grandmother's comment. But Meghan didn't have time to point this out. She was reeling from the knowledge that Harold had not only gone to her family and blamed her for the wrecked wedding, but he'd also gone to the press with his pack of lies too. The revelation hit her like a sucker punch.

"Why would he do that?" she muttered. Her public persona was her livelihood. Was he trying to wreck her career?

"Maybe if you talked to him you could straighten things out."

She shook her head. At last she was seeing past Harold's smooth talk and fancy airs to the self-centered man beneath the designer suits. "He doesn't want to hear what I have to say. Not after what happened."

Cash's gaze was filled with questions, but she wasn't up for answering them. Right about now she would gladly give her diamond ring just to have a shower and a glass of ice-cold water.

"Could we get out of the sun?" she asked.

Cash's brows rose, as though he'd realized he'd forgotten his manners. "Sure. My house isn't far down the lane."

Alone with this cowboy. It didn't sound like a good idea. In fact, it sounded like a really bad idea. She eyed him up. He looked reasonable. And his grandmother certainly seemed to think the sun revolved around him. So why was she hesitating? It wasn't as if she was moving in. She would figure out a plan and be out of his way in no time.

"You're safe," he said, as though reading her thoughts. "If you're that worried about being alone with me, you heard my grandmother—you can sleep on her couch. Although, between you and me, it's a bit on the lumpy side."

His teasing eased the tenseness in her stomach. He'd been a gentleman so far. There was no reason to think he'd be a threat.

As she stood there, contemplating how to climb up into the passenger seat again, Cash said, "Let me give you a hand."

She knew without having any money or her own trans-

portation she was beholden to him, but that didn't mean
she had to give up every bit of self-reliance.

"Thanks, but I've got it." She took her time, hiking up
her dress in one hand while bracing the other hand on the
truck frame. With all of her might she heaved herself up
and into the seat without incident. While he rounded the
vehicle she latched her seatbelt.

"The lane," as he'd referred to the two dirt ruts, contained a series of rocks and potholes, and Meghan was
jostled and tossed about like a rag doll.

"Did you ever consider paving this?" She clutched the
door handle and tried to remain in her seat.

A deep chuckle filled the air. The sound was warm and
thick, like a layer of hot fudge oozing down over a scoop
of ice cream—both of which she could easily enjoy on a
regular basis. Ice cream had always been something she
could take or leave, but suddenly the thought of diving
into a sundae plagued her, as did pulling back the layers
of this mysterious cowboy.

In the next instance she reminded herself that she didn't
have the time nor the energy to figure him out—not that
she had any clue about men. She'd thought she'd understood Harold. The idea of being a parent must have scared
him—especially since he'd never planned on having kids.
It scared her too. They could have talked about it. Supported each other. But for him to cut and run at the last
minute, leaving her all alone to deal with this… That was
unforgivable.

She'd been so wrong about him.

And that was the real reason she found herself at this
out-of-the-way ranch. If she'd been so wrong about Harold
she didn't trust herself to make any more big decisions.

She glanced over at Cash. Had she been wrong to
trust him?

She smothered a groan. This was ridiculous. She was overthinking everything now. She wondered if this cowboy had ever questioned his every decision. She studied the set of his strong jaw and the firm line of his lips—everything about him said he was sure of himself.

He turned and their gazes connected. His slate-gray eyes were like walls, holding in all his secrets. What kind of secrets could this rugged cowboy have?

CHAPTER THREE

CASH PULLED TO a stop in front of his two-story country home and none too soon. Meg was giving him some strange looks—not the kind he experienced from the good-time girls in the local cowboy bar. These looks were deeper, as though she had questions but didn't know how to phrase them. Whatever she wanted to know about him, he was pretty certain he didn't want to discuss it.

This ranch had become his refuge from the craziness of the rodeo circuit, and now he couldn't imagine living anywhere else. Here at the Tumbling Weed he could be himself and unwind. Though the house had been built a few years ago, he'd never brought home any female friends. He didn't want any misunderstandings. He made it known that he was a no-strings-attached cowboy. Period.

"Thanks for everything," Meg said, breaking into his thoughts. "If you hadn't helped me I don't know what I'd have done."

"I'm certain you would have made do. You don't seem like the type of person who goes long without a plan." When she didn't say anything, he glanced over. She'd bitten down on her lower lip. "Hey, I didn't mean anything by the comment. You're welcome here until you feel better."

"I don't want to get in the way."

"Have you looked at this house?" He pointed through

the windshield. "I guess I got a little carried away when I had the plans drawn up. Tried to talk Gram into moving in but she flat-out refused. She said all of her memories were in her little house and she had no intention of leaving it until the good Lord called her home."

"Your grandmother sounds like a down-to-earth lady."

"She is. And the best cook around."

He immediately noticed Meg's lips purse. He'd momentarily forgotten *she* was some kind of cook. He'd bet his prize mare that Meg's scripted cooking couldn't come close to his grandmother's down-home dishes, but he let the subject drop.

Meg reached for the door handle. "Before I leave I'd love to hear about some of her recipes."

He'd met women before who only had one thing on their minds—what they could freely gain from somebody else. He didn't like the thought of the Jiffy Cook using his grandmother's recipes to further her career. If he had his way that would never happen. And the sooner he got her settled, the sooner she'd be rested and on her way.

"Shall we go inside? I'll see if I can find something for you to change into."

"That would be wonderful. Every girl dreams about their wedding dress, but they never realize how awkward it can be to move in."

"I couldn't even imagine."

He rushed around the truck, but by the time he got there Meg had already jumped out. Seemed she'd gotten the hang of rustling up her dress to get around. The woman certainly had an independent streak. What had convinced her to chain herself to Harold?

Love. That mythical, elusive thing women wanted so desperately to believe in. He refused to buy into hearts and Valentines. There was no such thing as undying love—at least not the romantic kind. His parents' marriage should have been proof enough for him, but he'd given it a shot and learned a brutal lesson he'd never forget.

He led Meg up the steps to the large wraparound porch. This was his favorite spot in the whole house. Weather permitting, this was where he had his mid-morning coffee, and in the evening he liked to kick back to check out the stars.

"This is really nice," she said, as though agreeing with his thoughts.

"Nothing better than unwinding and looking out over the pasture."

"You're lucky to have so much space, and this view is awesome. How big is the ranch?"

"A little more than sixteen hundred acres. Plenty of room to go trail riding."

"It's like having your own little country."

He chuckled. She'd obviously spent too much time in the city. "It's not quite that big. But it's my little piece of heaven." He moved to the door and opened it. "Ready to get out of that dress?"

Color infused her cheeks and she glanced away. He tightened his jaw, smothering his amusement over her misinterpretation of his words.

Meg kept her head down and examined the dirt-stained skirt. "Shame that all it's good for now is the garbage."

"Why would you want to keep a dress from a wedding you ran away from?"

A flicker of surprise showed in her eyes and then it was gone. "If you would show me where to go, I'll get out of your way."

"The bedrooms are upstairs."

She stepped toward the living room and peered inside. "This is so spacious. And the woodwork is beautiful."

Her compliment warmed his chest, and whatever he'd been meaning to say floated clean out of his head. This was the first time he'd shown any woman other than Gram around the house he'd helped design and build. He noticed how Meg's appreciative gaze took in the hardwood floors, the built-in bookcases and the big bay window with the windowseat.

Why in the world did her words mean so much to him? It wasn't as if they were involved and he was out to impress her. She was merely a stranger passing through his life.

"I'll show you upstairs," he said, anxious for a little distance. "I'm sure I'll have something you can change into. Might not fit, but it'll be better than all of that fluff."

"I'm sorry to put you to such bother. If you are ever in Albuquerque you should look me up. The least I can do is take you to dinner." She followed him to the staircase. "Didn't you say your grandmother is a fan of the Jiffy Cook?"

He stopped on the bottom step and turned. What was she up to? He hesitated to answer, but the twinkle in Meg's eyes drew him in. "She watches the show religiously. That's why she was thrilled to get an invite to the wedding."

"So why didn't you attend? You could have gone as her escort."

His gaze moved to the floor. "I don't do weddings."

"Is that from personal experience?"

His hands clenched. What was it with this woman, making him think about things he'd rather leave buried in the dark shadows of his mind? Refusing to reveal too much, he said, "Marriage is for dreamers and suckers. Eventually people figure out there's no happily-ever-after, but by then it's usually too late."

"You can't be serious! I've never heard such a cynical

view on marriage. And especially from someone who has never even tried it."

"Don't always have to try something to know it's a sham."

He didn't want to go any further with this conversation. He didn't want to think about the kids of those unhappy marriages that had no voice—no choice.

He turned his back and started up the stairs. Not hearing her behind him, he stopped to glance over his shoulder. She remained in the foyer and shot him a pitying look that pierced his chest.

"That's the saddest thing I've ever heard anyone say."

He knew better than to discuss romance and marriage with a woman. He'd thought a runaway bride would have a different perspective on the whole arrangement, but apparently today hadn't been enough to snuff out her foolish childhood fairytales.

"There's no such thing as Cinderella or happily-ever-after." He turned and climbed the rest of the stairs, certain she would follow him with that silly dejected look on her face as if he'd just told her there was no tooth fairy or Easter bunny.

Her heels clicked up the hardwood steps. There was a distinct stamp to her footsteps, as though she resented him pointing out the obvious to her. True, she had had a hard day, but what was he supposed to do? Lie to her? He didn't believe in romance. Plain and simple.

"Let's get you settled," he said, coming to a stop in the hallway. "Then we'll see about grabbing some chow…if you're up to it?"

"Actually, I'm feeling better now. And something to eat does sound good."

He opened the door and stepped back to let her pass.

"Is this your room?" she asked. "I don't want to put you out."

"No. Mine's at the other end of the hallway. This happens to be the only other bedroom I've gotten around to furnishing."

"You decorated this?" Her eyes opened wide as she began inspecting the green walls with the white crown molding.

"It isn't anything great, but I figured if I was going to have a shot at talking Gram into moving in here she might be persuaded by a cheerful room."

"It's definitely cheerful. You did a great job. And I just love the sleigh bed. It's so big you could get lost in it."

He nearly offered to come find her, but he caught himself in time. Apparently Meg's thoughts had roamed in the same direction as color flared in her cheeks and she refused to meet his gaze.

He smiled and propped his shoulder against the doorjamb. "This room has its own bathroom, so feel free to get cleaned up. I'll go find you something to change into. I'll be back."

"Thanks. Seems like I've been saying that a lot. But I mean it. I don't know what I'd have done if you hadn't been at the church."

One minute she was strong and standing her ground and the next she was sweet and vulnerable. She left his head spinning.

"I'll get those clothes."

He slipped into the hallway and strode to his bedroom. What in the world was he supposed to give her to wear? There really wasn't that much to her. She was quite a few inches shorter than him. And he recalled spying high heels when she lifted her dress.

Then there was her waist. She wasn't skinny, but still

none of his pants would even come close to fitting. Not even if they were cinched up with a belt. No, he'd have to think of something else.

Cash rummaged through his closet but found nothing suitable. Then he started sorting through his chest of drawers. He made sure to dig to the bottom, hoping to find something he'd forgotten about. He couldn't believe he was doing all of this for a woman who was obviously still in love with what's-his-face. Cash's hands clenched tight around the T-shirt he'd been holding.

So, if she still loved this guy, why had she run out of the church? He was tired of contemplating that question—he resolved to try again and ask her straight up what had happened. Get it out in the open. Once he understood he'd... he'd give her advice—you know, from a guy's perspective.

With a plan in mind, he grabbed a pair of drawstring shorts and a T-shirt. He knew she'd swim in them but it was the best he could do.

He returned to the guestroom and found the door shut. He rapped his knuckles against the wood. "Meg?" He waited a few seconds. Nothing. "Meg? It's me."

He didn't hear anything. Guessing she'd opted for a shower, he decided to leave the clothes on the bed before heading down to the kitchen to scrounge up some food.

With a twist of the doorknob he swung the door open and stepped inside. His gaze landed on Meg sprawled over the bed and he came to an abrupt halt. What in the world?

She was lying on her stomach in nothing more than white thigh-high stockings, a garter belt and lacy bikini panties that barely covered her creamy backside...

He swallowed hard and blinked. The sexy vision was still there. He shouldn't be here, but his feet refused to cooperate.

A soft sigh escaped her lips, snapping him from the

trance. He dropped the clothes on the cedar chest at the end of the bed and hightailed it out of the room. The image of her draped over the bed would forever be tattooed on his memory.

CHAPTER FOUR

MEGHAN SHOT UPRIGHT in bed. Something had startled her out of sleep. Her heart pounded in her chest. She shoved the flyaway strands back from her face and looked around. Where was she? Her gaze skimmed over the unfamiliar surroundings.

A knock sounded at the door. "Meg, it's dinnertime. Gram's expecting us."

The male voice was familiar. Cash. Flashes of the day's events came rushing back to her.

The wedding that would never be.

The narrow escape from the press.

Being sick on the side of the road.

And, lastly, her ride home with Cash and his grandmother.

Thanks to him she was safe. Her breath settled as the beating of her heart eased to a steady rhythm.

An insistent pounding on the door ensued. "Meg? Are you okay? If you don't answer me I'm coming in."

She glanced down at her scant bra and white lace panties. "I'm fine."

"You sure?"

"I fell asleep." She leaned over and grabbed the quilt she'd turned down earlier. With it snug over her shoulders, she was prepared in case Cash charged into the room.

"It's getting late." His deep voice rumbled through the door. "We should get moving."

Her bedraggled wedding dress lay in a heap on the floor. She never wanted to put that dress back on, but she couldn't go around wrapped in this quilt either, no matter how pretty she found the mosaic of pastel colors.

She worried at her bottom lip. Her gaze slipped to the window, where the sinking sun's rays glimmered. "But I don't have anything to wear."

"I left a few things on the cedar chest."

Relief eased the tension in her body. "Thanks. Give me five minutes to get changed."

She waited for his retreating footsteps before scrambling out from beneath the quilt. She couldn't believe she'd fallen asleep for—what? The whole afternoon? For the past couple of weeks if she hadn't been sick, she'd been tired. She wondered if it was the stress of the wedding or the baby. She pressed her hand protectively to her abdomen.

She rushed into the bathroom to wash up. When she'd finished, she stared in the mirror at her fresh-faced reflection. She had a rule about never going in public without her make-up—but that was before her life ran straight off the rails. The time had come to rethink some of those rules.

Back in the bedroom, she found the clothes where Cash had said he'd left them. Her face warmed as it dawned on her that he would have had to enter the bedroom—while she was sprawled across the bed in the lingerie she'd planned to wear on her wedding night.

The thought of the sexy giant checking her out sent a tingle of excitement zinging through her chest. A part of her wondered what he had been thinking when he realized she'd stripped down to her skivvies before sleep claimed her. Yet in the very next second a blaze of embarrassment rushed up from her chest and singed the roots of her hair—he'd seen her practically naked. Could this day get any worse?

She gave herself a mental shake and gathered the borrowed clothes. His earthy scent clung to the shirt. Her mind conjured up thoughts of the tall, muscular cowboy. If circumstances were different—if her plans were different—she wouldn't mind moving in for an up close and personal whiff of the man.

As quickly as the notion occurred to her she dismissed it. She didn't have room in her messed-up life to entertain thoughts about men. Right now she should be concentrating on more important matters, like trying to figure out her future. She had to make careful plans for the little baby growing inside her.

Not wanting to keep Cash waiting longer than necessary, she slipped on the clothes. Though the shorts and T-shirt were about five sizes too big for her, they were at least clean, and much cooler than the tattered dress she'd attempted to shove in the wastebasket.

In the bathroom, she gave her appearance a quick once-over, knowing there was no way she could make herself look good—presentable would have to do. She rushed to the top of the stairs and glanced down to where Cash was pacing in the foyer. His handsome face was creased as though he were deep in thought—probably about how soon she'd be gone from his life.

Her empty stomach rumbled. After only some juice and toast early that morning, her body was running on empty. She started down the steps.

Cash stopped and turned but didn't speak. She paused on the bottom step as his intense perusal of her outfit made her stomach flutter. Was he remembering what he'd seen upstairs when she'd been sleeping? For a moment she wondered if he'd liked the view.

She forced a tentative smile. "Ready to eat?"

He didn't return her friendly gesture. In fact, his face lacked any visible emotion. "I've been ready."

"Do you always eat at your grandmother's?"

He shifted his weight. "With it just being me here, and Gram all alone, I like to keep tabs on her. Sharing meals allows me to make sure she's okay without it seeming like I'm checking up on her. Speaking of which, we'd best get a move on."

Meghan glanced down and wiggled her freshly manicured, pink-painted toes. "I don't have any shoes."

He sighed. "Wait here. I think I have something that'll work."

She couldn't imagine what he'd have that would fit her size seven feet. A glance at his impressive cowboy boots confirmed her feet would be lost in anything he wore.

When Cash returned from the kitchen he was toting a couple of large bags. He stopped in front of her and dropped them at her feet. "Take a look in those."

Confused, she peeked inside, finding both bags full of clothes of varying colors. "I don't understand. Where did these come from?"

"This afternoon Gram needed some stuff in town. So while you were napping I drove her. We picked up some essentials. Whatever doesn't fit can be returned or exchanged."

Her mouth gaped. She wasn't used to such generosity. Harold had always been a stickler for keeping their expenses separate. At first she'd found it strange, but she didn't mind paying her own way. In fact she'd soon learned she liked being self-reliant and the freedom that came with it.

"But I can't accept these," she protested.

Cash frowned. "Why not?"

"I don't have any money to pay you back…at least not on me."

"It's okay. I can afford it."

She shook her head. "I didn't mean that. It's just you hardly know me and you've already opened your home up to me. I can't have you buying me clothes too."

His brow arched. "Are you sure that's the only reason? After all, they aren't designer fashions."

"I'm not a snob. Just because I'm on television doesn't mean I'm uppity—"

"Fine." He held up his palms to stop her litany. "Consider this a loan. You can pay me back when you get home."

The idea appealed to her. She really didn't have too many options. "It's a deal."

She bent down and dug through the bag until her fingers wrapped around a pair of bubblegum-colored flip-flops. A little big for her, but it didn't matter. They fit well enough and they'd be cool in this heat. Double win.

Outside, he held open the truck door for her. She really wanted to walk and enjoy the fresh air and scenery but, recalling they were running late, she didn't mention it. Suddenly her plans to flee this ranch as soon as possible didn't seem quite so urgent. This little bit of heaven was like a soothing balm on her frazzled nerves. In fact Cash was making her feel right at home.

The bumps on the way to his grandmother's house didn't bother her so much this time, and thankfully it didn't kick up her nausea. She was feeling better after that nap. Amazing how sleep could make a new person out of you.

Cash pulled to a stop and turned to her. "Before you go inside, I know you're a fancy cook and all, but my grandmother is a simple woman with simple tastes. She's proud of her abilities. Don't make her feel bad if her food isn't up to your TV standards."

It hurt that he'd immediately assumed she'd be snooty about dinner. She might be on TV, but she loved home-cooking the same as the next guy.

Heck, if Cash knew she was pregnant and the father had dumped her on her keester, he probably wouldn't worry so much. However, she had no intention of telling him her little secret. He'd already witnessed her at her lowest point—she wasn't about to confirm that her entire life was completely out of control.

"I'd never say or do anything to upset your grand-mother. I'm very grateful for her kindness."

"You swear?"

She blinked. He didn't trust her? "I promise."

He eyed her, as if to discern if she were on the level. Apparently she passed his test because he climbed out of the truck and she met him on the sidewalk.

The fact he didn't trust her without even giving her a chance bothered her. Why did he seem so wary of her? Because she was on television? What did he have against TV personalities? Or was it something else?

She most likely wouldn't be here long enough to fig-ure it out. After she'd had something to eat she'd think up her next move. Yet it made her cringe to think of facing her mother and telling her that she was pregnant and the father didn't want her or the baby.

Cash trailed Meg into his grandmother's house. Even the sweet sashay of her rounded backside wasn't enough to loosen the unease in his chest. In fact it made the discom-fort worse.

His mind filled with visions of her bare limbs sprawled across the bed while her assets were barely covered with the sheerest material. It'd taken every bit of willpower to

quietly back out of the room and shut the door. No woman
had a right to look that tantalizing without even trying.

He couldn't believe he was letting her get to him. He
thought he'd become immune to feminine charms. Take
them or leave them had been his motto. And the way this
little redhead could distract him with her shapely curves
and heart-stopping smile were sure signs he should leave
her alone.

"Remember what we talked about," he said.

"I'm not a child. You don't have to keep reminding
me—like I'd *ever* be so rude."

"Good."

He followed her up the steps to the porch. He wanted to
believe Meg, but he'd been lied to by his straight-faced ex-
girlfriend. In his experience, when women wanted something badly enough they could be sneaky and deceptive.
Now he preferred to err on the side of caution.

After all, Gram had been preparing for this meal ever
since they'd returned from town. It'd only take one wrong
look or word from the Jiffy Cook, his grandmother's favorite television celebrity, and Gram would be crushed.

Cash rapped his knuckles on the door of the modest
four-room house before opening it and stepping inside.
"Gram, we're here. And, boy, does something smell good."

His grandmother came rushing out of the kitchen wearing a stained apron, wiping her hands on a towel. "Good. I
threw together a new dish. I hope you both like it."

"I'm starved," Meg said.

"Okay, you two go wash up. Cash can show you to the
bathroom."

He nodded, then led the way. In silence, they lathered
up. Even standing next to her, doing the most mundane
thing, he couldn't relax. Every time he glanced her way
he started mentally undressing her until she had nothing

on but that sheer white underwear. His throat tightened and he struggled to swallow.

What was wrong with him? He barely even knew her, and he had absolutely no intention of starting up anything. His focus needed to be on rebuilding this ranch, not day-dreaming about a brief fling with the tempting redhead next to him.

Back in the kitchen, Gram said, "I'll warn you—dinner's nothing special."

Cash held back a chuckle at his grandmother's attempt to downplay this meal. He wished she'd made one of her tried-and-true dishes instead of taking a chance on something new to impress their guest. But no matter what it tasted like he would smile and shovel it in.

"What did you make?" Meg asked.

"I tried something a little different. I was hoping for your opinion."

"My opinion?" Meg pressed a hand to her chest and the light glittered off the rock on her ring finger. The wedding dress might be gone, but the impressive engagement ring remained. Obviously she wasn't quite through with what's-his-name.

"You're the expert."

Remembering his manners, he pulled out a chair for Meg. Having absolutely nothing to add to this conversation, he quietly took his usual seat.

"I'm no expert." Sincerity rang out in Meg's voice. "I just cook and I hope other people will like the same things as me."

"I'll let you in on a little secret," Gram said, leaning her head toward Meg. "I watch your show every day and I jot down the recipes I think Cash will like."

Meg leaned toward Gram and lowered her voice. "And does he like them?"

Cash wasn't so sure he liked these two women putting their heads together to discuss him. "You two *do* remember that I'm in the room, right?"

"Of course we do." Gram sent him a playful look. "Yes, he likes them."

So now he understood why he'd been eating some strange dishes for the past year—Gram had been imitating Meg. Interesting. But he still preferred Gram's traditional recipes, such as homemade vegetable barley soup and her hearty beef stew.

"Dinner isn't quite ready," Gram said. "The shopping today put me a little behind. I have some fresh bread in the oven, and I have to add the tortellini to the soup."

"Anything I can help with?" Cash offered, as he did at each meal.

Usually she waved him off, but today she said, "Yes, you could get us some drinks."

"Drinks?" Their standard fare normally consisted of some tap water. On really hot, miserable days they added ice for something special.

"Yes. I picked up some soda and juice at the store." Gram turned to Meg. "I'm sure you're probably used to something fancy with your meals, like champagne or wine, but I'm afraid we're rather plain around here. If you want something we don't have I'll have Cash pick it up for you the next time he's in town."

"That won't be necessary. You've already been too generous with the clothes. Thank you for being so thoughtful."

"I didn't know what you would wear, and Cash wasn't much help."

"I haven't had a chance to go through them." Pink tinged her cheeks. "I slept longer this afternoon than I'd planned…well, I hadn't planned to go to sleep at all."

"I'm sure you were worn out after such a terrible day. You poor child."

"You can help yourself to drinks," Cash said, trying to offset his grandmother's mollycoddling.

"Oh, no, she can't. She's our guest. You can serve her."

Cash swallowed down his irritation. The last thing in the world he'd wanted to do was upset his grandmother.

Gram and Meg discussed the Jiffy Cook's show while he kept himself busy. He opened the cabinet and sorted through a stack of deep bowls, trying to find ones that weren't chipped on the edges. He'd never noticed their worn condition before today. A sense of guilt settled over him like a dense fog. He'd been too focused on the rodeo circuit and hadn't paid enough attention to the small things at home. He made a mental note to get his grandmother some new dishes.

When Gram turned her back to check on the bread in the oven Meg held out her hands for the bowls. Cash handed them over. No need to stand on ceremony. It wasn't as if she was an invited guest or anything. He had no idea why Gram was treating the woman like some sort of royalty—even if her burnt-orange curls, the splattering of freckles across the bridge of her nose and the intense green eyes *were* fit for a princess.

He gathered the various items they'd need for dinner and laid them on the edge of the table. When he turned around he found Meg had set everything out accordingly. Maybe she wasn't as spoiled as he'd imagined.

Again the light caught the diamond on her hand and it sparkled, serving as a reminder of how much she liked nice things—expensive things. And, more importantly, that she was a woman who didn't take off her engagement ring after calling off the wedding—a woman with lingering feelings for her intended groom.

Cash's jaw tightened. Best not get used to having her around. After dinner he'd drive her wherever she needed to go.

Gram stirred the pot and set aside the spoon. "These are a couple of recipes that I pulled from one of my new cookbooks. Don't know how they'll turn out. If nothing else, the bread is tried and true. Cash can attest to how good it is."

"You bet. Gram makes the best fresh-baked bread in the entire county. With a dab of fresh-churned butter it practically melts in your mouth."

"You don't have to sell me on it." A smile lit up Meg's eyes. "I had a whiff of it when she opened the oven. I can't wait to eat."

"Well, if you're hungry we can start with the salad." Gram hustled over to the fridge and removed three bowls with baby greens, halved grape tomatoes and rings of red onion. "This is the first time I've made blue cheese and bacon dressing from scratch."

"Sounds good to me," Meg said. "But you know you didn't have to make anything special. Your usual recipes would have been fine."

"But those dishes aren't good enough for a professional chef."

"I'm not a chef. Just a cook—like you. And I'm sure your salad will be delicious."

Gram turned back to the fridge and pulled out a plastic-wrapped measuring cup. She moved it to the table before retrieving the whisk from the counter. In an instant she had the dressing unwrapped and was stirring the creamy mixture. Cash's mouth began to water. Okay, so maybe Gram didn't have to go to all this trouble, but he had to admit some of her experiments turned out real well, and this dinner was slated to get star ratings.

Cash passed the first bowl to Meg. He noticed how

the smile slid from her face. And her eyes were huge as she stared at the salad. He wanted to tell her to drown it in black pepper—anything so she would eat it. With his grandmother by his side, he was limited to an imploring stare.

For some reason he hadn't thought a chef—or, as she called herself, a *cook*—would be opposed to blue cheese. Was it his grandmother's recipe? Had Gram made some big cooking blunder?

"Eat up, everyone." Gram smiled and sat across the table from him. "There's more if anyone wants seconds."

He immediately filled his fork and shoveled it in his mouth. The dressing was bold, just the way he liked it. But *his* impression wasn't the one that counted tonight. He cast Meg a worried glance. He couldn't let this meal fall apart. He moved his foot under the table and poked Meg's leg.

"Ouch!" Gram said. "Cash, what are you doing? Sit still."

"Sorry," he mumbled. "This is really good."

"Thank you." Gram's face lit up.

It was Meg's turn to chime in, but she didn't. Her fork hovered over the bowl. *Eat a bite,* he willed her. *Just take a bite and praise my grandmother.*

"Excuse me." Meg's chair scraped over the wood floor and like a shot she was out of the room.

Cash inwardly groaned as he watched her run away. He turned back to find disappointment glinting in his grandmother's eyes. It didn't matter what he said now, the meal was ruined. Meg had gone and broken her word to him.

His fingers tightened around the fork. He should have listened to the little voice in his head that said not to trust a spoiled celebrity—one who hadn't even seen fit to stick around for her own wedding.

CHAPTER FIVE

A SPLASH OF cold water soothed Meghan's flushed cheeks but did nothing to ease her embarrassment. She was utterly mortified about her mad dash from the dinner table. One minute she'd felt fine, but after the stern warning from Cash to enjoy the dinner and his constant stares her stomach had twisted into a gigantic knot. The whiff of blue cheese had been her final undoing.

"Thank you for being so understanding," Meghan said, accepting a towel from Cash's grandmother.

"I've been there, child. I remember it as if it were yesterday. I was sick as a dog when I was carrying Cash's father."

"But I'm not—"

Martha silenced her with a knowing look. "Honey, there's no point trying to close the gate when the horse is obviously out of the corral."

There was no sense carrying on the charade. Meghan sank down on the edge of the large clawfoot tub. "I wanted to keep the news to myself for now. It's the main reason I'm here. The thought of being a single mother scares me, and I need a plan before I go home."

Martha patted her hand. "I won't say a word to anyone. And you can stay here as long as you need."

"But Cash—"

"Don't worry about him. He's gruff on the outside but he's a softy on the inside."

"I don't know… He already thinks I'm spoiled and self-centered. I can't tell him about the baby and have him thinking I'm irresponsible too."

"Give my grandson another chance. He can be extremely generous and thoughtful."

To those he loves, Meghan silently added. She admired the way he looked after his grandmother. Everyone should have someone in their life who cared that much.

Where she was concerned he wasn't so generous. She was an outsider. Although she had to admit he had willingly opened his home to her, and for that she was grateful.

Feeling better, Meghan agreed to try a little of the soup. Martha looked pleased with the idea and rushed off to dish some up for her.

Meghan moved to the mirror and inspected her blotchy complexion. She looked awful and she didn't feel much better. No one had ever warned her being pregnant would feel like having a bad case of the flu. She groaned. Or was it a case of overwrought nerves? The pressure and warning looks from Cash had made her entire body tense.

She shrugged and turned away. Either way, she'd gone back on her word to him and ruined the dinner. How in the world would she make it up to him?

She eased out of the bathroom and found him pacing in the living room. "I'm really sorry about that."

His brows drew together and he gave her a once-over. "You feeling better?"

She nodded, but didn't elaborate.

"Good. But you should have told me you still didn't feel well. I wouldn't have dragged you to dinner. I would have explained it to my grandmother."

Meghan eyed him. Was this the cowboy's way of apologizing for those death stares at the dinner table? The tension in her stomach eased. Something told her apologies, even awkward ones, didn't come easily to him.

"Apology accepted. But I was feeling fine and then it just hit me at once. I told Martha I would try a little broth and bread. Have you finished eating?"

"No."

"Sorry for disturbing everyone's dinner. If you want, we can try again."

On her way back to the kitchen her gaze roamed over the house, admiring all the old pieces of oak furnishing. Everything was in its place, but a layer of dust was growing thick. Definitely not the perfect home appearance her mother had instilled in Meghan. Her mother had insisted that the perfect house led to the perfect life and the perfect future. This motto had been drilled into her as a child. If only life was that easy.

She worried about how she'd scar her own child. How in the world would she instill confidence in them? Especially when she struggled daily with the confidence to follow her own dreams?

"You sure you're okay?" Cash asked just outside the kitchen.

"Yes, I'm fine."

She really should level with him about her pregnancy, but she couldn't bring herself to broach the subject. She didn't want him to look down at her—a single woman, dumped at the altar by her baby's daddy as if he was tossing out a carton of sour milk.

Definitely not up for defending herself, she stuck with her decision to keep her condition to herself. Besides, it was none of his business. Soon she'd be gone and their paths most likely would never cross again.

With Cash acting friendly, Meghan relaxed and savored

every drop of the delicious broth. She even finished every morsel of the thick slice of buttered bread. "That was delicious. I'd love to have more, but I don't think I should push my luck."

"Still not feeling a hundred percent?" Cash asked, concern reflected in his eyes.

The fact he genuinely seemed worried about her came as a surprise. "Not exactly. Would you believe I'm ready to go back to sleep again?"

He didn't say a word. Instead he kept his head lowered, as though it took all his concentration to slather butter on a slice of bread.

Martha reached out and patted her hand. "Cash can run you back to the house so you can rest."

His head immediately lifted. Deep frown lines bracketed his eyes and lips.

"I don't want to overstay my welcome," Meghan said. She wasn't sure what alternatives she had, but she'd come up with something. "If you could just give me a lift to the closest town."

Was that a flicker of relief that she saw reflected in his eyes? She'd thought they'd made peace with each other, but perhaps she'd been mistaken.

As though oblivious to the undercurrent of tension, his grandmother continued. "Nonsense. You barely made it through dinner. You're in no condition to go home and face those reporters. Cash knows all about how merciless they can be. Isn't that right, Cash?"

His blank stare shifted between his grandmother and herself. He merely nodded before dunking his bread in the remaining soup in his bowl.

Meghan couldn't stay where she wasn't wanted. If Cash wouldn't set his grandmother straight she'd have to do it herself. "But I can't…"

Martha's steady gaze caught hers. The woman quietly shook her head and silenced her protest. Maybe the woman had a point. Stress definitely exacerbated the unease in her stomach. But if Cash didn't want her, where would she spend the night? She'd already eyed up Martha's small couch with its uneven cushions. Her back hurt just from looking at it.

"So how long can you stay?" Martha asked.

"I do have two weeks of vacation time planned. It was supposed to be for my honeymoon."

"Well, there you have it. Plenty of time to rest up. We'll make your stay here as pleasant as possible." Martha got to her feet. "Cash can drive you back to his place."

Cash looked none too happy with his grandmother's meddling. "I will as soon as the kitchen is straightened up."

This wasn't right. She didn't want them going out of their way for her. "I'll stay on one condition."

His brow arched. "And what would that be?"

"I refuse to be waited on. I want to do my share—starting with cleaning the dinner dishes."

He shrugged. "Fine by me. I don't have time to wait on you with a ranch to run."

She nodded, understanding that he had his hands full. "I think your grandmother should go in the living room and put up her feet after she's slaved away all afternoon making this fantastic meal."

The older woman's gaze moved back and forth between her and her grandson. Meghan braced herself for an argument. She might be down and out right now, but that didn't mean she was utterly pathetic and in need of being waited on hand and foot.

"Thank you." Martha started for the doorway. "There's a classic movie on tonight and I don't want to miss it."

The woman slipped off her sunflower-covered apron and hustled out of the room without a backward glance.

Cash's gray eyes filled with concern. "Do you think she's okay?"

"I don't really know her, but she seems okay to me. Why do you ask?"

"It's not like her to leave the work to others. She's normally a very stubborn woman who won't rest until the house is in order."

During the meal, Meghan had noticed the kitchen needed some sprucing up, and the windows needed to be wiped down inside and out. Maybe his grandmother needed some help around the place. A plan formed in her mind as to how she could carry her weight while at the Tumbling Weed and keep from dwelling too much on her problems.

"Maybe she figured there was enough help in the kitchen and she wasn't needed. I wouldn't worry. Just be glad she's taking a moment to rest. She deserves it."

"She certainly does. I've tried to get her to slow down for years now, but instead I think she does more. Heck, a lot of days she invites the ranch hands to the house for lunch. And then she fights with me when I insist on helping with the clean-up. And when any of the neighbors need a helping hand she's the first to volunteer, whether it's to cook for another family or to care for a sick person."

"Your grandmother is amazing. I wish I still had my grandmothers, but one died before I was born and the other passed on when I was in grade school."

"Gram is definitely a force to be reckoned with. Maybe you can help keep an eye on her while you're here? Make sure there's nothing wrong? As you can tell, I'm not good at reading women. I had no idea that you were still sick."

He glanced down, avoiding her stare. "I thought you didn't like my grandmother's cooking."

She glanced over her shoulder to make sure they were alone and then lowered her voice so as not to be overheard. "Actually, I was going to suggest that I could earn my keep by being housekeeper and helping with the cooking. I'm thinking it's been a while since your grandmother's house has been washed top to bottom, so I could clean here. It would give me something to do all day."

"I don't know."

She pursed her lips together and counted to ten. "I'm not some spoiled actress. I'm a local television cook. Period. I still do everything for myself."

He stepped closer. "Then I'd say you have yourself a job. Do as much as Gram will let you."

With him standing right in front of her, she was forced to crane her neck to meet his gaze. When he wasn't scowling at her he really was quite handsome, with those slate-gray eyes, a prominent nose, stubble layering his tanned cheeks and a squared jaw.

And then there was his mouth. She found herself staring at his lips, wondering what his kisses would be like. Short and sweet? Or long and spicy? When his mouth bowed into a smile she lifted her gaze and realized she'd been busted. She grew uncomfortably warm, but she didn't let on.

This was a way to earn her keep and extend her time here, allowing her a chance to think. She liked the idea. This way she wouldn't feel indebted to the sexy cowboy who made her feel a little off-center when he stood so close to her—like he was doing now.

The next morning Meghan awoke to a knock. Had she slept in again? Her eyes fluttered open and she sat up in bed to find herself surrounded by darkness.

It was still the middle of the night. What in the world was going on?

"Cash, is that you?"

"Who else were you expecting?"

"No one." She yawned and stretched, enjoying the comfort of the big bed. "It must be the middle of the night."

"It won't be dark for long. You planning to sleep the day away?"

"The day? The sun hasn't even climbed out of bed."

"It'll be up before you know it. That's why a rancher has to get an early jump on the day."

Meghan groaned. "Fine. I'll be downstairs in a half hour."

"Ten minutes, tops."

"Ten?" she screeched before scrambling out of bed. The coldness from the bare wood floor seeped up her legs and shocked her sluggish body to life.

She didn't care what he said. She was getting a shower. Otherwise there was no way she'd make it through the day. She rushed into a hot steamy shower before sorting out a pair of blue jeans and a T-shirt, both of which were a little big. She supposed in her current condition that was a good thing. She pressed her hand to her almost non-existent baby bump. Shortly after she returned home she'd most likely be getting herself a whole new wardrobe—*maternity clothes, here I come.*

The assortment of supplies in the bag was quite extensive. Meghan located a hairbrush and ponytail holders. She made quick use of them, pulling her unruly curls back. Without worrying about her lack of make-up, she ran downstairs.

Cash reached for the doorknob. "It's about time."

"I hurried," she protested, still feeling a bit damp from

her shower. "Especially considering it's the middle of the night."

He chuckled, warming her insides. "Hardly. Gram probably already has breakfast started."

"Well, then, lead the way. We don't want to keep her waiting." And she had a job to do—a means to earn her keep.

"Are you feeling better this morning?"

"Much better. The sleep really helped."

He studied her. "Your stomach is okay?"

She nodded, touched by his concern. "In fact I'm ravenous. Now, quit with the overprotective act and get moving."

He grinned at her. "Yes, ma'am."

Her empty stomach did a somersault. How could his smile do such crazy things to her insides? She refused to dwell on its meaning as she rushed to the pickup. The short ride to Martha's house was quiet. Without caffeine, Meghan lacked the energy to make idle chitchat, even though Cash's mood appeared to have improved.

When he pulled to a stop in front of the steps leading to his grandmother's house Meghan glanced over to him. "Aren't you coming inside?"

"Later. Right now I have the animals to tend to."

"But don't you need something in your stomach?"

"I had a mug of stiff black coffee while I waited for you." He patted his stomach and rubbed. "It's the fuel this cowboy runs on."

Meghan scrunched up her nose. "I never learned how to drink that stuff straight up. I always add milk and sugar."

"Gram should have everything you need to make yourself a cup. I'll see you soon. Remember our deal."

"I won't forget. Your grandmother is my first priority." She didn't want to think about her other priorities—

not at this unseemly hour. "Maybe later I can help you in the barn."

"And break those pretty nails? I don't think so."

She held out her hands and for the first time noticed she was still wearing Harold's ring. She wanted to rip it from her finger and toss it out the window, but instead she balled up her hands and stuffed them back in her lap. Disposing of the ring now would only evoke a bunch of questions from Cash—questions she didn't want to answer.

"My nails aren't long. They can't be. Remember I'm a cook?"

"Long or short, you weren't born and bred to this kind of work. A pampered star like yourself will be much better off in the kitchen with my grandmother."

"I'm not pampered."

She pursed her lips together. She didn't like being told what she could and couldn't do. Harold had told her she needed to be a television personality because she was too pretty to hide in some kitchen. Looking back now, she wondered if he hadn't pushed her into taking the television spot, if she'd have chosen that career path for herself. Her love had always been for the creative side of cooking, and it rubbed her the wrong way to have recipes provided for her merely to demonstrate.

"I'll bet I can keep up with you in the barn," she said. Her pricked ego refused to back down.

He raised his cowboy hat. "You think so, huh?"

"I do."

Humor reflected in his eyes. "Maybe we'll put you to the test, but right now you're needed in the kitchen."

"I know. I haven't forgotten our deal. But that doesn't mean it's the only thing I can do."

She hopped out of the truck and sent the door swinging shut. With her hands clenched, she marched up the walk.

Just because she hadn't been fortunate enough to be born into such a beautiful ranch with dozens of horses, it didn't mean she couldn't learn her way around the place.

The time had come to prove to herself that she could stand on her own two feet. With a baby on the way, she needed to know she could handle whatever challenges life threw at her.

If earning her keep meant cleaning up after this cowboy and his horses, she'd do it. After all, it couldn't be that hard—could it?

CHAPTER SIX

CASH SAT ASTRIDE Emperor, a feisty black stallion, as the mid-morning sun beat down on his back. He brought the stallion to a stop in the center of the small arena. He'd spent a good part of the morning working with this horse in preparation for its new owner.

The stallion lowered his head, yanking on the reins. Cash urged the horse forward, which in turn raised Emperor's head, allowing him to retain his hold on the reins. Cash's injured shoulder started to throb, but he refused to quit. This horse was smart and beautiful. He just needed to remember who was the boss.

They started circling the arena again. The horse's hooves thudded against the dry earth, kicking up puffs of dirt that trailed them around the small arena. With the horse at last following directions, Cash's thoughts strayed back to the redhead with the curvy figure. It wasn't the first time she'd stumbled into his thoughts. In fact she was on his mind more than he wanted to admit.

"Nice horse. Can I ride him?"

The lyrical chime of a female voice roused him from his thoughts. Cash slowed Emperor to a stop and turned. He immediately noticed Meg's pink and white cowboy hat—the one he'd picked out for her. She looked so cute—too cute for his own comfort.

She wouldn't be classified as skinny, which suited him just fine. When he pulled a woman into his arms he liked to feel more than skin and bones. But she wasn't overweight either. She was someplace between the two—someplace he'd call perfect.

His pulse climbed. All he could envision was wrapping his arms around her and seeing if her lips were as soft as they appeared.

Meghan rested her hands on the fence rail. "After that challenge you threw down this morning about how I couldn't be a cowgirl because I wasn't born on a ranch, I came to prove you wrong."

He couldn't help but chuckle at the fierce determination reflected in her green eyes. This woman was certainly a little spitfire. And at the same time he found her to be a breath of fresh air.

"You wouldn't want to ride Emperor. He can be a handful. If you're serious, I'll find you a gentler mount." He turned Emperor loose in the pasture and joined her by the fence. "But what about our arrangement? Shouldn't you be helping my grandmother?"

"I did. After we cleaned up the breakfast dishes I ran the vacuum, even though Martha complained the entire time about how she could do it all herself. And then I dusted—before your grandmother shooed me out of the house, insisting her morning cooking shows were coming on and she didn't want to be disturbed. I'll go back and do more later."

"My grandmother does like her routines."

Meg climbed up and perched on the white rail fence. Her left hand brushed his arm as she got settled. He noticed something was different about her, but he couldn't quite figure it out—then it dawned on him. She'd taken off the flashy diamond. The urge to question her about the missing ring hovered at the back of his throat but he swallowed down his curiosity—it shouldn't matter to him.

"The horse you were riding is a beauty. You're lucky to own him."

"He isn't mine."

Her brows lifted. "He isn't?"

"No. I train horses and sell them. So technically he's mine, but only until the buyer shows up later this week to collect him."

"That must be tough. Spending so much time with the horses and then having to part with them."

He shrugged. "It's a way of life I've grown up around. You have to keep your emotions at bay when it comes to business. Now, don't get me wrong. I have my own horses and there's no way I'd part with *them*. They're family."

"I've heard about men and their horses." She eyed him speculatively.

"Yep, we're thick as thieves."

"Are you up for that ride now?" she asked.

Her jean-clad thigh had settled within an inch of his arm. It'd be so easy to turn around and nestle up between her thighs. He'd pull her close and then he'd steal a kiss from this woman whose image in lacy lingerie still taunted his thoughts.

What in the world was he thinking? He bowed his head and gave it a shake, clearing the ridiculous thoughts. It was then that he noticed her old cowboy boots. His grandmother must have lent them to her. He considered explaining how he needed to keep on working, but he liked her company—even if it were purely platonic—and he didn't want her to leave quite yet.

"I'll give you a quick tour of the ranch."

She leveled him a direct stare and then a smile tugged at those sweet lips. "I already like what I've seen."

His heart rammed into his windpipe. Meg's eyes filled with merriment as her smile broadened. Was she flirting with him? Impossible. She was only being friendly. After all, she was still hung up on what's-his-name. And that was for the best.

Cash cleared his throat, anxious to change the conversation to a safer subject. "We'll start here. This is the arena where I do a lot of work with the horses. And over there—" he pointed to an area behind the barn "—is a smaller corral where we break in the young ones."

"Can I watch you sometime?"

"Sure." He longed to show her some of his skills. He cleared his throat. "And this way leads to the barn."

Out of habit, he worked his sore shoulder in a circular motion. The persistent dull ache was still there—it was always there, sometimes better and sometimes worse. Right now it was a bit better.

"When did you hurt your shoulder?" Meg asked as she rushed to catch up with him.

He didn't like talking about that time in his life. When he'd been discharged from the hospital he'd made tracks, putting miles between him and the press. All he'd wanted to do was forget the whole scene and the events that had led up to his accident. And it wasn't something he wanted to delve into with this television personality. Sure, she was just a cook, and highly unlikely to be able to use any of the information he gave her, but she was closely linked to people who would love a chance to revisit the scandal. After all, it wasn't as if it was ancient history. It'd only happened a little more than three months ago.

He carefully chose his words. "It happened at my last rodeo in Austin."

"You're a rodeo cowboy?" A note of awe rang out in her voice.

"Not anymore. I walked away from it a few months back."

"Did your decision have something to do with your shoulder?"

He shrugged. "Maybe a little."

"What happened?"

"I made good time out of the gate, but the steer I drew stumbled during the takedown and we hit the ground together. Hard. I landed on my shoulder at exactly the wrong angle."

"Ouch." Meg winced. "Shouldn't you be resting and letting it heal?"

"I did rest after the surgery."

"Surgery? What did they have to do?"

"Pop a pin in to hold everything together. Not a big deal." He knew guys with far worse injuries, but it was best not to mention that to Meg. "I did my stint in rehab and now I'm back on horseback."

"I can't imagine loving something so much that you would take such risks."

"Don't you love being in front of the cameras, cooking up something new for your fans?"

Seconds passed, as though she were trying to make up her mind. "The fans are great. It's the rest of it that gets old. Watching what I eat because the camera puts fifteen pounds on me is pure drudgery. And it's frustrating being told what will and what won't be in each segment instead of having a voice in the show's content."

"I thought the stars were in charge?"

She shook her head. "Maybe if you're Paula Deen or Rachael Ray, but not for some no-name on a local network."

So she wasn't as big a star as his grandmother had built her up to be? Interesting. He wondered what else he had got wrong about her.

"If you were no longer a television personality, what would you do with your life?"

She paused and stared at him. Their gazes locked and his heart thump-thumped in his chest. His eyes dipped to her lips. What would it be like to kiss her? Maybe if he swooped in for a little smooch then he'd realize his imagination had blown her appeal way out of proportion.

"I...I don't know." Pink tinged her cheeks.

Could she read his mind? Was she having the same heady thoughts? Would it be so wrong to steal a kiss?

She glanced away. "Right now I'm rethinking everything. With my marriage being off, my life is about to take a very different direction, and I have to start planning what I'm going to do next."

The reminder of her almost-wedding washed away his errant desire to kiss her. She'd already run out on the guy she'd promised to marry—she was the kind of woman who'd let a man down without a second thought. And he didn't need someone like that in his life.

In no time at all Meghan was sitting astride Cinnamon, a gentle mare. Cash led her on a brief tour of the Tumbling Weed. She couldn't help but admire all the beautiful horses in the meadow, but it was the cowboy at her side that gave her the greatest pause. With his squared chin held high and his broad shoulders pulled back, he gave off a definite air of confidence. She couldn't help but admire the way he moved, as if he were one with the horse.

"Tell me a little about yourself," Cash said.

"You don't want to hear about me. You'd be bored senseless."

"Consider it part of you getting the job. After all, there'd normally be some sort of interview where I'd get to know at least the broad strokes of your life."

He had a point. If *she* had a stranger working and living with her, she'd want some background information too. But opening up about herself and her family didn't come easily to her.

Her mother had taught her to hide their family flaws and shortcomings from the light of day. And never, ever to let the man in your life know of them—not if you wanted to plan a future with him. Meghan had foolishly followed that advice with Harold and held so much of herself back. As a result they'd had a very superficial relationship.

She never wanted that to happen again. If a man was to love her, he had to see her just as she was—blemishes and all.

But that didn't make revealing her imperfections any less scary. Thankfully she could take her first plunge into honesty with a man she had no intention of getting romantically entangled with.

"Let's see—you already know I'm a professional cook. I grew up in Lomas, New Mexico. I have two younger sisters. And my parents were married almost thirty years before my father died of cancer this past winter."

"Are you close to your family?"

The easy answer teetered on the tip of her tongue, but she bit it back. The point was to learn to open up about herself. "The family splintered apart after my father died. Since I'm the oldest, I know it falls to me to keep everyone together. But too much happened too fast and I...I failed."

Seconds passed before Cash said, "I don't know about your particular situation, but in my experience I've learned some families are better off apart."

Sadness smothered her as the truth of his words descended over her. She didn't want that to be true of her family. But, more than that, she wondered what he'd lived through to come to such a dismal conclusion.

She wanted to ask. She wanted to offer him some hope. But she couldn't let herself get drawn into his problems when she had so many of her own.

Instead, she changed the subject. "How many horses do you have?"

"Fifty-one. I aim to have close to a hundred when all is said and done."

"That's a lot."

"Sure is. But with thousands of cowboys roaming through the West, and the right sort of advertising, I'm thinking soon I'll have more business than I can handle."

"Do you have a business plan?" She was curious to know if a cowboy could also have a mind for business.

"I do. Why do you ask?"

"Just curious. So, do you advertise?" She almost blurted out that she'd never heard of the Tumbling Weed before yesterday, but she caught herself in time.

"I have a website, and I've taken out ads in various publications, but the best form of advertising by far is word of mouth."

So he knew his stuff. She was impressed. She had a feeling that some day soon everyone in the Southwest would know of the Tumbling Weed.

"But don't you get lonely out here by yourself?"

A muscle in his cheek twitched. "Not at all. There are ranch hands to talk to and there's always Gram."

"But what about…?" Meghan bit down on her bottom lip, holding back her intrusive question.

"You surely aren't going to ask me about my social life, are you?"

Heat blazed in her cheeks. "Sorry. None of my business. An occupational hazard."

His dark brows rose, disappearing beneath the brim of his Stetson. "Do you interview people on your show?"

"Sometimes. It's always fun to have local celebrities on as guests. I really shouldn't have pried into your private life. I was just trying to get to know you."

"If it makes you feel better, I don't have a girlfriend or anyone special. I'm not into serious relationships."

His answer put her at ease. However, the fact that his status mattered to her at all was worrisome. He was her temporary boss—nothing more. As a single expectant mother, she didn't have any right to notice a man—even if he *was* a drop-dead sexy cowboy.

Tuesday's late-morning sunshine rained down on Meghan, warming her skin and raising her spirits. She had come to anticipate her daily walks to Martha's house. It provided her with a chance to stretch her legs and inhale the sweet fresh air. At this moment her problems didn't seem insurmountable. She could…no, she *would* conquer them.

Upon reaching Martha's place, she knocked on the door. From the beginning, Martha had insisted she not stand on formalities and let herself in, so Meghan eased open the door and stepped inside, finding the house surprisingly quiet.

"Hello? Martha? I'm here to help with lunch," she said loudly, in case her dear friend hadn't heard the knock. "I also have a question for you—"

The words died on her lips when she stepped into the kitchen and found it vacant. A closer inspection revealed lunch hadn't been started, which was quite unlike Martha, who always stayed a step ahead of everyone. Meghan's stomached tightened into a hard lump.

Please don't let anything have happened to her.

A search of the remainder of the house turned up nothing. Where in the world had she gone? Martha hadn't mentioned anything at breakfast. This just didn't make sense.

On her way out the door Meghan noticed a folded piece of paper propped up on the kitchen table. Her name had been scrawled across the front. She grasped the page and started to read.

Meg,

Sorry to leave in such a rush. Amy Santiago just gave birth to triplets and is having complications. She has no family in town, so I'm going to stay with them until their relatives arrive in a few days. Cash will make sure you have everything you need.

See you soon.
Martha

Meghan refolded the paper and slid it in her pocket. She couldn't help but wonder if this would change things with Cash. Would he want her to stay on? Or would this be the perfect excuse for him to send her packing?

CHAPTER SEVEN

"What do you mean, Gram's gone?"

Cash's spine straightened as every muscle in his body tensed. Why would Gram disappear without talking to him? Had it been an emergency? His chest tightened.

"You didn't know?" Meg asked, surprise written all over her delicate features.

"Of course not." He swung out of the saddle of a brown and white paint. In three long strides he reached the white rail fence where Meg waited. "Would I be asking you if I did?"

"It's just that I would have thought she'd tell you…would have asked you for a ride."

"Quit rambling and tell me where my grandmother went."

Meg yanked a piece of paper from her back pocket and held it out to him. He snatched it from her, eager to get to the bottom of this not-so-fun mystery.

His gaze eagerly scanned the page. Relief settled over him as he blew out a sigh of relief.

"Don't worry me like that again." He handed the paper back to Meg. "Gram is fiercely independent. And sometimes she gets herself into trouble."

"If you don't mind me asking, what sort of things does she do?"

"You wouldn't believe it." He shoved up his Stetson and ran a hand over his forehead. "One time I actually found her on the roof."

"The roof?" Meg's eyes rounded. "Why in the world was she up there?"

"She said it was the only way she could get the upstairs windows cleaned. There was a smudge, and she couldn't reach it from the inside. With her, I never know what's going to happen next."

A smile lifted Meg's lips, which stirred a warm sensation in him. He shoved aside the reaction, refusing to acknowledge that she held any sort of power over him.

"What did you do about your grandmother while you were away on the rodeo circuit?"

"I worried. A lot. I tried to call home every day, and I had Hal, my foreman, check in a couple of times a day."

"I can't even imagine how tough that must have been for you." She paused and her gaze lowered. "I suppose with your grandmother away you'll want me to pack my things?"

The thought hadn't crossed his mind until she'd mentioned it. Her leaving would certainly make his life a lot easier. He'd no longer have to worry about the press tracking her down. And he could relax, no longer tormented by his urge to see if she tasted as sweet as she looked.

He cleared his throat. "If you give me a chance to clean up, I can give you a lift wherever you want to go."

Her gaze didn't meet his as she shook her head. "I don't want to be a bother."

"You aren't. I'm the one who offered. Where do you want to go? Home?"

She caught her lower lip between her teeth. When she lifted her head, he saw uncertainty reflected in her green eyes. She didn't have any clue what her next move would be. Sympathy welled up in him.

No. This wasn't his problem. She'd be fine.

Or would she be?

He couldn't just kick her to the curb. If his grandmother had dismissed *him* as not her problem he'd have ended up as a street urchin at best… At worst— No, he didn't want to go there. He'd slammed the door on his past a long time ago.

Against his better judgment he heard himself say, "On second thought, if you aren't in a hurry to go I could use your help."

Surprise quickly followed by suspicion filtered across her face. "I don't need charity."

She still had her pride. Good for her.

"What I have in mind is purely business. With you here acting as housekeeper and cook I've been able to get more work done than ever before. Besides, my grandmother won't be gone long."

The stress lines eased on her face. "Are you sure?"

Absolutely not. It was crazy to invite this sexy red-head to stay here…alone…with him. But what choice did he have?

"I'm sure," he lied.

A hesitant smile spread across her face, plumping up her pale cheeks. "Since it's just the two of us, maybe we could christen your new kitchen?"

"Fine by me."

She climbed down from where she'd been perched on the fence. "Any special request for dinner?"

"Meat and potatoes are my favorite, but the fridge and pantry are almost bare. So whatever you come up with will do. I'll pick up a few things in town later today."

"I noticed there isn't any wine. Sometimes I like to cook with it. Would you mind picking up some red and white?"

Cash clenched his jaw. He knew it wasn't her fault. She didn't know about his past, and that was for the best. If only she'd let the subject drop.

"You *do* like wine, don't you?" Her gaze probed him. "If you tell me your preference—"

"I don't drink," he said sharply.

She jumped. Regret consumed him for letting his bottled-up emotions escape. But he couldn't explain himself. He couldn't dredge up the memories he'd found so hard to push to the far recesses of his mind.

"Uh…no problem. I can cook without it."

He lowered his head and rubbed the back of his neck. "I didn't mean to startle you."

"You didn't."

She was lying, and they both knew it, but he didn't call her on it. He just wanted to pretend the incident hadn't happened.

Meg had turned to walk away when he called out, "If you'd make up a store list it'll be easier for both of us."

She glanced over her shoulder. "I'll do it first thing."

"Good."

"I'll have to remember to add a pie for dessert." She turned fully around. "You *do* like pie, don't you?"

His previous tension rolled away. "I thought the Jiffy Cook would whip one up from scratch."

"Not this girl. I can cook almost anything, but when it comes to baking I'm a disaster. Trust me, you wouldn't want to try one of my pies. Last time I tried the crust was burnt on the edges and raw in the center."

"Hard to believe someone as talented as you can't throw together a pie."

Color infused her cheeks. "My younger sister, Ella, got all the baking genes. In fact she runs her own bakery."

"If she bakes half as good as you cook, her pies must be the best in the land."

Meg's beaming smile caught his attention. His gaze latched onto her lips—her very kissable lips. His stomach dipped like it had when he was a kid riding a rollercoaster.

Damn. What had he gotten himself into by agreeing to let her stay?

A slight tremor shook Meghan's hands.

Why in the world was she letting herself get so worked up about this meal? So maybe she'd experimented a bit? That wasn't anything new. She'd been putting her twist on recipes since she was a kid.

But this was her first attempt to cook for Cash without his grandmother taking charge of the meal. Tonight's menu was spicier than anything they'd had since she'd arrived. She could barely sit still as she waited for his opinion.

"What do you think?" she asked as the forkful of flat enchilada slipped past his lips.

His eyes twinkled but he didn't answer. She watched as he slowly chewed. When his Adam's apple rose and fell as he swallowed she couldn't stand the suspense.

"Well—tell me. Did you like it?"

He rested the fork on the side of his plate, steepled his fingers together and narrowed his eyes on her. Her nails dug into her palms as she awaited his verdict. Patience had never been one of her strong suits.

Unable to stand it anymore, she blurted out, "Enough with the looks. Tell me the good, the bad or the ugly. I can take it."

She couldn't. Not really. His opinion meant more to

her than a judge's at a national cooking competition. Her breath was suspended while she waited.

"So you want my real opinion, right?" he asked, poker-faced. "The unvarnished truth?"

She pulled back her shoulders and nodded.

"The enchiladas were…surprising. I wasn't expecting a fried egg inside. And the sauce was tangy, but not hot enough to drown out the Monterey Jack or the onion." He broke into a smile. "Where did you find the recipe? I'll have to try it sometime."

The pent-up air whooshed from her lungs. "Honest? I mean you aren't saying this just to be nice?"

"Me? Nice? Never."

She started to laugh. "Would you quit joking around?"

"You still didn't say where you got the recipe."

She sat up a little straighter. "That's because I didn't have a recipe. I made it up."

He grabbed her fork and held it out to her. "Then I suggest you try your own dish."

He had a good point. She'd been so wrapped up in his reaction that she'd forgotten to have a bite. How could she let this man's opinion matter so much to her? When had he become so important?

By dwelling on this current of awareness sizzling between them she was only giving it more power over her. And the last thing she or her baby needed was another complication—even if this complication came with the most delightful lips that evoked spine-tingling sensations.

She stared down at her untouched food.

Concentrate on the food—not the cowboy.

Even as a portion of the casserole rested on her plate it held its shape. Of course, she'd let it cool for about ten minutes before serving. Presentation was half the battle. No one wanted to slave away in the kitchen and have their masterpiece turn out to be a sloppy, oozing mess on the plate. And you never wanted one dish to flow into the other. That would be enough to ruin the whole meal.

So aroma and presentation passed. Now for texture and taste. A dish that turned to mush was never appetizing, nor would it be fulfilling. There had to be solidity. Kind of like Cash, who was firm and solid on the outside, but inside, on those rare insightful moments, his soft center showed.

Oh, boy, now she was comparing the man to her culinary creation. Yikes, was she in trouble?

She lifted the fork to her lips. The dish was good, but it was those riveting eyes across the table that held her captive. If only she could create a dish that made a person think they'd floated up to the heavens with each mouthful—like Cash could make her feel whenever his gaze held hers—then she'd be the most famous cook in the world.

"Something wrong with the food?" His brows creased together.

"Um…no." Heat crept into her cheeks. Thank goodness one of his talents wasn't reading minds.

"You should be writing your own recipes."

His statement triggered a memory. "You know, it's funny that you mention it. There was this book editor once who wanted to know if I'd be interested in writing a cookbook."

"What did you tell her?"

Meghan shrugged. "That I'd think about it."

"If this is any indication of your other recipes I'd say you'd be a big hit." He helped himself to another heaping forkful of enchilada.

She couldn't hold back a grin. She did have a lot of fun creating unique food combinations. She couldn't imagine it'd be too hard to come up with enough recipes to fill a book. In fact it might be fun, now that Harold wasn't around discouraging her.

"You know, I received an email from the editor not too long ago."

"Why don't you talk to her and see what she has to offer?"

Cash was so different from Harold. Where Cash encouraged her to follow her dreams, Harold had insisted writing a cookbook would be a waste of time. She'd been so intent on pleasing him—on earning his love—that she'd gone along with his decision. She'd been willing to sacrifice her dreams to fulfill her mother's wish for her to become the perfect wife. The memory sickened her.

"I'll get back to her," Meghan said with conviction.

For a while they ate quietly. Meghan tried to focus her thoughts on anything but the sexy cowboy sitting across the table from her. Giving in to this crush would not be good. Soon she would be leaving the Tumbling Weed, and she needed to keep her focus on her baby and her options for the future.

"So what happened?" Cash asked, drawing her back to the here and now. "What made you run away from your own wedding?"

Wow! That had come out of nowhere. Her fork clanked onto her plate. She sat back and met his intense gaze. She'd suspected he'd ask sooner or later, but this evening she'd wanted it to be all about the food—the one thing she could do well. Not about her failings as a woman.

"We…we wanted different things."

His gaze continued to probe her. "You guys didn't talk about the future and what each of you wanted?"

She stared down at her still full plate. "We did. But things changed."

"And Harold wasn't up to handling change?"

What was up with all of these questions? Why the sudden curiosity? She pulled her shoulders back and lifted her chin. The determined look in his eyes said he wasn't going to let the subject rest until she'd answered him—but it didn't have to be the whole truth.

"A couple of weeks before the wedding I told him about some changes to our future and…and he seemed to accept it. It wasn't until the day of the wedding that he called everything off."

"I don't understand. If he called off the wedding why were you both at the church? Why did you walk down the aisle?" Before she could say a word, Cash's eyes widened. "Wait. You mean he waited to dump you until you were standing at the altar in front of your family and friends?"

She nodded, unable to find the courage to add that Harold had not only rejected her, but their unborn baby too. The memory of the whole awful event made her stomach churn.

"The jerk! How could he do that to you? You must have been horrified. No wonder you ran. You must hate him."

"No," she said adamantly. When Cash sent her a startled look, she added, "I can't hate him. It…it wasn't all his fault."

She'd been the one to forget her birth control pills. She'd strayed from their perfectly planned-out life. Maybe the problem was that they'd planned everything out *too* well—leaving no room for the unexpected.

"How can you stand up for him after what he did to you?"

She couldn't spout hateful things about the father of her baby—no matter how hard it was to smother the urge. "I don't want to talk about him."

"You mean you're still hung up on this guy?"

She didn't answer as she picked up her dinner plate and

headed to the kitchen. Maybe she should have told Cash about the baby. Guilt gnawed at her over this lie of omission. But she couldn't see how revealing her pregnancy would change things for the better.

The last thing she wanted was for Cash to look at her as if she was an utter fool. She valued his opinion and needed him to respect her. If only she could keep her secret for a little longer he'd never have to know.

CHAPTER EIGHT

MEG'S STOMACH FLUTTERED with nerves. What had gotten into her yesterday when she'd promised Cash that she'd contact the book editor?

What if the woman had already found someone else? Or, worse, what if the editor had completely forgotten about the offer *and* her? This wasn't a good idea.

But she had promised, and she always tried to do her best to keep her word. So she sat down at Cash's computer and started it up.

Without her cell phone she felt totally disconnected from the world—cocooned in the safety of the sprawling Tumbling Weed Ranch. The thought of having to face the reality of her life and the aftermath of the wedding disaster made her heart palpitate and her palms grow moist.

Staring at the blank screen, she realized she was being melodramatic. It wasn't as if anyone was going to know she was online and confront her.

Slowly her fingertips poked at the keyboard. As was her ritual, she visited the discussion thread on the Jiffy Cook's television show website.

Any other day she'd log on to find out how people had responded to her previous broadcast. Today was different. Today her morbid curiosity demanded to know how her fans were reacting to her wedding debacle.

What would happen to her television career if her followers bailed on her? The thought of being jobless and pregnant had her worrying her lower lip. That wouldn't happen. It couldn't. Her show was doing well.

Meghan scrolled down to find over nine hundred comments. *Wow!* That was a record. Apparently people had a lot of emotions concerning her runaway bride act. Now the question remained: did the majority side with her or the groom?

She clicked on the comments and waited for them to load on the screen.

Jiffy Cook Discussion—Comment #1
Hey, Jiffy Girl, hang in there. You did what you had to do. Now stick to your guns. We're behind you.
SexyLegs911

The message brought a smile to her lips. SexyLegs911 had been Ella's screen name for years. It was a private joke since her sister had inherited their mother's short legs. And with Ella being a baker she wasn't skinny. A point their mother stressed regularly. But that didn't keep the young guys from turning their heads when Ella strolled by. It just went to show that some men liked curves on their women—no matter what their mother said.

Meghan continued skimming over the comments until she spotted a heart-stopping link: *Fickle Cook Bails on Groom for Hotter Dish.*

The backs of her eyes stung. Part of her just wanted to shut down the computer and run away, but a more powerful urge had her clicking on the link. In seconds, a picture popped up on the screen. It was from a distance, but it showed her as she'd run out the church doors.

Meghan's face flamed with heat and she blinked repeatedly as she read the malicious article. They accused her of running out on Harold for a hottie from her stage crew.

It was libelous! Outlandish! Horrible!

But it also had thousands of hits. Her shoulders slumped. By now even her own mother must think she was a two-timer with no conscience.

An internet search of her name brought up another trashy article. It included a picture of someone claiming to be her, and with the picture being slightly out of focus observers just might believe it really was. Her look-alike was on some beach, making out with a tanned, muscular guy that she'd never laid eyes on before in her life. And this headline was even more outrageous: *Jiffy Cook Dishes up New Dessert on Solo Honeymoon.*

What in the world was her family thinking after reading that scandalous trash? Her once stellar reputation was beyond tarnished—singed beyond repair. What was she to do now?

Cash was in the middle of exercising Emperor when he spotted Meg walking down the lane. He was about to turn away, but there was a rigidness in her posture—an unnatural intensity in her movements—that didn't sit right with him.

Something was wrong—*way* wrong.

"Hey, Hal!" he called out to his ranch foreman. "Can you finish up with Emperor? I need to take care of something."

Hal cast a glance in Meg's direction. "And if you don't hurry, at the pace she's moving, you'll need the pickup to catch up to her."

Cash didn't waste time responding. He swung out of the saddle and ran, vaulting over the fence. All the while he searched his memory to recall if he'd done something wrong. He couldn't think of anything. In fact she'd seemed to be in a good mood at lunch, having created a delicious frittata recipe.

"Racing off to any place in particular?" he asked, taking long strides to keep pace with her short, quick steps.

"Like you'd care," she said in a shaky voice.

Cash grabbed her arm, bringing her to a stop. "Whoa, now. What has you so riled up? And, by the way, I do care. Now, out with it."

She glanced up at him with red-rimmed eyes. The pitiful look tugged at him, filling him with a strong urge to pull her to his chest and hold her. But her crossed arms and jutted-out chin told him the effort would be wasted.

"I'm waiting," he said. "And we aren't moving until I know what's going on."

A moment of strained silence passed. "You'll think it's stupid."

"I doubt that."

"Why?"

"Because you don't strike me as the type to get this upset over something trivial."

Surprise closely followed by relief was reflected in her bloodshot eyes. "I went online to contact the book editor and…"

"She turned you down that fast?"

Meg shook her head. "There were these articles online…about me. They were…awful. Full of lies."

Her shoulders drooped as she swiped at her eyes. He inwardly groaned at his own stupidity. If he hadn't urged her to contact the editor she wouldn't have run across the bad press.

He had to make this better for her. Throwing caution to the wind, he reached out and wrapped his hands around her waist. Surprisingly, she came to him without a fight. Her cheek pressed to his chest.

His heart hammered as he ran a hand over her silky hair. She felt so right there. So good.

"I'm sorry," he murmured.

She yanked out of his hold. "Why should you be sorry? You didn't write those malicious lies."

He lifted his hat and raked his fingers through his hair. "No, but I've been on the receiving end of the tabloid press. I know how bad it can hurt."

She eyed him. "Is that why you hide away here—all alone?"

"I'm not hiding." Or was he? It didn't matter. This wasn't about him. "Don't try and turn the tables on me."

"Just seems, with you being a good-looking guy and all, you wouldn't have a hard time finding someone to settle down with."

His heart thumped into his ribs. She thought he was good-looking?

Now wasn't the time to explore what that might mean. Right now she was upset and trying her hardest to change the subject. But he couldn't let the press stop her from having the brilliant future she so deserved.

"Meg, this isn't about me and my decisions. You have to ignore the lies. Because the more you say about the matter, the more headlines you'll make for them. And you don't want them to make a bigger deal of this, do you?"

A fire lit in her eyes. "Of course not."

"Good. Anyone who knows you will know it's nothing but a pack of lies. Give it a little time and they'll move on to the next story."

The stress lines eased on her face, which in turn eased the tightness in his chest. He wanted to go online and call those people out on their lies—he wanted to tell the whole world that Meg was the kindest person he'd ever met. She'd no more intentionally hurt someone than he would return to the grueling life of the rodeo circuit.

He fought back the urge. He couldn't make this any worse for her. All he could do was be there for her when she needed a friend.

Not liking the thought of her returning to a career where the press took potshots at her, he asked, "Did you contact the book editor?"

Meg shook her head, letting the sunshine glisten off the golden highlights in her red hair. "I was going to, but then I saw those awful articles—"

"Don't dwell on them. They aren't worth it. Pretend they don't exist and go ahead with your plan to email the editor."

"But if my reputation is already smeared in the press, what's the point?"

He *hated* that some lowlife had made Meg doubt herself. "Trust me, those articles aren't such a big deal."

Her gaze narrowed. "Really? Or are you trying to make me feel better?"

"I'm serious." And he was. He doubted anyone would give those headlines any credence. "Now, promise me you'll contact the editor."

A wave of expressions washed across her pale face. Seconds later her shoulders drew back, her chin tilted up and her gaze met his. "I'll do it."

Late the next afternoon, Cash stared down at the large check made out to the Tumbling Weed and couldn't help but smile. Emperor's new owner had just picked up the black stallion. The sale couldn't have come at a better time. The ranch could certainly use a few more profitable sales like this one.

He couldn't wait to share the good news with Meg. His

strides were long and fast as he made his way to the house. Inside, he found some pans on the stove, but no sign of his beautiful cook.

"Hey, Meg?" Nearly bursting with pride over his biggest sale to date, he searched downstairs for her.

"I'm in the family room."

In his stockinged feet, he moved quietly over the hardwood floors. Meg turned as he entered the room. Her smile was bright like the summer sun. It filled him with a warmth that started on the inside and worked its way out. He tamped down the unfamiliar response. He couldn't let himself get carried away.

"You never told me you were a world champion steer wrestler." A note of awe carried in her voice as she held up a trophy. "I'm not sure this room is big enough to display all of your accomplishments. Shame on you for hiding all of these awards in a box in the corner."

His chest puffed up a little. "You really like them?"

"I think they're amazing—*you're* amazing. And very brave."

Brave? No one had ever used that word to describe him. He could tell her some horror stories from his days on the rodeo circuit, but he didn't want to ruin this moment. He felt a connection to her—something so strong he wasn't sure he'd ever experienced it before.

"I was lucky," he said. "I retired before anything too serious happened to me."

"I'm glad." She picked up another trophy. "Any particular place you want these?"

"Wherever you think is best works for me."

She immediately turned and began positioning the two awards on the mantel. "What did you come rushing in here to tell me?"

Oh, that's right. He'd gotten so caught up in Meg and

her compliments that he'd forgotten his big news. "The buyer just picked up Emperor. I've made my first big sale. And the man promised to be back for more."

"That's wonderful! Congratulations. I've got some good news too."

"Are you going to make me guess?"

She grinned like a little kid with a big secret. "I followed your advice and found the email from that book editor. I reread it. She sounded very excited about the project. I can only hope she's still interested. I emailed her and now I'm waiting to hear back."

Cash basked in Meg's happy glow. He'd never seen anyone look so excited and hopeful. With all of his being he willed this to work out for her.

"The editor's going to jump on this opportunity."

"We need to celebrate," she said. "And I just happen to have your favorite meal started in the kitchen. I'd better go check on it."

She remembered his favorite meal? He paused and looked at her. He couldn't deny it. He was impressed. She was a diligent worker—in fact his house had never been so clean, with a fresh lemony scent lingering in the air— she'd befriended his grandmother in record time, and she was thoughtful.

He liked this—he liked *her*. There was so much more to Meg than he'd originally thought possible for a television celebrity. She wasn't at all concerned about herself, but she cared for others.

He trailed behind her into the kitchen. His gaze latched onto her finely rounded backside as she sashayed across the room. His blood warmed at the sight, bringing his body to full attention.

His gaze slid down over her shorts to her bare legs. He stifled a murmur of approval. Still, he couldn't stop his mind from imagining what it would be like to run his hands over her creamy smooth skin.

She turned to him and heat flamed from beneath his shirt collar, singeing his face. His mouth grew dry and he struggled to swallow.

He should turn away, but he couldn't. He liked staring at her too much. Every day he swore she grew more beautiful. She was like a blooming flower. Even the dark circles under her eyes had faded since she'd been here. He'd also taken note of her increased appetite. For the second time the blue skies and fresh air of the Tumbling Weed had worked its magic and healed a broken person—he'd been the first, when he'd returned here a few months back.

Meg rushed around the kitchen. "Do you see the hot mitts?"

He spotted them on the counter and moved into action. "Let me get the food from the oven."

"I've got it." She snagged the mitts from his hand, moved to the oven and removed the aluminum foil from a casserole dish. "Not yet. The roast needs a few more minutes."

"Sure smells good," he said, making small talk since his grandmother wasn't around to fill in the silent gaps.

"Thanks." She adjusted the oven and reset the timer. "I hope you like it."

"If it tastes half as good as I think it will, you don't have a thing to worry about."

She grabbed a serving spoon from the ceramic canister on the counter and turned to him. Her smile sparked a desire in him that raced through his body like wildfire, obliterating his best intentions.

The tip of her pink tongue swiped over her full bottom lip. "I experimented with it. You might be taking your life in your hands by trying it."

"Where's the fun if you don't take a risk now and then?" His gaze never wavered from her mouth. "Have I thanked you properly for all you've done?"

"No, you haven't." Her eyes grew round and sparkled with devilry. "What did you have in mind?"

He stepped up to her and wrapped his hands around her waist. Any lingering common sense went up in smoke. With a slight tug, she swayed against him. Her hands splayed across his chest. Could she feel the pounding of his heart? Was hers pounding just as hard?

Her voluptuous curves pressed against him and all he could think about was kissing her...holding her...having her. His gaze met hers. The want...the need...it was written in her smoldering eyes. Was this the way she'd stared at Harold?

Cash froze. His chest tightened. The thought hit him like a bucket of icy water. The last thing he wanted to think about was old what's-his-name. And he certainly didn't want to think about him or anyone else kissing Meg.

The brush of her fingertip along his jaw reheated his blood. Dismissing the unwanted thoughts, he gazed back at Meg. Before he could make his move she stood up on her tiptoes and leaned into him. Was this truly happening? Was she going to kiss him? Or had he let his daydreams run amok?

Her breath tickled his neck and her citrusy scent wrapped around him. This was certainly no dream. And if by chance it was he didn't want it to end. Meg fit perfectly in his arms, like she'd been made for him.

With her pressed flush against him he was helpless to hide his most primal response to her. Her mouth hovered within an inch of his, but she stopped. Had she changed her mind?

When she didn't pull away he dipped his head. His lips

brushed tentatively across hers. He longed for a deeper, more intense sampling, but he couldn't rush her. This moment had to be right for both of them. He'd never wanted someone so much.

A slight whimper met his ears. He hoped it'd come from her, but at this point he couldn't be sure. He took the fact she was still in his arms as an invitation. Their lips pressed together once again and there was no doubt in her kiss. She wanted him too. His hold on her waist tightened until no air existed between their bodies.

She tasted sweet like sun-warmed tea. He didn't want to stop drinking in her sugary goodness. Their kiss grew in intensity. His fingers worked their way beneath her top. Her skin was heated and satiny smooth. He wanted to explore every inch of her. Here. Now.

He'd never met anyone like Meg—a woman who could drive him to distraction with a mere look or the hypnotic sway of her luscious curves. Yet in the next moment she could make him want to pull his hair out with her fierce determinedness.

Now, as her hips ground into his, he wanted nothing more than to shed the thin layer of clothing separating them and make love to her right there in the kitchen. What would she say? Dared he try?

His fingers slid up her sides until his fingertips brushed over her lacy bra. He'd slipped his hands around to her back, anxious to find the hook, when an intrusive beeping sound halted his delicious plan.

"The food!" Meg pushed him away and rushed over to the oven. "I can't let it burn."

If anything was burning it was him. His body was on fire for her and his chance of being put out of his misery had slipped right through his fingers.

He strode across the room, stopping by the window—

as far as he could get from Meg without walking out on her. His clenched hands pressed down on the windowsill. His gaze zeroed in on the acres of green pasture. But it was the memory of Meg's ravaged lips and the unbridled passion in her eyes that held his attention. He raked his fingers through his hair. What was he doing? He hadn't been thinking. He'd merely acted on impulse.

As he cooled off he realized that for the first time in his life he'd let his desires overrule his common sense. Meg had teased him with those short-shorts and tempting lips, and he'd forgotten that she was a runaway bride, hiding out here while she pieced her life back together. The mere thought of how he'd lost control shook him to the core.

Thankfully they'd been literally saved by the bell. Otherwise she still might be in his arms, and things most certainly would have moved beyond first base. He expelled a long, frustrated sigh. He'd really screwed up. How in the world were they supposed to forget that soul-searing kiss and act like housemates now?

CHAPTER NINE

MEGHAN FLOPPED ABOUT her bed most of the night. She couldn't wipe that stirring kiss from her memory, but it was Cash's reaction—or rather his lack of a reaction—since then that ate at her. Life had merely returned to the status quo.

She rose long before the sun and hustled through her morning routine. With her energy back and her stomach settled, Meghan couldn't stand the thought of spending another day cooped up in the house. Besides, Cash made her job easy since he had a habit of picking up after himself. She appreciated the fact he didn't take advantage of her being the housekeeper. He was such a gentleman.

He'd certainly make some woman a fine husband—if only they could lasso him. A frown pulled at her lips. The thought of another woman in his arms left her quite unsettled.

Still, with his stirring kisses it was only a matter of time before someone took him permanently off the market. She'd certainly never experienced such passion in a kiss before. Not even close. So what was different? What was it about Cash that made her insides do gymnastics? Or was it simply that the grass was greener on the other side of the fence?

She tried to recall her first dates with Harold. They

were hazy and hard to remember. Not a stellar commentary on the man she'd almost married and the father of her unborn baby.

The harder she thought about it, the more certain she was that Harold had never once excited her with just a look. He'd never watched her with such rapt interest. They had simply started as good friends with parallel goals. Somewhere along the way they'd gotten caught in a dream of being the perfect power couple.

But, even though Cash's kiss had touched her in a way no other kiss ever had, she had to put it out of her mind. With no firm plans in place to return to her life, she needed to make sure things were all right between her and the sexy cowboy.

The allure of the stables and the horses called to her. Heck, she could work a shovel and wheelbarrow with the best of them. She'd used to help her mother every spring by turning the soil in the vegetable garden—a garden which had expanded each year. How different could it be cleaning up after horses? What she didn't know, she'd learn.

Dressed in blue jeans and the borrowed boots, she trudged to the barn, ready for work. She glanced around the corral but didn't spot Cash. The doors were open on the stables, as they had been since she'd arrived here. Shadows danced in the building as a gentle breeze carried with it the combination of horses, hay and wood. The rustic scents reminded her of a certain cowboy and a smile pulled at her lips.

Cash stepped out of a stall leading a golden-brown mare. He stopped in his tracks. "Did you need something?"

"Point out what needs to be done out here and I'll get started."

"You mean you want to shovel horse manure?" When

she nodded, he lifted his tan cowboy hat and scratched his forehead. "Don't you have enough to do inside?"

She crossed her arms and didn't budge. "I need a change of pace."

"Wait here," he said. "I'm taking Brown Sugar outside."

"No problem. Growing up, I spent a lot of time at my best friend's ranch. I loved it and wished I'd grown up on one." She shrugged. "Anyway, I still remember a thing or two."

Cash walked away, leaving her alone except for the few other horses still lingering in their stalls. The place was peaceful. She understood why Cash loved this ranch. Perhaps if the cookbook deal worked out and she made some extra money she could buy a small plot of land for herself and the baby. The thought filled her with hope.

Meghan strolled down the wide aisle, peering into the empty stalls. At the far end she made her way over to one of the occupied stalls. An engraved wooden plaque on the door read "Nutmeg." The mare stuck her head out the opening and Meg ran her hand down over the sleek neck.

"Hey, girl. Ready to stretch your legs?"

The horse, as though understanding her, lifted her chin.

"Have you made a new friend?"

The sound of Cash's voice caused Meghan to jump.

She whirled around to face him. "You startled me."

He held up both hands in defense. "Sorry. But you've got to pay more attention to your surroundings if you intend to spend time around the horses."

"Where would you like me to start?"

He eyed her up. "You're really serious about this?"

She nodded.

"Do you think you're up to walking Nutmeg out to the corral?"

"Definitely. We were just becoming friends."

When he stepped closer to help with the horse the quivering in her stomach kicked up a notch. No man had a right to be so good-looking. If he smiled more often he'd have every available female in New Mexico swooning at his feet. And she'd be the first in line.

Meghan got to work. She wasn't here to drool over him. She wanted to earn her keep and prove to him that they could still get along.

Cash watched as she led the mare outside. Meg's curly ponytail swished from side to side. He couldn't turn away. He drank in the vision of her like a thirsty man lost in the desert. There were no two ways about it: he was crazy to agree to work with this beautiful redhead who could heat his blood with the gentle sway of her hips.

He should have turned her away, but when her green eyes had pleaded with him he'd folded faster than a house of cards in a windstorm. He sighed. No point in beating himself up over his weakness when it came to Meg. Besides, maybe it'd do her some good, having a chance to live out her childhood dream of living on a ranch. He wondered how real life would compare. Probably not very well.

When he'd first arrived at the Tumbling Weed he'd believed all his problems were in the past. Not even close. As a child, he hadn't had the capacity to realize his father had most likely got his mean streak from Cash's grandfather.

Cash had started for the tackroom when the sound of an approaching vehicle had him changing directions. He couldn't think who it would be—perhaps a potential buyer? His steps came a little faster. Slowly but surely the reputation of Tumbling Weed had been getting out into the horse community, drawing in new customers.

He stepped out of the stable and a flash went off in his face. He blinked, regaining his vision only to find a stranger with a camera in his hand. A growl rose in the back of Cash's throat. He didn't need anyone to tell him that this smug-looking trespasser was a reporter.

"Aren't you Cash Sullivan, the two-time world steer-wrestling champion?" The man, who appeared to be about his own age, approached him with his hand extended.

Cash's shoulders grew rigid. His neck muscles tightened. He'd bet the whole ranch this reporter wasn't here to do an article on his horse-breeding business. He crossed his arms and the man's hand lowered. "What do you want?"

"A man who gets straight to the point. Good. Let's get down to business—"

"You can start by explaining why you're on my ranch."

The man's brows rose. "So you're admitting you're Cash Sullivan? The man who started a life of crime at an early age? What was it?" He snapped his fingers. "Got it. You held up a liquor store with your old man."

The muscles in Cash's clenched jaw throbbed. This reporter had certainly done his homework and he wasn't afraid to turn up the heat. Cash refused to defend himself. No matter what he said it'd be twisted and used against him in the papers.

When silence ensued, the reporter added, "And weren't you a suspect in the rodeo robbery earlier this year?"

Cash lowered his arms with his hands fisted. Every bit of willpower went into holding back his desire to take a swing at this jerk. A little voice in the back of his mind reminded him that an assault charge certainly wouldn't help his already colorful background.

With all his buttons pushed, Cash spoke up. "Funny how you forgot to add the part where I was never charged with either crime. If you guys don't have a good story you conjure one up. Now, get off my property."

The man didn't budge. "Not until you tell me if you've stolen another man's bride."

Cash glared at the man. Did this fool have a clue how close he was to being physically removed from the Tumbling Weed?

"How do you know her? Have you two been lovers all along?"

Cash flexed his fists and stepped forward. "For your own safety, leave. Now."

The man's eyes widened but he didn't retreat. "So my question struck a chord? Where are you hiding the runaway bride?"

The man peered around. Cash wanted to glance over his shoulder to make sure Meg hadn't followed him out of the barn, but he couldn't afford to give anything away. There was no way he'd let this man get anywhere near her.

"I don't know what you're talking about. There's no woman around here."

"You don't remember being at that church at the time of the bride's mysterious escape?"

Cash's gaze narrowed in on the man. This was the reporter who'd asked him if he'd seen which way Meg had gone. How much did he know?

"Why bother me? Shouldn't you be checking out her home? Or speaking with her family?"

What had led this man to his doorstep? Were there more reporters behind him? A sickening sensation churned in his gut.

The reporter rubbed his stubbled jaw. "The thing is she hasn't been home and her family doesn't have a clue where she is. Seems you're the last person to see her. I'm thinking she tossed over the groom for her lover. I'll just have a look around and ask her myself."

Cash's open hand thumped against the guy's chest,

sending him stumbling back toward his car. "You're trespassing. If you take one more step on my ranch you'll be facing the sheriff."

The man narrowed his gaze on him, as though trying to figure out if he was serious. Cash put on his best poker face, meeting the man's intense stare dead-on. At last all those late nights of card playing out on the rodeo circuit had paid off.

"What if my publisher was willing to make this worth your while?"

"I don't have anything to tell you. You're sniffing 'round the wrong cowboy and the wrong ranch. You've been warned."

The man yanked a card out of his pocket. "If you change your mind, call me. Don't take too long. If the rumors and public interest die so does my offer."

When Cash didn't make a move to accept the card, the man reached out and boldly stuffed it in Cash's shirt pocket. Finally the man turned and climbed back in his car. Cash didn't move until the vehicle had disappeared from sight.

He pulled the card out and ripped it up. This wasn't over. As sure as he was standing there on this red earth the rumors would begin to swell. His past would be dug up—again.

No matter what he did, he'd never escape his past. In the end he would only end up damaging Meg's reputation even more. If he'd ever needed a reminder of why he was better off alone this was it.

He'd never be a good boyfriend, much less husband material.

This fact stabbed at his chest deeply and repeatedly.

Cash turned and headed for the barn. At least Meg had

had the presence of mind to stay hidden while the reporter had been snooping around.

"Meg, you can come out now."

He detected a whimper. His eyes took a moment to adjust to the dim lighting after being in the bright sunshine.

"Help me..." Meg's voice wavered.

He scanned the area and saw her lying on her side. His heart galloped faster than his finest quarter horse. He rushed to her side and crouched down.

"Did you break something?" Her watery eyes stared up at him. He wished she'd say something—anything. "Meg, you've got to tell me what's wrong."

"I was running to hide from the reporter and...and I slipped." Her bottom lip quivered.

He reached out and tucked a loose strand of hair behind her ear before letting his hand slide down to caress her soft cheek. "Do you think you can get up?"

"I...I think so. But what if I hurt the baby?"

The baby? A shaft of fear sliced into him. He snatched his hand back from her. She sure didn't look pregnant.

"How...how far along are you?"

"Not very. But I can't lose it." A silent tear splashed onto her pale cheek.

"I'll call an ambulance." He reached for his cell phone.

"No—wait."

"You're in pain. You should go get checked out right away."

"Help me up." She held out a hand to him.

"You sure that's a good idea?"

"Never mind." Exasperation threaded through her weak voice. "I'll do it on my own."

Figuring he couldn't make things any worse than having her struggle to get up on her own, he moved swiftly and slipped his hands under her arms. She was a solid girl, but he easily helped her to her feet. His hands lingered around her as he studied her face for signs of distress.

"Any pain?" If she said yes he didn't care how much she protested. He was throwing her in his truck and rushing her to the emergency room.

She shook her head.

"You're sure?"

She nodded.

He wished she'd talk more. It wasn't like her to be so quiet. "Let's get you inside."

Guilt and concern swamped his mind, making his head throb. This whole accident was his fault. He should have kept a closer eye on her. He'd never forgive himself if something happened to her or her baby.

A baby. Meg was pregnant. The fragmented thoughts pelted him, leaving him stunned. What was he supposed to do now?

Once the shock wore off Meghan breathed easier. Thank goodness there was no pain or cramping. Before she could take a step toward the ranch house Cash swung her up in his arms.

"What are you doing? Put me down."

He ignored her protests as he started for the house at a brisk pace. Her hands automatically wrapped around his neck. A solid column of muscle lay beneath her fingertips. A whiff of soap mingled with a spicy scent teased her nose.

She wanted to relax and rest her head against his shoulder, but she couldn't let herself get caught up in the moment. Cash had so many walls erected around his heart that she doubted a wrecking ball could break through. With all her own problems she didn't need to toy around with the idea of getting involved with someone who was emotionally off-limits.

He carried her into the family room and approached the leather couch. Meghan glanced down. A manure smudge trailed up her leg. "Don't put me down here. I'm filthy."

"It'll clean up."

"Cash, no."

Ignoring her protest, he deposited her with the utmost care onto the couch. The man could be so infuriating, but she wasn't up for an argument. Once she'd rested for a bit, assured herself everything was all right with the baby, she'd grab the leather cleaner and spiff everything up. After all, it was her job.

"Can I get you anything?" he asked, breaking into her thoughts.

"No, thanks. I'm okay now."

He sat down on the large wooden coffee table and leaned forward, resting his elbows on his knees. "No aches or pains? The baby—?"

"Is fine." When Cash made no move to leave, she added, "You don't need to sit there the rest of the day, staring at me."

He leaned back and rubbed the stubble lining his jaw. "You have to tell me the honest truth. Do you need a doctor?"

She reached out and patted his leg, noticing the firm muscles beneath his denim. "Other than needing another shower, I feel fine. If things change you'll be the first I tell."

"Promise?"

Her hand moved protectively to her abdomen. "I've got a little one to protect now. I'll do whatever it takes to give him or her the best life."

"Does that include sticking by the father even if he doesn't deserve your loyalty?"

CHAPTER TEN

MEGHAN STUDIED CASH'S face, wondering what had given him the idea she was in any way standing by Harold. After the thoughtless, hurtful manner in which he'd dumped her, nothing could be further from the truth.

"Why in the world would you think I feel loyalty toward Harold?"

Cash's dark brow arched. "I don't know. How about because you wanted to save your wedding dress? You wore your engagement ring until you started doing housework, and you refuse to say a bad word about him."

Oh, she had a whole host of not-so-nice things to say about Harold, but she refused to give in to the temptation—it'd be too easy. And she didn't want her child exposed to an atmosphere where animosity was the *status quo*.

However, Cash had opened his home to her, and he hadn't needed to. And once he'd gotten to know her he'd been kind and generous. It was time she trusted him. He deserved to know the unvarnished truth.

She inhaled a steadying breath and launched into the events leading up to her mad dash out of the church, including how Harold had rejected not only her but also their baby.

Cash's eyes opened wide with surprise. "He doesn't want his own baby?"

She shook her head.

Cash's expression hardened and his eyes narrowed. "How can he write off his own kid as if it was a houseplant he didn't want? Doesn't he realize how lucky he is? I'd give anything to have my baby..."

The impact of his words took a few seconds to sink in. Dumbfounded, she stared at him. Lingering pain was reflected in his darkened eyes.

At last finding her voice, she asked, "You're a father?"

His head lowered. "I never got the chance to be. My ex didn't want to be tied down."

Meghan squeezed his hand. His fingers closed around hers and held on tight.

"I'm so sorry," she said. "But maybe someday—"

"No. It's better this way." He released his hold on her and took a step back. "Are you sure you want to be a mother?"

Meghan nodded vigorously. "Besides, even if I had done what Harold wanted he still wouldn't have married me. It just wasn't meant to be."

"So there's no chance of a reconciliation?" Cash's direct gaze searched her face.

"Absolutely none." Instead of pain and regret, all she felt was relief.

"I guess this is the part where I'm supposed to say I'm sorry it didn't work out, but it sounds like you were lucky to find out the truth before you married him."

Meghan sighed. "My mother wouldn't agree with you. She had this perfect wedding planned. In fact, she expected me to be the perfect wife to the perfect husband and live out the perfect life."

"That's a tall order, considering nothing and no one is perfect."

"Try explaining that to my mother. She likes to run

with the 'in' crowd and pretend our family is better than we are. No matter how hard I've tried I've never earned her approval. But when I started dating Harold she became a little less critical of me and she smiled a little more."

"I'm guessing she isn't happy about the wedding being called off."

Sadness over not being able to turn to her own mother during this trying time settled over her. "Once again I've disappointed her. And she doesn't even know that I'm about to become a single parent."

"Doesn't sound like your mother is going to be much help with the baby. What will you do?"

"For the time being I'm going to keep my pregnancy under wraps and go back to my job as the Jiffy Cook."

"I thought you didn't like the job? Why not try something else?"

"I can't. I'm pregnant. I no longer have the freedom to pick and choose what I do for a living. I have to do what is best for my child."

Cash's brow arched. "And you think being the Jiffy Cook is the best option?"

"It provides a comfortable income and excellent health benefits."

"But if you aren't happy—"

"I don't have a choice."

"What about Harold? He's still the baby's father."

The thought of her child growing up without a father deeply troubled her. Both of her parents had played significant roles in her life. Her mother had given her the gift of cooking, for which she'd be forever grateful, and her father had taught her to keep putting one foot in front of the other, day after day, no matter the challenges that lay ahead. How in the world would she ever be enough for her child?

"For the baby's sake I'll make peace with Harold. We'll work out visitation. Or, if he really wants nothing to do with the baby, I'll have him sign over his rights."

Cash nodded in understanding. "Sounds like you've been doing a lot of thinking since you've been here. You know there's still the press to deal with? Seems they're more fascinated with you than I first thought."

The memory of why she'd slipped and fallen came rushing back to her. "What did you tell the reporter when he was here?"

"Nothing." Stress lines marred his face. "The reporter was the same man I spoke to at the church when we were leaving. I don't think he knows anything definite, but I can't promise he won't be back."

She noted how his lips pressed together in a firm line. In his gray eyes she spied unease.

"What else is bothering you?"

The silence engulfed them. She wouldn't back down. She had to know what was eating at him.

Cash got to his feet and paced. He raked his fingers through his hair, scattering the short strands into an unruly mess. He stopped in front of her, resting his hands on his waist.

His intense gaze caught and held hers. "Fine. You want to know what keeps going through my mind?" She nodded and he continued. "You didn't tell me you were pregnant."

He was right. She'd been lying by omission. And none of the excuses she'd been feeding herself now seemed acceptable. She'd never thought about it from his perspective. "I...I'm sorry. The timing just never seemed right. I shouldn't have let it stop me. I should have worked up the courage to be honest with you—"

All of a sudden there was a movement in her abdomen. Her hands moved to her midsection.

Cash rushed to her side and dropped to his knees. "Is it the baby? Are you in pain?"

She smiled and shook her head. It was the first time she'd ever felt anything like it.

"Meg, talk to me or I'm calling an ambulance."

Pulling herself together, she said, "I swear I'm not in pain."

"Then what is it?"

She grabbed his hand and pressed it to her tiny baby bump. "There it is again."

He pressed both strong hands to her stomach. His brows drew together as though he were in deep concentration. "I don't feel anything. Was the baby kicking?"

"When I found out I was pregnant I started to read a baby book. At nine weeks the baby's too small to kick, but there was a definite fluttering sensation."

"Sounds like you have a feisty one in there." His expression grew serious. "Promise me you'll be more cautious from now on? That little one is counting on you."

She blinked back a sudden rush of tears and nodded. She wasn't a crier. It must be the crazy pregnancy hormones that had her all choked up.

When Cash moved away a coldness settled in where his hands had been pressed against her. She didn't want him to go. Not yet. But she didn't have a reason for him to stay.

"Don't move from that couch until I return." He bent over and snatched his cowboy hat from the coffee table. As he stood, his gaze met hers. "I won't be gone long. I have to speak with Hal and let him know if he needs me I'll be right here, taking care of you."

His orders struck her the wrong way. "No."

"Meg, don't be ridiculous. You need to rest. And I'll be here to make sure that you do just that."

The idea of listening to him sounded so good—so

tempting. But the fact she wanted to let him take charge frightened her. She couldn't need him—want him. The last time she'd leaned on a man he'd taken over her life. This time she needed to make her way on her own.

She swallowed hard. "I can take care of myself."

"Quit being stubborn."

"Just leave me alone," she said, struggling to keep her warring emotions in check. "I don't need you. I don't need anyone. I can take care of myself and my baby."

Cash expelled an exasperated sigh but didn't say another word.

His retreating footsteps echoed through the room. Once the front door snicked shut a hot tear splashed onto her cheek. She dashed it away with the back of her hand, but it was quickly followed by another one. These darn pregnancy hormones had her acting all out of sorts.

She refused to accept that her emotional breakdown had anything to do with her wishing Cash was her baby's daddy, not Harold. Because if she accepted that then she'd have to accept she had feelings for him. And she didn't have any room in her life for a man.

Cash stomped out to the barn, tossed his hat on the bench in the tackroom and raked his hair with his fingers. His thoughts kept circling over the conversation he'd had with Meg. He was trying to figure out where it'd run off the tracks. One minute he was offering to help her and the next she was yelling at him.

No matter how long he lived, he'd never understand women. They'd be mankind's last unsolved mystery. He kicked at a clump of dirt, sending it skidding out into the aisle.

What was he supposed to do now? The thought of Meg packing her bags and leaving played on his mind. Worry inched up his spine. He hoped she wouldn't do anything so foolish.

He was thankful for one thing—Gram wasn't here to witness how he'd screwed things up. If Meg left early because of him...because he'd overstepped the mark...his grandmother wouldn't forgive him—he wouldn't forgive himself.

His cell phone buzzed. He didn't feel like talking to anyone, but with a ranch to run he didn't have the luxury of ignoring potentially important calls. "Tumbling Weed Ranch."

"Cash, is that you?" Gram shouted into the phone as though she were having a hard time hearing him.

"Yep, it's me. Ready to come home?" Talk about lousy timing. What he didn't need at this moment was a lecture about how he'd blown things with Meg.

"I'm not ready to leave yet. Amy's mother had problems catching a flight, but she's supposed to be here by next week. I agreed to stay until then. How are things there?"

Talk about a loaded question. He couldn't tell Gram about Meg—not over the phone. Besides, Gram already had her hands full caring for a new mother and her babies. She didn't need to hear about *his* problems.

"Cash?" Gram called out. "Cash, are you still there?"

"I'm here. Things are going well. Not only has Meg finished cleaning your house, but she almost has mine spiffed up too."

"You aren't working that poor girl too hard, are you? She needs to take care of herself and get plenty of rest."

Gram *knew* Meg was pregnant. The knowledge stole his breath. Why had he only just learned about it? A slow burn started in his gut. He'd been the last to know when his mother and father had run out of money. And the last to know when his dad had planned to hold up a liquor store.

Then, earlier this year, he'd been the last to know when his girlfriend, who'd worked in the office at the rodeo, had been in cahoots with a parolee. Behind his back they'd ripped off the rodeo proceeds and framed him for the job. She'd claimed he owed her. Instead of giving her his prize money, to fritter away at the local saloon, he'd always sent it home to Gram for the upkeep of the ranch. Thank goodness he'd had an alibi.

And now this. Meg had confided in his grandmother about her condition but she hadn't seen fit to share it with him, even though he'd opened his home up to her. His hand tightened on the phone.

"When did she tell you?" he asked.

"Tell me about what?" Gram asked a little too innocently.

"Don't pretend you don't know she's pregnant. You've known all along."

A slight pause ensued. "It wasn't my place to tell you."

"What else have I been kept in the dark about?"

"Nothing. And why does it bother you so much? It's not like you're the father."

Gram paused, giving him time to think. He might not be the biological father but he already had a sense of responsibility to this baby and its mother. His jaw tightened. He knew it'd lead to nothing but trouble.

"Cash, you're not planning to get involved with Meghan, are you?"

"What?" He would have thought his grandmother would be thrilled with the idea of him settling down with Meg, not warning him against it. "Of course not."

"Good. I know you've had a rough life, and trusting people doesn't come easily to you. That girl has been through enough already, and with a baby on the way she doesn't need another heartbreak. She needs someone steady. Someone she can rely on."

His grandmother's warning shook him. He wanted to disagree with her. But she was right. This wasn't his baby.

"Don't worry," he said. "Nothing's going to happen. Soon she'll be gone."

"I didn't say to run the poor girl off. She has a lot to deal with before she returns home. I have to go. One of the babies is crying. Tell Meghan I've come across some unique recipes while I've been here. We can try them out when I get home."

Without a chance for him to utter a goodbye the line went dead. Gram was expecting Meg to be here when she returned. If Gram found her gone she'd blame *him*. He'd already caused his grandmother enough heartache for one lifetime. He didn't want to be responsible for Meg leaving without Gram having an opportunity to say good-bye.

CHAPTER ELEVEN

THE WARM GLOW of the afternoon sun filled Cash's bedroom. Meghan swiped a dust rag over a silver picture frame with a snapshot of a little boy cuddled in a woman's arms. She pulled the picture closer and studied the child's face. The familiar gray eyes combined with the crop of dark hair resembled Cash. She smiled back at the picture of the grinning little boy. Was the beautiful woman gazing so lovingly at the child his mother? Meghan wondered what had happened to her. And where was Cash's father?

So many unanswered questions. She shoved away her curiosity. None of this was any of her business. She ran the rag over the frame one last time before placing it back on the dresser.

His bedroom was the last room to be cleaned. She gave the place a final inspection, closed the windows and dropped the blinds. Sadness welled up in her as she pulled the door shut behind her. With both houses clean she needed to make plans to leave—especially after her total meltdown the day before.

Even so, she'd come to love this house and ranch so much in such a short amount of time. She'd been able to relax here and be herself. If only she could get her life back on track—back to normal. Whatever *that* was. Then she'd be just as comfortable back in Albuquerque as she was here. Wouldn't she?

After putting away the cleaning supplies and grabbing a quick shower she realized it was five o'clock and she still hadn't started dinner. With exhaustion settling in, she decided to go with an easy meal. Spaghetti marinara with a tossed salad.

While the sauce simmered, Meghan took a moment to check if there'd been a response from the book editor. This time she made a point of avoiding any blogs or articles about herself. Her empty stomach quivered in anticipation as her fingers clicked over the keyboard.

She opened her email account, finding a bunch of new messages. The third one down caught her attention. It was from Lillian Henry, the editor. Meg's heart skipped a beat before her nerves kicked up a notch. Was Lillian still interested? Or had the bad press swayed her decision? Questions and doubts whirled through Meghan's mind as her finger hovered over the open button.

Taking a deep breath, she clicked on Lillian's name and the email flashed up on the screen.

To: JiffyCook@myemail.com
From: Lillian.Henry@emailservice.com
RE: Cookbook
Hello, Meghan. I was surprised to get your email, considering everything that's been happening in your life. I'm happy to hear you're interested. Let me know when you're available to discuss a theme for the book series. I'm looking forward to some sample recipes. Lillian

Meghan jumped to her feet and did a happy dance around the kitchen island, laughing and squealing in delight. *A series. Wow!* Things were looking up for her at last. She couldn't stop smiling.

She'd need to rethink how to fit in enough time to work up additional recipes and figure out themes for these books. There was so much to plan—but then again, planning things was her forte. Now, with a baby to care for, a demanding television show and books to write, she'd definitely need a new strategy to make time for everything.

She started for the door to tell Cash, but as her hand touched the doorknob she paused. Since she'd told him to leave her alone, he'd done just that. Other than a couple of inquiries about her well-being and the baby's, no words had passed between them.

Meghan's excitement ebbed away.

With no one to talk to, Meghan returned to the computer. She scrolled down through the list of unrecognizable names until she came across one from her producer at the TV studio.

To: JiffyCook@myemail.com
From: Darlene.Jansen@myemail.com
RE: Urgent!
Meghan, where are you? What happened? We need to talk right away. Call me. Darlene Jansen

Guilt washed over Meghan. She'd been MIA longer than was appropriate, but her time at the Tumbling Weed had been so nice—so stress-free. Now it was all about to end.

She grabbed the phone and dialed her producer. On the second ring she picked up.

"Where have you been?" Darlene asked, cutting straight to the chase. "Do you know what has been going on around here? The suits upstairs were real unhappy when the television special about your wedding fell through. All the buildup and the money we spent on advertisements to pique viewer interest and we ended up having to air a rerun. Ratings plummeted."

A baseball-sized lump swelled at the back of Meghan's throat. She swallowed hard and it thudded into her stomach. Television was a ratings game. Up until this point her ratings had been impressive—so impressive they'd been working on moving the Jiffy Cook to a larger audience.

"I'm sorry, Darlene." Now wasn't the time to remind her producer that she had been opposed to promoting the wedding week after week. They'd covered everything from floral arrangements to choosing the right wedding dress. It'd just been too much.

"Couldn't you have gone through with the ceremony?" Darlene asked. "If you really didn't want to be married, you could have had it annulled later."

Meghan's mouth gaped. Was she *serious?* Sure, she might have been planning to marry Harold out of obligation to their child, but that was different than saying "I do" to impress the public while planning an annulment the next morning.

Trying to smooth the waters, Meghan said, "Listen, I'll be back in town tomorrow. How about we get together for lunch and discuss how you want to handle things for the next show?"

Ignoring the lunch invitation, Darlene plowed on. "Why did you walk out on the ceremony when you knew it was being taped to air on the next show?"

With her job on the line, Meghan decided it was time she came clean and let the broken pieces of her life fall as they may. Surely Darlene would sympathize with her after she'd heard the details.

"I'd just found out I'm...I'm pregnant."

A swift intake of air filled the phone line, followed by an ominous silence. Not at all the reaction Meghan had been expecting. Darlene had always been friendly and supportive before. She obviously didn't know her as well as she'd thought.

Too late to turn back, so Meghan ventured forth. "Harold waited until we were at the altar to tell me he didn't want…the baby." She exhaled an uneven breath. "He didn't want me. I…I couldn't think about anything but getting away from him…from the church."

A tense silence ensued. Unsure what else she could say in her own defense, Meghan quietly waited.

"This won't help us," Darlene said in a firm tone. "After you ran out on your wedding, the execs got the impression you're fickle. They're not going to pick up the show on a national basis."

"But they don't know the circumstances. The wedding was personal, not business."

"None of that matters to them. They believe you're spoiled and selfish. That you'll balk at the first rough spot."

Meghan's body tensed. "Who gave them that impression?"

"Doesn't matter."

She didn't need confirmation. Her gut said it had been Harold. He could be a wonderful ally, but if he thought someone had crossed him he wouldn't rest until he'd leveled his enemy. Apparently he truly believed she'd intentionally gotten pregnant and he'd done her out of her job. How could he be so vindictive?

She paced back and forth, needing to keep her rising temper in check while she approached this conversation from a different direction. "But I've been working toward this point in my career since I took my first waitress job when I was sixteen. I've always worked in the food industry."

"Your work history is a long list of pitstops before you moved on to the next rung on the ladder. It doesn't display any stability."

Meghan's hand spread over her abdomen. "There has to be a way to renew my show in its former spot. Surely they'll understand. I can bring the numbers back up."

"Your old time slot has been filled. You knew it was going to be a gamble when we put the show out there to be picked up on a larger platform."

Meghan's mouth gaped and she sucked in a horrified gasp. She remembered the meetings about moving the Jiffy Cook from her half-hour spot for a small audience around Albuquerque to an hour-long broadcast for a national audience. She'd met with Darlene and the executives. And then she'd discussed it with Harold. Everyone had been in agreement that with the rising ratings the sky was the limit. Now the sky was raining down all over Meghan, and there wasn't an umbrella big enough to protect her.

"You've been great to work with," Darlene said in weary voice, "and I thought you had a bright future ahead of you. But the suits want what they were promised—a career-oriented woman. Now, with the ratings at an all-time low, I have to tell the execs that your priorities will soon be split between your career and being a single mom."

Meghan blinked away the sting at the back of her eyes. "I can manage a career and a family."

"They don't care. All they care about is the bottom line. That's why I've been trying to reach you. Word came down on Monday to shut down the show."

A sob caught in the back of her throat as her eyes burned with unshed tears. This couldn't be happening. Her life kept spinning out of control and she didn't know how to stop it.

* * *

Cash strode up to the house late that evening. He'd put off talking to Meg as long as possible. But a sandwich and chips just didn't go far when you were spending the afternoon breaking in a horse. And not even the most stubborn stallion could erase his thoughts of Meg. In fact at one point he'd lost his hold when the horse had bucked and nearly landed on his injured shoulder. Another slip like that and he'd be back in the hospital—a place he hoped never to see again.

A part of him knew he'd let himself begin to care about Meg more than he should, but this silent treatment was a bit of overkill. Maybe he should apologize…but for what?

His temples began to throb. He didn't know what he'd done wrong. Could he have overreacted when he found out about the baby? That had to be it. He'd apologize and they'd make peace.

He hoped.

Cash quietly let himself into the mudroom at the back of the house. His motions were slow after his rugged workout. His shoulder ached from the repeated abuse. He rubbed the tender area with his other hand.

He pulled off his dirty boots and set them aside. In his stockinged feet, his footsteps were silent as he crossed to the entrance to the kitchen. He spotted Meg with her back to him. The soft glow of the stove light illuminated her curves. His immediate reaction was to go to her and wrap his arms around her before nuzzling her neck. But he held himself to the spot on the hardwood floor. He didn't need to muddy the waters by sending her mixed signals.

Cash took a closer look and noticed the way her head was bent and her shoulders slumped. Had she been lying when she'd told him she was okay after the fall? Was something wrong with the baby? Or maybe this was just one of those pregnancy hormone fluctuations?

A sniffle caught his full attention. His chest tightened. If there was something wrong with her or the baby and he'd left her alone all day he'd never forgive himself.

He strode over to her. "Are you okay?"

Her spine straightened, but she kept her back to him. "I'm fine. Your dinner is ready."

He placed his hand on her shoulder. "I'm not interested in the food. It's you I'm concerned about. Turn around and talk to me."

She didn't budge. "Go wash up."

Alarm sliced through him. *Please don't let anything be wrong with the baby.*

The child might not have his DNA but he felt a connection to it. He knew what it was like to be rejected by your biological father. No child should ever go through that pain.

The fact the baby was part of Meg had him conjuring up an image of a little girl. Cute as a button with red curls and green eyes just like her mother. But soon Meg was leaving, and he'd never get the chance to know the baby.

"Meg, you aren't listening to me. I don't want dinner. I want you to face me and tell me what's wrong."

"Nothing. Just leave it alone." The pitch of her voice was too high.

"I'm not moving until you start giving me some answers."

Not about to continue talking to her back, he tightened his hand on her shoulder as he pivoted her around to face him. Her eyes were bloodshot and her cheeks tearstained. He didn't take time to consider his next action. He merely reached out and pulled her into his embrace.

Her lush curves pressed against his hard length. He was surprised when she willingly leaned into him. Her arms draped around his midsection while her head drooped against his chest. She fit so perfectly against him—as though she'd been made for him.

Her emotions bubbled over and he let her cry it out of her system. He pressed his lips to her hair and breathed in her intoxicating scent. His hand moved to the length of red curls trailing down her back. For so long he'd ached to run his fingers through the silky mass and at last he caved in to his desire. Nothing should feel so soft or smell so good. He took a deep breath, inhaling the faint floral scent. It teased his senses, making him want more of this woman.

His body grew tense as he resisted the urge to turn this intimate moment into something much more—a chance to caress her body and chase away those unsettling tears. He knew it was wrong—she was pregnant, and a local celebrity, totally out of this broken-down cowboy's league. But that didn't douse his longing to protect and comfort her. Nor did it diminish the mounting need to love away her worries.

When her tears stopped, he mustered up all his self-restraint and moved so that he was holding her at arm's length—a much safer distance. What she needed now was a friend, not a lover. If only his libido would listen to his mind.

"Meg, if it's not the baby, what has you so upset? Let me help you."

She shook her head. "You can't."

CHAPTER TWELVE

CASH REFUSED TO give up. Meg needed him, and he intended to find a way to make things better for her. "If this is about me overreacting about the baby, I'm sorry."

She pulled back to look up at him. "It doesn't have anything to do with that."

Her eyes shimmered with unshed tears and her face was blotchy. Her pouty lips beckoned to him. If only a kiss could make her worries disappear he'd be more than willing to ride to her rescue. He gave himself a mental jerk. A kiss would only complicate matters.

"Will dinner be okay for a little bit?" he asked, wanting to get her off her feet.

She nodded. "I turned the burners off."

"Come with me." He led her to the family room, where they sat side by side on the couch. "Now, tell me what has you so worked up."

When a fresh tear splashed onto her cheek, his body tensed. Not sure what to do, he grabbed a handful of tissues from the end table and stuffed them in her hand. His gaze strayed from her to the door. He stifled the urge to make a beeline back to the stables. Out there, he knew what to do. In here, he didn't have the foggiest idea if he should hold her again or sit by patiently until she stopped sniffling and started talking.

"Did someone die?" he asked, needing to know the severity of the situation.

She hiccupped and shook her head. "It's nothing like that. I think the pregnancy hormones have me overreacting."

He let out a pent-up breath and squeezed her hand. "It's okay. You just worried me."

Long seconds passed as Meg dashed away tears with a tissue and blew her red nose. "I heard back from the book editor."

Oh, no, had the editor changed her mind? The woman had to be crazy, because Meg made the most delicious dishes. He should know—his waistline was increasing from the second and third helpings he had regularly at each dinner.

"What did she say?" he asked, already searching for words of support.

"She wants to get together and discuss the idea of writing a series of cookbooks."

Confused, he said, "Sounds like good news to me."

"You think so?"

"Of course I do. Otherwise I wouldn't have encouraged you to contact her."

"That's one of the things I like about you—your straightforward answers."

One of the things she liked about him implied there were more. A warm sensation filled his chest and made his heart pound. He wanted to know what other things she liked, but resisted the urge to ask.

He was having trouble figuring out her problem, but he didn't want to say too much and get the waterworks flowing again. He was certain if he waited she'd tell him more. Women liked to talk about what bothered them—wasn't that what his grandmother had told him?

Meg balled up the tissue in her hand. "While I was checking my email I came across one from my television producer." The color drained from her cheeks. "She needed to talk to me so I called her. She…she told me the deal to move my show to a bigger platform had fallen through."

Ah—now he understood. "I'm sorry." His sympathy did nothing to ease the pain etched on her face. He should say something else—something to calm her worries and give her hope. "Maybe if your show keeps doing well they'll make the change next year?"

She shook her head. "You don't understand…there's no show. *The Jiffy Cook* has been cancelled. I was worried this might happen if we went ahead with plans to move to a larger platform, but Darlene assured me with the ratings the show was generating it'd be a sure thing. And I believed her. I thought she was my friend. I thought wrong. I've been so wrong about so many people in my life."

Cash sat back on the couch, resisting the urge to pull her back in his arms and kiss her until she forgot her problems. He didn't want to end up being another person who let her down. And leading her on when they had nowhere to go would certainly qualify.

"What am I going to do?" She threw herself back against the couch and hugged her arms over her chest. "I need those health benefits."

Secretly, he thought this was for the best. Meg could find a better job—a more stable one. A job that would make her happy.

He glanced over at her. The light had gone out in her eyes. It knocked him for a loop. Meg was a gutsy woman. Someone he'd come to admire for her spunk and determination. Until now, he'd never seen her utterly give up—not even after the father of her baby dumped her at the altar.

This reaction had to be some sort of shock. She'd snap out of it. He just might have to give her a nudge.

"Don't let this defeat you," he said with conviction. "You can make new plans. Let me help you."

Her chin lifted. "I have to do this on my own."

"But why? I've got friends and they've got friends. Surely someone needs a fabulous chef?"

She shook her head. "I let myself rely on Harold and look where that got me. This time I have to do it my way."

Was she comparing *him* to Harold? The thought stung. He was nothing like that self-righteous, pompous jerk. He wanted to call her out on her comment, but the wounded look in her eyes subdued his indignation. This was about Meg, not his wounded ego.

"There's still the plan to work with the book editor," Cash offered.

Meg's green eyes opened wide and at last a little light twinkled in them. "That's true. And she didn't seem to be fazed by the wedding falling through. She said she's looking forward to receiving sample recipes."

"Sounds promising."

"I just can't believe she wants to do a whole series. How in the world will I come up with so many new dishes?"

As quickly as the light in her eyes flicked on, it dimmed again. Meg leaned back on the couch. Her emotions were bouncing up and down more than a bucking bronco. He raked his fingers through his hair. Pregnancy hormones should be outlawed. He didn't know what reaction to expect from her.

"How about we grab some food?" he asked, anxious for a distraction. "I always think more clearly on a full stomach."

"I *am* hungry." Meg rose to her feet. Her shoulders

drooped, as though every problem in the world was weighing on them. "I'll set the table."

He grabbed her hand. Her fingers were cold—most likely from nerves. His thumb stroked her smooth skin as he guided her down next to him. Just a mere touch quickened his pulse. He pulled his hand away.

"You've done more than enough today. You stay here and put up your feet." He picked up the remote for the large screen television and held it out to her. "Find us a good show to watch."

He was at the doorway when Meg called out, "Cash, thank you."

"No problem. After all, you cooked it."

"Not for dinner. For listening to me and not judging me for losing my job." She got to her feet and moved until she stood directly in front of him. Her emerald eyes held a sadness which tugged at his heart. "I feel safe here with you—like I could tell you anything and you'd understand."

Her words touched a spot deep inside him. He swallowed hard, feeling a thump-thump in his chest. It was a place he'd thought had all but died, but Meg had shown him that his heart might be damaged but it could still feel the intensity of her words. Maybe somewhere, somehow, with Meg around, there was a spark of hope for him.

"We'll get through this together." He pulled her into his arms and held her close, drawing on her strength to bolster his own. "I won't let you down."

"I know you won't."

Her faith in him made him want to move the sun and the stars for her. But what was he doing, making promises to a pregnant woman? Especially promises he didn't know if he could keep—if he *should* keep.

* * *

Meghan's bare feet were propped up on the coffee table, exactly where Cash had placed her after the comforting hug. How had she gotten so lucky to have someone so caring in her life?

She flipped through the various television stations. She wasn't used to a man waiting on her. Her father had been old-fashioned and had expected to find dinner on the table. Then there had been Harold, and he'd liked to be waited on as though he were royalty. At first she hadn't minded. She'd thought he'd eventually do the same for her. But he had never returned the gesture. And she'd begun to wonder if all men expected to be catered to.

Cash had renewed her belief that there were still gentlemen in this world. She hoped when the right lady came along and landed him she would realize what a wonderful man she'd married. The thought of another woman sitting here, waiting to share a cozy meal with him, brought a frown to Meghan's face. She was being silly. It wasn't like she had any claim on him. They were friends. Period.

"Here you go." Cash held a big plate of spaghetti in one hand and the salad in the other. "I'll be right back with your drink."

When he handed over the food their fingers touched. Awareness pulsed up her arm and settled into a warm spot in her chest. As he returned to the kitchen she found herself turning to appreciate his finer assets. How had this man managed to stay single all these years?

The fact he didn't mind treating her like a princess only added to his irresistibility. In that moment she knew the man she married would have to have this quality. Thoughtfulness went a long way in her book. But, sadly, this sexy cowboy no more fit into her city life than she could be a world-famous cook on an out-of-the-way ranch.

At last they settled side by side on the couch with their feet up. Meghan worked the remote, scanning the television stations. When they stumbled over a crime series she paused and turned a pleading look to Cash. "Do you like this?"

"It's fine by me."

She grinned. "I love this show. But you have to guess the killer."

"I do?"

She nodded, excited to have someone to share her favorite television show with at last. "It's no fun otherwise."

He glanced over at her with an arched brow. "And what if—?"

"Shh…it's on. We'll miss the clues."

He chuckled as he settled back against the couch. She couldn't remember the last time she'd been home to catch an episode. It seemed as though the past year of her life had been one long string of dinners out on the town or mandatory appearances at various events.

An hour later the empty dishes were piled at the end of the coffee table because neither wanted to risk missing any of the show. Each threw out guesses about the villain's identity, and at the end Cash got it right.

"Since you guessed the killer, I'll clean up," Meghan said, getting to her feet.

"I don't think so." He picked up the stack of dishes and started for the kitchen. "You cooked. I'll take care of the rest."

This man was offering to clean up? Had she died and gone to heaven? Even if all he did was rinse them off and stack them in the dishwasher she'd be tickled pink.

She followed him. "Are you serious?"

"Would you quit acting so shocked?" He sat his load on the counter and turned to her. "It isn't that big a deal."

"If you're sure." He nodded and she added, "I should give my sister a call."

He momentarily frowned. "Is this sister the one you called right after the wedding?"

"Yes. Ella is a couple of years younger than me. We used to be really close."

"Maybe with the baby on its way it'll draw you two back together."

She smiled at Cash's encouraging words. He reminded her of her father and his peacemaking tendencies. "I hope so. I'm pretty sure my mother will want nothing to do with me or the baby after the way I screwed up the wedding."

Disappointment and frustration welled up in her as she faced the fact that she'd come so close to receiving her mother's approval at last, only to have it snatched away. She promised herself never to be so hard on her own child.

"I take it your sister won't be so judgmental?" he asked.

"I don't think so. You should meet her sometime. I think you'd like her." She regretted the words as soon as she spoke them.

He smiled and the dimple in his cheek showed. "I'd like that."

His comment implied they had a future, but she knew that wouldn't be the case. Once she left the Tumbling Weed she'd never be back. She'd mail him a check for all the clothes and then this part of her life would be done—over—a memory.

Sorrow settled in her chest. So many doors were being closed to her. She needed to start throwing open some windows until she found a way out of this mess.

...

CHAPTER THIRTEEN

CASH YAWNED AS he strolled to the kitchen early the next
morning and flicked on the ceiling light. He wanted to help
Meg, but she'd told him point-blank not to. It just wasn't in
his nature to stand by and not lend a hand. What would it
take to get that stubborn redhead to see reason?

He moved to the cabinet where he usually kept the
coffee grounds but found none. Funny…he'd just picked
some up at the store. They must be around somewhere. A
quick search revealed they were on the bottom shelf of the
fridge. He smiled. Little changes had been made all over
the house but he didn't mind a bit. It was nice to share the
place with someone.

"Morning." A long yawn followed Meg's greeting. "I
slept in."

He turned, ready to shoo her back to bed, but when his
gaze landed on her cute pink cotton top and sleeper shorts,
all rational thoughts fled his mind. His gaze lingered on
her skimpy outfit, which revealed her smooth, bare legs.
His blood stirred. With each heartbeat his temperature
shot up another degree.

Realizing he was staring, he jerked his line of vision upward. Another yawn overtook her and she stretched. The
tiny T-shirt rode up, giving him a glimpse of her creamy

midriff. He shifted uncomfortably, fighting the urge to go to her.

"Sorry I'm still in my PJs. When I saw the time I rushed down here. I didn't want you to skip breakfast."

"You should go back to bed." He forced himself to turn away from the tempting view. He breathed in a deep, calming breath before he proceeded to add grounds to the coffeemaker. "I've got everything under control."

With the machine armed with coffee and water, he switched it on. Having regained his composure, he turned to find her heading for the refrigerator.

"Stop," he said. "You aren't cooking this morning."

She paused. The overhead light made her squint as she turned to him, but it was the return of the dark shadows beneath her eyes that concerned him.

"Of course I am."

"Did you get any sleep last night?"

She shrugged. "After I talked to my sister I had trouble falling asleep."

And he knew exactly what had kept her awake—the loss of her job. His hands clenched and his jaw tightened. He could help alleviate some of her worries if she'd just let him.

Unable to keep his mouth shut, he said, "I'll make some calls today and see if I can track down some leads for you."

Her shoulders squared and her hands balled and rested on her hips. "We talked about this, I don't need charity. If I'm going to be a mom I've got to learn to do things on my own."

"But it's just a little help—"

"No. Thank you."

He'd certainly give her credit for fierce determination to gain her independence. And, as much as he wanted to argue with her, the pursing of her lush lips and the slant of her eyes told him he needed to find another tactic.

All this stress couldn't be good for her or the baby. If she wouldn't let him help her find a job, he could at least help distract her from her problems for a little bit.

"You know, you've been working too hard around here," he said. "When we made our agreement I never meant for you to clean the house top to bottom."

"But I wanted to do it. You didn't have to open your house up to me but you did. And I'm extremely grateful."

"And I'm glad I was there to help. But I don't want you to overdo it. Especially with the baby and all…"

Pink tinged her cheeks. "I am a little tired."

"Then go crawl back in bed."

"But what about breakfast—?"

"I can grab something to eat. I'm not helpless." Not giving her time to protest, he added, "If you do as I ask I've got an offer for you. How would you feel about packing us a picnic lunch?"

"A picnic?" Her face lit up.

"I'll saddle up a couple of horses and we'll take off about eleven. What do you say?"

"I say it's a date." Another yawn had her covering her mouth. "It's been years since I was on a picnic. I can't wait."

She sauntered out of the kitchen. His gaze followed the pendulum movement of her hips until she turned the corner. He expelled a sigh of regret.

Soon she'd be gone and, boy, was he going to miss everything about her. No one but his grandmother had ever gone out of their way for him. His house not only sparkled, but bit by bit she'd made it into a home. Somehow he would find a way to pay her back.

* * *

Meghan sat atop Cinnamon, trying not to frown. In between preparing food for the picnic she'd searched the online job notices. She hadn't found any openings for a chef, but she refused to let it defeat her.

She'd taken the time to update her résumé and sent it out to a number of restaurants in Albuquerque. It was only after she'd hit "send" that the nerves had settled in. What if none of them called her? What would she do next?

She'd deal with that later.

Right now, with the sun's rays warming her back and the handsomest cowboy on her left, she made a concerted effort to shove her problems to the back of her mind. It wasn't every day such a sexy guy asked her out on a picnic.

With a gentle breeze at their backs, they quietly rode along with no particular destination in mind. Out here it was just them, their horses and an abundance of nature. Meghan inhaled deeply, enjoying the fresh air laced with the scent of grass and wildflowers.

Cash was easy to be around. He talked when he had something to say, but never just to hear himself talk. And he listened to her—really listened. He made her feel special. She only wished she could make him feel the same way.

He worked so hard, from dawn until late in the evening, never once complaining, but instead insisting on helping her with the dinner dishes. That was why she'd worked extra hard on this picnic lunch. He deserved a special treat.

After riding for an hour or so they came upon a winding creek. Off to the side was a lush green pasture, just perfect for a secluded picnic—a romantic rendezvous. Was it possible Cash had more in mind for today's outing than just food? She cast him a sideways glance. He wasn't acting any different than normal.

"Can we stop here?" she asked.

Her overactive imagination conjured up an image of her spreading out a blanket and sinking down into Cash's arms. His gaze would catch hers, stealing her breath away. And before she knew it his lips would be pressed to hers. The daydream sparked heat in her cheeks.

The level of her desire for him struck her. She'd never hungered for a man in her life. She worried at her bottom lip. She was carrying one man's baby and craving the touch of another. Did this make her some sort of hussy?

"Why are you frowning?" His voice cut into her troubled thoughts. "Did you change your mind about stopping?"

"No, this is fine. In fact it's beautiful. You're so lucky to own this little bit of heaven on earth."

"Really? Because you looked like something was bothering you."

"Nothing." She forced a smile. "Although I'm getting hungry. How about you?"

"Definitely. The aroma of fried chicken has been pure torture."

She was being silly and worrying for no reason. But when he helped her out of her saddle she noticed how his hands lingered a little longer than necessary. His gaze caught hers and his Adam's apple bobbed.

In the next breath he pulled away. "I'll grab the food."

In no time Cash set the supplies down at her feet. They included a container of homemade potato salad, macaroni and cheese and some deviled eggs. "If you don't need anything else, I'm going to take the horses down to the creek."

"Go ahead. I'll be fine here. Lunch will be ready when you get back."

"I won't be gone long." His gaze paused on her lips,

causing her insides to flutter. "Promise you won't start without me?"

She swallowed and tried to maintain an easy demeanor. "Now, would I do something like that?"

He strolled over to the horses. Wise or foolish, she couldn't ignore the magnetic attraction pulling at them. Cash felt it too. She was certain of it.

And it wasn't just now that he'd felt it. This morning in the kitchen she'd caught his hungry glances. And there had been other times when he'd eyed her up, all the while thinking she hadn't noticed.

She licked her dry lips. She'd most definitely noticed.

No more than ten minutes later Cash had tended to the horses and was heading back to join Meg. The aroma of fried chicken floating along in the gentle breeze was tempting, but not as tempting as having a taste of Meg's sweet kisses. This picnic was his best idea so far. And Meg looked more delicious than the cherry pie she'd packed for dessert.

When he entered the clearing she flashed him a smile. His chest puffed up. No one had ever looked at him quite that way before.

She got to her feet and moved to meet him partway. Her beauty mesmerized him, from the pink tingeing her cheeks to the spark of mischief in her emerald eyes.

"Thanks for bringing me here," she said, stopping in front of him. "I didn't think it was possible, but I'm feeling much better."

"That's great. I thought a change of scenery might help."

Her palms rested on his chest. Could she feel how her mere touch made his heart beat out of control? He hoped not. The last thing either of them needed was to let this physical attraction get out of hand.

"It's not the scenery," she said, her voice growing soft with a sexy lilt. "It's you."

Before he could make sense of what was happening she leaned closer. He couldn't let this happen—no matter how much he wanted it. He turned his head and her lips pressed against his cheek.

Meg jumped back. Her face flamed red. His gut knotted with unease. He knew that he was responsible for her embarrassment and was unsure where this would leave them.

"I thought you…um…don't you like me?" she stammered.

He lowered his head, realizing he'd been too obvious with his interest in her. "You're wonderful. It's not you, it's me."

"Seriously? You're going to throw that tired old cliché at me?" She stepped forward and raised her chin so they were making direct eye contact. "You like me. You're just afraid to admit it."

"Drop it." He tried to walk away but she grabbed his arm.

"Admit it. Admit that you can't forget about that kiss we shared back at the house. Admit that you want to do it again."

She was right. He did like her. And he thought about that stirring kiss far too often for his own sanity. Heck, he'd offer up his prize stallion to taste her lips once more—but he couldn't—they couldn't.

"Meg, stop it! This—you and me—it can't happen."

He pulled away from her touch. He had to convince her that he wasn't good enough for her. She could do so much better.

He strode over to the picnic area.

A blue-and-white quilt was spread over the ground with the food in the center. He stopped next to the blanket, unable to tear his gaze from the familiar hand-sewn material. His throat tightened and the air became trapped in his lungs.

"Why can't we happen?" Meg persisted.

He knelt down on the edge of the quilt. His outstretched fingers traced over the interlocking blocks of material. This was a physical reminder of why he had to stop this romance with Meg before it got started.

"You don't know me," he said.

Her intense stare drilled into him. "Then tell me. I'm listening."

He didn't want to have this talk—not with her—not with anyone. But he'd already said too much, and now he might as well fill her in. Maybe then she'd understand why they could never share more than a few kisses—no matter how much he longed for more.

"This quilt is older than me. My great-grandmother made it for my mother. It kept me warm in the winter, but most of all it kept me safe from the war between my parents. When I was hidden beneath it I pretended no one could see me."

He paused, wondering how many people described their parents' relationship as a war. He sure hoped not many. No child should ever live through what he'd endured. No one should ever feel the need to become invisible to stay safe.

Meg opened her mouth, obviously to offer some unwanted sympathy, but when he turned a hard gaze to her she pressed her lips back together and knelt down beside him. He'd never get it all out if she showered him with compassion. He needed to say this once and for all. Revealing his past was necessary. It'd set both of them free from this magnetic attraction.

His muscles tensed and his stomach churned as he reached into the far recesses of his mind, pulling forth the memories he'd tried for years to forget. "My mother wasn't a bad person. But she was young when she became pregnant. She wasn't ready for a husband and a child. And my father...well, he was a piece of work."

"Your mother must have been a brave woman. I'm scared to death about bringing a child into this world."

"You don't need to be afraid. You'll make a wonderful mother."

Her eyes lit up with hope. "You really think so?"

He nodded. He envisioned Meg with a baby in her arms—a baby with red hair and green eyes just like her. Sadness welled up in his chest when he realized he'd never witness mother and child together. Once she left the Tumbling Weed there'd be no looking back for either of them—it had to be that way.

"Tell me some more about your mother," she said, with genuine interest in her voice.

"She was the most beautiful woman I'd ever seen. I remember her singing me to sleep. She sang like an angel."

Meg's hand moved to her stomach. "I hope my son or daughter will have such wonderful memories of me."

Cash shook his head. "It wasn't all good. She tried to be a good mother, but she couldn't stand up to my father. He blamed her for his washed-up rodeo career. Heck, he blamed her for everything that went wrong. I'll never understand why she didn't just leave him. When the money ran out she sold our possessions—anything that would buy us food for just one more day."

"I can't imagine not knowing where your next meal was going to come from," Meg said softly. "So this is why you treat the people in your life like the horses you sell. By holding them at arm's length they can't hurt you."

"You don't understand." His hands clenched. "There's

more to it. Some people shouldn't be allowed to reproduce, and my father was one of them."

Cash threw his hat down on the blanket and stabbed his fingers through his hair. Memories bombarded him. He chanced a glance at Meg. Her features had softened and her eyes were warm with…was that *love?*

His heart skipped a beat. No, it couldn't be. It had to be compassion. If it was love, they were in far more trouble than he'd ever imagined. He had no choice now but to get the rest of his past out in the open.

"When there was nothing left for my mother to sell or barter, my father's answer wasn't to get a job. Not him. Instead he loaded the family up in the car and we headed into town. We pulled up to a liquor store and he made me get out…"

Cash drew in an unsteady breath, refusing to meet Meg's unwavering stare. What was she thinking? It didn't matter. Nothing she'd imagined could come close to the horror of his dreadful tale.

"I didn't want to go. I was a frightened nine-year-old who wanted to stay in the car with my mother. My father grabbed me by my collar and yanked me out of the backseat." Cash rubbed his hand over the back of his neck, still able to recall the burn where his shirt had been pulled taut across his skin. "He dragged me to the liquor store door, pulled it open and pushed me inside. I knew by the fierce look on his face that it was going to be bad. I had no idea how bad. I was shaking when he shoved a handgun at me."

Meg expelled a horrified gasp. "What on earth was he *thinking?*"

"Probably about how to get his next drink." Cash spat out the bitter words. "When I didn't take it, he forced it into my hands. I think he said if anyone tried to come in the door I was to shoot them. I'm not real sure. I'd started crying by then."

Meg reached out to him, but he jerked back before her fingers touched his.

He gave her a hard stare, which stopped her hand in midair. "You wanted to know why I'm damaged goods, so I'm telling you."

"I don't care what you say. You're a good person."

He ignored her protest while he dredged up the courage to finish telling her this nightmare. "I stood in the liquor store, crying and shaking. The gun dangled from my fingertips. My father yelled at the salesclerk and the next thing I heard was a gunshot. I ran out of the store and kept running until my mother pulled me into the car."

Meg placed a hand on his jean-clad thigh and this time he didn't move it. He needed her strength to get through the next part—the part that had haunted his dreams for years.

"I can't imagine how scared you must have been." Meg's soft voice was like balm on his raw scars.

"My father had left the car running, so when he ran out of the store and jumped in he punched the gas pedal. He ranted about what a wimp I was and I believed him. If I had been stronger I would have stayed by his side. I climbed into the backseat to get away from him. I knew all too well what the back of his hand felt like. In no time there were sirens behind us but my parents continued to fight. I hunched down on the floor to keep out of his reach. He started chugging stolen whiskey. That stuff always made him meaner. When he couldn't grab me, he smacked my mother. The car jerked and my mother screamed. The next thing I knew the car was wrapped around a tree and both of my parents were dead."

"That's the saddest story I've ever heard." Pity echoed

in her voice, making him feel worse. "Nobody should ever have to put up with a bully like him."

"It wasn't until I was a teenager, after being around my grandfather, that I realized the apple hadn't fallen far from the tree. Both of them were tough men to get along with under the best of circumstances, but put some liquor in front of them and they became mean."

"So that explains it," Meg said.

"Explains what?"

"The reason there's no liquor in your house or Martha's. And why you reacted so negatively to my suggestion of picking up some wine in town."

"When he had the money Dad always started his evenings with a cheap bottle of wine at dinner. From there he'd move to the stronger stuff."

"I'm sorry. I should have figured there was a reason both houses are completely dry. I just wasn't thinking."

This time it was Cash who reached out and squeezed her hand. "There was no way for you to know. But now that you do you have to understand, with a father like mine, why I'm better off keeping to myself."

CHAPTER FOURTEEN

WATER SPLASHED ONTO the back of Meghan's hand. Had it begun to rain? She glanced up at the clear blue sky. There wasn't a cloud in sight. Then she lifted a hand to her cheek, finding it damp.

She didn't know when during that sad story she'd begun to cry, but it didn't matter. All that mattered now was Cash.

She sat there in the meadow, wanting nothing more than to ease his pain. She stared across at him, noticing how the color had drained from his complexion.

What did you say to someone who'd lived through such an abusive childhood? *I'm sorry* seemed too generic—too empty. She wanted him to know how much she cared about what had happened to him. Still, words of comfort remained elusive.

She got to her knees and leaned forward. Unwilling to let the firm set of his jaw or his mask of indifference deter her, she wrapped her arms around him. With a squeeze, she wished she could absorb his pain.

"Cash, you can't beat yourself up for something that happened when you were a kid. You were a victim…not an accomplice."

He unwound her arms from his neck. "You don't understand. The bad stuff—it's in my genes."

"I don't believe it. You're nothing like your father or

grandfather. But if you let the past rule your future it won't matter. You'll miss out on all of the good bits—"

"I've got to check on the horses." Cash jumped to his feet.

"Wait. Don't go." Her heart ached for him. She once more held out her hand, hoping this time he'd grab on. He had to know he wasn't alone. "I'm here for you."

Inner turmoil filtered across his tanned face. He glanced at her hand. She willed him to take it. Instead he turned and, like a wooden soldier, marched away without so much as a backward glance.

She lowered her hand to her lap. This trip down memory lane hadn't brought them closer together. In fact she'd wager their talk had only succeeded in confirming Cash's belief that he should remain a lone cowboy. The thought left a sad void inside her.

His story was so much worse than she could have ever imagined. The fact he'd lived through such horrific events and still turned out to be a caring, generous soul amazed her. But it explained why he distanced himself from everyone in his life. He was afraid of being hurt again.

Her heart clenched. She knew all too well what *that* felt like.

Giant chocolate chip cookies.

That was Meghan's answer to Cash's stony indifference. Since he'd revealed that intimate part of his life yesterday he'd locked her out. Other than a nod here or a glib answer there, they hadn't really interacted.

At dinnertime the back door clattered shut a few minutes before six. Meghan tossed a clean kitchen towel over the large platter of still warm cookies. Then she placed a homemade Mexican pizza smothered in Monterey Jack and cheddar in the oven.

With the timer set, she dusted off her hands and turned. "Dinner's just about ready."

His gaze didn't meet hers. "There's no rush."

"I made something special for dessert." She held her breath, hoping it'd pique his interest.

"That's nice." He headed out of the room, most likely on his way to get cleaned up.

The air rushed out of her lungs. Not a smile, not a glimmer of interest in his eyes or even some basic curiosity. So much for getting to a man's heart through his stomach. Obviously the person who'd made up the saying had never encountered anyone as stubborn as Cash.

She pressed her fingers to her lips, holding back a litany of frustration. She'd had it with him. If only she hadn't made such a fool of herself back at the picnic by throwing herself at him they'd still be friends. Life would still be peaceful.

With the salad made, she had twenty minutes to herself. Time to see if her résumé had hooked any interested employers. It was high time she got out of Cash's way—permanently.

She rushed to the computer. Her fingers flew over the keyboard. Though the thought of never seeing Cash again bothered her, she refused to dwell on it. Maybe by the end of the week she'd have an interview lined up—no, make that two or three.

Out of habit, she started to type the address for the Jiffy Cook website. She stopped herself just before hitting "enter." That was her past. Her future was waiting for her in her inbox.

With the correct address entered, her fingers drummed on the oak desktop. At last the screen popped up. She had a number of new emails. She held her breath in anticipation as she opened the first one:

To: JiffyCook@myemail.com
From: admin@TheTurquoiseCantina.com
RE: Employment
Thank you so much for considering the Turquoise Cantina in your employment pursuit. However, at this time we don't have any openings. We wish you the best with your continued endeavors.

Disappointment slammed into Meghan. She hadn't realized until that moment how much she'd been counting on an eager reception to her inquiries.

She swallowed hard. There were still other responses. She opened each of them. One after the other. All were polite. But each held the same message: thanks, but no thanks.

Meghan's eyes stung as she stared at the monitor.

"Ready?"

The sound of Cash's voice jarred her from her thoughts. After a couple of rapid blinks she shut down the computer. She'd figure out what to do tomorrow. It'd always seemed to work for Scarlett O'Hara.

"I'll get your dinner," she muttered through clenched teeth. With her shoulders rigid, she strutted past him to retrieve a plate from the cabinet.

"Aren't you eating too?"

She could feel his curious stare drilling into the back of her head, but a girl could only take so much rejection without it getting to her. Cash hadn't just rejected her kiss, he'd then proceeded to treat her like she had the plague. She slammed the plate on the table.

"Would you talk to me?" Cash's voice rumbled with agitation. "Tell me what's bothering you."

With only seconds to go on the timer, Meghan turned

off the oven and pulled the pizza out. She placed it on the stovetop and threw down the hot mitts.

Her patience stretched to the limit, she swung around to face him. "That's rich, coming from you. You've done nothing but give me the cold shoulder since I mistakenly tried to kiss you."

Cash crossed his arms, his face creased into a deep frown. "I thought I explained why starting anything between us would be a mistake. I should never have suggested the picnic. I'm sorry. Now, will you join me for dinner?"

"I'm not hungry."

He stepped closer. His voice lowered. "Listen, I know I've been a bear lately—"

"A bear with a thorn in his paw."

His lips pressed into a firm line. "I guess I deserve that. But if I promise to be on my best behavior will you eat dinner with me? After all, you have the baby to think of."

She shook her head. "I've got more than that on my mind."

"Such as?"

Her gaze met his. Genuine concern was reflected in his eyes. At last Cash was being his usual caring self. She breathed easier, knowing that the grouchy version of him was gone. Still, she wasn't so sure she was up for sharing her latest failure.

"Meg, I'm not going anywhere until you spit it out."

His unbending tone let her know that he was serious.

"Fine. If you must know I just got a slew of responses to my job search. Seems no one needs an out-of-work Jiffy Cook."

Cash stepped forward. His hands rose as if to embrace her. She glared at him. She didn't want his pity. Not now. She needed to hold it together. His arms lowered.

"Maybe I gave up on my television show too soon. I should ask—no, *beg*—for my job back."

"Don't do that. You already told me it didn't make you happy."

She clenched her fists. His calm, reasonable tone grated on her last nerve as panic twisted her stomach in knots. "But I don't have much savings. And with the baby coming I need a steady paycheck."

Cash pulled out a kitchen chair and helped her into it. He knelt down in front of her. "You tried—what? A half-dozen restaurants?" When she nodded, he continued, "There are dozens more you haven't contacted. Keep going. Keep trying. You'll find the right position in no time."

He was right. Her search had only just begun. Her stomach began to settle. "I know you're right. But with the baby on the way it's just so scary not to have a reliable job."

"Quit worrying. You and that little one will be just fine. My offer still stands. Any time you want some help—"

She shook her head. "I'm fine now. I can do this. But thank you."

He got to his feet. "Stay there. I'll get you a plate. And no protests. That little one you're carrying is hungry."

Cash amazed her with his ability to be so supportive. No one in her life had ever rallied behind her like he had. The others had barged in and told her what to do.

But not Cash. He was willing to step aside and let her find her own way. How would she ever repay him?

Cash chugged down his third mug of coffee and trudged off to the barn. Another yawn plagued him. After his talk with Meg the previous evening he'd been troubled by his conscience.

He'd spent a sleepless night, staring into the darkness,

wrestling with what he should do: honor his word to Meg and let her find a job on her own? Or make a few phone calls on her behalf?

After witnessing the toll her unemployment was taking on her, he couldn't imagine that the ensuing stress was any good for the baby. And the knowledge that she was considering begging for her television job back tipped his decision.

He'd made a lot of contacts while working the rodeo circuit. After all, he was a world champion twice over. He'd had influential sponsors. He'd never asked for any special favors in the past so he had a few chips to cash in.

He was hesitant, though, to reconnect with that part of his life. He had always thought that when he'd decided to walk away after that last scandal selling horses to cowboys would be the extent of his involvement with the rodeo crew.

However, there was more here to consider than his own comfort. Meg and her baby deserved a good life, and if he could do anything to make that happen he had to at least try.

He grabbed for his phone. The echo of Meg's determined voice filled his mind. Surely she'd forgive him? After all, he was only offering her a helping hand.

He dialed the phone number scrawled on an old slip of paper. "Hey, Tex. It's Cash. I was hoping you could help me out with something…"

Meghan sat down at Cash's computer with her bottom lip clenched firmly between her teeth. A couple of days had elapsed since she'd received that handful of passes on her résumé, but after Cash's pep talk she'd contacted more potential employers. Now it was time to see if anyone was willing to give her a chance.

She sent up a short, hopeful prayer and opened her

email. The first few were more of the same—"thanks, but no thanks" notes. The fourth email was from someone whose name and address she didn't recognize.

To: JiffyCook@myemail.com
From: Tex.Northridge1@emailRus.com
RE: Inquiry
Ms. Finnegan, it has come to my attention that you're looking for a position in the restaurant industry. I'm currently in the process of establishing the Golden Mesa Restaurant, a 5-star culinary delight in Albuquerque. If you were to forward me your résumé and a list of references, I'd like to consider you for our kitchen staff.

At last her luck was turning around. She couldn't quit grinning. She squealed with delight.

Cash ran into the room. "What's wrong? Is it the baby?"

"Nothing's wrong. Nothing at all."

She jumped to her feet. In a wave of happy adrenaline she rushed over, threw her arms around his neck and hugged him. At first he didn't move, but then his arms snaked around her blossoming waistline to give her a squeeze. It'd only take the turn of her head for them to be lip to lip.

He was so tempting.

So desirable.

So...

No. She couldn't set herself up to be rebuffed once again. If he wanted her, he'd have to make the first move.

She pulled back. Pretending not to be affected by their closeness, she explained to him about the email she had just received. "I don't know how the owner got my name, though."

Cash's throat bobbed. "Hey, you're a celebrity. I'm sure

the word is out that your talent is available to the right restaurant."

"You really think people in the know are talking about me?"

"Of course I do. Did you email back?"

"No. I was so excited I forgot. But with it being Friday I probably won't hear back until Monday."

In that moment she realized her two weeks at the Tumbling Weed were almost over. She'd been hoping that by the time she had to face her family and friends she'd once again be gainfully employed.

"Don't worry," Cash said, as though reading her troubled thoughts. "We'll get through the weekend together. Maybe there will be some more murder mysteries on television for us to guess the culprit."

She smiled. Her chest was filled with a grateful warmth over the way he'd so smoothly made it possible for her to stay on a little longer without putting her in the difficult position of having to ask.

It'd all work out. She wasn't worried. She had a good feeling about this job—a real good feeling.

With a thump, she settled back into the desk chair. It was time to put her best foot forward. She began to type an eager response.

CHAPTER FIFTEEN

HE'D CHICKENED OUT.

After witnessing Meg's excitement over the job inquiry Cash hadn't been able to bring himself to snuff out her glow by confessing that he might have opened the door for her with Tex. Besides, all he'd done was make a few phone calls and throw out her name. It would be Meg's talent that landed her that job. And he had no doubt she'd get it.

In all honesty, it hadn't been easy to convince Tex to consider Meg. News of her canceled television show and the ensuing bad press hadn't died down yet. In an effort to counter the negativity Cash had mentioned in confidence Meg's upcoming cookbook deal, assuring Tex that the public would love it. In addition, Cash had thrown out the idea of having a large press presence and a sizeable crowd for the ribbon cutting. Tex had liked the thought of creating some media buzz about the grand opening. Now Cash was in over his head. But he couldn't back out.

Tex had held up his end of the deal by taking Meg into consideration for executive chef. Now Cash had to come through with his part of the deal. And he wasn't looking forward to it.

But the thought of Meg and the baby with a secure future would make it tolerable. He'd do almost anything for them.

He'd done some research on the internet and now he had a plan of action. Only it'd take more manpower than he could muster single-handedly in such a short space of time. Remembering Meg's sister's phone number was still on his cell phone, he strode outside for privacy and placed a call. He could only hope her sister was as trusting of strangers as Meg.

A warm voice answered.

"Is this Ella? Meg's sister?" he asked, hoping he wasn't about to make a fool of himself.

"Possibly. And who would this be?"

She was cautious. Good for her.

"This is Cash Sullivan. I think your sister might have mentioned me."

"Is Meghan all right?" Ella asked in a rushed, anxious voice.

"Yes, she is. I didn't mean to alarm you. There's a problem, but it has nothing to do with her health."

"Did one of those reporters track her down? I told her eventually they'd find her. They're worse than bloodhounds."

His gaze moved to the empty country lane. "So far she's avoided them. The reason I'm calling is because I need your help if we're going to get your sister a new—a *better* job as the celebrity chef of a new five-star restaurant."

"I still can't believe they canceled her show." A note of anger rumbled through the phone. "You know, I saw Harold talking to some TV executives at the church. I'm certain he's somehow mixed up in this. I never did understand what Meghan saw in him."

That made two of them. But Cash didn't want to get started listing all Harold's faults or they might be there all evening. They had more pressing matters to discuss.

"Your sister is returning home soon, but it's going to be

tough for her to face her friends and family with no husband and no job." He didn't elaborate on her need for this job because he wasn't going to spill the beans about the baby. Meg had a right to her privacy, as his grandmother had pointed out. "I have a plan, but we'll need to act fast."

"*We?* As in you and me?" Her tone sounded doubtful.

"Yes." His neck and shoulders tightened as he thought of the way this must sound to her.

"But I don't even know you."

"True. But what devious motive could I have by helping Meg get a job?"

A slight pause ensued. "Are you in love with her?"

What? Talk about a crazy idea—this ranked at the top of the list. It was a physical attraction between them—pure and simple.

"Of course not. Your sister has been a big help to me and my grandmother. All I want is a chance to pay her back."

"I'm listening."

"There's one condition, though. Would you be willing to keep this from Meg until we work out all the details?" He almost mentioned how the stress wouldn't be good for the baby. Instead he settled for, "After the wedding she was so upset she ended up physically sick. I don't want to get her worked up again, especially since she doesn't quite have the job yet."

"Aren't you rushing things, then?"

"I have faith in your sister's abilities."

"Are you sure there isn't something else going on between you two?"

Her suspicion made him uneasy. Memories of the steamy kiss they'd shared stirred his body. Did that constitute something going on? No. He'd certainly made it to a lot more bases in the past without any strings attached. This was no different.

"I'm certain. She's a friend. Nothing more," he lied.

"If you say so."

She didn't sound as though she'd bought his line. Her warm voice was a lot like Meg's and, just like her sister, she wasn't easily swayed.

He brushed off Ella's suspicions. They had more important matters to address, and soon Meg would come looking for him for dinner. "The thing is, this will take more coordination and planning than I have time to do on my own. Will you help?"

"Depends on what you have in mind. Start talking."

Her interest in hearing him out eased his tension. With some help, his plan had a real chance. He prayed it would all work out the way he envisioned. Then Meg and the little one would have a stable, happy life—something *he* could never offer them.

Talk about a joyous homecoming.

Meg pulled up to the ranch house at Tumbling Weed after returning from her job interview on Tuesday morning with Tex Northridge. She smiled as she recalled how well the meeting had gone. She'd left him with a sample menu and he'd assured her that he'd be in contact "real soon."

She climbed out of the truck to find Cash standing on the porch as though he'd been there for a while, waiting for her. The thought filled her with warmth and her smile broadened.

"I'd ask how the interview went, but by the look on your face I'd say you have the job."

"Not quite. But I have a good feeling about it."

"I never doubted you could pull it off."

She climbed the steps and stopped next to him. "That's one thing I love about you." When surprise was reflected in Cash's gray eyes she realized her poor word choice hadn't gone unnoticed. Not wanting to make an even bigger deal of it, she continued, "You're always so encouraging and optimistic…about my life. I just wish you'd take some of your own advice. Forget your past and make a future for yourself."

He looked at her thoughtfully. "You still think that's possible after everything I've told you?"

"I honestly do. The trick is you have to believe it too."

Cash shuffled his feet. "We best get moving or we'll be late for lunch. And you know how Gram likes to eat on time."

"She's home?" Meghan grinned.

Cash nodded and led her back to the pickup.

She couldn't wait to see her dear friend. It felt like she'd been gone for a month or more. What was she going to do when she returned to Albuquerque? The thought of never seeing Martha—or Cash—deflated her good mood.

Lunch was filled with nonstop talk about Meghan's interview and Amy Santiago's babies. Cash remained unusually quiet and ducked back out the door before he even swallowed his last bite of sandwich.

After the dishes were washed and the kitchen put to rights Martha shooed her out. "Go and work on some new recipes for that cookbook."

"Are you sure? I could stay and help you unpack, or do laundry."

"Nonsense. You have more important things to do. And it's great you're putting my grandson's new kitchen to use."

"I can work on the recipes another time," Meghan insisted, preferring to stay here and talk.

"Go," Martha said, chasing her through the door. "I'll be over for dinner at six. Yell if you need any help."

My, how things were changing. Dinner at Cash's house and *she* was in charge of the meal. As Meghan strolled up the lane she realized those meals were numbered. She'd already stayed beyond what they'd originally agreed to. Once she heard back from Mr. Northridge, which was supposed to be by the end of this week, she'd be gone.

Sure, she could keep finding excuses to stay longer, and Cash was too much of a gentleman to boot her out. But it wasn't fair to him, and it was high time she stood firmly on her own two feet. If this job didn't pan out she'd find another.

She might have lost her television career, but her life wasn't over. In fact it was just beginning.

But somewhere along the way she'd started picturing Cash as part of that new beginning. Not a good thing to do with a man who'd shut himself off from love. If only she could get through to him...

Once she stepped into the kitchen she concentrated on creating fabulous new recipes. She whipped up sauces and marinades. She discarded the ones she'd classify as merely "good." She was looking for something with a "wow" factor. She knew Cash liked her cooking, but tonight she planned to knock his boots off.

All too soon the back door banged shut. Her gaze shifted to the wall clock above the sink. Half past five. When had it gotten so late? Martha would arrive soon and she wasn't ready.

Meghan dropped a hot mitt to the counter and ran a hand over her hair. After slaving over the stove all afternoon she must look a sight, but it was too late to go spruce herself up.

Cash strode into the kitchen. "Something sure smells good."

"Thanks. Umm...I didn't have a chance to clean up. I was working on recipes for the cookbook."

"Does this mean we're going to dine on another of your soon-to-be famous recipes?"

"Are you offering to be my guinea pig again?"

His dimple showed when he smiled. "If it's as good as your other creations, count me in."

"You know I won't be around much longer to tempt your palate?"

The light in his eyes dimmed. She'd thought he'd be relieved to know he'd soon have the place back to himself. Was it possible he wasn't anxious for her to go?

Before she could figure out how to ask him such a delicate question he excused himself to go wash up for dinner.

He was so sweet and kind. It was a shame he had no intention of letting some lucky woman into his life. Next to her father, he was the most dependable man she'd ever known.

Meghan had finished setting the dining room table when Cash strolled back into the kitchen, looking fresh and dangerously sexy with his damp hair. His Western shirt was unbuttoned, giving her a glimpse of the light smattering of dark hair on his chest. Heat rushed to her cheeks and she glanced away, trying to focus on cleaning up the kitchen island.

He approached her and she inhaled a whiff of his spicy cologne. It was darn near intoxicating, and she nearly dropped the mixing bowl she'd intended to place in the sink. He reached out to take the bowl from her and their fingers connected.

The heat of his touch zinged up her arm and settled in her chest. She turned her head to him. His very kissable lips hovered only a few inches from hers. Would it be so wrong to take one more sizzling memory with her when she left?

She tried to tell herself this wasn't right—for either of

them—but the pounding of her heart and the yearning in her core drove her beyond the bounds of caution.

The breath caught in her throat and the blood pounded in her veins. She was totally caught up in an overwhelming need to have him kiss her—here—now. For just this moment she wanted to forget their circumstances and lose herself in his arms.

His hungry gaze met and held hers. He wanted her too. She'd never experienced such desire. Her stomach quivered with excitement. But she held herself back. She'd promised herself the next time *he'd* be the one to make the first move. She couldn't risk being shunned again—no matter how much she wanted him.

As though reading her thoughts, he lowered his head. Thankfully she didn't have to test her resolution. As light as a breeze, his lips brushed hers.

He pulled back ever so slightly. A frustrated groan clogged her throat. He couldn't stop yet. She needed more. Something hot and steamy to fill the long lonely nights ahead of her.

"Kiss me again," she murmured over the pounding of her heart. "Kiss me like there's no tomorrow."

His breath was rushed as it brushed her cheek. "You're sure?"

"Stop talking and press your lips to mine."

In the driver's seat, she reveled in the exhilaration of telling Cash what she desired. His eyes flared with passion before he obliged her by running his lips tentatively over hers. A moan swelled inside her and vibrated in her throat.

When he pulled back and sent her a questioning gaze, she said, "Again."

His mouth pressed to hers with urgency this time. As their kiss deepened excitement sparked and exploded inside her like a Roman candle. He sought out her tongue with his. He tasted fresh and minty. Her arms trailed around his neck and she sidled up against him. She wanted more of him—so much more.

In the background, she heard a bowl hit the countertop with a thud before his hands slid around her waist. His fingertips slipped beneath the hem of her top to stroke her tender flesh. She lifted her legs and wrapped them about his waist, never moving her mouth from his. His kisses were sweeter than honey and she was on a sugar high. She'd never get enough of him. *Ever.*

Just then it sounded like someone had cleared their throat, but Cash didn't miss a beat as he rained down sweet kisses on her. Obviously she'd been hearing things. She let herself once again be swept away in the moment.

"Excuse me?" The sound of Martha's voice startled Meghan, ending the kiss. "I hate to intrude, but I think something is burning."

Meghan lowered her feet to the floor as a blaze of heat flamed up her neck and set her cheeks on fire. She felt like a naughty teenager, having just been busted making out with the hottest guy in school.

"You need to do something with the stove." Martha pointed over Meghan's shoulder. "Dinner is going to be ruined."

"Dinner!" Meghan shrieked, coming out of her desire-induced trance.

She rushed to the stove, glad to have a reason not to face Martha. She had no excuse for losing her mind and begging Cash to kiss her. Between the steam from her sauce and the heat from her utter mortification she thought she was going to melt.

"Gram…we…um…didn't know it was so late," Cash stuttered.

"Obviously. Good thing I showed up before this place went up in smoke."

Martha's voice held a note of amusement, which only added to Meghan's discomfort.

Though the bottom layer of the Dijon sauce was burnt, she was able to ladle off enough for the three of them. Thankfully Martha didn't make a fuss about the scene she'd walked in on. In fact she seemed rather pleased with the idea—mistaken though it was—that they were a couple.

Someone needed to set Martha straight, but with Meghan's lips still tingling and her heart doing double-time she couldn't lie to the woman. There was no way she'd be able to convince anyone that the kiss had meant nothing to her. In fact it'd shaken her to her core.

Instead of saying goodbye, it had been more like hello.

Please ring.

Meghan lifted the phone Friday morning and checked for a dial tone. Satisfied it still worked since she'd checked it a half hour ago, she hung up. What was the problem? Why hadn't she heard about the job yet?

Maybe it was bad news and they were dragging their feet about making an uncomfortable call. Her stomach plummeted. Or it could be good news and they were notifying all of the other candidates first. Her spirits rose a little.

She sighed. Staring at the phone wouldn't make it ring. She needed to get busy if she was going to maintain her sanity. After all, there was a pile of dirty laundry with her name on it.

She'd just started up the stairs when the chime of the phone filled the air. Like a sprinter, she set off for the kitchen.

She paused, gathered herself, and blew out a deep breath.

"Hello?" She hoped her voice didn't sound as shaky as she felt.

"Good morning, Ms. Finnegan. This is Tex Northridge…"

In her frenzied mind his words merged into an excited blur. However, she caught the most important part—she'd got the job!

Her heart thump-thumped with excitement. She grinned until her cheeks grew tired. She couldn't wait to tell Cash the news.

In the end, the position had come down to her and one other. It was her sample menu with its unique flair which she'd thought to include with her résumé that had tipped the balance in her favor. *She* would be the executive chef.

Still in a daze, she hung up the phone. At last she had what she'd wanted since she'd arrived at the Tumbling Weed—a new beginning for herself and the baby. She should be bubbling over with joy, but as her gaze moved around the room which had come to feel like home to her the smile slid from her face.

It was more than the house—it was Cash. Now that she had a job the time had come for her to leave…leave *him*. The thought tugged at her heart.

She shoved aside her tangle of feelings for the cowboy and forced her thoughts back to her new job. Her mouth gaped open when she realized in her excitement that she'd forgotten to ask how soon Mr. Northridge would need a full menu to approve. She immediately called back.

"I thought Cash would have told you," Mr. Northridge said. "We have the ribbon cutting coming up in a few weeks. We need to have everything in place by then."

Cash was involved in her getting this job? Her heart

rammed into her throat, choking her. *How? Why?* Questions bombarded her. She choked down her rising emotions. There had to be a mistake.

"Cash knows?"

"Well, sure. We go back a long way, to when he was a rodeo champ. So when he called me about you I was eager to help."

Stunned to the point of numbness, she asked, "This was his idea?"

"You're lucky to have a man who'll go out of his way for you. He's really outdone himself arranging press coverage. They're all anxious to find out what the Jiffy Cook is up to. It was a brilliant idea to reveal your upcoming cookbook deal at the restaurant opening."

She blinked repeatedly, holding back a wave of disappointment. Feeling as though someone had ripped out her heart, she hung up the phone.

Meghan sank down in a kitchen chair and rested her face in her hands. Cash was behind this whole job offer. He had gone behind her back and done exactly what she'd asked him not to do.

Her chest ached and her head throbbed. How could he have done this? She'd trusted him.

He was no better than her ex. He'd manipulated her into doing what he thought was right for her—or was it what worked for *him?*

CHAPTER SIXTEEN

THE CLOSER CASH got to the house, the faster he moved. He was a man on a mission and his plan was beginning to fall into place. The night before, when he'd taken Gram home, he'd explained about his involvement in getting Meg the interview. No arm twisting had been necessary to convince his grandmother to call her friends and invite everyone to attend the upcoming ribbon-cutting ceremony. The only part she'd balked at was keeping his involvement a secret from Meg, but upon revealing how Meg had refused his offer of help Gram had relented.

With it being almost lunchtime, he slipped off his boots and stepped into the kitchen, expecting to find Meg hard at work on a new recipe. The room was empty and the counters were spotless. He supposed it was possible she'd never returned from Gram's house after breakfast. He wouldn't know as he'd been busy in the tackroom, making phone calls and fighting with the internet to push ahead with advertising the big event.

"Meg?" No response. "Meg, are you here? It's time to head over to Gram's for lunch."

His mood had lifted ever since that kiss—the kiss Meg had insisted upon—the one that had spiraled so wonderfully out of control. If Gram hadn't intervened dinner wouldn't have been the only thing overheated.

The memory made his mouth go dry. The last thing he should do was stir up the embers, but he'd loved how he hadn't been the only one getting into the moment. Meg had been demanding and it had only heated his blood all the more.

"What are you smiling about?"

Meg's serious tone wiped the grin from his face.

"Nothing. Are you ready for lunch?"

"It can wait." She crossed her arms and her brows knit together in a frown. "We need to talk."

Oh, no. What had happened? His body grew tense.

"Why don't we eat first?" Somehow food seemed to calm people. "Gram will be waiting."

"I phoned Martha a while ago and explained that we'd be late." Meg didn't wait for him to say a word before she turned on her heels and headed for the family room.

His body tensed as he followed her rapid footsteps. What was bothering her? He couldn't think of anything he'd done wrong, but that didn't mean he hadn't missed something.

He followed her as far as the doorway, where he propped himself against the doorjamb. She paced in front of the stone fireplace, her forehead creased as though she were in deep thought.

His gut churned with dread. "Whatever it is, just spit it out."

She stopped and stared at him. "I got that executive chef position...but I'm sure that's no surprise to *you,* since Mr. Northridge said you went out of your way to make it happen."

Cash rubbed at the tightness in his chest. So much for keeping his involvement off the radar. And now that Meg knew she sure didn't look grateful. He'd guessed that one wrong.

"You aren't going to deny it?" When he shook his head, she continued, "How could you do it?"

Justification teetered on the tip of his tongue, but he knew it would be a waste of breath. He'd been busted. And it didn't matter that he'd had the best of intentions—he'd broken his word to her.

"I asked you to leave my employment issue alone, but you couldn't trust me to handle it. I was *so* wrong about you. You're just like my ex. Both of you think you know what's best for me. And you don't!"

Her comparison between him and Harold was like a sucker punch to the gut. "That's not true. I'm not like that jerk. It isn't like I dumped you at the altar. I only tried to help."

Meg pulled her shoulders back and jutted out her chin. "How? By helping me out the door?"

"That's not true."

"Why?" Her lips pursed together. "Are you saying you want me to stay?"

He couldn't give Meg the answer she wanted—the words inside his heart. It was impossible. He was crazy even to contemplate the idea.

The Sullivan men repeatedly hurt those around them. He thought of the physical and mental anguish he'd witnessed between his parents. And then how he'd come to the Tumbling Weed, where his grandfather had verbally abused him. The men in his family lacked the ability to be gentle and caring. But Meg had showed him that he wasn't like them. He was different. So what was holding him back?

Clarity struck with the force of a sharp blow to his chest. All this time he'd had it backward. It wasn't that he feared hurting her, but rather he feared that by letting her in she'd let him down—like most everyone else.

"Cash, say something." She wrung her hands. "Are you saying we have something beyond an employer/employee relationship?"

He wanted to say yes. He wanted to trust her and believe what she was saying. But once bitten, twice shy…

He swallowed hard. "Weren't you listening the other day in the meadow? I'm not good for you—for anyone."

"You're hiding away from life here on this ranch!" she shouted. "Any man who takes such loving care of his grandmother and takes in a total stranger is a good man."

Meg continued to cling to the idea that he could fit into her life like a dog clutching a bone. Cash's neck tensed. He had to get her to forget about this foolish notion.

"Meg, listen to me. I'm not the man for you. My past isn't dead and gone. It still haunts me. It will ruin your future."

"No, it won't. It's old news. The only one keeping it alive is you."

He wished she was right, but the reporter who'd visited the ranch proved his point. Now he had no choice but to reveal his latest embarrassing scandal.

Cash sucked in a deep breath and straightened his shoulders, feeling the heavy weight of his past pushing down on him. He slowly blew out a breath, all the while figuring out where to start.

"Remember how I told you I left the rodeo after I busted my shoulder?" When she nodded, he continued, "That wasn't the only reason I pulled out. My ex-girlfriend framed me for a robbery in Austin. Being a child armed robber sticks to a person worse than flypaper. The rodeo circuit is a small world and people have long memories. Even that reporter who showed up here knew all about my past. He accused me of moving from robbing liquor stores and rodeos to stealing the bride from her own wedding."

Sympathy was reflected in Meg's luminous green eyes as she stepped closer. Her tone softened but still held a note of conviction. "You've got to stand up and prove to everyone—most of all to yourself—that there's more to you than those nasty tabloid stories. You're a strong, hardworking cowboy who cares deeply about his family."

Cash had never thought anyone would fight for him— certainly no one as special as Meg. In the time they'd spent together she'd snuck past his defenses and niggled her way into his heart, filling it up—making him whole.

But she didn't belong here at the Tumbling Weed. Her future was in the spotlight. Soon she'd realize that and then she'd be miserable here.

The thought of what he had to do next turned his stomach. He met Meg's determined gaze head-on. She refused to back down.

You can do this. It's the best thing for her.

"I need you to listen to me," he said. "You've read too much into what we've shared."

She shook her head. "I *know* you felt that strong connection too."

He had, but that was beside the point. Right now it was about getting her to see sense.

"It was a physical thing," he forced out. "Nothing more."

He stood rigid, resisting the urge to turn away and miss the pain that was about to filter through her emerald eyes. It would serve as his punishment for letting himself get too close to someone—a lesson he would never forget.

You can do this. You're almost there.

Soon Meg would be set free to have the wonderful life she deserved.

He swallowed. "I knew things were getting out of control between us. That's why I contacted Tex. It's…it's time you got on with your life—"

"Stop." She held out a shaky hand. "I don't want to hear any more."

Her eyes shimmered with unshed tears. She pressed a hand to her mouth and fled the room.

He felt lower than pond scum. What had he done?

He followed, but she'd already made it to the second floor. The resounding bang of her bedroom door shattered the eerie silence.

"I'm so sorry. I only wanted what was best for you and the baby."

The too-late words floated up the empty staircase and dissipated. He felt more alone in that moment than he had ever felt in his life.

Meghan sat by the bedroom window as tears fell one after the other. Stupid hormones had her crying over every little thing. It wasn't like Cash had told her anything she didn't already know. Of *course* there was nothing between them.

Memories of the moments she'd spent in his arms flooded her mind. The kisses they'd shared—had they all been a fleeting fancy for him? How could that be?

They'd been so much more for her. Why, oh, why had she read so much into his soft touches and passionate embraces?

Every time she replayed how he'd admitted he'd found the job for her so she'd leave, the aching hole in her chest widened. She blamed her out-of-control emotions on her pregnancy. In the future she'd work harder at keeping them under wraps.

When she saw Cash jump into his pickup to head over to Martha's for lunch she knew her time at the Tumbling Weed was up. She needed to head home and face the music—or, in her case, face her mother and any lingering reporters.

CHAPTER SEVENTEEN

ONE LONELY, MISERABLE week stretched into two...then three.

All alone, Cash stood in his kitchen, holding a mug full of coffee. His thoughts strolled back to the day Meg had left him, leaving only a brief note thanking him for his hospitality. Instead of asking him for a ride into town she'd called upon his ranch foreman, Hal, whom she'd befriended during her stay. Cash hated how she'd slipped away without so much as a "good to know you," but he couldn't blame her after his not-so-gentle letdown.

Without her around, the house was so quiet it was deafening. There was nowhere to go, and nothing he did let him escape his thoughts. He couldn't hide behind the excuse that by turning her away he'd done the right thing. The glaring truth was he'd let her go because he was afraid of taking a chance on love.

He gazed out the kitchen window as the late evening sun glowed liked a fireball, painting the distant horizon with splashes of pink and purple. Still he frowned.

A sip of the now-cold brew caused him to grimace and dump the remainder down the drain. Food no longer appealed to him. It was just one more reminder of Meg. Not even Gram's down-home cooking stirred his appetite. Everything tasted like sawdust.

Everywhere he looked he saw Meg's image. Next to the stove, serving up eggs and bacon. In the laundry room, folding his clothes. In the family room, watching television. Even the stables didn't provide him with an escape. Her memory lurked in every inch of the Tumbling Weed.

While doing some overdue soul-searching he'd realized he had accomplished something his father never had—he owned his own home. And he couldn't imagine ever demeaning anyone the way his grandfather had done.

Could Meg be right?

Had he avoided the Sullivan curse?

Cash sighed. What good did the knowledge do him now? He'd already turned Meg away, and each day he regretted that decision even more.

He'd tried to move on with his life, but it was so hard when he was working night and day to make her new career a huge splash in all the news outlets. It was his parting gift to her and the sweet baby she was carrying. Sadness engulfed him as he thought of all he would miss.

The telephone buzzed, drawing him from his list of regrets. He grabbed the phone, but before he could utter a greeting he heard, "Cash, what exactly did you do to my sister?"

The female voice was familiar, but it definitely didn't belong to Meg. "Ella? Is that you?"

"Of course it's me. How many women do you have calling you about their sister?"

The implication of her initial accusation sank in. "What's wrong with Meg? Is it the—?"

He stopped himself before blurting out about the baby. He recalled how Meg had planned to keep the pregnancy to herself for a while. The last thing he wanted to do was further complicate her life.

"The baby is fine," Ella said, as though reading his

thoughts. "She had a doctor's appointment earlier this week and she got a clean bill of health."

"What's wrong with Meg?"

"She doesn't laugh," Ella said in an accusatory tone. "She doesn't smile. She wasn't this way until she stayed at your ranch. What happened? Did you break her heart?"

Was it possible Meg missed him as much as he missed her? Was there still hope for them?

Nonsense. She'd hate him by now.

"Meg will be fine." It was what he'd told himself every day since she'd left the Tumbling Weed. "She's probably just nervous about the new job. Wait until she sees everything that's planned for the ribbon-cutting ceremony."

"That's another thing. Do you know how hard it's been to keep her away from the internet? I think we should let her in on all of the details."

"Is everything in place?"

"Yes."

He supposed there was no longer a reason to keep Meg in the dark. "Go ahead and tell her how her publisher has agreed to go public at the ceremony with news of her three-book deal. It'll cheer her up."

"I hope so. Nothing else has." Ella sighed. "I could show her the outpourings of caring viewers on the new blog we set up for the Jiffy Cook cookbook series. The response has been huge. I can't believe we pulled this off."

"You did most of it," he said, not wanting to share the spotlight. He preferred to remain the man behind the curtain.

"You know that's not true. You've worked round the clock, drumming up support and lining up press coverage. It's amazing what you've been able to accomplish in such a short amount of time. When Meghan finds out how you went above and beyond for her she'll be indebted to you."

"No."

"What do you mean, *no?*"

"I don't want her to know I'm still involved. She'll think I'm trying to control her life."

"No, she won't. She'll be grateful."

"Trust me. I know your sister, and the less said about my involvement the better."

"You're acting just as strange as Meghan. I'm thinking there was a lot more cooking at your ranch than those recipes for the cookbook."

"The past is the past. Leave it be. After tomorrow afternoon Meg won't have time to think about her stay at the Tumbling Weed. She'll have a classy kitchen to run and a baby to plan for."

"You're going to be at the ceremony, aren't you?"

He shouldn't go. For his sake as well as Meg's. But the thought of seeing her just one more time—even from a distance—was too tempting to pass up.

"I promised my grandmother I'd drive her."

Meghan rushed into the bedroom of her Albuquerque apartment, clutching the now signed custody papers. She'd just come from a meeting with Harold. He hadn't changed his mind about the baby—he didn't want to be involved in any part of its life, and had willingly signed away his rights.

She couldn't believe she'd come so close to marrying a man so different from herself. And then there was Cash, who'd missed out on a chance to be a father—something he wanted. She was certain he'd make a fine parent if he would give himself the chance.

"About time you got here," Ella said, entering the bedroom. "You'll have to hurry or you'll be late for the ceremony."

Meghan stuffed her copy of the custody papers in her purse before going to touch up her barely there make-up. Her hand trembled, smearing brown eyeliner.

With the custody issue settled she should be focused on her career, but all she could think about was Cash. Every time her phone rang she hoped it would be him. But not once in the past few weeks had he attempted to contact her.

Was it possible he'd dismissed everything they'd shared so easily? The thought whipped up a torrent of frustration. Did he *have* to be so stoic and resolute about his lonely life?

Her wounded pride was willing to wallow in his rejection, but her heart wasn't ready to lie down and accept defeat. His spine-tingling kisses had contained more than raw hunger. They'd been gentle and loving. And she recalled how he'd opened up to her about his past. He'd let her in and revealed his vulnerable side. He wouldn't have done that with just anyone. He cared about her, and somehow she had to get him to admit it.

"I'm so nervous I can't hold my hand steady enough to put on my make-up." Meghan tossed the eyeliner pencil on the counter. "At this rate I'm going to look like a clown."

Ella walked over, handed her a tissue, and propelled her toward the bathroom. "Wash off your face and we'll start over. We don't want the Golden Mesa's executive chef looking anything but phenomenal in front of the press."

"I can't believe you pulled all this together. I couldn't have asked for a better sister."

"Hey, what about me?" chimed in her little sis Katie.

Meghan peeked her head around the doorway. "Correction. I couldn't have asked for *two* better sisters. You guys rock."

She added a few drops of water to the tissue and some facial cleanser. Even though she'd made a mess of her life her sisters were right there, rallying behind her. Thank goodness. At last her siblings had set aside their problems and banded together. Why in the world had she thought she had to go through all this alone? She should count her blessings, but a part of her wished Cash could be there for her too.

Her mother, on the other hand, had been mortified when she'd learned the reason for Meghan's disappearing act. Meghan scrubbed at the messed-up make-up with more force than necessary. Her mother hadn't been quiet about her disapproval over the way Meghan had handled the situation with the wedding. In fact she'd flat out refused to attend today's ribbon cutting.

What surprised Meghan the most was her ability to accept her mother's decision to stay away. She might love her mother, but it didn't mean they were good for each other. They'd always had a strained relationship. There was no reason to think it would change now…or ever.

"If you scrub your face much longer there won't be anything left," Ella called out. "And we've got to go soon."

Meghan glanced in the mirror at her blotchy complexion, noticing the dark shadows under her eyes. Her sister had her work cut out for her if she was going to make her look more human again instead of like something the cat dragged in.

"What's up with you? You sure don't look thrilled about finding such a great job," Katie said.

Ella elbowed their younger sister, frowning at her to be quiet.

Meghan pulled her shoulders back and tried not to frown. "Sorry, guys. I just have a lot on my mind."

"I thought landing the top position at a five-star restaurant would be a dream come true." Katie flounced down on the bed next to her and crossed her legs. "I'd love it if someone would give *me* a kitchen to run. Can you imagine all of the chocolate desserts I could create?"

Meghan found herself smiling at her little sister's different take on life. "We could swap places today."

Both sisters froze. Their smiles faded and they turned startled glances in her direction.

"Would you guys quit staring at me like my face has broken out in an ugly rash?" Meghan pressed her fingers to her cheeks, relieved to find no hot bumps.

Ella turned to grab some foundation from the dresser. "It's just that we've never heard you talk like this before. Your career has always been so important to you."

"Yeah," Katie chimed in. "You don't seem the least bit excited about today."

Meghan mentally admonished herself. Her sisters had chipped in with her boss to make this grand opening a huge event, and she was being nothing but a downer. "I think it must be these hormones. They have me moody most of the time."

Ella dabbed make-up on her cheeks. "I'd be willing to bet it isn't hormones. In fact I'd wager my bakery that your problem has something to do with a cowboy named Cash Sullivan."

"I agree," Katie piped up as she started to brush Meghan's hair.

The breath stilled in her lungs. How had they found out? She'd made sure to say very little about him since she'd come home. "What do you two know about him?"

Ella flashed her a guilty look. "I promised not to tell you, but..."

CHAPTER EIGHTEEN

"STEP ON IT, Cash," Gram insisted.

He chanced a startled glance at his grandmother. "Aren't you the one who usually tells me to slow down?"

"This is different. It's an emergency."

Since when had a ribbon-cutting ceremony qualified as an emergency? But he wasn't about to argue. He pressed harder on the accelerator. It felt like an eternity had passed since Meg had left. Enough time for him to realize that she'd not only invaded every part of his life but most especially his heart.

He'd finally had to accept that life was a series of choices. And now he had to face the most important choice of his life. Stay secluded on the Tumbling Weed and miss out on the good things life has to offer, or go after the woman he'd come to love—the woman who'd given him the desire and courage to admit he wanted to be a family man.

He chose to have Meghan in his life.

One question still remained: would she still want him?

His chest tightened with nervous tension as he braked for yet another red light. They were only seconds away from the Golden Mesa Restaurant.

Until now he'd been so anxious to set things straight with Meg that he hadn't taken time to contemplate the scene he'd have to face. The parking lot would be swarming with press. He'd made sure of it.

With each passing second the churning in his gut grew more intense. When the light changed, he tramped on the gas pedal. He'd wanted Meg to get as much coverage as possible to undo the damage her canceled television show and runaway bride episode had done to her reputation. While he'd been talking to the reporters over the phone about the ceremony he'd been able to cover up his own identity. But once he stepped anywhere near Meg the camera flashes would start, followed by probing questions.

His hands grew moist against the steering wheel. But he had to do this—there was no backing out now. Meg had finally opened his eyes and he accepted that he could never have anything worthwhile unless he was willing to accept the inherent risks.

He didn't want to end up a lousy husband, like his father and grandfather. All he could do was promise Meg to do his best not to fall into bad habits. With her at his side, he believed he could be a husband and father worthy of his family's love.

Parked cars lined both sides of the street. Couples, families, young and old all filed down the sidewalk headed toward the restaurant. The turnout was phenomenal.

"There!" Gram shouted. "Someone's pulling out. Grab that parking spot."

"But it's a hike to the restaurant. I'll drop you off and then park."

Gram smacked his arm. "I'm not a helpless old lady. And we don't have time for you to play the thoughtful gentleman. You have to find Meghan and set things straight."

His grandmother was right. He was running out of time to find Meg before she took the stage. He glanced at his watch. Seven minutes until the ceremony began. The twisted knot inside him ratcheted tighter, squeezing the air from his lungs.

They parked and Cash rushed to help his grandmother out of the vehicle. Gram still got around quite well for her age, but as they started down the walk her modest pace held him back. He checked the time again. It would all work out. He forced a deep breath into his lungs.

"What are you doing?" Gram grumbled.

"Walking with you. What else would I be doing?"

"How about hurrying to the woman you love? Unless you've changed your mind about marrying her?"

He shook his head. He had doubts about being here, around all this press, but he didn't have any doubts about proposing.

"Then go," Gram said. "Don't let her get away. Tell her how you feel."

"Are you sure you'll be all right walking on your own?" he asked, not wanting to leave her alone in this crowd.

"I promise I won't get lost."

"Thanks, Gram." He kissed her cheek.

He sprinted up the walk, weaving his way through the throng of people. He couldn't miss this chance to prove to Meg that he'd changed—that at last he was ready to take a chance. A chance on *them*.

The number of supporters in the Golden Mesa parking lot was impressive. Ella had been right about advertising free giveaways—who didn't like something for nothing? They were also providing finger food, balloons and a Mariachi band. It was a very festive gathering, with lots of smiles.

The attendance surpassed Cash's wildest estimations. In fact there were so many people he had trouble threading his way to the stage. Tex Northridge stood in the spotlight, holding the microphone as he extolled the virtues of the newly opening Golden Mesa. Cash didn't have time to stop and listen.

He moved faster, bumping into people in his haste, yelling an apology over his shoulder. His gaze scanned left and right. Where in the world *was* she?

"Cash?" a female voice called out.

He stopped and turned, finding a woman waving her arms over her head. She looked familiar, but he couldn't put a name to the face. He considered ignoring her, but she might know Meg's whereabouts. He sidled over to the stranger and gave her a puzzled look. When she smiled, she bore a striking resemblance to Meg.

"Are you Ella?"

She eyed him and then smiled. "Good guess."

"Do you know where Meg is?"

She eyed him again. "What do you want with her?"

He deserved her suspicion. He just didn't have time to answer all her impending questions. "Let's just say I came to my senses. Now, where's your sister?"

"Well, it's about time you admitted it. She's over there."

He followed the line of her finger and spotted Meg just as she stepped onto the stage. The only way to convince her that he was willing to do whatever was necessary to make this relationship work was to step up on that stage with her. He had to show her that he was stronger than those tabloid stories—that at last he was willing to step forward and take chances.

The closer he got to the stage, the more his gut churned. His gaze swept over the sea of unfamiliar faces and the army of cameras. His chest tightened to the point where he could barely suck in a breath. Maybe he should wait here in the shadows until Meg had given her speech.

Yet if he fell back into his old routine and shied away from the public…if he didn't make the choice to step outside of his comfort zone…how would he prove that he'd changed? If he couldn't make the right choice now, what made him think he'd have the courage, the strength, to do right by Meg and her baby?

Meghan stood in front of the microphone. "Thank you all for coming here today." She swallowed, easing the tickle in the back of her throat. "I'm so honored to have been offered the awesome position to head up the kitchen at the Golden Mesa, as well as to be offered a cookbook deal. Dreams really do come true!"

A round of applause filled the air.

Meghan's insides quivered with nerves. As she stood there she was more certain than ever of what she had to do. She was about to tell everyone how much she appreciated their support, but she couldn't accept the Golden Mesa position.

When Ella had spilled the beans about Cash being the mastermind behind this amazing ceremony it had confirmed that he still had feelings for her.

In the past couple of months she'd learned that life didn't always have to follow a plan—sometimes the best things in life came when you least expected them. Her mind filled with Cash's image. She knew exactly what she wanted—Cash. But first he'd have to admit he loved her. And the only way to find out was to go back to the one place she'd been happiest.

Frustration knotted up her stomach when she realized that for all of her best intentions—her attempts to put herself out there and chase after her dreams—she'd failed to do the most important thing of all.

She'd never spoken the actual words "I love you" to Cash.

Tex Northridge took control of the microphone. "Wait

until you see the carefully planned menu we have to tempt your tastebuds!"

Meghan caught sight of Cash stepping onto the stage. What was he doing here?

"Ladies and gentlemen," continued Mr. Northridge, "in order to share this culinary experience with many of you, we have a number of gift cards to give away to some lucky winners."

Another round of applause and whistles filled the air, but all Meghan heard was the pounding of her heart. Her gaze remained glued to the rugged cowboy stepping into the spotlight. The fact he was willing to push past his fear of standing in front of a swarm of reporters to get to her made her love him all the more.

She wanted to run to him and shield him from the cameras, but her rubbery legs refused to move. A hush fell over the crowd. Even Mr. Northridge paused as Cash crossed the stage. He dropped to his knee and took her left hand in his. Camera flashes flared in the background, lighting up the sky like the Fourth of July.

"What are you doing?" she whispered.

He smiled up at her, causing her stomach to flutter and rob her of air. "I came here to stake my claim on the woman I love."

The fluttering in her chest increased and she grew giddy. Had she heard him correctly? She stared into his unwavering gaze. He was perfectly serious. "But you didn't have to come here. In front of everyone."

"Yes, I did. You taught me that I can't run or hide from my past. I no longer need to lurk in the shadows, always worrying about someone digging up ancient history."

"Oh, Cash." She swiped at her moist cheeks. "You're a great man, inside and out. Anyone who can't see that is blind."

His grip on her hand tightened. "Miss Meghan Finnegan, I love you."

This was her chance to put herself out there in front of everyone and reach for her dream—her happiness. "I love you too."

His confident gaze held hers. "Would you agree to be my bride?"

Her free hand pressed on her abdomen. The public didn't know she was in the family way, and she didn't want to announce it here, but she hoped Cash would know what she meant.

"Are you sure? I come with a lot of baggage."

"I wouldn't have you any other way. I love you and all of your baggage."

She pulled on his hand until he got to his feet, and then she held up her index finger for him to wait. She turned back to Tex Northridge and retrieved the microphone.

"Wow! I can't believe this day. I think I must be—no, I *know* I am the luckiest woman in the world. Thank you, everyone, for sharing this special moment with me." Tears of joy slipped down her cheeks.

Her new boss's brow arched. "Are you sure you want to pin your future on this cowboy?"

She couldn't think of anything she wanted more. She grinned. "I'm absolutely positive."

"Then let me be the first to congratulate you both." Mr. Northridge's tanned face lifted into a smile as he leaned toward Meghan. Loudly he said teasingly, "I hope Cash knows what a wonderful woman he's getting."

Cash stepped up and placed an arm around her waist. "I'm the luckiest man in the world."

Her unwavering gaze held his.

The crowd broke out into applause, shouting, "Kiss her!"

Cash swept her into his arms. "I've wasted enough time. What would you say to a brief engagement?"

He pulled her close for a deep, soul-searing kiss that gave way to a round of hootin' and hollerin' from the onlookers.

"I'd say when do we leave on the honeymoon?"

* * * * *

Look out for
Mills & Boon® TEMPTED™ 2-in-1s,
from September

*Fresh, contemporary romances
to tempt all lovers of
great stories*

A sneaky peek at next month…

Cherish™

ROMANCE TO MELT THE HEART EVERY TIME

My wish list for next month's titles…

In stores from 16th August 2013:

☐ A Marriage Made in Italy — Rebecca Winters

& The Cowboy She Couldn't Forget — Patricia Thayer

☐ Miracle in Bellaroo Creek — Barbara Hannay

& Patchwork Family in the Outback — Soraya Lane

In stores from 6th September 2013:

☐ The Maverick & the Manhattanite — Leanne Banks

& A Very Special Delivery — Brenda Harlen

☐ The Courage To Say Yes — Barbara Wallace

& Her McKnight in Shining Armour — Teresa Southwick

Available at WHSmith, Tesco, Asda, Eason, Amazon and Apple

Just can't wait?

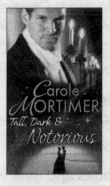

Join the Mills & Boon Book Club

Want to read more **Cherish**™ books?
We're offering you **2 more** absolutely **FREE!**

We'll also treat you to these fabulous extras:

- **Exclusive offers and much more!**
- **FREE home delivery**
- **FREE books and gifts with our special rewards scheme**

Get your free books now!

visit www.millsandboon.co.uk/bookclub
or call Customer Relations on 020 8288 2888